**First edition May 2021**
**© Cherry Publishing**
**71-75 Shelton Street, Covent Garden,**
**London WC2H 9JQ, UK**

**ISBN 9781801161060**

# Foreplay on Words

E.L. Koslo

Cherry Publishing

Subscribe to our Newsletter and receive a free ebook! You'll also receive the latest updates on all of our upcoming publications!

You can subscribe according to the country you're from:

You are from...

**US**:
https://mailchi.mp/b78947827e5e/get-your-free-ebook

**UK**:
https://mailchi.mp/cherry-publishing/get-your-free-uk-copy

# ONE

### Chase Rodgers
*Pen name: Chastity Rose*
*Occupation: Romance novelist*

**Boston**

"Oh, come on. You can't expect me to hold some rookie writer's hand," I complained as I sat in a chair across from my editor, Isobel, in her office.

We'd worked together for the past several years after I'd been assigned to her in the romance novel division of the publishing house I signed with.

"I can, and I do."

"No. Not happening. I don't have time to walk some amateur through developing a sex scene," I adamantly refused with a shake of my head. She arched an eyebrow at me, and I knew I was fighting a losing battle.

"He's not an amateur. He's already been published, quite a bit actually." The way she said it piqued my interest but I remained skeptical of being roped into a project when I didn't have extra time to spare.

"Then what do you need me for?" I rolled my eyes. My new project was supposed to be starting and I didn't have time to take on some charity case for Isobel, no matter how much I enjoyed our working relationship.

"You're our highest grossing romance novelist right now."

"And?" I'd worked my ass off to get where I was, and I wasn't derailing my career for someone I didn't even know. She didn't need or want to inflate my ego, but I wasn't seeing my value in this situation. I was a novelist, not a writing consultant.

"He's currently got two books on the Times bestseller list." My eyes narrowed at her smirk as I sat up straighter in my chair. Exactly who was she wanting me to work with?

"Cut the shit, Is. Why do you need me to hold this guy's hand?" I was irritated, but I had to admit the idea was starting to sound intriguing. This wasn't some rookie writer, this was a pro. Maybe they'd be on my level, but I'd yet to clear the top 100 on the same list.

"He's having some trouble with character development in his new novel." The nonchalance in her shoulder-shrug tried to keep her body language casual, but there was an edge to her voice. She needed me on board with this.

"I have a deadline. I don't have time for this. Can't you throw a junior editor at him?"

"The higher-ups were thinking more about collaboration," she responded casually, as if she hadn't just told me I not only had to work with this guy, but I also had to share the credit when he was the one who needed me.

Oh, hell no. I was not tying my brand to some other author and then practically writing their book for them. I was halfway through book two on a three-book contract and still needed to do some research to flesh out the male lead. I'd gotten more comfortable in writing from the male perspective in my career, but I always wanted to make sure it didn't come off as forced.

"He could probably give you some help with your book," Isobel hinted as she gave me an imploring look.

My hackles rose as I clenched my fists. "I don't need help. I need my editor not to drop a babysitting gig in my lap."

"I promise you'll like this one," she smirked as she tossed a hardback book across her desk and pulled open the cover to show me the book jacket. "Meet Evan..."

"You mean Stone Evans? What does a mystery writer's new book have to do with this conversation?"

"God, Chase," she sighed loudly as I interrupted her, "quit being a royal pain in my ass and let me get through a sentence."

"Go on." I motioned as I sat back heavily into my chair and crossed my arms.

"Stone Evans is a pen name. His real name is Evan Stineman," she explained as I continued to look at the black and white picture. "He's writing a new thriller and one of the main characters is a call girl."

"I do *NOT* write porn," I stressed as I stared at her, unimpressed.

Isobel smirked at me from across the desk. "You write erotic fiction."

"There is a difference between a book with a romantic plot and writing about a prostitute."

"Is there?" she asked, clearly amused. "Is there really?"

"I'm leaving," I huffed as she burst into laughter and threw a pen at me. I'd dealt with a lot of bullshit stereotypes in my day and thought she had more tact than this.

"Sit down, you know I'm just joking."

"Why me?" I failed at keeping the whine out of my voice as she continued to laugh at me. "It's not like pretty boy Evan needs help reeling in the chicks. I'm sure he could go find a lady of the night to help him with his 'research'."

"He is pretty, but..." she trailed off and clenched her teeth.

"Oooh, is he gay? I mean, that's totally cool and would explain why he's having trouble if he doesn't understand lady parts..."

"No!" she practically shouted at me from across the desk. "For the love of God, Chase, stop talking."

"But how...?"

"He doesn't get out much."

"What does *that* mean?" This was starting to sound suspicious again. Even with the black and white photo, it was clear that Evan had a set of piercing light blue eyes, framed by long dark lashes, and a chiseled jawline dusted with a light layer of facial hair. If I ran into him out on the street, I'd do a double take at that face.

"He doesn't have contractual appearances. I don't think he really dates either," she said nonchalantly as she avoided eye contact. She was keeping something from me.

"Is he a..." I leaned in close and looked towards the door to make sure no one was walking by to overhear me before I whispered to her across the desk. "Virgin?"

Isobel lost it again and slapped her hand down, inadvertently pushing Evan's book off the edge of her desk. I caught it before it hit the floor and I propped it up on my lap to study his picture again.

"I don't think he is, but maybe."

"How old is he?"

"Twenty-seven," she replied. So only a few years younger than my thirty-one. At least he wasn't too much younger; I think I'd feel dirty consulting with him otherwise.

"There's no way. But he's so..."

"So..." she coaxed with a curious smile.

"Cute?" Her smile grew as my voice rose. He was more than cute; I think we both knew that, but I wasn't telling her about the very visceral reaction I'd had to seeing his picture.

"So, you'll meet him?" she asked as she glanced down at her phone laying on the desk.

"Why are you so desperate for this?" I was wondering how Isobel had gotten dragged into this too. I knew Evan wasn't one of her writers, so there had to be a reason besides my acumen for romance that was drawing the both of us into this project.

"His new series is assigned to Adrian. He sent me some pages. It's..."

"The scenes are too rough?" I interrupted when she didn't finish her thought right away. Most men who didn't know how to write a passionate scene used aggressive male archetypes to try to make it seem sexier. As a romance novelist who'd written hundreds of drafts of sex scenes over the last ten years, it physically hurt to read male writers forcing a sexy scene.

"Not exactly. More like too awkward." She pulled a face and handed me a page from a manuscript. As I scanned the dialogue and the interaction between the two characters, I really had a hard time believing this had been written by a bestselling author. It was choppy and the actions didn't flow. I felt myself cringing more than getting turned on.

"Is he in a slump? Surely his books have had sex scenes in them before." Suspense writers often had tumultuous affairs between characters to build up some of the relationships in their plots.

"Not really. He's always written very well-researched mystery novels. The plots haven't lent to romantic storylines."

"None? Not even a hot scene with the protagonist nailing someone out of frustration or because they were in danger?" That seemed to be a popular one in more than one mystery or suspense book. When in danger, fuck a stranger.

She shook her head at me, and I was a little taken aback. I knew that sex was pretty much a prerequisite in my genre, but others drew on sexual encounters too. There was a reason the phrase 'sex sells' existed.

"So, what exactly am I supposed to be helping him with?"

"He obviously needs someone who's used to writing something more graphic that draws the reader in," she explained, "the plot is there, but he needs help getting the passion on paper."

"Does he know that you're pulling in a consultant on his book?" I didn't want to be put into an awkward situation if I wasn't wanted. "Isn't he going to be pissed at Adrian?" Everyone was pissed at Adrian at one point or another, but still.

"He does," she nodded with a sly grin. "He asked for you."

"Adrian asked for me?" He was another editor in the mystery/action/suspense/thriller (MAST) portion of the publishing house. He was not a fan of mine, but he did have a huge crush on Isobel.

"No," her smile grew. "Evan asked for you."

"Me?" I clarified, confused. "Has he even read my work?"

"He has. Adrian said he wasn't willing to meet with anyone else."

"Have I met him before? You'd think I'd remember that face, but I know sometimes the book jacket doesn't match up to the person."

Even in the black and white, I could see the way his light eyes sparkled with hidden mystery. It seemed fitting that the mystery writer would have an allure to his appearance. His hair was curled slightly, an open expression that wasn't quite a smile. He was an incredibly attractive man, but there was something more...

"He doesn't do the industry events."

"Writer's conferences?" I had no idea how he would even know who I was if we didn't run in any of the same circles. Being the talent for the same publisher didn't mean that authors knew one another. Sometimes there were hundreds of authors just in your own genre.

"Nope."

"And you're sure he requested me?" I repeated, a little baffled.

"Positive."

"Not Chase Matthews?"

"Chase Matthews is a guy who writes sci-fi novels," she laughed, "He knows how aliens get freaky, not humans."

I laughed as I pictured the writer she was talking about. He was 5'5" — a full two inches shorter than me — was balding, had a paunch, and had been sporting adult braces as long as I'd known him.

"Now *he* might be a virgin." We both laughed until she took a deep breath and put on her 'I'm a serious businesswoman' face.

"He wants to meet you the day after tomorrow. He's got some specific scenes drafted that he wants you to work with him on," she told me.

"So, coffee shop? Park? Where does he write?" I personally liked to sit in a quiet corner of the library or a park if the weather was nice.

"Well..."

"Spit it out, Is," I urged.

"He needs you to come to his house." It seemed like a simple enough request, but the way she said it made it sound like it wasn't something I would readily agree to willingly.

"And that's bad?"

She sighed as she avoided looking up at me again. "Not exactly, no."

"Hey, Is?"

I turned my head towards the door as a knock sounded and Adrian stepped into the door frame. If I didn't know what an egotistical jerk he was, I would have thought he was handsome. His athletic frame filled the space inside the doorway, broad shoulders and an impeccably fitted suit clinging to the obvious muscles in his arms.

"Yes?" she responded, and I glanced between the two of them. There was always tension in the air whenever they were in the same room.

"Oh, hey Chase. Did Is ask you about...?" He asked as he stepped fully into her office and sat down in the chair next to mine.

He was classically handsome, tall, full head of slightly wavy dark hair, gorgeous blue eyes — it really was a shame he was such an asshat. Isobel said it was a trait that only I seemed to bring out in him, but I was skeptical. He just seemed to hate most romance writers based on genre alone.

"Evan? Yes." I nodded as he sat up straighter in his chair and turned to face me fully.

"And?"

"Well, she said..." Isobel interrupted. I held up my hand to cut her off and turned back to Adrian.

"She said, what is the benefit of doing this favor for your author?"

"You really need to ask that?" he asked as he looked over at me like I was crazy. "You'd be getting byline credit for consulting on a Stone Evans book. He blows his nose, and it hits the Times list."

"I'm not exactly struggling to get my name out there," I bristled at his tone, arching an eyebrow in his direction. He didn't need to know I'd already agreed to hold Evan's hand.

"Yeah, but your demographic is a little bit different than his," he laughed. Jackass.

"What's that supposed to mean?" Isobel inquired as she shot daggers at him with her narrowed eyes.

"Um." He cleared his throat and his cheeks colored as he looked over at Isobel. "Just that the female nineteen to thirty-five demo is a little bit less *selective* than the whole twenty to sixty male-female that Evan pulls in. His draw is bigger."

"It may be a larger pool to pull readers from, but there are a lot of female readers ages nineteen to fifty-five. I don't just pull the YA demo."

"I know you don't, but his books have just that little wider reach. This could be good for you. Get your name out there to some new potential readers." The arrogance was back in his voice. Now I was starting to second guess my decision because it meant working with Adrian.

"Because I obviously have an issue with my hundreds of thousands of readers."

This was why I didn't get along with Adrian. He was a literary snob. He had his head so far up the asses of the Mystery Action Suspense Thriller writers that he couldn't see romance as a real genre. It didn't escape me that most of his MAST writers were male. All waving their dicks around. He saw me as some vapid bodice-ripper writing airhead.

"OK kids, simmer down," Isobel interjected. I think she could tell I was about to lay into him. "Chase already agreed to meet your precious Evan. She just needs an address."

Isobel was always amused by our banter. She thought it was kind of hilarious how wound up I could get Adrian with a few well-placed barbs. It took all my self-control not to reveal that he was more than capable of doing the same to me.

"Oh, she did?" He asked as he studied me with a knowing smile. He knew I could never say no to Isobel, no matter how much I despised her ability to get me to bend to her will. I was good at writing sex scenes; she was good at subtle manipulation of all the little pawns in her life. Adrian and I were merely pieces on a chess board to her.

"Don't look so smug. Someone needs to throw that poor kid a bone. Those pages were just awful," I said with faux sympathy.

"Hey, he's got more bestselling books under his belt than you have notches on your bedpost."

"Hey! Break it up before I get the hose." Isobel's voice rose and we both looked in her direction. "Chase, stop riling him up." She pointed a finger at him with a raised eyebrow. He'd gone too far this time.

"Adrian, quit slut-shaming and get out of my office before I stab you with my letter opener," she picked up said letter opener and replaced the finger-pointing at him with her little metallic weapon. "1950 called and they want their misogynistic bullshit back."

The laughter burst out of me as he turned to her with a look of shock mixed with what I was sure was arousal. Gross.

"You need us. Don't be a dick. Just email Chase the address and a time and she'll be there."

Adrian let himself out of the office quietly and I turned back on Isobel before she could avoid my question again.

"So, what is so bad about Evan's house?"

"It's not the house that's the problem." She laughed at the face I made because I still obviously was not getting the joke. "It's the fact that he rarely leaves it."

"Ever?"

"Pretty much." Even she couldn't hide the cringe and I felt a stab of apprehension climb up my spine.

Shit. What did I just get myself into?

# TWO

**Evan Stineman**
*Pen name: Stone Evans*
*Occupation: Mystery novelist*

**Connecticut**

"Ugh. Why am I so terrible at this?" I growled as I pushed my laptop off my lap and onto the cushion next to me.

Swinging my legs off the side of the couch, I leaned forward with my elbows on my knees, scrubbing both my hands across my face.

I was stuck. Writer's block had never been an issue for me before. The words had always just appeared. Half the time I didn't even consciously formulate the plot in my head, it just flowed onto the paper. My editor, Adrian, called me his ringer. Whenever he was having trouble with another author, he relied on me to knock one out of the park.

"Speak of the devil," I muttered as my phone started buzzing on the coffee table.

He was hounding me for pages. I had the whole book drafted — I knew it needed work, but he'd basically told me that my sex scenes were shit. And for once in his life, Adrian was right.

"Yes?" I swiped the screen to connect the call and let my eyelids fall closed.

"Any word on when you'll have new pages in my inbox?"

"I'm working on it," I sighed as I glared at the laptop sitting next to me.

"So, you're still hung up on the first edits I sent you?"

"No," I lied.

Yes. How could I not be? The last time we'd spoken, he'd basically insinuated I needed to get laid in order to be able to finish my book.

"Man, you gotta snap out of this. I get that you're not a fan of people, but you're a good-looking guy," Adrian coaxed.

Oh shit, not this again.

"If you need a wingman, I can drive out this weekend," he laughed. "We can call in at that little pub down the road from your house, talk to some ladies..."

The thought of going in there made my palms sweat. There was a reason I lived in a small town in rural Connecticut. No crowds, no subways, no people if I didn't want to see them. I needed to derail this train of thought. I preferred my privacy, and I could only take so much of Adrian's bravado in person.

"I'm in the research phase, I've got it handled."

Literally. With my hand.

I may have had a slew of incognito tabs open on my tablet with Redtube videos I'd marked for reference.

"So, my boss floated an idea by me — it's not a bad one, but you might not be a fan," he said evenly.

Missing your initial deadline was such a headache. The editors were on your ass, their bosses were on their asses. It was a giant clusterfuck.

My outline and chapters were way ahead of schedule, but they wanted a polished excerpt to put in the next run of my last book. I was the dumbass who decided to use a prostitute as the main character. Of course, I couldn't avoid using the trappings of literary sex. It sold — it sold big — and I had managed to avoid anything graphically sexual in my last eight books.

Fade to black in a mystery novel wasn't uncommon and often readers were there for the plot and not the word porn.

"Our portfolio also includes some pretty solid Romance writers, we thought maybe with a little help you could push through this."

"You think I need a writing consultant?"

Fuck, it was worse than I thought.

"Just someone to bounce ideas off of, work with on structure and flow," he explained.

"I'm not letting a ghost writer take over my book," I told him. I'd worked too hard to let someone come in and rewrite everything.

"She won't. She'll just be there to point you in the right direction."

"So, you have someone in mind?" I still wasn't sure I trusted his judgment, but I was running out of options.

"We have a few candidates. I express posted you a box. I know you like to flag references, so I thought hard copies might be easier."

"You sent me a box of erotic novels?" I asked dryly.

"They're not all erotic — OK, some of them are. But it'll give you an idea of the material they write."

"What if I don't like any of them?" I hadn't had time to read for recreation in years. I wasn't sure I had the attention span to sit through a whole box of books. I always had too many characters itching to get written to focus on reading.

"Those chapters need total rewrites. You need help or you need to get some hands-on experience to draw from," he raised his voice and huffed over the line. I knew I was becoming a source of frustration for him.

"I'm not going to go have rough sex with a random stranger."

His deep laugh resonated through the speaker and I was so glad he got amusement out of my situation. "Any sex with a stranger would probably help."

"Dick," I muttered.

"Yes, you supposedly have one, go use it," he laughed.

"How you are considered a grown professional is beyond me."

"You love me," he teased.

"No, I really don't."

"The package will be there later today. Put down the laptop and get reading. I need a name sooner rather than later."

"Fine," I sighed heavily.

"Good."

"I'm hanging up on you now," I threatened as my finger hovered over my phone screen.

"Have fun with your research!"

I pressed the little red button on my phone and pushed it across the table.

"Ugh."

I needed a distraction until the UPS man came in a few hours. That box was like an axe hanging over my head. I did not want help with this, but I obviously needed it. It had been a while, but it's not like I was totally inexperienced. I had girlfriends in high school and college.

Although, back then I'd been more confident and self-assured. I didn't second guess every other word out of my mouth. Paper was easier. I could just let my fingers fly and eloquent words would fill the paper — or the screen. The things that came out of my mouth, not so much. I could be charming on paper when I was pretending to be someone else.

"OK, let's see if I can figure out which authors he will be sending me books from."

I switched out of incognito mode and opened a new Chrome tab on my tablet.

The publisher's website had author bios listed by genre in a very easily accessible format. I clicked on the romance link and was overwhelmed at the listing of authors. There were a lot of authors who wrote under pen names.

I had my own, but the Romance writers had some flowery ones. One in particular caught my eye, but it wasn't so much the name as the picture thumbnail beside it.

Now I was aware of the makeup artists, stylists and flattering lighting that went into taking a photo for a book jacket, but she was stunning. *Chastity Rose.* Hmm. She made me think some thoughts that were anything but chaste. The smirk on her full lips and the subtly concealed curves drew me in and I knew I needed to investigate this reaction to her. For all I knew, she could be a horrible writer with a pretty face.

"What do you write, hmm?"

I tapped my finger on the link to see her books, and heat surged through me as the thumbnails of her book covers popped up.

*'Candace was still reeling from her divorce when her friends signed her up for an online dating website. Will young Marc help her get back out there?'*

"Looks like it from the cover." It showed a barely clothed, very muscular man embracing a woman who looked like she was in her forties.

*Damn.*

*'Retired rodeo cowboy, Luke, settles down on a dude ranch as a horse trainer to escape after a devastating injury. Will the ranch owner's daughter help him with his recovery?'*

"Doesn't seem too injured to me," I muttered. This cover featured a shirtless cowboy bending a young woman in a cowboy hat backwards over his arm.

*'Rival CEOs Carson and Melody hate each other with a passion. Will things heat up when a merger throws them together?'*

"Love — hate, classic set up." Another hot cover with a barely clad woman in a sexy pencil skirt peeling a dress shirt off a man sitting on the edge of a desk.

*'Coffee shop owner Blake is too focused on work to find love. When a clumsy barista falls over the threshold of his café, will they be able to create the perfect blend?'*

"Male POV, interesting choice for a female writer." A woman wearing a man's shirt with the sleeves rolled up to her elbows was sitting on a countertop with a shirtless man's face buried in her neck.

The last thumbnail didn't load, so I clicked on it to see if it was just my tablet being glitchy. I nearly swallowed my tongue when the image finally loaded.

*'Kayla has never had a problem with confidence, but she's never felt fully satisfied. Will a mistaken address on a catering gig lead her to find someone who's able to finally put her in her place? Caution: Mature Themes and BDSM'*

Fuck. There it is. She wrote a book about BDSM.

I needed someone to fine tune rough sex scenes, this might be the author to help me. Blowing out a heavy breath and adjusting my now tighter lounge pants, I hesitated before I clicked on the extended excerpt link.

A dialogue box warning that this content was for mature readers and a little drop-down menu to input your birthdate appeared.

I scrolled through to find my birthdate and braced myself as the page viewer app loaded.

"What the hell am I getting myself into?"

*Kayla could feel the atmosphere in the room change, her skin blossoming with goosebumps as she anticipated his next move.*

*She'd known that Michael enjoyed exuding power in his professional life, but she never anticipated how deep-seated his need for control was.*

*The blindfold shifted slightly as she blew out a breath and tried to keep herself still. Her whole body was aware of every little sound that his bare feet made on the floor across the room.*

*He was making her wait - building up the tension - and trying to see if he could get her to shift out of her position.*

*It took control and patience to kneel — hands bound behind her back — with silk lined handcuffs pulling her arms into a position that thrust her uncovered chest forward. She was thankful for all* the 6:00 am gym sessions she'd attended over the last two years as her muscles flexed slightly to try to maintain her posture.

Michael had been extremely specific. Knees shoulder width apart, tops of her feet flat on the floor, head relaxed forward but not drooping, shoulders back, arms extended, wrists resting over the small of her back and chest and shoulders raised to the sky.

"You've done well, my pet." His deep voice rasped as she felt something soft touch her shoulder.

It traced across her shoulder blades and down her arms - stopping briefly on the cuffs before it lifted from her skin. It was soft, smooth, and flexible. She found herself running images through her mind of the things she'd seen laid out in the open drawer as she'd walked in the room earlier in the evening.

"Very well..."

She could hear the floor creak as he slowly circled her in his appraisal.

"Uhhh," she moaned as she felt the crack of the leather riding crop bite at the sensitive skin on the side of her breast.

"Ah, ah, ah. Quiet now, pet. You wouldn't want me to stop," His feet stopped pacing and she felt the soft leather kiss the skin on her chin as he pushed up lightly. "Should I stop?"

"No," she breathed out as her whole body was pulled taut. She was throbbing as she waited for his next move.

"Is that how you address me?"

The swift smack to her nipple caused her chest to jerk and she bounced in place before she caught herself.

"Nnn no, Sir."

"Should I leave you here to think about your behavior?"

Kayla shook her head slightly before she was able to find her voice again.

"No, Sir."

"Speak freely pet. What do you need?" he instructed.

"You."

*Her chest started to heave as the soft leather caressed the waistband of her silk panties. Back and forth, back and forth. Occasionally stopping, but never striking.*

*"What do you need from me, pet?" he asked in a low, sultry voice.*

*Her mouth dropped open as she tried to come up with a confident answer. He was going to wait her out. Driving her half mad with desire as he stood completely still.*

*She could imagine his cool blue eyes looking down on her, that passive look on his face as he patiently let her figure out what she needed. He'd told her that she could take from him what she needed, she only had to ask.*

*"Your cock, Sir. I need your cock."*

"Holy fucking shit. I need to meet this girl."

I set my tablet down and closed my eyes for a moment before I picked it back up and tapped the screen a few times going back into my incognito tabs.

My hand was shaking as I shifted the waistband of my lounge pants down. Reaching into the little pocket in the front of my boxer briefs, I pulled myself out and ran my hand down the rigid flesh. My other hand pressed play and I closed my eyes and imagined Chastity's intriguing eyes and light hair as moans filled the air around me.

"Fuck yes," I moaned as my hips involuntarily shifted into the rhythm of my hand as my wrist moved faster.

The guttural female moans on the tablet intensified the sensation as I felt myself getting closer. Images of blonde hair covered by the strap of a blindfold danced on the inside of my eyelids as my whole body tensed and I let go in streams across my hand and bare chest.

My heart was hammering in my chest as I opened my eyes and grabbed the tablet. I pressed stop and threw it on the coffee table as I grabbed my cell phone and opened the texts.

*Evan:* Chastity Rose
*Adrian: Done. That was quick.*
You have no idea, Adrian, no fucking idea.

# THREE

## Chase

**Boston**

"Laptop, check."

"Where is that damn cord?" I rummaged around in the bottom of my messenger bag. I was constantly losing charging cords. For everything. My phone...laptop...tablet. If it had a cord, I could lose it. I had an abundance of extra battery packs dispersed around my condo, but the cords that plugged into the wall — gone.

Isobel hated how disorganized my condo was, but it was ordered to me. Sort of. The clutter didn't bother me. Most days I was too absorbed in my characters to put away laundry or sort through things I needed to donate. It was clean, it was just a mess. Kind of like my social life.

My friends all thought that I had some spectacular sex life given that they thought I wrote lady porn — but in reality it'd been a while.

"Ah-ha!" I exclaimed as I pulled on the little C connector that I could barely see sticking out from under the couch cushion. For some reason, I apparently thought storing a laptop cord under a couch cushion was a good idea, but I wasn't always the most logical person.

My phone started to ring, and my eyes scanned all the flat surfaces in my apartment for the hot pink case before I felt the vibration against my leg.

Whoever invented yoga pants with pockets was a freaking genius. It kept me from losing my phone most of the time. When I remembered that it was in said little pocket.

"Is?" I asked as I wrapped up the cord and shoved it into my messenger bag.

"Did you find it?" Her voice was amused, but I didn't remember telling her I was looking for something.

"Find what?"

"Whatever it is that is making you late? You should have left forty minutes ago."

*Shit.* I looked at the tiny clock in the corner of the cell phone before I held it back to my ear. I'd thought I was doing well on time, but obviously I was not. She hated it when I went off her little itineraries.

At least it was just meeting another author, not a book signing. My head would be on a pike if I were ever late to one of those again.

"I don't know what you're talking about. I always know where my things are." She laughed so loudly that you'd think it was the funniest thing she'd heard all year. "Yeah, yeah. I'm hilarious. Laugh it up."

"Hilarious — delusional — either one," Is said in her usual dismissive tone.

"Was there a reason you're bothering me?" Other than to point out how hopeless I am.

"Just wanted to confirm that you'd gotten the PDFs with the scenes Adrian pulled for you."

They'd come through last night. To say that I was underwhelmed was being generous. Even the very first awkward sex scenes I'd written as a university student were not this bad. Romance writer 101. If you've never done it in real life, then don't try to bravado your way through it. Research on the Internet could only get you so far — sometimes you needed to experience it.

"I got them," I sighed, shaking my head. Evan needed more help than she'd originally led me to believe.

"You're awfully quiet. I thought you'd have all kinds of things to say about those pages."

The character he'd developed had already gotten under my skin. She was strong, which I'd guess you'd need to be living as she did, but she also had this intense sense of loneliness that resonated with me.

It made me think about the man behind the story. Was he as lonely as this girl? What had happened to him?

She'd aged out of the foster system and done what she needed to survive. Kallie had been dealt a shit hand, but what was Evan's story?

I wasn't proud of myself, but I'd tried Facebook-stalking him. Other than an author page clearly managed by Adrian and a couple of fan groups, I came up empty.

He was a ghost. I knew he'd been a soccer player his first year at Stanford, but he'd disappeared after that. It'd also coincided with the publication of his first novel.

Was that the reason for his seclusion?

He'd obviously relocated to the East Coast from California, given the Connecticut address, but his story was a puzzle I wanted to put together.

"You're hooked, aren't you?" Isobel sounded amused; she knew I liked to figure out how people worked.

"Huh? What? Nooo." I cringed as my voice took on that squeaky tone that I hated.

"You are! You've got a crush on the mystery writer!"

"I haven't even met him. How would I already have a crush on him?" I denied — weakly.

"So, if I went through your search history, I wouldn't find anything about Evan?" Goddammit. Was I that transparent? She knew I was a sucker for the tortured artist type.

"Nooo."

"Liar! Get your shit together Chase. You need to get in, do your thing, and get out," she warned.

"Do my what?"

"Get in there, show him how to make his characters angry fuck, and get back to the city." I could just see her rolling her eyes at me from her desk.

"You make it sound so easy. You're not the one that needs to teach a guy how to channel sexuality as a woman."

She started laughing again — my pain amused her to no end. I had no idea what I was walking into. Fame did all kinds of weird things to writers. He could be a pompous asshole for all I knew. Add in the fact that he was antisocial and there was a whole other level of shit. I'd agreed to two weeks. Who knew how long it'd really take?

"You'll be fine," she coaxed. "I've yet to see you intimidated by any man."

Despite it being an industry of mostly female writers, my first editor had been a man. Now *he* was a pompous asshole. Why he'd been assigned to edit Romance novels was a mystery.

He was in his late forties, divorced twice, and thought that he was a god. He did have an excellent grasp of the written word, but interpersonal relationships were not in his wheelhouse.

As soon as I'd met Isobel at a book release for another author, I'd begged for a transfer.

"Finish getting your mess packed and get on the road. You'll end up sleeping in your car if you miss your check-in."

There hadn't been any major chain hotels within ten miles of Evan's address. He really was taking the writing in seclusion a little too seriously.

There also didn't seem to be any chain stores of any type within the same radius of his little town. How that existed just a few hours outside of three major cities astounded me, but maybe leaving the metropolis of Boston for a while would be good for me.

"I know, I'm going. I found my laptop cord; my suitcase has been packed for hours."

"Looking forward to getting updates, have a safe drive," she sang like she hadn't just been making fun of me.

"Thanks, Is. I'll text you when I get there."

She hung up and I looked around my apartment to make sure that I hadn't forgotten anything. Living alone was nice, and my building didn't allow pets, but it was also a little sad that nothing would change between now and whenever I returned.

Maybe, despite living in a major city and having the modern world at my disposal, I was just as alone as Evan.

Once I got out of the city traffic, the drive was quite pleasant. Both Massachusetts and Connecticut had some stunning scenery.

I wasn't sure exactly what I was getting myself into as I ventured further into the increasingly rural countryside. It was only a few hour's drive, but it was like being on another planet. I was used to modern and historic blending together seamlessly in an urban environment.

There was nothing modern about Ashford. It was a quaint little town with lots of historical markers, a few summer camps, and only four thousand or so residents. If you wanted to be left alone, this was probably the place to do it.

The bed and breakfast that Isobel had booked for me was exactly what you'd expect from the pictures. An old colonial farmhouse that'd been restored to cater to the tourist traffic they got during the fall. It was gorgeous and I was already getting the itch to start writing. Something about the quiet scenery was inspiring me.

The owner was extremely sweet and was happy to take me on a tour of her lovely home and surrounding acreage, explaining the history of the three-hundred-year-old property. She told me about several pubs and restaurants available within a twenty-minute drive and left me in my room with a promise to see me at breakfast.

I knew Is would be waiting to hear that I'd checked in, so I fired off a quick text to her before I forgot.

*Chase: I've arrived. It's lovely.*

She didn't respond right away, so I put my phone down on the bed and pulled the printed-out packet of information that Adrian had sent me. It had a post-it note on the top with Evan's cell phone number listed, as well as his address.

Evan knew I was driving in today, but we hadn't communicated directly yet. Isobel and Adrian had been our go-betweens. I'd been too nervous to contact him, not knowing exactly where I stood. Writers could be very possessive of their work and I knew I needed to tread carefully.

"You're a big girl, Chase. You can do this," I reminded myself.

I picked up my phone and opened a new text screen. Carefully tapping the numbers on the paper into the keyboard, I tried to compose a message in my head before my fingers started moving.

*Chase: Hi, Evan. I'm here.*

No, too vague. He might not even have my number in his phone. I deleted the message and bit my lip before I typed in a new one.

*Chase: Evan, this is Chase. I'm at my hotel now.*

No, it sounded like an invitation. Ugh. Shit. Had Adrian even told him my real name? I had no idea.

I closed his text screen and opened Isobel's.

*Chase: Does he know my real name?*

I saw the little dots show up and then disappear. She'd seen the message, but she wasn't responding.

*Adrian: 4 pm, the address I gave you. Don't be late, he's expecting you.*

So, Isobel was with Adrian. Why wasn't she responding?

I didn't even know if he knew who I was.

"Shit, shit, shit. Why am I being so ridiculous about this?" I moaned.

I knew why. I was *nervous*.

There was something about the look on his face in that picture that intimidated me. I already wanted to know more about him, and that was dangerous. That wasn't why I was here.

It was just after three, so I had about twenty minutes to get myself ready to leave. The maps on my phone said it took about fifteen minutes to get to his house from here. It was also in a pretty rural area that backed up to a state park, so I didn't want to get lost.

What did one wear to meet a colleague? A dress? I obviously couldn't wear my yoga pants, tank top, and slouchy sweater.

I finally settled on a loose-fitting denim shirt dress and a pair of ankle boots. It was dressier than my normal writing attire, yet still casual.

The maps on my phone were useless ten minutes into the drive and I was glad that Adrian had included turn-by-turn directions to Evan's house. I was going to die out here if I was left to rely on modern technology.

The last turn wasn't paved and had a gravel road that cut a narrow path through the trees. I couldn't even see any other houses nearby.

It said to follow the road for 1.4 miles until it stopped. So, I was literally on a road to nowhere.

His house was not at all what I expected. Not by a long shot. Just over a mile in, the trees started to thin, and then it appeared — totally out of place with its surroundings.

There was a small lake situated behind it, the trees open to the water. I'd been expecting something along the lines of a rustic log cabin, but I guess when you sell enough books you can afford to build yourself a nice modern farmhouse in the middle of the forest.

The lights were on, so he was obviously home. With all those windows, he was probably watching me — wondering why I hadn't gotten out of the car yet.

Grabbing my messenger bag from the backseat. I began the walk to his front door.

It was so quiet. No industrial noise, no cars, only the sounds of nature. I was so used to the background noise of city life that it was a little unsettling.

My palms were sweating as I approached the door, and my heart was pounding in my chest. Quickly glancing at my watch, I noticed it was 3:58 pm and I mentally patted myself on the back for being a few minutes early. Isobel would be so proud.

I wiped my hand on my dress and knocked on the door before I psyched myself out.

Footsteps echoed through the door and I tried to force myself to remain calm as I waited. They stopped and I stared at the doorknob as it started to turn. My eyes snapped up as the door swung open.

*Shit.* He really was as attractive as his photo. This was not good. He was wearing a pair of loose-fitting athletic shorts with a fitted gray shirt. He'd obviously been doing something strenuous as I noticed a bead of sweat make its way down the side of his neck.

His hair was a shade of medium brown, slightly wavy with little highlights of a lighter hue. His skin had a golden glow to it; he obviously spent a lot of time outdoors. Deep blue eyes with a lighter ring right around his pupil peered back at me. Just like in the book jacket photo, they had a certain edge of vulnerability. A light layer of scruff covered his face and jawline, framing full, pink, soft-looking lips.

"Hey." His voice was a little strained as he took an earbud out and pulled the door open wider.

"Hi, uh, am I early?"

He just stood there, chest heaving as he looked at me for a few moments. "Oh...no. Sorry. Shit." I held in my laughter as he started to look a little flustered. "No, I lost track of time." He looked at his wrist and his eyes widened as he took in the time.

"I can come back?" I offered, motioning over my shoulder towards my car.

"No! No. That's OK. I was nervous so I went for a run. I guess I didn't realize how long I'd been on the treadmill."

His rambling was kind of adorable.

I shifted the strap of my bag on my shoulder as we continued to look at each other. His whole body was blocking the door and I didn't want to just invite myself into his home.

"So...?"

"What?" He pulled the other earbud out and moved to the side. "Shit, sorry. I'm sorry, Chastity. Come in." He stepped back further as I crossed the threshold and took a few steps inside.

"Chase."

His brow furrowed as he looked at me, confusion marring his handsome features.

"My name."

He continued to stare at me.

"Chase. My name is Chase."

"Oh god, I'm sorry. I guess I just got so used to seeing Chastity Rose on all your books..." He trailed off as his cheeks darkened with a rosy flush.

"All my books, huh?"

He scratched the back of his neck and averted his eyes.

"Exactly how many of my books have you read?"

It somehow seemed natural to tease him. And it secretly thrilled me that he'd read my work — and more than just one book by the sound of it.

"A few." He cleared his throat and looked into my eyes. "I wouldn't be a good writer if I didn't do my research."

And then it was my turn to blush. Check and mate, Evan Stineman.

# FOUR

## Evan

**Connecticut**

I couldn't believe that I lost track of time. I had so much nervous energy pent up that I knew I just needed to run it off. Chastity — correction, Chase — had been the only thing on my mind the whole day.

When the box from Adrian had arrived, I'd plowed through the two books of hers that he'd included. I didn't even look at the other half dozen books in there by other authors, because I'd already made up my mind.

After I was done with those, I'd spent the next day on my tablet buying all the rest of her books on Kindle. I couldn't stop.

I'd saved the book with Michael and Kayla for last and had finished it in a matter of hours. I couldn't put it down. Well...that wasn't entirely true. I'd put it down a few times when I was so rock solid that I couldn't focus anymore and had taken matters into my own hands.

Oh god, don't think about masturbation while she's standing two feet in front of me. These shorts hid nothing.

Fuck. I was all sweaty. I probably smelled. Such a great first impression, you moron.

"Research is always good," she smirked, a dimple appearing in her left cheek. Oh god, was she something to look at. Her blondish-brown hair was down around her shoulders in soft waves. Long dark eyelashes framed bright blue eyes. She was tall, but still a good six inches shorter than me.

Shit. I was just staring at her again.

"Um. You can take a seat in the living room or out on the back patio if you want to. I should probably take a shower."

She smiled at me and nodded as her gaze slowly ran down my torso. I'd started to sweat through my shirt, and it was stuck to my chest in a few places. When her eyes lingered at my waistband, I knew I needed to get out of here before I rose to the occasion.

"Make yourself at home while I, uh...get cleaned up," I told her nervously.

"OK. I might go check out the lake. Your property is really gorgeous."

No, you are really gorgeous.

"That way?" she asked as she pointed to the door that led to the sunroom.

Shit. I was staring again.

"Uh. No."

She looked at me expectantly and I felt my cheeks heat up again. "Over there. The double doors lead to the patio. You can walk down the hill to the dock from there."

"Got it."

We both just smiled at each other again and I shook my head as she giggled.

"Well, I'll uh...just go then."

"See you soon," she nodded with an indulgent smile.

I walked myself back towards the hallway that led to my bedroom, only backing into the corner of the kitchen island once, eliciting that giggle from her again. I pivoted and turned away from her, taking a few long strides towards my bedroom door. I needed to regroup.

"Fuuuck..." I cursed under my breath. This was exactly why I hid from people. I always managed to say or do something completely mortifying.

Chase was out there waiting for me, probably wondering why she'd been sent out into the woods to babysit an imbecile.

Stop. Just relax. I was a good writer. I knew that. I wasn't questioning my ability to weave a well-planned out plot. I was entirely questioning my ability to interact with women. Serena had really done a number on my self-esteem and I was still beating myself up over it three years later.

"You can do this." And now I was talking to myself again.

As I walked into my bathroom, I toed off my shoes, stripped off my shirt and my shorts, and threw my sweaty clothes into the hamper.

It'd be easy to become a slob living hidden out here by myself, but I'd always respected order.

That's probably why writing had always come easy to me. It was second nature to outline my stories. I had numerous diagrams, outlines, and character summaries filling folders on my laptop. I always knew exactly where the plot was going before I typed the first line of text.

Maybe that was why I was having such a hard time with these sex scenes. I could outline them, move the characters how I wanted them to move, but my words only seemed to skim the surface.

It was mechanical, choreographed. I had a hard time making it seem spontaneous or passionate.

Now the sex scenes that Chastity — Chase — wrote were a different matter. They drew you in, pulled you in to observe, and then made you feel what the characters were feeling in a sensual way.

I could feel a stirring in my briefs as I imagined the scene in Michael's playroom where he had Kayla suspended mid-air with her hands bound and attached to a hoist while he fucked her from behind, ramming himself inside her as he held onto her hips.

How did she even come up with that? I knew you could research things on the Internet, watch videos on YouTube — and other places — and try to immerse yourself into the experience, but the way she wrote it made me feel like she'd experienced it.

Was Chase into bondage? Did she do more in-depth research into the lifestyle?

"Stop it," I growled at myself in the mirror. Thinking about it was just making things harder. Much harder.

If she wasn't here, in my home, I would just take care of it in the shower, but that would just be weird right now.

Turning the faucet to just barely warmer than room temperature, I hopped in and lathered myself up. Practicing my breathing techniques under the tepid blast seemed to help calm me down.

It also meant I'd taken the fastest damn shower I'd had in a while.

"Where did she go?"

I was standing in my kitchen, looking out the windows that lined the back wall of my house.

She obviously wasn't in the living room, and the patio was empty. I could only see the very end of the dock from the windows, so she must be somewhere down the hill.

"Chase?"

The sun was just barely starting to droop in the sky, but I knew it'd be pitch black in a few hours. I hadn't really known what to plan for our meeting, but I guess I could offer to cook her dinner. The fridge was usually well-stocked because I lived so far out of town. The market in Ashford was small and quiet, so I made a weekly trip in and stocked up on groceries.

I heard humming as I walked down onto the grass-covered hill that led to the water. It was technically a pond, but resembled a small lake, and I knew when I toured the acreage that this was where I wanted to build my house.

"Chase?"

She was seated with her legs outstretched, about halfway down the grassy hill. Her phone was lying next to her, earbuds in her ears, an old school composition notebook balanced on her lap.

I watched her for a few moments, her pencil flying across the page. Obviously, this place inspired her as much as it did me. There was a firepit closer to the water where I did most of my writing when the weather cooperated.

I didn't want to scare her, but she'd probably be more frightened of me standing a few feet behind her, just staring like a creeper. She had to already think I was a little strange since I used my obviously stellar conversational skills on her earlier. Talking to people had never been my favorite thing, but around women — especially beautiful, sexually attractive women — I got flustered.

I took a few steps a little further down the hill and I could see the moment she noticed me. Her hand halted and the pencil slipped on the page. Her head shot in my direction and she yanked her earbuds out with a nervous smile on her face.

"Sorry." She smiled as she squinted up in my direction. "How long have you been standing there? I didn't mean to stay out here this long, but I just couldn't help myself."

"Not long," I replied, my voice rough. Watching her had intrigued me.

She nodded as she tossed her notebook into the grass and pushed herself up from the ground.

"It's one of my favorite places to write too," I confessed quietly, clearing my throat.

I tried not to stare at her ass as she bent over to pick up her things, but it was right there. I couldn't look away.

She was different than I expected — curvier. That was a good thing, I hated it when women were afraid to enjoy food because of their figure. Food gave people pleasure too; why deny yourself in order to wear a smaller size? I'd never had issues with overindulgence, and my compulsive need to run to clear my head helped keep me in shape.

I shoved my hands in the pockets of my jeans to resist the urge to run my hands down the curve of her hips and averted my eyes as she straightened out and turned to face me.

"So..." She smiled as she bit her lip.

"So..." I was so lame.

"I'm sorry, I'm not usually this awkward," she laughed a little and rolled her eyes.

"I am." It was the goddamn truth.

A grin pulled at my lips as her laughter rang out. She had a nice laugh.

"Shall we go inside? I can make us some dinner."

"A man who cooks *and* writes. You're a dangerous one, Evan," she teased, and I felt my face heat up a little.

"I don't know about that," I laughed as she smiled at me. "Cooking for yourself kind of becomes a necessity when you live in the middle of nowhere."

"I'd be in trouble then." She smiled and the dimple in her cheek deepened.

"You can't cook?" I asked curiously.

"No, I can. I just choose not to most of the time."

I could understand that. She didn't seem like the type to spend her evenings on domestic chores.

"The Chinese food delivery person told me he uses my weekly delivery to remember what day of the week it is," she confessed with a guilty smile.

"I don't think I was ever that bad. Although the girl at the coffee shop near my last apartment did have my order ready when I walked in the door each day, and my name was spelled correctly on the cup each time," I recalled from when I still lived in the city. It felt like a literal lifetime ago.

"That probably wasn't because of a routine." Her laughter rang out again as I stared at her. "If I could look at you each morning, I'd make sure your coffee was ready when you walked in the door too."

I looked away and scratched the back of my head. It sounded like she was flirting with me, but I didn't want to read too much into it. I wasn't always the best at picking up the signals.

"I'm sorry. I didn't mean to make you feel uncomfortable," she said quietly, tilting her head to look into my downturned eyes.

"You didn't."

"Okay." She didn't look so certain, a small frown flickering across her face.

"I'm just not the best at this."

"What 'this' are you referring to?" Her voice sounded equal parts amused and curious.

"This," I said, gesturing my hand between the two of us.

"Talking? You seem to be doing fine to me," she smiled.

"Not talking exactly. Banter, witty conversation. I usually just end up saying something embarrassing." Or just staring and not saying anything at all.

"I thought I had the market cornered on that one," she giggled.

I liked talking to her. She didn't seem to have an agenda. It also helped that she was a little self-deprecating. I could relate to that.

I turned towards the house and started walking, Chase falling into step a few feet to my side.

"So, what are we having?"

"I hadn't planned that far ahead," I shrugged. "What are you in the mood for?"

She grinned at me again and arched an eyebrow. "You ask dangerous questions too."

"Maybe you're just reading into things," I teased back.

"Are you sure about that?"

So she *was* flirting with me. I wasn't sure how I felt about that. Was she like this with everyone? It seemed like she was the type that enjoyed getting people wound up.

"Chicken?" I needed to change the subject before she realized how much of a doofus I was.

She laughed and stopped as we reached the back patio. "It's not nice to call me names, we just met."

"For dinner," I turned and rolled my eyes dramatically at her. "Would you like chicken?"

"If you're cooking, make what you'd like. I'm easy," she shrugged.

"Is that so?" Oh my god. Did I just pull off flirting back with her?

"I'd put just about anything in my mouth right now, I haven't eaten since I woke up this morning."

My mouth went dry as I looked at her lips. She bit her bottom lip and looked into my eyes. My hand was frozen on the knob of the back door.

"Well, we can't have that," I cleared my throat and glanced down briefly before my eyes were drawn back to hers.

Her stomach growling broke the trance and I looked away as she laughed again. "Told you I was hungry."

I pushed the door open and led her into the open living space. "Take a seat. Would you like something to drink?"

She continued to follow me and sat down on a stool at the kitchen island instead of staying in the living room.

"Water?"

"Is that all you want?" I asked curiously. She seemed like the type that liked to curl up with a book and a glass of wine.

"What are you offering?"

"I could open some wine," I nodded to my small countertop rack that displayed several bottles.

"Maybe another night? I have to drive back."

I smiled at the implication that she intended to be here for another meal. I liked the sound of that. Eating alone for months on end was mildly depressing.

"How far do you have to drive?" I didn't even know where she was staying. I just got a text yesterday from Adrian telling me she'd be here at 4:00 today.

He knew I had a routine I liked to keep in the morning, and I usually wrote for a while after lunch. My days were all pretty much the same.

"Not far. Only about fifteen minutes. But I'm not sure how well I'll navigate out of here in the dark." Her voice had a slight tinge of worry. It was intimidating to drive out here where there were lots of places to get lost and turned around.

"No streetlamps to guide you. I'm sorry. Maybe we should have met at your hotel."

I started to pull ingredients out of the fridge while we talked. It was nice to have someone here with me. Chase was surprisingly easy to talk with.

"No, it's OK. The bed and breakfast Is reserved for me is actually really nice."

"I just feel bad that I'm the reason you had to come out here and you have to do all the work," I sighed.

"It's all being written off as a corporate expense," she shrugged before she leaned forward on her elbows, propping her chin on her hands as she watched me. "I really don't mind it. The quiet out here in and of itself is nice. I'm so used to the sound of traffic I'd forgotten what true quiet really was."

I glanced back at her with a smile. It made me happy that she enjoyed being out here. Not many city dwellers could appreciate a slower life.

"It was hard for me to adjust to at first, but now I'm not sure I could sleep without the quiet," I nodded.

"Where did you live before you moved here?" she asked curiously, her attention focused squarely on me. Normally, I would have started stuttering by now, but I liked her watching me.

"Chicago, California. Boston for a little while, but I needed to get away from the city."

"It can be a bit of a pain sometimes, but everything is so accessible," she smiled.

We continued talking about places we'd lived and places she'd traveled as I chopped vegetables and sautéed the chicken.

I liked listening to her voice. She had an interesting way of describing things and I could see how she'd translated that ability to her books.

We ate at the island, side by side, our knees and elbows occasionally brushing. I found myself eating slower, trying to prolong my time with her. As soon as this meal was over, she'd probably be leaving. The sun was already starting to set.

"Well," she yawned as she stretched her arms above her head and swiveled her stool to face me. "That was amazing. You've officially spoiled me. You'll have to teach me some tricks while I'm here."

My pants started to feel a little snug as I thought about tricks being taught in my kitchen. My kitchen island was probably the perfect height to...

"Are you still with me?"

"Hmm?" I hummed, "Oh, sorry." I must have been quiet too long while I was fantasizing about bending her over the counter.

"I should probably get going. Have to get some sleep before I come back tomorrow to whip you into shape." She laughed as I felt my cheeks turn pink at the images her words conjured in my head. My mind strayed to a particularly graphic scene she'd written between Michael and Kayla involving a flogger.

"Hopefully, you'll take mercy on me," I chuckled as I looked over at her naughty smile.

"Oh, don't you worry, I'll be gentle."

I sure hope not.

She started to gather our dishes to carry them to the sink. A surge of something electric raced up my palm as I laid my hand on top of hers to stop her.

"I've got it. You should probably go before it gets too much darker."

"Are you sure?" she asked quietly.

"Positive."

"Okay. So, what time do you want me?"

All the time.

"Tomorrow morning?" she asked again.

I must have been staring again.

"Oh. I get up between six and six-thirty. Any time after that should be fine," I told her, and she shook her head.

"Well, I'm not getting up that early, but I could probably make it here after eight."

"That works for me. I'll be here."

Waiting impatiently.

"It was nice to meet you," she said softly, with a little smile on her face.

I smiled back at her as we reached the door. She paused in the threshold and looked toward me. "I wasn't sure what to expect, but this has been really nice."

"It has. I'm glad I picked you." I couldn't imagine anyone else here in her place.

"Me too," she laughed as she gave me a little wave and turned towards her car.

I stood in the doorway as she drove away and found myself wishing it was the morning already. I didn't think I'd be getting much sleep tonight knowing she'd be back here tomorrow.

# FIVE

## Chase

**Connecticut**

Despite being totally flustered as I drove away from Evan's house, I made it back to the B&B without crashing in a ditch somewhere. It was *so* dark. I'd never realized how much light pollution big cities had. It got dark at night, but this was a whole next level of dark.

The house was quiet as I walked up the private entrance to my suite. Normally I'd be excited to jump in a big comfy bed and pass out for hours, but I was a little keyed up.

Maybe Isobel was right; my being here, interacting with Evan might help my new book. As I'd waited for him to get cleaned up earlier — and tried fruitlessly not to think about what he looked like naked in that shower — I'd written several pages of dialogue.

It's like the character's voices just needed my head to be quiet to start pouring out of me.

Tomorrow was going to be hard — no pun intended.

Evan and I had gotten along well, not having too many moments of awkward quietness. He was easy to talk to and didn't seem offended by my teasing. I found flirtatious things coming out of my mouth without even trying. I probably should have tried to be more professional, but I just couldn't stop.

He was attractive. OK, that may be an understatement. He was fucking gorgeous, and I'd had a hard time keeping drool from sliding out the corner of my mouth when he opened the door all sweaty and out of breath.

"Ugh. How am I going to survive this?"

Writing about sex had never bothered me. Even when I'd been new to having it myself, it'd never embarrassed me to talk or think about it. My parents were still disgustingly in love after thirty-six years and they never made me feel like sex was a shameful thing.

They'd been an open book — sometimes too open — and answered questions for me without pretense or agenda. That was probably why I'd been a little bit of a late bloomer with the actual act. And the fact that I had two fiercely protective older brothers who would have preferred to see me placed in a nunnery rather than a regular high school...

I'd done my fair share of under-the-clothes fumbling in the back seats of cars and in parents' basements, but my parents taught me to respect myself enough to set my own timeline. My high school dates had only been interested in one thing, and I'd taken great satisfaction from being the one girl they couldn't manipulate or pressure into doing something I wasn't ready for.

The ultimate honor had gone to my second college boyfriend, who had quite a few repeat performances and I'd still give a standing ovation if his wife wouldn't murder me. He was more than happy to let me explore his body — learning what things he liked — and he was always up for trying new positions.

He was older and had scored a single room in the dorm next to mine. We'd had plenty of privacy for our anatomy study sessions. He was also the first guy to blindfold and spank me. I wasn't fully into doing all the things I'd researched and written into my fifth book; but limited sensory deprivation and corporal punishment excited me.

It was also fun to work with a real-life Dominant to learn about all that went into what they did. Once, he'd tied me up and suspended me from the ceiling, with no other sexual contact involved.

"Oh, god..." What if Evan read that book?

No wonder he had a hard time making eye contact with me. My own mother had a hard time making eye contact with me after that book was released.

Changing into my pajamas, I curled up in my bed with my laptop and my notebook. I started transferring dialogue into a new text document and tweaking it to fit my current characters. It was going to be interesting to see if I could keep writing like this once I started to help Evan.

I had a feeling that if I was taking on breaking down the character of Kallie, she was going to invade my brain.

"OK, I need help," I admitted to myself.

After I'd finished getting my writing onto the computer, I dug around in my suitcase for my melatonin spray. I was never going to sleep with all the conflicting voices running through my brain.

Anyone else who said that would probably need to be medicated, but authors always understood what it meant to have voices in your head that were not your own.

The next morning, I woke feeling rested. Sometimes I had trouble sleeping, and I was worried it'd continue while I was sleeping in a strange bed.

"What time is it?" I blindly reached behind me to the nightstand for my phone. I probably should have set an alarm to make sure I didn't sleep the morning away, but I was so anxious it hadn't occurred to me last night. Did I mention that authors also commonly spoke to themselves?

"Oh, wow." It was still early — 7:18 am. "Guess I'm up early enough for breakfast."

The owner had told me the previous day that she served a home-cooked breakfast each morning, and I was enjoying having other people cook for me on this trip.

I wasn't sure what to wear today, but finally settled on a pair of skinny jeans paired with a white button-down shirt tied at the waist. Evan was going to have to get used to me wearing clothes that weren't dresses. My usual writing attire was leggings and a baggy sweater, so this was dressy for me.

I could already smell something delicious as I came down the main staircase. The dining room was set up with several smaller tables, neatly set, and waiting for diners.

"Hello?"

"In here!" I heard a shout from the room adjacent to the dining room. I assumed that was where the kitchen was located.

"Good morning," I greeted the owner of the inn, Marian. She was standing over a gas range, turning a sizzling piece of thick-cut bacon over as a pot with poached eggs simmered on another burner.

"Morning dear, you're up earlier than I expected."

"I was a little surprised too," I laughed, as I watched her move effortlessly around the space.

"I hope you're not a vegetarian."

"Nope, I'm a big fan of meat."

She laughed and smiled at me over her shoulder.

"It'll be done in a few minutes. You're welcome to chat with me for a few moments or you can sit in the dining room and I'll bring it out to you."

"If I'm not in the way, I can wait in here." I'd feel weird sitting by myself in the other room just waiting for her to serve me.

"Just sit on one of the stools and you can tell me about why you're here," she nodded over to the side of the kitchen island.

"Well...I'm a writer," I started. It was still awkward for me to out myself to people.

"Hmm. Anything I may have read?"

"Maybe?" I shrugged. "I write under a pen name."

"And...?" she laughed a little as she turned briefly in my direction.

"It's um, Chastity Rose," I mumbled. I wasn't ashamed of my writing, but I never knew how people were going to take it.

"Oh, you write some racy stuff! That last one was quite the page-turner."

I blushed and bit my lip. That book was usually the one people remembered. My other books had been steamy, but the whips and chains in the last book had really gotten people's attention.

"Thank you?"

"So, are you working on a new book?" she asked without pause, and I let out the breath I'd been holding. Living up to others' expectations of my writing was always difficult for me.

"Yes, but that's not why I'm here. I was sent to help another writer fine-tune his next novel."

"Ah, the mystery writer," she replied knowingly.

"You've met him?" I asked her curiously. He'd seemed normal to me, despite Is' warnings about his reclusive nature.

"Not technically. I've seen him in town, and he's bought produce from the farmer next door occasionally. He keeps to himself."

"I've heard." I nodded.

"So, did you meet him yet?" The little smile she aimed in my direction was more than curious. I think Marian thrived on gossip.

"Last night." I nodded with a little smile.

"And? Is he as mysterious and intriguing as the young ladies in this town seem to think he is?"

I smiled as I thought about how uncomfortable it'd probably make him to have people imagining that he was some mystery to be solved, like his novels. "He is a little bit of a mystery to me, but he seemed pretty normal. Quiet. He likes things to be orderly."

"I think the fact that he never talks to anyone and only shows his face a few times a month makes them all endlessly fascinated."

"His land and house are amazing," I sighed, mentally recalling the peaceful scenery that I'd enjoyed the previous day.

"He backs up to a state park. I was kind of surprised when I found out he was building a house out there. They had to run fiber optic cable out to his property just so he'd have Internet."

"Yeah, I don't think most of us could survive without the Internet nowadays," I laughed.

"I could do without it," she shrugged, "but I have to cater to the clientele." She pointed to a wireless router that was mounted to the wall above one of the cabinets.

"Us spoiled tech-obsessed city folk."

"Something like that," she chuckled, as she drizzled a thick, creamy, light yellow sauce over the meal she'd been assembling on the counter. "Do you want to eat inside or out? Are you a coffee drinker?"

"Outside would be amazing. And yes! One hundred thousand percent yes," I laughed at the thought that people were capable of surviving without extra caffeination.

"I have a travel mug you can borrow while you're here. No Starbucks for miles around." Marian chuckled at the way my eyes widened at her comment about Starbucks.

"That would be amazing!"

The food she served me was phenomenal, a rich hearty interpretation on Eggs Benedict with crispy bacon, cooked to perfection. I wanted to live here. This was already the best trip ever.

By eight I was stuffed, my laptop was in the car, my travel mug of brown liquid gold was in my hand, and I was ready to go.

"Here I come, Evan. I hope you're ready for me."

"Hey," I smiled as he met me at his front door.

"Hey."

Damn, he's beautiful.

We both just kind of stood there in his open front door and stared at each other. This seemed to be a thing we did. I wasn't opposed to it, but we weren't going to get any work done standing in the doorway.

"So, you ready to get down to it?" I laughed as I rubbed my palms together.

"Hmm? Oh, yes. Sorry. I'm doing it again. Come in." He stepped to the side and waved me into the house. "So...I'm not sure where you want to start. Adrian sent you some pages?"

"Yup," I nodded. "Where do you want me?"

His eyebrow arched as his gaze slowly drifted lower. "Inside or outside?"

Oh god, he just kept dropping the bait. Be good Chase, don't pick it up.

"Where does the magic happen?"

Let's see how he likes it.

His eyes drifted down the hallway towards what I was assuming led to his bedroom.

Not that kind of magic, sweetheart.

"Um, uh. Outside?" he stuttered, as he looked away from me and scratched his head.

"Exhibitionist, nice," I teased.

A nervous laugh escaped him before he scratched the back of his neck again, clearing his throat. "It's nice out. I usually sit down in the lounger at the firepit."

"Cozy. Lead the way," I gestured for him to go ahead of me.

He stopped to put on some shoes, then grabbed his laptop off the table along with a folder full of papers.

I took a deep breath and slowly exhaled as I followed along behind him. I could see why he loved being out here.

"Um, there's just the one seat down here, do you want me to go grab a chair off the patio, or..."

"I'm a big girl. I can share," assured him.

A quick nod was all I got before he walked over and set his laptop down on the edge of the unlit firepit.

"Where would you like to begin?"

"I don't know. Do you want to explain to me how it all happens?" His voice was sharper today, more nervous. This really took him out of his comfort zone.

"Well...when a boy and a girl decide the other one is attractive, they take off all their clothes, but not always, and then..."

"Stop," he looked up at me with mild panic, waving his hand. "No...god. I know how that works."

"Which scene do you want to start with? Your writing process is probably different than mine, so what works for me may not be useful for you." I decided that maybe I'd give him a little slack, although I loved teasing him, especially as he was so jumpy.

"The scene with the detective is kind of the pivotal point in their relationship, but it's towards the middle of the book."

"So, start there?" I asked quietly, watching his face for any indication of where he wanted to go.

"That one has more emotions involved. The ones at the beginning of the book are with her..." he trailed off, his cheeks reddening a little.

"Clients? Johns? Hole fillers?" I bit my bottom lip, waiting for the blush to go nuclear.

There it is.

"Clients. We can call them clients." He was fighting not to laugh, but I could tell he wanted to. I was trying to get him to relax.

"OK, do you want me to be completely honest with my impression of these, or do you want me to hold your hand?" I pulled out the stack of papers from my bag and put them on my lap. There were multiple colors of post-it flags hanging from the sides and red pen pretty much covering the pages.

"That bad?" he cringed as he looked down at my notes.

"Well...it could be worse?" I trailed off. It could be, but not much. I felt like I was an English teacher telling someone they failed an essay.

"Shit. Might as well rip me a new one." He shook his head as he closed his eyes. He pinched the bridge of his nose and I felt a little twinge of sympathy.

"I promised you I'd be gentle," I coaxed, hoping I didn't break his spirit on day two.

# SIX

## Evan

**Connecticut**

"OK, like this part here. You might have just as well typed 'insert tab A into slot B'." Chase frowned at the paragraphs describing their interaction. "Does the word insert sound the least bit sexy to you?"

"I guess not. Are you going to pull out your porno thesaurus and give me a better synonym?" If she was going to continue to tease me, I could give it right back.

"As a matter of fact," She picked up her phone and started typing something quickly before she held it up for me to see.

"Urban thesaurus. What is that?" I frowned. Urban dictionary was a little wild; I couldn't even imagine what the thesaurus would hold.

"It's a dirty thesaurus," she grinned, as she started typing something into the search field.

There was a listing of random words — some obviously sexual — underneath where she had typed the word missionary into the search field.

"What does an angry orangutan have to do with sex?" I asked dumbly, I was obviously way out of touch.

"Click on it," she giggled and then bit her lip, holding in an amused smile.

Well, that was a little messed up.

"Oh my god. Do you actually use this stuff to write?" My voice was a little astonished but mostly appalled.

"No," she shook her head, her light curls bouncing around her shoulders. "Usually, I just consult it when I want a laugh. People are into some weird shit."

I couldn't help but laugh at her assessment. People were into some weird things, but it wasn't my place to judge.

"OK. So clinical sounding words like 'insert' need to be the first things to go," she told me as she pointed back to the marked-up pages in her lap.

"And what do I use in its place?"

She didn't even hesitate as she started listing off words. "Glide, slide, slip, push, thrust, drive. Depends on the context."

"You are like a walking thesaurus," I marveled. Those verbs were obviously not even in my toolbox of words to describe physical interactions.

"It's one of my many talents." Her wink threw me a little off guard, but I could only imagine what other talents might lie in that curvaceous body of hers.

"So, what else?" I asked, clearing my throat, trying to force myself to stay on topic. She was here to help me, not be objectified.

"The whole goal of a scene like this is to draw the reader in and capture their attention. If their heart doesn't start beating faster as they read it, it's not hot enough."

I watched her eyes dilate as she looked up at me and wanted to be the reason her heart started beating faster.

"What makes it hot?" I felt like I was completely clueless.

"Using provocative words, describing a sensation...you want them to be picturing the act as it unfolds." Her voice took on a breathy quality, and I pictured some things I wanted to unfold with her.

The writer's best friend was the human imagination. If you could paint a picture vivid enough for the reader, they could truly immerse themselves in the story.

"OK, so run your finger down the side of your face slowly," she instructed as she turned to face me and tucked one leg underneath her.

"Why am I doing this?" I asked as I watched her skeptically.

"Just humor me." I tried not to laugh as she made an impatient huff. "Now close your eyes. Take a deep breath. Do it again and tell me what you feel."

I did what she told me to and tried to think of the sensation I was feeling.

"A finger on my face?"

"Alright, smartass."

My eyes were still closed, but I could just tell she was rolling her eyes at me.

"Fine," she huffed, and I jumped as I felt a tickling sensation along my sideburn and over the stubbly hair on my cheek.

"Tell me what you feel," she said in a low, sultry voice. Or maybe I was just imagining it was sultry.

"Warmth...it's soft...makes my breath catch in my chest."

"Good. Keep thinking of how the touch makes you feel," she urged. I wasn't sure where she was going with this, but I was strangely enjoying it.

Her finger traced across my lips and I could feel the hairs on the back of my neck rise in response. It slowly trailed to my jaw and behind my ear. Her fingers cupped the back of my neck and my mouth went dry. I felt a stirring in my groin as her thumb started to slowly trail up and down, tickling the hair above my collar.

"Do you get it now?" The sultry voice was back.

My head slowly nodded up and down as she continued to caress my skin. I was fighting the urge to open my eyes. I wanted to see if her touch was affecting her as much as it was me. My pulse jumped as I felt her put a little pressure on the back of my neck.

I leaned in and could feel her hair brush against my cheek. Her hot breath was caressing the side of my face.

"You described the mechanics of their interaction. That was just the physical action. You want to describe to the reader the sensations that the actions cause, and the feelings they invoke." Her voice was low, and I could feel my heartbeat pick up further in response to the warmth of her breath blowing against my ear.

My entire body was fully aware of her proximity. She smelled good, her hair was so soft, and the thumb on my neck felt like it had a direct line to my cock. The slow action of it tracing the hairs on my neck was creating a chain of sensation I could feel in my whole body.

"I uh..." My voice was much deeper than normal, and I had to lick my lips before I tried to talk again. "I think I understand what you mean."

"Good." And then her hand disappeared.

When I opened my eyes, she was sitting perfectly upright next to me, like she hadn't just been whispering in my ear and stroking my skin.

"So, do we want to work through this blow by blow, or would you like to try to adjust it and then have me critique?"

The already precarious situation in my pants throbbed as she said the word blow. My eyes were immediately drawn to her soft pink lips. I needed to adjust something.

"Can I try to see if I can fix it?" I meant the writing, of course. Once she explained it to me, I started to see where I'd disconnected from the writing.

"It's your book," she laughed, with a shrug.

"I know, but if it got published today the critics would eat me alive."

"That's why you've got reinforcements," she smiled. "We'll pop this cherry and make a man of you yet."

I shook my head at her, laughing as I pulled my laptop onto my legs and propped it up by placing my feet up on the bricks.

"My erotic literary virginity is delicate, you promised to be gentle."

I loved listening to her laugh. She made me feel funny, charming in a way I hadn't felt in a long time. It was easy to just say what I was thinking to her without worrying about filtering it.

"That I did," she promised, her lip quirking into an amused smile.

"OK, quit distracting me." I mock-glared in her direction.

"Touchy. All you virgins are the same." I loved her sarcasm. It helped keep me from overthinking things.

"Shhh," I scolded.

She stuck her tongue out at me and pulled out the pencil and composition notebook again. I could respect a writer who drafted on paper. All my initial outlines are on paper. You never knew when a story idea was going to hit you, so being able to quickly write it down was key to remembering things.

When I looked at the scene again, I immediately went in and changed the vocabulary for several sections. She'd told me to be provocative. Then I broke down the actions and tried to add in more descriptive words.

The feeling of the rough upholstery of the couch against the front of her thighs.

The way her back arched when he grabbed ahold of her hair.

Once I knew what I needed to remedy, the scene flowed better and became a little less choppy.

"That's probably as good as it's going to get on a first try," I nodded as I saved the document.

"You're done?" she asked distractedly as she finished what she was writing and closed her notebook.

"Take a look." I passed the laptop over and she settled it on her thighs, tucking her pencil behind her ear before she adjusted the screen. Waiting for her feedback was making me antsy.

"Do you want a drink?" I asked quickly, hating the anticipation of her approval...or disapproval.

"Hmm?" She was really focused on the screen. I wasn't sure if that was a good thing. A little line appeared between her eyebrows as she concentrated.

"I'm going to run up and grab a water from the fridge. Can I get you one?" I asked again.

"Sure," she answered absentmindedly.

I rose from the lounger and quickly walked up the stone path to the hill, glancing back to look at her before I went. The line was still there.

When I returned with our waters a few minutes later, she had a new notebook with a bright red cover open on the arm of the chair.

"I'm just jotting a few notes," she told me as her pencil flew across the page.

"Take your time," I sighed, but I think she could hear the nerves in my voice.

"It actually wasn't bad," she mused, glancing up briefly with a small smile.

"I assume it's not good if you're writing me notes." I nodded at the notebook.

"These are more suggestions on places to dive deeper on. I feel like now it's bouncing around instead of just sliding along the surface."

"Better or worse?" I cringed.

"Better, much better. They seem like real people now and not sex robots." The smile she gave me wasn't merely indulgent; I think she was pleased that I'd not been completely hopeless to her tutoring.

"That's a whole other book," I laughed, and she shook her head,

"Oh, diving into sci-fi next, are we?"

"What, you're the only one who gets to play with other genres?" I shot back without even thinking.

Her eyebrow rose as she looked up at me.

"You get leather and blindfolds, why can't I have robots?"

The way her eyes widened after I said that almost made me feel guilty, but the way her pupils dilated as she looked at my lips afterward made it totally worth it.

"So, you read it?"

"I couldn't put it down." It was the truth, her words had sucked me in, and I couldn't stop turning the pages on my tablet. It was the quickest I'd devoured a book in years. I usually got so distracted by my own characters I couldn't finish books written by other writers.

She was quiet for a few moments before she stood up next to me. "Will you show me something?"

Images of her on my bed flitted through my mind as I watched the light breeze dance with her hair.

"Sure."

"Take me on a walk," she requested quietly. "You have to have explored this place."

"I've cleared some trails around the pond," I told her as I pointed to a break in the trees.

"Let's take a break," she urged as she put the notebooks to one side.

"You sure we shouldn't keep going? We just got started." I was confused at her sudden need to explore my property.

"I'm here for two weeks, we've got time. Come on." She started to walk down towards the water's edge.

It really was amazing how clear the water stayed. I'd spent a lot of time looking out over it trying to make sense of the words in my head.

I nodded towards a break in the trees, and she followed me.

"How long have you lived here?" Her voice was quiet but curious.

"Three years."

"Why here?" I don't know if anyone had ever asked me that question. Adrian hadn't cared, he'd just been upset that I wasn't as accessible outside of the city.

"I was taking some grad level courses at UConn."

"I thought you lived in Boston before you moved here?" It thrilled me that she listened when I talked.

"I did." I nodded.

"Why did you come to UConn? You couldn't have gone to Boston College?"

"I could have. But I didn't want to stay in the city anymore." It was too toxic for me to stay there.

"Because you wanted a quieter life?" she asked as she glanced over at me.

Not exactly.

"I didn't want to have to find a new apartment." I knew I was being cryptic, but I hated that part of my life.

"So, you moved to Connecticut?" She narrowed her eyes and studied my face. "It seems like there's a story there."

"There is." A story I had no interest in telling her.

"And?" I should have been annoyed that she was prying into parts of my life I didn't like thinking about, much less talking about, but I had a hard time being irritated with her.

"Ex-girlfriend wanted the apartment. I wanted to get away from her."

"That's all I get?" she laughed.

"What about you? How long have you been in Boston?" I changed the subject.

"Since college." Her coy smile let me know that she knew I was avoiding.

"Creative writing?" I guessed.

"Am I that obvious?" She rolled her eyes.

"Nah, it's just what most of the writers I know who went to Boston College majored in."

"What about you? Does Stanford have creative writing?" she asked with a smirk.

Ah, so she'd done her research. "Someone's been Googling."

"Oh, shut it. I can't help myself. Cyber-stalking is my superpower," she laughed, but I could tell by the pink on the high points of her cheeks that she was embarrassed.

"So, what did you find out about me?" I was genuinely curious to see how deep she'd dug into the Internet.

"Not much. Still play soccer?"

I couldn't help but laugh as we stopped beside a place where the trees opened to the water.

"I'm not sure if I should be flattered or scared?" I mused, shooting her an amused smile.

"How have we not met? We were in the same place at the same time and have the same publisher," she asked as she looked over at me.

"I'm not sure, but maybe me being horrible at describing sex wasn't such a bad thing." If we'd met under different circumstances, I knew that my guard would have been up. I'd have never talked to her like I was doing now.

"Full disclosure...I didn't want to come here," she confessed quietly.

"Then why did you?" I knew our editors were pushing it, but they could easily have sent someone else.

"Is begged me, and..." She stopped talking abruptly and her cheeks turned a little pink.

"And?"

"Then she showed me your picture." The vulnerability in her voice as she came clean made my pulse jump. She'd come here for me.

"And that alone didn't frighten you off?" I teased.

"Hardly," she scoffed. We had drifted closer to each other, our shoulders touching. I could feel the plastic from the water bottle she was holding brushing against my knuckles.

"I looked at yours too."

Her face turned in my direction as I whispered my confession.

"Should I be scared?" she teased.

"I wouldn't be," I laughed quietly. "You looked hot."

"Did you fall down the rabbit hole too?"

"I didn't Google you, no," I shook my head. "But I may have..."

"You may have what?" Her eyes narrowed suspiciously.

"Never mind." I shook my head, suddenly nervous.

"No, tell me," she coaxed.

"Not important."

"Oh, come on. I told you that I tried to look for you on the Internet before I'd even met you. You can tell me." She turned those beguiling blues eyes up at me and pled in a quiet voice. "Please?"

She was looking at me under her eyelashes and my eyes were having a hard time looking anywhere but at her lips.

"Let's just say my Amazon account took a hit earlier in the week." Her ability to get information out of me was dangerous. She was climbing past all my walls.

"Meaning?" The pleading look turned to suspicion.

"I invested in some reading materials."

"Oh god." Her eyes widened. She stepped back and turned away from me.

Before I could even process the motion, I'd grabbed her elbow and tugged her back in my direction. The move surprised both of us; I typically was not assertive, at all.

"I don't even want to know what you..."

"All of them," I blurted out, interrupting her. "I read all of them."

She was looking up at me, searching my eyes for something. "Uh..."

"In two days. I read all of them in two days." My pulse pounded as I waited for her reaction. It could go either way.

"Wow." Her eyes were wide open and vulnerable.

My hand tightened on her elbow and I pulled her closer until our chests were barely apart. At this point, I was just moving on instinct.

"They were captivating. You...you're..." I hesitated.

"I'm?" Moisture glistened on her lower lip as her tongue peeked out, my eyes drawn to the motion.

"You're captivating."

Her expressive blue eyes fluttered closed seconds before I cupped the back of her neck and captured her lips with mine, finally giving in to the feelings she had awoken in me.

# SEVEN

## Chase

**Connecticut**

There had been quite a few first kisses in my life, but never one that felt like this one did. Drunk kisses, awkward kisses, slobbery kisses, dry-lipped kisses, some passionate kisses, but this kiss...

It was by far the most unexpected, yet simultaneously most right kiss I'd felt so far. There was something about Evan that drew me in, and he had since I saw that picture in Isobel's office. Maybe it was because he wasn't trying to charm me. Maybe it was because he was so goddamn adorable with the staring.

Whatever it was, when he told me that he'd read all my books and looked at me with those slightly uncertain deep blue eyes... I was lost.

My hands clutched the sides of his denim shirt as his other hand slipped along the side of my face and cradled my jaw as he deepened the kiss. His lips were so soft, and when he nipped at my bottom lip I gasped into his mouth.

Evan's hand tightened on the back of my neck as he tilted my head and eased his tongue past my lips. I was almost drowning in sensation as I pressed myself against his chest.

"Fuck...you're so sexy," he panted in a raspy voice as his lips trailed across my cheek and down my neck.

"Oh god, Evan," I moaned as he sucked on a particularly sensitive patch of skin near my shoulder blade.

"Which one is it? God or Evan?" His deep rumbling laugh vibrated into my neck as he held me there, his face buried into my hair and me arched against him.

"Maybe both?" My chest shook with unrestrained laughter. He thought he was awkward, but he was smoother than he gave himself credit for.

"Mmm, I'm okay with being compared to a god."

I giggled and pinched his side.

"Hey, don't hurt me. I'm trying to impress a woman with my godlike skills," he teased.

"You're terrible!" My face was buried in his neck as he straightened us up and smoothed his hand down my back. "What happened to the kissing? I was enjoying that part."

He pressed his hand into my hip as he pulled his face back from my hair, ghosting his lips across my cheek.

"Oh, you were?" he teased as he pecked my lips once, and then eased back.

"Where do you think you're going?" My hand grasped his shirt and pulled him forward again.

"Nowhere." And his lips were on mine again, hard and insistent. Heat coiled up my spine as his hand slid down further and cupped my ass, pushing my hips into his.

His other hand was tangled in the hair at the base of my neck, tugging slightly as he eased his tongue back inside my mouth.

I may have only just met him, but our chemistry was undeniable and we were obviously attracted to each other. It would probably be too presumptuous to assume we'd be jumping into bed anytime soon, but if the subtle gyration of his hips against mine was any indication, we'd be compatible there too.

My heart was bounding in my chest as he finally released me and stepped back, sliding one of his hands into my own. "Should we continue our walk?"

"I don't know if I *can* walk," I laughed as I tried to regain my bearings. His kisses had me beyond flustered.

He tugged on my hand and continued the trail, slowly caressing my fingers with his thumb.

"So, what's going on here?" I asked curiously. While I wasn't a prude, I also didn't go around making out with male coworkers I met a day earlier in the woods, for instance. A girl has got to have standards.

"I honestly have no fucking clue." He aimed that unintentionally charming grin in my direction.

"Do you think we possibly crossed a line we shouldn't have?"

I didn't, but I wasn't sure where this put us. We were supposed to be working together and I lived in Boston, where I was returning in two weeks.

"Do you?" He stopped and turned me to face him, his hands framing my hips.

"No. I don't." My hair fell into my face as I shook my head and he reached up to tuck it behind my ear.

"Good, neither do I." He pecked my lips once, gazing down at me. "I can honestly say that I probably started fantasizing about what it'd be like to kiss you the moment I saw your picture."

Damn. For someone who claimed he was so awkward, he said all the right things.

"That's a lot for a girl to live up to." His answering smile did things to my heart. "Did I stand up to the fantasy?"

"Oh, you blew the fantasy out of the water." He pulled me into him and kissed me again. We didn't seem to be making much progress on this walk.

"We probably need to actually try to get some work done," he sighed heavily, and I shared his disappointment.

"This doesn't count as research?"

"You have read all the pages, right?" I nodded as I smiled up at him. "Does Kallie strike you as the type to take long walks and engage in sensual kissing?"

"Sensual, huh?" I raised an eyebrow. Fuck hot seemed a more apt description, but we could go with sensual.

"You keep telling me to use provocative words," he smirked.

"Smartass."

"You seem to like my ass," he teased as he wiggled it in my direction. Playful Evan was back. I liked him.

"Whose hand was on whose ass earlier, mister?" I pretended to be affronted, but let's be honest...it was hot.

"You liked it," his voice was taunting as he narrowed his eyes at me.

"I never denied that." My shrug pulled another amused chuckle out of him.

"Come on." His pace was steady as he led me along the trail on the far side of the lake. I could barely make out parts of his house through the trees.

It was a nice little trail, and he'd taken care to spread river rock on it to keep it from being reclaimed by the forest.

"So, do you own all this? The pond and everything?"

"Everything the light touches," he joked. "My property starts at the main road where you turn in and stops about ten feet that way," he said, pointing toward the woods that ran away from his house and disappeared into the distance.

"Past that is all part of the state park," he told me. "I liked that I wouldn't have neighbors close by. The park kind of wraps around my land."

"Your books must be selling well to afford all this."

He nodded as he smiled over at me. "I've been very blessed. I went to college on an athletic scholarship and wasn't sure how I was going to pay room and board."

That hadn't turned up in my Google search.

"My parents helped as much as they could, but we grew up knowing that we needed to work for what we wanted."

"We?" There wasn't much on his family in the things I'd read about him.

"I have a sister. She's still in Chicago."

"I have two brothers in Minnesota," I offered. He didn't ask, but I felt like he appreciated not having to drag information out of me.

"You're from Minnesota?"

I nodded. I hadn't lived there in over a decade, but it was home. "South of Minneapolis. I'm the baby."

"Sorry, didn't mean to sidetrack you. I'm a chronic over-sharer," I apologized, and he gave me an indulgent smile.

"That's fine. I'm glad you're still talking to me."

I may have looked at him like he was crazy.

"I don't have the best track record with women."

"I find that hard to believe." He was beyond charming in his own special way, and the outside package was quite appealing as well.

"When I get nervous I either clam up and do that staring thing or I just start rambling." My heart clenched at the broken look on his face. "It used to drive Serena nuts."

"Is that the ex?"

He nodded. I could tell he didn't like to talk about her.

"So, anyway," he redirected, "I was a poor ramen-eating college student. I sat down one day of my freshman year and started turning a short story I'd written for an assignment into a book."

"Were you a writing major too?" I knew writers came from all sorts of backgrounds, but I was curious about how he got started.

"No." He shook his head. "I was actually a chemistry major."

"Then how did you come to write a short story for an assignment?" Last I checked; chemistry majors spent all sorts of time in science labs, not computer labs.

"Fine arts core requirement. I took a writing seminar. I'd always been a fan of writing, but I also had dreams of becoming a forensic detective."

"Ah, so that's how you got into mystery novels."

He winked at me and pressed his finger on his nose.

"So why didn't you continue with forensics?"

"My roommate told me I should enter my book into a writing contest and it actually got noticed," he shrugged.

"That's lucky." I'd had a pile of discarded manuscripts in my closet before I'd gotten signed to my first contract deal.

"I didn't win, but one of the judges was an editor. He liked my first draft and submitted it to his company."

"And it got published?" Talk about luck.

"I was offered a three-book contract with another one optioned based on sales," he told me, looking a little embarrassed.

"Holy shit. That's like the unicorn of writing contracts." I couldn't hide my jealously. "I was book to book for my first two."

"I was totally shocked. But my parents encouraged it," he sighed. "With the advance from my second book, I was able to fast track my degree and graduate a little early."

"You completed your studies?"

"My parents told me that I needed to follow it through," he nodded.

"Good parents." Mine hadn't been thrilled with my major, or the rocky start to my career.

"So, my first book was published while I was still in school and then the second right after I graduated."

"I didn't get published until after I'd been out for two years." I was a little envious of how his career had essentially dropped into his lap.

"But you seem to be popular. I read some of the reviews of your first book and the critics seemed to love you," he frowned over at me and I shrugged.

"That wasn't my first book."

"You mean there's more?" He looked a little eager at this information. I wouldn't have thought a chemist who wrote mystery novels would be into romance.

"Trust me, you don't want to read them." He laughed as I shook my head.

"Oh, come on, they can't be that bad," he scoffed.

"They were before I got picked up by a bigger publisher. There's a reason I changed my pen name."

"I'll find out eventually," he told me cryptically.

"No, you won't. I buried them where no one can find the bodies." He'd better not enlist Adrian to dig!

"That sounds like something I'd write," he joked. I smacked him in the arm and narrowed my eyes as he laughed at me.

A few moments later, we crossed into the open space at the opposite side of his house. I was disappointed that our walk had ended, but not what had transpired while we were on it.

"Are you hungry?" He was doing the shifty eyes and neck scratching again.

"Are you OK?"

"Yeah, I just wish we had more time to talk. I like listening to your voice." He looked a little shy and a lot vulnerable at his admission.

"Are you kicking me out?"

He shook his head slowly.

"Then we've got plenty of time."

He smiled at me as I headed towards the house.

"So, what are you going to feed me?" I asked excitedly. It was a treat to get all these amazing meals I had no hand in.

"Am I your personal chef now?" he scoffed, pretending to be offended.

"You're the one who mentioned food!"

"I did," he nodded with a little wink.

"Do you have an apron? That'd really make the personal chef fantasy complete," I teased.

"Oh, we're talking fantasies now?" He looked all sorts of intrigued by that topic. I was curious as well.

"No, I just think you'd look hot in an apron," I shrugged. Maybe with no pants.

"Because aprons are so sexy." The exaggerated eye roll he gave made me bite my lip to contain the laughter.

I stopped in the open doorway from the patio and winked at him over my shoulder.

"Who said you'd be wearing anything else."

He made a sound that was halfway between choking and whimpering and I cracked up laughing as I sauntered in and took a seat at the island.

"So, is naked chef a new character I can expect from you?"

"Not in this book, but I wouldn't be opposed to starting my research early." The banter with him was becoming my new favorite activity.

"It's a little bit early in the day for a striptease."

"So, you'll give me one later?" I asked eagerly.

He stopped pulling ingredients out of the refrigerator and braced himself with both arms outstretched in front of him on the island. "It depends."

"On?" I was genuinely curious.

"How much work we get done today. We still have two more scenes you haven't looked at yet." Well, that was a buzzkill. All work and no play made Evan a clothed boy.

"I looked at all the pages Adrian sent me." I frowned. I'd already marked up all the copy to let him have as a reference.

"These weren't included in that." Hmm... there was more.

"I thought the manuscript was finished."

"I felt inspired," he shrugged. "I wrote another chapter last night."

"Inspired by what?"

He winked and turned back to the fridge. "I'm sure you can figure it out."

My eyes widened and I fanned myself with my hand.

Was it getting hot in here?

# EIGHT

### Evan

**Connecticut**

The rest of the day we sat side by side out by the firepit, passing the laptop back and forth. We got most of the scenes edited and I was preparing a PDF to send to Adrian. I knew they weren't quite finished, but we wanted some feedback to figure out what we needed to work on next.

I was surprised at how much we were able to accomplish, but once the initial tension between us was broken, I didn't feel as distracted by her. It wasn't that she lost allure, but now that I knew what it felt like to kiss her, and I could kiss her when I wanted, thinking about it didn't consume me.

"So back here bright and early tomorrow morning?" she asked as she packed her notebooks back into her laptop bag.

"I'll be up early again, so whenever you'd like to show up."

"I could probably come a little earlier, but I'm definitely not missing Marian's breakfasts." The dreamy smile that crossed her face made me a little jealous.

"Oh, I see how it is, already replacing me."

"Well, she does have a pretty fabulous apron," she teased.

"Using her for research?"

"Definitely not. I can't say that I imagine what she'd look like naked." The look she gave me over her shoulder was almost predatory.

I walked around the side of the couch and placed my hands on her hips, turning her around to face me.

"You think about me naked?" I was unable to mask the huskiness in my own voice and her eyes widened.

She ran her hands up my chest and pressed herself up against me as I pulled her hips snugly against mine. There was no question that I wanted her, but I wasn't sure if all her teasing was just that.

"It's all I can think about," she whispered as she looked up into my eyes.

"You could stay tonight."

Her breath caught as her fingers gripped my shirt tighter. "I, uh..."

Shit. I'd come on too strong. This was insane. I'd only met her yesterday. "Sorry. Shit."

One of her hands gripped the back of my neck and pulled my face towards her. My whole body shuddered as her lips gently caressed mine. Our lips met tentatively a few times before she tugged my hair and pulled me into her.

It escalated quickly as she pushed up onto her toes and licked and bit at my bottom lip. My head spun as I pressed my tongue against hers and bent my knees, pushing my growing erection into her stomach.

I was fighting the urge to push her back onto the couch and strip her bare, but I knew that'd be pushing it too far.

After a few minutes, our lips slowed and she pulled back from me, resting her head above my galloping heart. "As much as I'd love to, maybe we should save that for another day."

I nodded and combed my fingers through her hair, willing myself to calm down. "That could be arranged."

She giggled and stepped back, picking up her bag by its strap and settling it on her shoulder.

"I should go." She reached up on her toes and kissed me once.

"I'll see you tomorrow." My lips pulled into an involuntary frown. Two days and I was already craving her presence in my life...in my home.

She stepped around me and I followed her to the front door. Leaning against the doorframe, I watched her pull away, her taillights gradually fading as she retreated down the tree-lined drive. I wasn't sure if I'd freaked her out, but maybe I needed to step back a bit. The only problem was I didn't want to slow things down.

I obsessively checked my email for the rest of the night, waiting for any response from Adrian.

A few hours later, I gave up and went to bed. Tomorrow would hopefully give me some clarity in what was developing between Chase and me.

My phone was pinging long before my alarm went off.

Who the hell was texting me at 5:00 am?

*Adrian: Did you get laid?*

*Adrian: Was it Chase?*

Of course, it was Adrian.

*Evan: No, and was what Chase?*

*Adrian: If you didn't get some, who wrote these edits?*

*Adrian: The scenes almost seem believable.*

*Evan: You're welcome?*

*Adrian: I thought you didn't want anyone else writing parts of your book?*

Fuck off, Adrian. I am a professional.

*Evan: She didn't write the edits, I did.*

Asshole.

*Adrian: How much porn have you been watching?*

No comment.

*Evan: ...*

*Adrian: I take it you two are playing nice?*

*Evan: Yes, I am capable of being nice to people...unlike someone I know.*

*Adrian: You love me ;)*

*Evan: No, I really don't.*

*Adrian: Maybe you won't need her the full two weeks after all.*

Shit...shit...shit.
*Evan: We still have a lot of material to get through.*
*Adrian: You may be able to pull this deadline off.*
*Evan: Did you mark up the PDF I emailed you?*
*Adrian: All business today, huh?*
*Evan: ...*
*Adrian: Yes. Isobel and I went through the draft. She sent you a separate email.*

By the time Chase arrived some hours later, I'd scoured both marked-up PDFs and started making the revisions they'd suggested.

I thought that maybe, at least on half of them, we'd accomplished what weeks of banging my head on my keyboard had not.

I felt myself behaving like an eager puppy as I answered the door, ushered her inside, urged her to sit down on the couch, and made her start reading.

"These look good. Especially compared to the original drafts. It's clear something has definitely clicked into place." She gave me a weak but reassuring smile as she leaned forward to settle the laptop onto the coffee table.

Her sigh was a little forlorn as she leaned back and curled up facing me on the cushion next to mine.

"Is something bothering you?" I wasn't used to this unsure, slightly sullen version of herself. She was usually so full of life and energy.

"I guess I just had it built up in my head that this would take longer," she sighed.

I knew exactly how she was feeling. I was happy that we accomplished our goal in record time, but that also meant that we probably didn't need to keep her here for the entire two weeks.

"Hear me out..." A plan started formulating in my head as she looked up at me. She was either going to think I was insane or a genius.

"I'm listening." Her face had brightened a little, but she was still skeptical.

"What if we sold you staying longer as a mutually beneficial situation?"

"What are you proposing?" she frowned.

"Maybe I have some expertise that will help you with your next book." I wasn't sure what that was, but Adrian and Isobel didn't need to know that.

"Naked chef?"

I laughed as she smiled at me, reaching forward to play with my fingers as our hands rested between us.

"Not quite. How do you feel about collaboration?" I knew we were both resistant to the idea of giving up control of our own work, but we'd meshed well in a matter of days. I wasn't ready to part yet.

"Like you being *my* consultant after I'm finished being yours?"

"No," I shook my head, "like a true collaboration. Shared byline."

"Are you saying?" She looked up at me with wide eyes.

"Write a book with me," I breathed out heavily and held my breath waiting for her answer.

"Isn't what I write a little too...soft...for what you normally write?"

"As in soft porn?" I almost felt bad for the loud laughter that burst out of me.

"Ouch." She sat up and pulled away from me, disappointment clear on her features.

"No...no!" Taking a deep breath, I calmed myself down and scooted a little bit closer to her, using my finger to push a loose strand of hair behind her ear. She sighed and closed her eyes, a shy smile on her face showcasing her dimple again. "What you wrote kept me anything but soft...for several days."

Her eyes popped open and flared with something akin to need as she scooted even closer to me.

"Is that so?" She slowly skated her fingers over my knee and up my thigh, causing me to shift a little.

"Mmhmm. Kind of like you're doing right now," my voice was a rough whisper as I felt all the blood pooling in my groin.

"Whatever will we do about that?" She fluttered her eyelashes at me dramatically and ran her fingernails across the fabric on my pants, dangerously close to my burgeoning erection.

"Are you trying to kill me?" I choked out as I tried to maintain the illusion of composure.

"*La petite mort*, maybe."

"Shouldn't we be brainstorming?" Her eyes had turned predatory again, and I was a little nervous about what was going on in that brain of hers.

"Maybe we need some 'hands-on' research..." By the time her hand had reached my zipper, I was solid and throbbing.

"Chase..." I warned her as she slowly started to pull the tab down, the teeth making a steady clicking sound as they slowly disengaged.

"Shh..." she soothed as she stared down at where her hands were at work, unbuttoning and spreading the fabric apart. "Just sit back and relax."

"Kind of hard to do when a girl has her hand in your pants," I laughed nervously. A woman had not touched or seen me like this in a long, long time.

"Oh, it's hard alright," she smiled deviously as she tugged at the waistband of my boxer briefs. I lifted my hips and helped her push my pants and briefs down my thighs.

"Are your sure about th...mfph..."

My cock was throbbing as she raised herself up on her knees and forcefully meshed our lips together, effectively cutting me off. Her tongue slid past my lips and she bit at my bottom lip as her hand closed around the base of me.

"Mmm..." I moaned in her mouth as she gripped me firmly and began to work my length.

My hands slid into the hair at the back of her neck as she kissed me passionately, while rhythmically pulling on my dick. The dual sensation of her hand pulling and her tongue massaging mine was making me dizzy.

It'd been so long since someone had touched me intimately, I was afraid I was about to spout off like a geyser. Then she started doing this thing where she alternated squeezing the base and twisting at the head.

"Oh my...fuuck...slow down," I broke my mouth from her and panted, throwing my head back against the couch.

She scooted back slightly, winking at me as she leaned down and licked around the head.

"Fuck..."

Her hand continued to tug at the base while she enveloped the tip in her mouth, sucking while she rubbed her tongue against the ridge of the head.

*Holy shit* did this feel amazing!

My heart was beating out of my chest as she brought one of her hands down below my shaft and gently rubbed my balls as she continued to lick and suck at the head. I was about to explode but was desperately trying to hold on to my dignity by not finishing too soon.

I rubbed my hand along her neck and back, leaning forward to grab her ass as she continued to go down on me.

"Mmmm..." she moaned as she took me almost all the way in, pausing before she started grazing her teeth along my length on the way back up.

"I'm close," I whimpered. My voice was husky and almost totally breathless as I grabbed her shoulder.

"Mmmm," she moaned again as she started bobbing her head quicker before taking me all the way in.

"Oh god..." I gasped as I tangled my hand in her hair and held on for dear life. Chase was trying to kill me.

I held on for as long as I could, but a man can only take so much torture. My guttural moan cued her in as she pressed her mouth as far as she could go down on my dick and sucked.

I came in a flurry of hair grabbing, moaning and whimpering as my hips lifted clear off the couch cushions. It was by far one of the most intense orgasms I'd ever had. I could lie and say it was just because it'd been a long time since someone else gave me one, but it was just the effect Chase had on me.

"I think you did kill me," I panted, as I lazily rolled my head to the side and looked at her through hooded eyelids.

She had the biggest smile on her face as she sat up and leaned her head against the cushion beside her, looking directly at me.

"But oh, what a way to go..."

# NINE

## Chase

**Connecticut**

I don't know what came over me, but apparently a hot guy asking me to write a book with him makes me lose my mind. Suddenly, I just needed to touch him. I hadn't intended to include a full oral happy ending, but I found myself wanting to taste him.

"You're quite proud of yourself, aren't you?" he smirked as he looked over at me.

"I guess someone doesn't want a repeat performance."

His head shot up from the couch cushion like I'd lit his hair on fire. "Definitely did not say that."

"I feel like I should start singing that song from Moana," I giggled, feeling empowered.

Evan looked at me strangely. Obviously, he never watched Disney movies.

"You're welcome," I sang, slightly off-key.

He did that staring thing again. Probably trying to decide if he just got fellated by a crazy person.

"Oh, come on, it's The Rock. Have you seriously never seen any Disney movies?"

"Not the princess ones," he shook his head. "Obviously, you have." He was laughing at me with a thoroughly amused look on his face.

"Laugh it up, dude," I rolled my eyes, the smile never leaving my face.

"You're adorable."

I rolled my eyes at him again and stuck my tongue out.

"I know where that's been," he told me, smirk firmly in place across his full lips.

"I didn't hear any complaining," I shot back.

"Only that it ended."

The teasing dynamic of our relationship clearly hadn't changed in the last twenty minutes.

"So, a book?" The prospect of teaming up with him was hard to resist. If we could channel our own chemistry into a book, I had no doubt that it would sell.

"Uh-huh." He smiled and then reached out and grabbed one of my hands, slowly tracing my palm. I had to admit, I'd never thought of the palm as being an erogenous zone, but it was starting to get me a little worked up.

"Any thoughts on content?" I was trying to let him steer me on this and not take over. He was the man with the plan.

"Obviously, something sexy." There was that little naughty glint in his eyes again. Evan wasn't quite as tame as he liked to portray.

"You finally write a decent sex scene and suddenly you think you're an expert?" I couldn't resist the urge to continue teasing him a little.

"I had a very gifted teacher," he smiled.

"Charmer," I said shyly, feeling a blush rising.

"Is it working?"

"You already got yours," I accused as I tried to play off the effect he was having on me.

"But you didn't get yours." He raised an eyebrow at me and made an obvious glance at my tight-fitting shirt. I was fairly sure my nipples were trying to burrow through the fabric.

"I thought we were trying to work here," I argued, but both of us knew that if he wanted to take things further that I'd jump on him in a second.

"You're the one who said we needed to '*do* research'." I'd obviously created a monster.

"Are you going to make this hard the whole time?"

"Give me a few minutes and I can make it plenty hard." Heat flared low in my belly as he turned the tables on me, and seductive Evan came out to play.

"I thought you were supposed to be the awkward one?" I teased as I stroked his finger suggestively.

"You apparently bring out the best in me."

My heart melted a little, even though his comment was clearly a little pervy.

"Work. We're supposed to be working," I tried to change the subject. "Genre?"

"Thriller?" he offered with a shrug. Obviously, that would be well within his comfort zone.

"Characters?" I was interested to see how he did the initial character development. Evan's brain was a curious place.

"Does Michael have any friends?"

My entire mouth went dry as my jaw dropped open.

Holy shit.

Evan wanted to write a sexy book with me about bondage. It's always the quiet ones.

"Are you saying...?" I wanted him to admit what he wanted.

"Maybe we write a thriller with a little bit of a kinky twist," he shrugged, but I could see the tension in his eyes.

"You're just full of surprises." Having read some of his older books, I knew that he tended to stay away from his characters being in tumultuous romantic entanglements.

"Maybe I'm ready to try something new." His readiness to jump right into this showed he was open to new possibilities, both with his writing and with me.

"More research?"

"If the right research partner comes along," he teased as he gave me a cheeky wink.

I pretended to be reluctant about his proposal, but I was so on board. "What does the job entail?"

"Lots of long...'*hard*'...hours." He stressed in that deep sexy voice that appeared when he was aroused. If I was a cartoon character, I would have fainted with little hearts flying around my head.

"You realize I'm not an expert, right?" I had more experience than he had, but I'd only seen the parts of the lifestyle that Emory had shown me.

"You know more than I do," he nodded. "We could learn together."

The thought of Evan coming with me to train with my Dom source was amazingly hot. Instead of having Emory tying me up and simulating the scenes I was trying to write...he could be teaching Evan what to do with me.

Is was going to have a field day with this. I go away for two weeks and bring back a new story pitch that's hotter than anything either one of us has written before. Adrian was going to have kittens. He was going to think I tempted his highest-grossing author over to the dark side.

"So how are we going to spin this?" Isobel was counting on me to finish my current project. Derailing my progress for a completely new project was going to piss her off.

"Honestly? Let's keep them in the dark," he said, looking slightly guilty. It seemed he knew Adrian would be protesting this match-up as well.

"You mean don't tell them until it's written?"

"Bingo," he winked.

"It could take months." It typically took me a few months to draft a book; I couldn't disappear for that long without drawing suspicion.

"Can you escape for that amount of time?"

"Won't you get tired of me?" I asked warily. That was a long time to spend with someone when you were used to being alone.

He shrugged and then pulled me closer to him on the couch. "I honestly don't know how this is all going to turn out, but if it means I get to spend more time with you, I'm all in."

"I'm having a hard time taking you seriously with your pants still undone."

He laughed and grabbed my sides, tickling me as he raised himself up over the top of me on the couch. We crashed back into the pillows and his mouth came down on mine in a calculated attack.

Evan's tongue and exploring fingers were erasing every doubt and hesitation that had been building up within me. I could feel him hot and hard pressing up against my stomach, his pants still halfway down his thighs.

My hands gravitated towards his bare cheeks as he slid his underneath the hem of my top, caressing the skin of my back. My breath was coming in harsh pants as I broke the kiss and threw my head back. His fingers delved under the cups of my bra and tweaked my nipples as I bucked my hips up into him.

"Oh god," I moaned as he started to thrust against the thin layer of my leggings, sliding one hand down the length of my thigh to hitch it over his hip.

"Come to bed with me," he growled into my hair as I dug my fingernails into his ass, causing him to jerk his hips into me.

I nodded my head frantically as he began to rain biting kisses down my neck and to my collarbone. "Yes..."

Before I could anticipate the motion, he pulled himself back and stood up, hitching his briefs and pants up over his tumescent cock — presumably so he could walk without tripping.

"Let's go." He held his hand out to me. I placed my hand in his and he yanked me up before he crouched down, banded his arms around my legs, and hoisted me over his shoulder.

"Evan!" I shrieked as he stood back up and stalked past the kitchen and down the hallway, me laughing into the back of his shirt as he held my thigh with one hand and my ass cheek with the other.

He was clearly a man on a mission as he kicked his bedroom door open. I saw it bounce lightly off the wall and then I was falling backward onto his bed.

That set off a new round of giggles as I scooted back towards the pillows. Evan was still standing beside the bed, kicking off his shoes before he ripped his shirt off over his head.

His chest was lean and lightly muscled with the perfect amount of hair on his pecs and abdomen.

"Is this my striptease?' I giggled as I propped myself up on my elbows and watched him unabashedly.

He smirked as he shoved his pants and briefs to the carpet, stepping out of them before his socks were discarded as well.

"I'll turn on the music next time," he laughed, as he grabbed me by the calf and yanked me towards his naked body.

Before I could even lift my hips to help him, he was pulling down the waistband of my leggings. He peeled them off with my panties and threw them to the floor before he pushed a knee up to the bed and hovered over the top of me.

This dominating side of him was turning me on. He wasn't going to have any problems at all with our 'research'.

He knelt straddling my legs as he took possession of my mouth again, sliding his hands up inside of my shirt and pushing my bra up my chest.

"Ahhh..." I moaned as he cupped my breasts and roughly dragged his thumbs over the nipples.

"Fuck, these are spectacular," he moaned as he pushed my shirt the rest of the way up to my armpits and dropped his head to my chest. My back arched up off the bed as he tugged at one of my nipples with his teeth.

"Off...off..." I insisted breathlessly as I tried to sit up and pull my shirt over my head.

He helped me take it off and released my bra clasp, throwing them both onto the pile of clothes on the floor. His eager mouth devoured my nipples as his big hands framed my breasts and pushed them together.

My hips were squirming on the bed as the twin sensations of his lips and the scruff along his jaw drove me towards madness.

"Oooo..." My hands grabbed his hips and urged him to lay down, his body covering mine.

"Ugh," he panted as he looked up at me, his hard length throbbing against my thigh.

My breasts were forgotten as he slowly shifted to the side, his hand tracing a path of fire up the inside of my thigh.

"You're so wet," he growled as he dipped the tips of his fingers inside of me and then began to rub my clit. My eyes rolled into the back of my head and my back arched as I pushed my hips towards his hand, seeking friction.

"I want to make you cum." His voice was rough in my ear as my eyes closed at the sensations he was stirring up inside of me.

One long finger slowly eased into me and I moaned loudly as it retreated and then slid back in. My leg was wedged in between his and I could feel him twitching against my thigh as he added another finger and began to build up speed.

"Ooo...fuck me," I moaned as I grabbed onto his arm and gyrated my hips into the movements of his fingers. It had never been this intense for me before.

"Come on, baby," he whispered as he nipped along my jaw. I started to spasm against him and grabbed ahold of the hair at the base of his neck and screamed out my orgasm.

"Fuck yes." His voice was gravelly as he raised himself up and settled between my legs. My eyes were screwed shut as I panted, my body completely overwhelmed with sensation.

"Chase?" he whispered as he ran his hands softly down my hair that'd spilled across his pillows.

"Mmm..." I moaned as I pushed my hips up towards his. He flexed forward and I could feel him poised at my entrance. He was hesitating.

"Open your eyes, baby."

I drowsily opened them, and he smiled at me before he ran a finger across my lips. "Protection?"

"Shot...I'm clean..." My voice was a whisper as he nodded quickly.

"Me too," he said quietly as he searched my eyes.

"Fuck me, Evan," I urged as I pushed my hips towards him.

We maintained eye contact as he slowly eased inside, causing us both to moan loudly into each other's mouths. He lightly caressed my lips with his as he pulled his hips back gradually and then pistoned them forward again. The pace of our hips increased, and he pressed his face into my neck as he lowered himself completely and began thrusting into me urgently.

"Oh my god," I moaned as one of his hands clung to my thigh firmly and changed the angle that he was grinding into me.

My hands were gripped onto the muscles of his lower back tightly as I began meeting his pounding rhythm with my hips.

"I'm close," I whispered as I turned my face into his ear, panting into him as he pushed a knee forward and began driving into me.

It was the most overwhelming thing I'd ever experienced, and as my orgasm shot through me, I found myself chanting his name. "Evan. Oh, Evan!"

"Yes..." he growled as he tilted his hips and pounded into my quaking body. "Fuck, Chase!"

His whole body seized, and he moaned into my shoulder as I clung to him, desperately trying to catch my breath. I was quite sure he was the one trying to kill me now.

# TEN

## Evan

**Connecticut**

There were no words.

Chase was curled up against my chest, fingers idly tracing the skin over my heart. I had no words that could adequately describe what had just happened. When I met her, I never expected to end up in bed with her a few days later — not that I hadn't fantasized about it.

"You're thinking awfully loudly up there," her quiet voice brought me back, and I kissed the top of her thoroughly sexed-up hair.

"I don't know what you're talking about. I'm fairly sure I've been stunned speechless." I didn't even recognize my own voice.

She smiled and kissed my chest. "What's the plan for the rest of the day?"

"I really want to get started on drafting an outline, but I still feel like the scenes with Kallie are missing something." I had a niggling feeling in my mind that we weren't quite done with them yet.

"How so?" she asked curiously.

"I know they sound believable now, but I keep thinking about what you said to me."

"I say lots of things," she laughed. "You're going to have to be more specific."

"I'm aware," I nodded, as I ran my fingers down her bare back. "The part about if your heart doesn't start beating faster while you're reading it that it's not hot enough."

"That's good advice." I smiled at the smugness in her voice. "You don't think you accomplished that?"

"I don't know," I sighed. "I just feel like maybe they could be more authentic."

"You're not going to abandon me to go chase down a prostitute, are you?" she teased. I doubted I could look at another woman and not compare her to Chase at this point. But it was way too early to be telling her that.

"Would you want to read the whole manuscript?" I normally didn't allow anyone but the editors to do that, but...

"You'd let me read it early?"

I'd let you do just about anything right now.

"If you knew the whole plotline maybe it'd make it easier for you to help me fix it." If she was going to be my partner, I wanted her to be completely in the loop. We could start with this.

"Won't Adrian have a fit?" she asked with a little bit of humor in her voice. I could tell she wasn't a fan of his. To be honest, sometimes neither was I.

"What he doesn't know..." I trailed off.

"OK." Her voice was quiet and guarded.

I blew out a nervous breath and turned my face into her forehead. She snuggled further into my embrace and sighed as my lips rested on her soft skin.

"Are you sure you trust me that much?"

Positive.

"Of course, Chase. I can't think of anyone else I'd rather... how did I phrase it before..." I mused, "rip me a new one."

She pinched my nipple before she smacked me in the chest.

"Do I need to pick up some lube on the way over tomorrow?"

"Oh, she's got more jokes," I teased as I squeezed her against me.

"I've always got jokes." I could tell she was rolling her eyes at me.

"I'll show you funny," I growled, as I flipped her over and began to nibble on the crease of her neck and shoulder. She was squirming under my weight, laughing hysterically as I rubbed my stubble along her soft skin.

"Ahhh. Stop!"

I eased back a little and began using my lips to kiss and suck along the same skin, eliciting a dramatically different reaction. She moaned and arched her neck as I readjusted myself to settle into the cradle of her thighs.

My cock slid along her lips and I angled my hips to ease inside of her with a slow, deep rhythm.

"Oh, Evan!" Her cries intensified as her hips began to meet mine. I moaned into her neck as she pulled her legs up and braced her feet flat upon the mattress.

The feeling of her body hugging mine so tightly made my head swim and I pounded her into the mattress until I felt her rhythmically clench down on me. Firmly gripping her hips, I slowly rolled myself to the side, pulling her with me. I eventually settled with my back flat on the mattress and her sitting astride my hips.

"Ride me," I urged as I bucked up from the mattress.

"You're in so deep," she panted as she began to swivel her hips, grinding down onto me.

As she picked up the pace, frantically sliding up and down, I met each movement with a firm thrust of my own.

It'd never been this hot for me.

Things had started to become infrequent and stale towards the end of my last relationship and once I caught her cheating, I was done.

Chase was a goddess, blonde hair mussed around her face and shoulders, eyes hooded, her curvy breasts bouncing, with cheeks flushed an enticing shade of pink. She was voluptuous and curvy and, judging by the sultry looks she was giving me, she was entirely comfortable with her own body and what she knew it could do.

Her innate sexuality turned me on immensely and I felt myself rapidly succumbing to the sensations she was stirring within me.

"Fuck. Go faster," I urged as I chased my orgasm, my cock about to explode.

"I'm cumming," she squealed as I gripped her hips and helped her slam down onto me. A few more particularly vigorous pulses of my hips and I roared out my orgasm, my neck straining against the pillows with the intensity of it.

She collapsed on my torso, her hair fanning out across my face and neck. Her heartbeat was pounding against my chest, the tempo almost as quick as my own.

"Shit. I can't breathe," I groaned as I panted.

"I don't think I can move," she laughed, as she lay across my chest.

My eyes closed as our breathing and heartbeats evened out. The last thing I remember is the amazing feeling of knowing how compatible Chase and I were with each other, and the anticipation of this happening again...and again.

Chase's body heat eventually pulled me out of sleep. My human blanket ran hot when she slept.

I didn't want to move her off me, I'd slept solidly for a few hours, but we probably needed to eat a late lunch and come up with a game plan. I didn't want her to go back to the bed and breakfast each night. Even though I truly did enjoy my privacy, it'd be so much better with her here.

I'd get to wake up to her attempts to overheat and smother me, we could write and brainstorm at our own pace, and maybe I could give her that naked chef demonstration that she wanted.

Mental note: order an apron on Amazon.

"Baby..." My whisper went unanswered, she really was out like a light. I wondered if she had trouble sleeping as I did sometimes.

My fingers skated down her sides, gently lifting her hips and attempting to ease her off to my side. She mumbled something and curled into the comforter as I finally freed myself. Lying on her stomach with her hair spread out around her, she looked sated.

Our chemistry — at least for me — was explosive.

I ached with the urge to climb back on the bed and slide into her from behind, but she was exhausted and probably a little sore.

My fridge was depleting quicker than normal with another person in the house, so I'd need to make another trip into town this week. Maybe Chase would accompany me.

That'd get the town gossips going!

"Might as well do something productive."

I found my laptop and worked on getting together a readable PDF of the latest re-draft of my manuscript.

My mind raced at the thought of her reading it, but I was also kind of dying for feedback from someone other than Adrian. He was paid to be nice to me.

"Hey..."

Arms encircled my shoulders over the back of the couch as Chase kissed my ear and hugged me.

"Someone was tired," I hummed as I leaned back into her embrace.

"I know. You slept forever," she yawned.

When she walked around the edge of the couch, I could see what she was wearing. She'd obviously raided my closet and was wearing a blue plaid flannel shirt. Her long legs were bare, but she had a pair of my socks on.

"Someone is making herself at home." I'm sure the smile I was wearing was ridiculous.

She tucked her hair behind her ear and looked at me shyly. I wasn't upset. She looked amazing in my shirt. It hugged her curves and hit mid-thigh. Showing off a sizeable amount of bare skin.

"It looked soft," she confessed as she rubbed one of the lapels against her cheek. She sat herself down on the opposite end of the couch.

"I'm never getting that back, am I?" And I was OK with that one hundred percent.

"Probably not."

This time when I stared across the space on the couch between us, it wasn't awkward or uncomfortable. My staring had to do with the fact that I couldn't and didn't want to stop looking at her, not my sometimes-intense awkward behavior. It hadn't seemed to bother her anyway.

"So, do we have a plan?" she asked as she nodded towards my computer.

"For?" I asked curiously.

"You're telling me you haven't planned out the rest of the day in your head?"

I picked up the tablet from the corner of the couch and slid it into her lap. "Well, you've got some reading to do..."

"And what are you going to do?" Her soft smile warmed something inside of me.

"I skipped my run for you this morning, so I probably need to get that in."

"Are you sure I can't just watch that instead?" she smirked.

"Fine," I teased as I started to tug the tablet towards myself, "if you don't want to read it then I guess I can take the tablet back."

"No! This is mine." She pulled it back and hugged it to her chest.

"I'll be on the treadmill in the sunroom," I told her as I stood up and went to go find my running shoes by the front door.

"You're not going to run outside? It's such a nice day."

"I usually alternate days, I'll run outside tomorrow." I shrugged as I looked over at her. "Do you want to run with me in the morning?"

"You probably get up obnoxiously early, right?" she sighed with a knowing look.

"6:00 am is not that early."

She pulled a face and shuddered. "It is when you don't fall asleep till midnight."

"Maybe you just need a good night's sleep," I teased.

"The bed at the B&B is comfortable. I slept like a baby in it last night," she sighed.

"I'm betting my bed is nicer." Especially with both of us in it... naked.

"Meh." She shrugged her shoulders. "The mattress was kind of hard and lumpy."

"I think you meant hard and chiseled... since you used me as a mattress," I teased, and her cheeks turned pink.

"You were warm."

"You know..." I hedged, trying to keep my voice even. "I was thinking."

"That's scary."

I ignored her and tried to keep going. "What if, in the interest of accessibility, you stayed here instead?"

"You want me to stay here because it would make me more accessible?"

Granted, it wasn't the best formulation of my argument.

"What if one of us gets inspired in the middle of the night?" I argued. "Wouldn't it be easier to write together if we could do it whenever we wanted?"

She seemed to be thinking it over.

"What's in it for me?" she teased but I could see her lip twitch.

"You get to look at my handsome face all day." I batted my eyelashes at her.

"Eh..." She shrugged her shoulders again. I pinched her side and she laughed.

"I'll cook your food?" I offered.

"If you throw in cooking while naked...then sold!" she giggled. She really was not going to let this naked chef thing go.

# ELEVEN

### Chase

**Connecticut**

Apparently, Evan's enthusiasm for my books had rubbed off on me. I couldn't put down the tablet. I'd even turned down taking a shower with his sweaty post-run self to keep reading.

Kallie's character had drawn me in, and I'd just gotten to the good part where she met Detective Peter Raines for the first time after witnessing a murder.

After he'd taken a shower, Evan pried the tablet out of my hands so we could leave, and thoroughly teased me on the car ride over. He'd ridden with me back to the B&B to check out and get my luggage.

I was going to miss my little private sanctuary but — even though I gave him a hard time — I was looking forward to cuddling up with him each night.

"The house is nice," he marveled, as I unlocked the door of the private entrance to my suite.

"I know. I was wary when Is told me there were no hotels anywhere near your house, but this place turned out to be so much better," I nodded. "It's quiet, and Marian's breakfasts are leaps and bounds from my usual stale bagels and yogurt served at other places."

"If you want to keep staying here..." he offered, but I cut him off.

"No."

He wrapped his arms around me from behind and kissed the side of my neck.

"I want to be with you. I think you're right. It'll help us get into the rhythm of it if we're not limited on time," I told him. He was right, inspiration didn't always hit during normal hours. There were times I woke up in the middle of the night and pages just poured out of me.

"There's another rhythm we can get into..." His hips pressed into my back and commenced a slow grind against my ass. "It's a pity we never got to break in this room..."

"You're naughty." I was enjoying this new side of him.

He slowly pushed my hair off my neck and laid hot kisses along the back of my jaw. His hands roamed my front as one slid down my stomach and into the waistband of my pants, while the other cupped my breast.

"Uhhh..."

The slow but firm motions of his fingers caused my breath to quicken. A heat pulsing through my veins.

"We've got some time. I'm in no rush," I moaned as I leaned back into his chest.

"The only rush I'm in is to get you out of these clothes." The low, urgent tone of his voice turned me on even more.

"By all means, don't let me stop you," I panted.

He backed up slightly and started to pull the fabric of my pants down my legs. Kneeling behind me, he kissed the backs of my thighs as he helped me pull off my shoes and step out of my pants. The socks and panties were eased off me too before he pressed on my back and bent me over the edge of the mattress.

I could hear rustling behind me and turned around to watch him unbutton his pants and shove them to the floor along with his briefs. My mouth watered as I took in his bare form. He was staring at my ass with an intensity that made me wet.

"Take your time..." I teased as I wiggled my ass at him and licked my lips.

"Fuck it," he growled as he gave up unbuttoning his shirt and grabbed me by the hips.

"That's the idea. Ohh," I moaned as he grabbed a hold of himself and rubbed the head of his cock through my opening.

"Someone is a little excited."

He kept dipping the head in and retreating. I tried rocking my hips backward, but he held my hips firmly with both hands as he tortured me. He continued this until I was a squirming mess, gripping the sheets on the bed above my head and biting my lip as I fought the urge to yell at him.

When I thought I couldn't take it anymore and was going to go insane, his grip intensified on my hips and he plunged in fast and hard.

"Oh god," I moaned as he pounded into me, widening the stance of his legs and angling his hips to hit me in just the right place that I almost screamed from the intense pleasure.

This reminded me vaguely of one of the scenes in his book, where the detective and Kallie finally gave in to the desire they had for each other.

A firm hand cracked down on my ass and I jumped as I moaned. "Ohh...fuck..."

"Again..." I moaned as he rubbed the tender skin and then switched which sides he was holding onto my hip with. His large hand smacked the other side and I grunted as I clenched around him.

Where had this come from? He didn't seem like the type to enjoy rough sex, but I was not complaining.

"God, you look so hot..." he groaned, and I turned my head to look at him. His eyes were focused on where we were joined as he continued the quick motions of his hips.

He lifted one hand and traced the place his hand had struck on my cheek that still stung a little bit, tickling the skin where he'd spanked me.

I laughed and then moaned as he gripped my hips again and picked up the pace. He was forcing my hips into the side of the mattress with every thrust, and I was just trying to hold on as my orgasm started to build.

"Ohhh..." I moaned as I felt him adjust himself to lean down over my back. He slipped a hand between my hips and the bed and found my clit while he continued ramming into me from behind.

The quick circles of his fingers, the rough pulsing of his cock, and his hot breath on the back of my neck set me off.

"Fuck...oh god..." My voice was muffled as I moaned into the sheets.

"Evan..." I keened as I clamped down on his cock and gripped the bed as my muscles started spasming uncontrollably.

"Yes...yes...ugh..." he groaned as he plunged into me through the spasms, not slowing the pace of his fingers.

I was moaning uncontrollably as he leaned himself back and gathered my hair into one hand, the motions of his hips never stopping. As he straightened himself back up, he pulled the hair in his fist lightly, causing my back to arch.

"Uhhh..." I moaned as he moved his hand back a little more and dug his fingers into my hip with the other hand. My body was on high alert as he manipulated me for his pleasure, and I felt myself start to build up again.

"Harder..." I urged, and the growl he let out as he snapped his hips forward and pulled on my hair stole my breath as another orgasm rolled through me.

"Fuck...fuck...fuck," he grunted as he punctuated each exclamation by slamming me back into his hips. I was out of breath and my entire body was tingly as he pulled me back into him one more time and groaned out as he held me tightly and pulsed inside of me.

"Oh my god," I moaned as I laid there face down on the sheets, my shirt stuck to the sweat on my back and thoroughly out of breath. I wanted to applaud his performance, but I couldn't move.

"Shit," he groaned as he slowly eased himself out of me and released my hair so he could rub his hand on my ass cheeks. They still stung a little bit, but I really did not mind.

"You alright?" He asked as he let go of me and I slumped against the side of the mattress.

"Mmm. I'm good." My voice was drowsy as I closed my eyes. He laughed as I heard him rustling behind me.

His pants were pulled up again when he lay down on the bed beside me and ran his hand down my hair. I cracked one eye open, and he laughed at me again as he propped himself up on his side and watched me.

"How am I the only one comatose?" I wasn't sure if I could make my limbs move, as numb and tingling as I was.

He shrugged as he began to run his fingers down my back, making me squirm.

"I hate you..." I mumbled as I looked at his smug face. He was a little sweaty, but he wasn't panting like me.

"Pretty sure you don't," he teased, the blue in his eyes alight with mischief.

"Grrrr..."

"Come on, get dressed. Don't make me spank that pretty ass of yours again," he threatened as he ran his palm over my thigh.

"What got into you? I never expected to see this side of you..." I rolled onto my side and scooted across the bed, so we were facing each other.

The content smile on his face turned more serious as he reached over and clasped my hand.

"Hey, it's OK..." I coaxed as I watched some of the light drain out of his eyes.

He was quiet as he took a deep breath and looked down at our interlaced fingers. "I've honestly never done that before."

"Really?" My eyes widened as I watched the pink stain of his blush grow on his cheeks.

"I'm surprised you didn't recognize what I was doing."

I thought back to how everything had transpired. It had been fairly like the way Detective Raines had bent Kallie over the arm of his couch.

"Maybe that's what we need to do..." My eyes widened.

"Um, I'm pretty sure we already did it," he laughed nervously.

"Shush..." I laughed as I squeezed his hand. "We need to recreate the scenes."

"From my book?" He frowned as a little line appeared between his eyes.

"Yes! Maybe that will give you the extra material you need to get those scenes where you wanted."

"Are you sure?" He did not look convinced this was a great idea.

"Am I sure that I want to recreate some pretty hot sex scenes with you? Hmm... let me think about it..."

"They aren't exactly romantic," he cringed.

"And slapping my ass and pulling my hair is?" I laughed.

His face turned bright red as he bit his lip and stared at me.

"Hey, don't get shy on me now. I obviously wasn't complaining."

"Where did you come from?" he breathed out as he stared at me incredulously. "I swear it's like someone just pulled you from my thoughts."

I smiled at him as I felt my cheeks heat up. "You already got in my pants; you don't need to pour on the flattery."

He slid himself a little closer to me and placed his arm across my waist. His fingers traced the bare skin along my spine, just under the edge of my shirt.

"I'm not kidding. I've never felt like this with anyone," he whispered. "Adrian makes fun of me and doesn't understand why I won't do book signings. My ex....well, she was just mean in general but..."

He stopped talking and got this forlorn look on his face. "She never made me feel comfortable when we were together."

"She sounds like a bitch."

He laughed as he leaned forward and kissed me softly. "She was, and she made me feel inadequate... sexually. I would have never felt secure enough in myself to do what we just did."

"But you are with me?"

He nodded. A soft smile forming on his lips. "I'm more relaxed with you than I've been in years. Normally, when a woman tries to flirt with me, or hell, even talks to me, I choke up and bolt."

"I'm glad you didn't bolt. Might have made it hard to finish your book." Perhaps my meeting him at his own house ensured that we at least had a level playing field. If I'd met him at an industry event, would he have even talked to me?

"As soon as I read your books and your author bio, I knew I had to get over myself and meet you."

Aw... he really was adorably perfect. I found myself feeling some intense things for him already.

"I don't know what to say. My words are going to fall short of yours today," I told him quietly.

"I wasn't looking for compliments," he shook his head as he looked over at me.

"I know, but I couldn't stop thinking about you before we met too. I wanted to know the man who wrote this incredibly strong character," I confessed quietly. "I wanted to know the person who could write so beautifully, but with this intense sense of loneliness. I wanted to give him a big hug and let him know he didn't need to be lonely anymore."

His eyes searched mine as he reached up and ran a strand of my hair in between his fingers.

"I'm not going to be able to let you go," he whispered as he leaned forward and captured my lips. His were soft and tentative, slowly encasing my bottom one and then retreating, just to dive right back in. He didn't try to deepen it or speed it up... just lazily kissing me until I felt dizzy.

After a few moments, he pulled back and rested his forehead against mine, closing his eyes. I reached up and cupped his jaw, running my thumb across his cheekbone. If I wasn't careful, this kind but awkwardly adorable man was going to steal my heart. And when he finally did, I wasn't going to want it back.

"Let's go home," he whispered, and my heart burst with affection that he was opening his life to me.

# TWELVE

### Evan

**Connecticut**

Having Chase in my house 24/7 was an adjustment. She was not an early morning person. The growl she unleashed on me when I tried to get her to run on the trail with me was both adorable and terrifying.

"Go away..." she groaned into the pillow she had a death grip on near her face.

"Come on, it'll wake you up. I always feel invigorated after a run."

I was wearing my athletic gear *sans* shoes and sitting next to her on the bed. My hand was combing through her tangled bed-head and she was groaning into the pillow.

"Good for you..."

"Please...I'll make it worth your while," I tried to coax.

"I hate you..."

"You seem to be saying that an awful lot. I might start taking you seriously," I smiled as I watched my grumpy girl.

"You're so annoying. Go take your morning person vibes somewhere else."

"Please..." I begged.

She rolled over onto her side facing me and squinted her eyes open. "I was promised naked cooking if I stayed here...if you don the apron and let me smack you with a wooden spoon, I'll go running with you..."

What...the...fuck...

My cock didn't know what to think. The thought of her swatting me with a kitchen implement both excited me and made me want to hide from her. She was kind of violent in the morning.

"Fine, you don't have to come this morning, but I will get you to go with me."

She laughed into the pillow as she flipped me off.

"Oh, come on, I won't hit you very hard."

"Go back to sleep." I kissed her cheek, and she closed her eyes again, pulling the comforter up to her chin.

I left her curled up in my bed and went to put on my running shoes. I especially needed to clear my head this morning. Chase had really done a number on me. I don't know if it was reading all her books, or my writing what I'd been writing this week...but I couldn't stop thinking about sex. More specifically, I couldn't stop thinking about sex with her.

Her idea to reenact the parts of my book I felt needed work was a good one, but some of the things Kallie and the detective did were rougher than I was used to. He liked rough sex and she did it for a living. My characters were obviously much more experienced than I was.

"Ugh...stop thinking about sex," I admonished myself. It was as if one of the characters in her books had invaded my brain.

I really needed to run. Although if my line of thought continued, I wasn't going to be able to with a rod in my shorts and I would have to go wake Chase up again. She'd probably growl at me, but I was sure I could persuade her with a few well-placed kisses.

"Stop it."

I could kiss her all I wanted after I got this run over with. Maybe I could get her to join me in the shower. I really did need to stop thinking about it. She had to be sore after last night. I'd gotten a little carried away before we came back to my house.

She said she liked it, but I saw her wince when she got redressed last night before we packed up all her things and said goodbye to Marian, who was very friendly and didn't stare at me like most of the other locals. I just liked my privacy; I wasn't a unicorn.

My feet pounded against the gravel trail, the crisp morning air permeating my lungs. I loved running. It always made me feel more alive. It was something I could do to tire out my body to clear my mind.

I found myself completing the trail at a pace that beat my usual time. My muscles burned as I grabbed my bottle of water off the patio. I was so wound up I could probably run another lap, but I wanted to shower and curl back up with Chase. Hopefully, she wouldn't be as grumpy by the time I rejoined her.

"'I'm a Barbie girl, in a Barbie world. Life in plastic, it's fantastic'."

What the hell? I hadn't heard Aqua's 'Barbie Girl' in years.

I crossed the threshold of my bedroom, tossing my empty water bottle onto the edge of the bed. It was empty, so apparently Chase had decided against sleeping in. She was evidently in my bathroom, singing very loudly.

I could also hear the shower running, so she hadn't waited for me. Hopefully, I could catch her in there. My shirt and shorts were quickly discarded in the hamper as I pushed the door open. A cloud of steam billowed out and I wondered how long she'd been in here. I was only gone a half-hour.

I wasn't proud to have the knowledge, but when she got to the part in the song at the end where Ken chimes in, I couldn't help myself.

"'Well, Barbie, we're just getting started.'"

"Arrgh!" She jumped and dropped the bottle of shampoo she'd been holding as I stood in the opening of my walk-in shower. I quickly crossed to her and grabbed her by the elbow as she started to slip backward.

The last thing we needed was for me to scare her into a concussion. That wasn't the kind of banging I wanted to be getting into with her.

"Holy fuck. You asshole," she laughed loudly. "You scared the shit out of me."

She continued laughing as I pulled her up against my bare chest and kissed her.

"I didn't know late 90s pop was your thing," I teased.

"It's obviously yours since you knew the lyrics!"

"I blame my sister," I shrugged.

"I blame my childhood," she snarked as she crossed her arms, and it pushed her breasts together enticingly.

"You were like ten when that came out. Your parents let you listen to that?"

She giggled as she snuggled up against me and ran a hand up into the hair at the base of my neck. "No...but my brother's girlfriend did."

"Corrupting young minds, such a shame."

"I thought you liked this corrupt mind," she smiled up at me.

"Oh, I do."

I was sure I more than liked it, but I was keeping that one close to the vest. She already knew I could be socially awkward. We didn't need to add 'clingy' to what she thought of me. I was serious when I told her I wasn't sure if I could let her go. I didn't want her to return to Boston.

My head knew it was inevitable for her to go home, but my heart... it'd already made a place for her here... with me.

"How was your run?"

"Fast," I laughed.

"Eager for something are we?" she teased as she pressed herself against me tighter, her nipples grazing my chest.

"Nope."

Her eyes shot up to mine and she pinched my nipple with the hand that was resting on my chest.

"So violent!" I laughed.

"You like it..." she teased as she ran her thumb over the peak softly. "Do I need to kiss it better?"

She was giving me a run for my money. I thought that she was a tease before things became physical between us, but now... she was insatiable.

"I mean, I'm not going to turn you kissing me down." I knew what those lips could do.

"Right answer," she said as she began to kiss and suck at my neck, working her way down my chest. Then she was nipping at the poor nipple that she seemed to enjoy torturing.

"Ahh!"

"Someone seems to enjoy it..."

Her warm, wet hand encircled my shaft, and I couldn't help but flex my hips into her ministrations.

"Fuck, you're driving me insane." But I was loving every minute of it. I never expected the reaction my body had to small amounts of pain.

"Now you know how I feel," she whispered as she licked a line up to the lobe of my ear. Her teeth tugged on it and I moaned louder as she continued the sweet torture on my body.

My palms found the swells of her breasts and slowly caressed them until she was moaning into my neck, continuing to pleasure me. This woman was a vixen, and I couldn't think around her, much less deny her desires.

"Let me touch you," I whispered in her ear as I began running my hand down her stomach.

"Oh! Evan...yes..."

My fingers slipped between her folds and, finding her drenched with desire, slid easily against her sex.

"Be gentle," she whispered as she rocked herself against my hand, the grip of her hand on me tightening.

"I don't want to hurt you," I whispered in her ear as I slowly eased a finger inside of her warmth, twisting and curling it to see if I could make her moan.

"Uhhh..." she moaned as she rose onto her tiptoes and my finger slid in further.

"Sit down, baby," I urged as I turned her around and pulled her hand from me.

There was a tiled bench seat along one wall, and I helped her sit and spread her legs apart.

"Put your feet up here." I tapped on either side of where her legs sat. She raised up her feet and settled them on either side of her. My hands pushed against the backs of her thighs and I pushed her further apart as I settled on the tile on my knees.

"Oh god!" she moaned as I leaned in and took a long, slow, lick in the crevice between her legs. I paused to suck on her clit as I slipped one finger inside of her, curling it slightly as I built up momentum.

"Yes! Fuck yes!" she practically screamed as I felt her clit start to throb against my lips. I could tell she was close because she'd grabbed my hair and held on tight as I drove her to the brink.

"Ahhh!" she shrieked as her walls clamped down on my finger and began to spasm. I pulled my finger out and kissed her clit one last time.

"That tickles a bit," she giggled as she released my hair and stroked my cheek.

I stood up and let the water rinse my face before I leaned down and kissed her. She looked sated, slumped against the wall behind the bench with a lazy smile on her face.

"Come here," she whispered as she reached forward and pulled on my hip, urging me close to her. "It's your turn."

"You don't..."

She shook her head and reached forward to grab my impossibly hard cock. She wet her lips with her pink tongue and then whispered the sexiest fucking thing I'd ever heard in my life.

"I want you to fuck my mouth."

My breath caught as she leaned forward and licked the head, causing it to jump between us.

"Ohhh..." I braced one hand on the wall above her head and grabbed myself with the other. She'd opened her mouth and placed both hands on the backs of my thighs as I guided my cock into her mouth.

I'd had women suck me off before, but to have her pull against my legs and encourage me to literally fuck her mouth was insanely erotic.

"Mmmm," she moaned as she dug her fingers into me and began to rub her tongue on the underside of me with each slow thrust.

"Fuck..." I groaned and slapped the tile with my hand as she grazed her teeth along the ridge at the head. My hips shot forward faster into her mouth. I was afraid I'd choke her, but she just moaned more as she increased the suction.

"I'm gonna cum," I moaned as I closed my eyes and threw my head back. My hips were on autopilot as I plunged in and out of her mouth, chasing my release.

"Mmm." As she moaned against me again, I lost control and pushed as far as I could, hitting the back of her throat.

"Yes!" My hand hit the tile as I clenched and then released, pulsing in streams down her throat.

My head fell forward and rested on the cool tiles as I panted, trying to catch my breath. I slipped out of her mouth and heard her take in a huge breath.

"That was hot."

I cracked open my eyes and gazed down at her.

She had damp hair plastered to the side of her face and her cheeks were pink, but she was the most beautiful thing I'd ever seen. It was situations like this that caused people to blurt out spontaneous declarations of love.

I wasn't going to...but I could see the appeal.

After we cleaned up in the shower, I got dressed and checked my phone. Adrian had blown it up with a flurry of text messages.

*Adrian: Tick-tock, quit playing with your cock. I need those pages.*

*Adrian: I know you're awake. Get your lips off Chase's ass and send me those edits.*

*Adrian: Don't make me drive down there.*

Oh, god no... that'd be a disaster.

*Adrian: I'm going to have Isobel harass Chase if you don't answer me.*

*Adrian: I've never been ghosted before... I don't like it.*

Adrian was such a dumbass.

Looked like Chase and I needed to buckle down and get some work done.

# THIRTEEN

## Chase

**Connecticut**

"Thank you! Just the package I've been waiting for," I thanked the delivery driver happily as I took the box from him. I was kind of surprised he'd deliver all the way out here, but Amazon Prime was never one to shy away from frequent deliveries.

Evan was going to either kick me out or laugh his ass off when he opened this box. I knew it was just a joke...mostly, but I had ordered him a sexy apron and a wooden spoon for myself.

It featured a cartoonish illustration of a hand and the phrase 'May I Suggest the Sausage?'

Why yes, Evan. You may suggest the sausage.

He had holed himself up in the bedroom going through more edits before he sent the manuscript back to be approved by Adrian. Apparently, I was distracting, and he needed to escape from me so he could finish. We needed to get started on our collaboration and he wanted all loose ends tied up.

Speaking of tied up, I needed to contact Emory and see when he was available to meet with us.

I wasn't sure if Evan would be comfortable driving into Boston, but we needed expert advice on this one. Neither one of us had the equipment readily available to start writing about a Dominatrix.

We'd agreed on a female lead and I was kind of scared of what Emory would make me do with Evan to get into character. I didn't want to scare him away.

*Chase: Hey. Got time for another consultation soon?*

Emory had been the Dom who tied me up so I could get into Kayla's head. He also loosely inspired the character of Michael.

Emory liked to follow rules and enjoyed teasing his subs to build up anticipation.

He was funny, always having a sarcastic comment for things when he was not in Dom mode. I'd loved working with him, and he'd only had one stipulation for offering his consultation services — he got to photograph me when he'd tied me up. He promised no pictures with my face in them, and I hadn't been fully nude, but Emory had seen quite a bit of me.

*Emory: Depends. I'm looking for a model...*

He was a fashion and art photographer during the day and a secret Dominant by night. He'd been a friend of a friend and I hadn't been able to use his name in my book dedication.

He wanted to keep his personal life separate from his professional one. I could respect that considering I wrote with a pen name.

*Chase: Bribery. Really?*
*Emory: I need a fresh face.*
*Chase: I thought we didn't do the face*
*Emory: You're walking right into this one.*
*Chase: Oh shut it, you perv*
*Emory: We both know that's not going to happen.*
*Emory: Don't make me find the paddle.*
*Chase: Brat.*
*Emory: Pretty sure you already hold that nickname.*

I sent him an emoji with its tongue hanging out, knowing he would react.

*Emory: What have I told you about the tongue?*
*Chase: Sorry...Sir*

I laughed as I enjoyed our usual banter. Despite being a successful artist, he wasn't pretentious at all. The only time he wouldn't engage in the fun back and forth was when he was acting as a Dom.

Then he was intimidating as hell. I'd initially been a little frightened of him, but he'd been clear when we set the ground rules that my safe word put me in ultimate control.

He'd initially let me sit in on his private sessions with his current sub. She was amazingly kind and fairly brash when she was outside of his studio.

I never would have taken her for the type to be submissive to anyone, but their chemistry was explosive. I had usually stepped out of the studio once they got to the final act, but her moans carried down the hallway despite the soundproofing. Maybe that's why my book was way over the mildly steamy point and was categorized as erotic fiction.

*Emory: Revisiting Michael?*
*Chase: No...*
*Emory: Intriguing... you going to tell me any details?*

I wasn't sure how much Evan wanted me to share with him. Evan didn't even really know that I planned to consult with my source again. But I knew that we needed real-life material to draw from.

*Chase: I have a writing partner...*
*Emory: Oh! Shit just got real...*
*Chase: Simmer down. You can't scare him off.*
*Emory: Him? Even better!*

And here comes the teasing.

*Emory: You hitting that? You going to fill me in? I bet he fills you in...*
*Chase: ...*
*Emory: Oh, come on!*
*Emory: You know I don't like to be kept waiting.*

I sat and stared at my phone for a moment and then looked down the hallway towards the door to Evan's bedroom.

*Emory: Is it anyone I'm familiar with?*
*Chase: His name is Evan.*

Emory: That's all I get?
Chase: ...
Emory: Chase!
Chase: You might recognize him by Evans...
Emory: ...

The screen was quiet for a few moments and then I saw the three little dots appear.

Emory: Fuck! You're bringing Stone Evans with you!
Chase: He's not as intimidating as I expected.
Emory: When did he get into the erotic stuff? He's usually a cockblock.
Chase: ...
Emory: Damn! Did you corrupt that poor man?
Chase: I'm not dignifying that with a response.
Emory: You totally got in his pants!
Emory: Should I be concerned I won't measure up?
Chase: I don't know! I've never seen your dick!

And Em was not seeing Evan's!

Emory: Not my fault... it's not like Talia would mind...
Chase: Keep that eggplant to yourself.
Emory: You know I like to share...
Emory: Actually, I don't :)
Chase: You've got to tone down on the flirty stuff.
Emory: Who me?
Chase: Seriously. I like him...
Emory: Aw! that's adorable. Chasey is smitten.
Chase: I can contact Nathan if you can't play nice.
Emory: Ouch. You know he'd never be as good as me. Although, he has been a switch lately. He could probably give your boy some pointers.
Chase: Who is topping him?
Emory: Grace.
Chase: Hell no!

Grace was a Dominatrix I'd met at one of the lifestyle showcases Em had taken me to. She was graceful alright, but she also carried a bullwhip and a penchant for collecting other people's pets. There was no way I was letting Evan anywhere near her. She took great joy from 'breaking in' new pets.

If Em didn't scare him, Grace surely would.

*Emory: Don't worry. He can be discreet. I can find another Trix to work with you.*

*Chase: You better.*

*Emory: What kind of timing are we looking at? Do I need to clear my schedule?*

*Chase: I need to talk to Evan. He doesn't know about you yet.*

*Emory: Pushing him right into the fire?*

*Chase: I just hope he doesn't run the other way.*

*Emory: He'd be an idiot if he let you go.*

*Emory: I've got shoots this week and next out of town. I can make myself available after that. Let me know.*

*Chase: I will.*

*Emory: Good luck! And don't forget you're mine when this is over.*

*Chase: I get veto on the wardrobe.*

*Emory: Drama Queen.*

*Chase: Yeah...yeah*

*Emory: Behave. I'll check in later. Have fun with your new toy.*

*Chase: Bite me.*

*Emory: Maybe later.*

I put down my phone and picked up my laptop. Isabel had sent me about three emails asking for my latest pages. There were also thinly veiled threats because she was mad; I was dodging her calls after all.

It wasn't necessarily intentional, but I didn't want to lie to her. I also didn't want to pop the bubble Evan and I were inside. We were just starting whatever this was, and I was attached. Going home was honestly the last thing on my mind.

I knew he wouldn't want me just moving in, but I wanted to see where this went. My heart was invested, and I couldn't walk away.

Large hands covered my eyes and I smiled as he kissed the back of my neck. "Being productive out here?"

"I'm trying. Someone told me they didn't want me getting into their head today."

I tilted my head to the side as I looked at him over the back of the couch. He kissed me softly and ran the pads of his fingers down the exposed skin on my neck.

"Now who is distracting who?" I raised an eyebrow.

"Fine...I can see where I'm not wanted." Evan started to back up from the couch and turn away.

I sat up and grabbed his arm before he got too far and pulled him back to me.

"I need to talk to you about something." Might as well get this over with.

"That sounds ominous."

His hands found my hips and he looked into my eyes before he leaned forward to kiss me softly. I hummed into his mouth as our lips languidly caressed each other.

"I promise it's not bad, but..."

"Lay it on me," he smiled.

"There's this photographer in Boston that I know. I'm trying to schedule a consultation with him."

"So, you need to go back?" He frowned and I hated that I may have upset him. "Why a photographer? New headshots?"

"He does want to photograph me, but no... He can help us with the book."

He looked at me quizzically. "New character? How does a photographer tie in?"

"That's his day job..." I trailed off.

His eyebrows raised. "And he's a serial killer by night?"

"Well, he does like to call himself the slayer sometimes... but not because he kills people," I giggled. He looked at me like I'd lost my mind.

"I'm so confused." His face pinched up.

I took a deep breath and put it all out there.

"He has a particular set of talents that he let me document to write Michael."

The look on Evan's face was priceless. Part arousal, part pure terror.

"And...uh...you..." He was scratching the back of his neck and avoiding eye contact with me.

"Hey, what's wrong?" I grabbed his chin and forced him to make eye contact with me. "Talk to me..."

"Will he touch you?" he whispered as he stared down at me. His eyes looked pained, and it startled me.

"Well, he'll need to if we want to make sure we've got the moves right." There was a certain amount of hands-on teaching that came with being a Dominant.

He pulled my hand from his face and turned around to stalk into the kitchen. He braced his palms out in front of him with his head hung low.

Shit.

I put down my laptop next to the box on the coffee table and cautiously walked up behind him.

"Hey," I whispered as I placed my hand carefully between his shoulder blades.

"Stop." His voice was low and gruff as he dipped his shoulders to shrug off my touch.

"What's going on in there?" I asked as I ran a finger across his temple.

"I guess I just thought..." The sigh he released was full of pent-up anguish.

"Thought what?"

He shook his head roughly from side to side. I could hear him taking shallow breaths and I was starting to get worried. "I thought you were mine..."

Oh!

He thought I'd been intimate with Emory. Shit.

"Do you want me to be?" My heart was pounding in my chest as I waited for his answer.

# FOURTEEN

### Evan

**Connecticut**

Fuck!

The thought of her letting another man touch her with me standing there made me want to punch something. I ran all those scenes with Michael back in my head, but with Chase as the one on her knees instead of Kayla.

I know she said it was just research, but I didn't know if this guy had touched her intimately. If he'd let his hands roam her bare body. It was killing me.

"Evan...?" Goddamn it. Of course, I wanted her to be mine. I didn't know how to tell her that and demand this prick didn't touch her at the same time.

I was constantly hard when she was near me and if he had the same reaction to her, then I was going to explode.

"Alright...maybe I should go...just for a bit." She sounded like she was on the verge of tears. I hated that I was making her cry. I had the words right there, but my damn mouth wouldn't work.

"Wait!" I growled as my hand shot out to grab hers.

"I don't know what exactly you think is going on, but I just want you to know that Emory and I have never..."

I leaned back and turned to face her, cautiously placing my hand on her hip. I still couldn't make full eye contact with her, but I was willing to listen.

"Never?" I asked, hating that I was this insecure.

"He's never seen me fully naked." She shook her head, but the way she phrased it didn't sound completely innocent.

Fuck. So, he's seen her partially naked.

"We don't...we haven't ever..." she bit her lip as she sputtered through a response.

"Fuck, just rip off the band aid and stop skirting around it. Who is this guy to you?"

"A friend."

"With benefits?" I deduced. Chase was an attractive woman, and some of those scenes were downright explosive.

She let out a humorless laugh and cupped my cheek, turning my face towards her.

"No! Seriously...just no." She shook her head roughly. "He really was just a consultant. He did tie me up a few times, but I was in shorts and a sports bra most of the time."

"Most of the time?" It sounded like there had been more between them, even if it was just as a photography subject in the context of her literary research.

"He's a photographer. He shot our session once." She wouldn't look in my eyes as she spoke softly.

"Were you naked?"

"Not entirely, no," she whispered, "and it wasn't sexual."

How could it not be sexual?

"He has never and will never touch me in a way that is anything other than as a friend who is helping me."

I scoffed.

"Stop being so stubborn and look at me," she urged, her voice getting stronger.

No...I knew if I looked in her eyes, I'd lose my resolve to be upset about this.

"Evan. I don't want anyone but you," she told me vehemently.

"What if he wants you?"

She laughed and I tried to pull away from her. "Stop. Just stop you idiot!"

"So, now I'm an idiot...thanks."

"For the love of..." she growled. "Shut up. Seriously. I can understand jealousy, but I'm trying to talk to you."

I leaned my hip against the kitchen island and crossed my arms on my chest. My eyes finally met hers and she looked irritated.

"Talk," I said flatly.

"Emory is a friend. I have never had sex with him. I never want to have sex with him." Her voice continued to rise with each word. "Despite being an outrageous flirt, with everyone, he doesn't want to have sex with me either."

The scoff came out unintentionally this time. Who wouldn't want to have Chase?

She smacked my bicep and narrowed her eyes at me. "And you're never going to have sex with me again if you don't stop being an ass."

"I don't want him to touch you."

"Caveman much?" she asked sarcastically.

"Let me rephrase that...the thought of him touching you makes me want to punch him."

"While that's adorable, it's completely unfounded," she scoffed. "When he touches me, it will literally only be to move my body into a certain pose so I can get into the character's head."

"For you maybe." I knew I was getting to the point where she was going to freak out and yell at me, but I'd never felt possessiveness like this. I didn't know how to process it.

"He doesn't want me like that!"

My eyes rolled and I turned my face to look into the living room.

"You are such a jealous little ass..." she growled as she pinched my arm.

"Fine! I'll answer your damn question!" I snapped as I turned back to her. "Yes! Of course, I want you to be mine. The thought of another man ever touching you makes me want..."

"Yes?" she asked with a satisfied smirk pulling across her lips.

I growled in frustration as I looked down at her.

"Talk to me," she coaxed as she stepped forward again.

The thought of another man made me want to claim her...for real. And for always. I was pretty damn sure I loved her. I barely even knew her, but god, did I love her already.

"I'm sorry." My whole body deflated as I tried to rein myself back in.

"I don't know what's going on in that head of yours, but you don't need to worry."

Easy for her to say.

"I want you to be mine too," she whispered as she looked up into my eyes.

"Fuck." I squeezed my eyes closed and pulled her into my chest, cradling her head against me. "I'm sorry."

"It's alright. You were a bit of a dick, but I can understand your reaction."

"It just makes me so angry to imagine..." I growled as I pulled her in a little tighter.

"Then don't imagine it, trust what I'm telling you. I will never want Emory, but I do want you."

We were quiet for a few moments. She put her arms around my back and squeezed me as we stood there. My heart was still pounding. The adrenaline amping me up a little.

"You alright?" She could probably hear it thumping through my chest.

"I'm just frustrated, and a little bit pissed off. I'll calm down. I just need a minute."

"Don't..." she breathed out quietly as she leaned back and gripped my biceps.

"Don't what?"

"Don't calm down. Channel this. The anger."

"What are you talking about?" I asked incredulously. I just acted like a jealous asshole and she wanted me to channel my anger.

"For the rough scenes, Kallie and the detective are furious with each other, right?"

Holy shit. She wanted me to push her up against a wall. My heart took off for another reason. Should we really do this?

"Chase, I don't know if this..." I trailed off as I felt beads of sweat pop up along my hairline.

"Don't overthink it. Just do it." She whispered, her eyes barely concealing her excitement.

"I..." Once again, I was at a total loss for words.

She reached down to take my hand in hers, stroking her thumb across my fingers. I searched her eyes. She was completely serious. I didn't see any hesitation.

Our joined hands gently raised to her throat and she moved my hand to grip it softly.

"Do I have to do the dialogue?"

She smiled at me and winked. "If that helps you."

I closed my eyes and flexed my hand on her neck as I tried to get myself into the character. The gasp she let out solidified it for me and my cock throbbed in anticipation.

I could do this. She was suggesting this, so it had to be consensual on her part.

"Safe word?"

Her neck jerked in my hand and she started laughing hysterically.

"Stop it. I don't want to take it too far. Please. Just give me something to work with here."

"Barbie," she smirked.

"What the...?"

She never failed to entertain me.

"OK. You're making this too hard," she rolled her eyes and held her hand on top of mine, trying to get me to concentrate.

"That's what he said!" I laughed.

"No man would ever say that." She rolled her eyes again. "Quit screwing around and fuck me."

Well, alright then...

I took several deep breaths and blew them out slowly with my eyes still closed.

The scene in Kallie's apartment near the climax of the book started running through my head like a movie.

"I can't fucking believe you!"

My eyes snapped open and locked onto hers. There was excitement there, and a little bit of fear. I felt myself dropping more into the character of Detective Raines and wondered if this was how actors felt.

"I don't see what the problem is. I got the information you wanted!"

I scoffed as I gripped the side of her neck firmly and started to push her back towards the wall next to the front door.

"I didn't tell you to use yourself as bait!" I shouted as I tried to channel my earlier anger.

"I was fine. I'm a big fucking girl, detective," she spat. "I can handle myself."

I growled as I pushed her head back into the wall. My hand moved to pull the hair at the base of her neck just hard enough that she angled her head up at me.

"He's killed people!" I yelled incredulously.

"So, have you!" she yelled back as she pushed at my chest with her small hands.

"Did he touch you?"

"I'm a fucking prostitute, of course, he touched me!" she said defiantly.

My eyes flashed to hers and I was surprised at the ferocity of her voice. She looked to be completely absorbed in what she was doing.

"Do you want to hear about how big his co...," she taunted.

My hand pulled harder, and her head snapped back. I waited for a minute and she winked at me.

Fuck.

"No, I don't want to hear about his damn cock. You shouldn't have even gone near it!"

I smacked the wall right next to her head forcefully and I could see her pupils dilate.

"You knew who I was when you got involved with me. Grow the fuck up!" she spat as she narrowed her eyes at me.

"You think I like knowing that you're going out there every night and putting yourself in danger...." I leaned in and whispered angrily as I pulled her head back again, aiming it towards the wall softly. Despite the situation, I wasn't going to hurt her. "I don't want you touching other men and I sure as fuck don't want them touching what's mine."

That seemed familiar.

She whimpered as she grabbed onto the front of my shirt with one hand. "I'm not yours! You're a damn prick! My body is the only thing that's kept me alive, and I can use it how I want!"

I pressed my hips forward forcefully, boxing her in with my body. She was shaking, with what I hoped was channeled anger, and it was so hot.

"If I want to fuck some guy who gives me what I want, I will. And there isn't a damn thing you can do about it!"

My cock throbbed as I pressed it into her stomach, forcing her back into the wall.

"I don't want you fucking anyone but me!" I yelled and I watched her eyes flare with anger.

She gritted her teeth as she growled at me and grabbed a hold of my dick through my pants. "You take me as I am, or you don't get me at all!"

"Goddamn it!" I growled.

She nodded as I leaned forward and pressed my lips to hers firmly. My hand yanked backward on her hair, eliciting a pained gasp. My eyes shot up to hers in a panic.

"I'm sorry..." I whispered, as myself this time.

"Shh. Don't break character!" Chase giggled.

I let out a nervous laugh and nodded my head.

"You're mine!" My teeth descended on the sensitive skin of her neck biting and sucking harder than I normally would. She was going to have marks left from this. When she moaned and yanked on my shirt, ripping the bottom part of it open, I knew she was with me regardless.

"Shut the hell up!" She grabbed my cock forcefully through the denim and squeezed, causing me to hiss and slap the wall again.

I was about to burst through my zipper.

"Not until you tell me what I want..."

"Fuck you," she whispered angrily as she tried to reach for my zipper.

I grabbed her hand and pinned it to the wall, my fingers tugging on her hair with the other hand.

"Tell me," I taunted as I pulled, and her neck arched backward.

"No!"

"Tell me or I'm leaving!" I threatened.

"You know you can't stay away from me!" she taunted back with a dark chuckle.

I growled. Both for the character and myself. She was right.

"Fine, get yourself killed!" I yelled, and I saw her flinch a little.

"I wasn't in danger! He was so distracted by my mouth on his..."

I cringed at the thump of her head back against the wall. She let out a little huff and looked up at me.

"Come on...it's getting to the good stuff..." she whispered as she slowly caressed my skin exposed by my torn shirt with the back of her fingers.

I rolled my eyes and shook my head.

"Evan, I'm fine," Chase insisted.

I took a few moments to get back into Raines' head. I didn't know how actors did this.

"The only cock I want in your mouth is mine!"

The moan she let out made my eyes widen.

It all sped up at that point.

My hand pressed down, sliding her head down the wall as she dropped to her knees. I held on tightly and stared as she unbuttoned me and yanked down the zipper. She didn't hesitate as she practically ripped my pants while she forced them down my thighs with my boxers.

My dick sprang free, and she immediately engulfed it in her hot, wet mouth. She wasn't gentle as she brought both hands around to my thighs and dug in her fingernails as she bobbed her head at a rapid pace.

I was close to losing it.

Detective Raines was supposed to yell out Kallie's name, but I didn't want to be screaming for another woman, not even an imaginary one.

"God. That mouth," I groaned as she started to scrape her teeth along the underside of my head.

She was really getting into character as she pulled herself forward by the backs of my legs and took me all the way down. I grabbed her by the hair again and pulled up.

She growled and released me, panting as I crouched down and picked her up by sliding my hands underneath her shoulders. Once she was standing, I yanked down her pants and underwear, flinging them across the room and ripping her shirt off over her head.

"Damn," I panted as she ripped my shirt the rest of the way open and used her foot to push my pants to the floor.

"Focus," Chase teased and I smiled at her and nodded.

I reached behind her thighs and hoisted her up, slamming her into the wall and biting on her neck. She moaned as she gripped the back of my head and my shoulder, digging her fingers into my skin.

"Fuck me!"

Her moan spurred me on, so I angled my pelvis and pushed inside her in one smooth thrust. My hips had a mind of their own as I started to snap them forcefully. She grunted with each thrust and held on as I pressed her into the wall.

"Stop fucking other men," I growled into her neck, continuing to keep up my punishing pace.

"What other men?" she moaned wantonly, gasping as she used my shoulders as leverage and grabbed onto my earlobe with her teeth.

"You're mine!" I shouted at Kallie.

I could feel her hips start to falter as she whimpered in my ear.

"Say it!" I yelled as my hips kept up their punishing rhythm.

We needed to get through this last bit of dialogue, but I was about to blow.

"No!" she moaned as she avoided eye contact with me.

"Say it!" I growled as I grabbed her chin in my hand and forced her to look at me.

"Fuck you!" she yelled.

I slammed her back into the wall and adjusted my hips to an angle that made her let out an impossibly sexy moan.

"Now!" My voice was deep and forceful.

"No!" She was keening in my ear and her nails were biting into my shoulders, marking me in the most primal way.

"You make me crazy!" I growled into her neck as I leaned forward. "Stop fucking torturing me!"

My muscles burned as I continued fucking her hard. She was pulsing on my cock and I knew that she was close. I was just waiting for it.

"Oh god! I'm yours! I'm yours!" she moaned as she clamped down on me, milking me for all I was worth.

"Chase!"

Flashes danced in my vision as I let go in streams inside of her. My hips slowed and I braced her gently against the wall and held her to me. I kissed her neck, and she stroked my hair as we came down from the high.

"Well, that was intense..." Her giggle jostled me inside of her and I bit my lip to keep from moaning. I was spent, but I was sure if I really wanted to, I could get it up again.

"Did I hurt you?" I whispered, trying to ease my hold on her.

"A little," she winced as she looked up at me.

"Shit."

"I kind of liked it," she smiled shyly, and I shook my head at her.

"Ugh. Stop it," She was deliberately trying to torture me.

"Can you let me down? My hip is sitting at a weird angle," she asked quietly.

"Sorry...I'm sorry." I shifted her and leaned back as I slipped out of her and gently lowered her to the floor.

She arched her back to stretch and winced a little as she touched her neck. It was red from my teeth and my stubble. It didn't look like I'd bruised her anywhere, but I felt bad for irritating her skin so badly.

"I'll be right back," she told me in a soft voice. She didn't seem all that upset with me.

I groaned as she slapped my ass on her way down the hallway.

"You might want to hydrate, we've still got a lot of material to cover," she giggled as she disappeared out of sight.

Cue the instant erection.

# FIFTEEN

### Chase

**Connecticut**

I didn't think it was possible, but I woke up two days after our novel sex marathon and didn't immediately want to jump Evan. It was probably because I was still walking like I was a rodeo cowboy. I'd ridden and been ridden hard and put away wet.

"Mmmm..." he hummed as his arm tightened around my waist and pulled me flush with his naked body. This had to be the best way to wake up in the morning.

His lips started trailing across the back of my neck.

"You put that away mister," I scolded.

He laughed as he pressed his hips into me.

"That's not what you were saying yesterday."

"Yesterday's Chase didn't feel like she'd been pounded."

His whole body shook with laughter behind me as he nipped at my ear.

"Yeah, she did." I loved...wait...well...I loved how playful he'd gotten.

"You stop it. I'm calling a ban."

He made a little whine and his hand started moving down my stomach.

"Quit it!" I whined.

"You like it," he whispered in the ear he'd been nibbling on.

"Seriously," I half moaned, half whined as I stopped the progress of his hand.

"I can make you feel good."

I knew he could, but my lady parts needed a break. I wasn't a machine.

"Please stop," I sighed. I wanted to; I just wasn't physically capable of keeping up with him today.

"Mmm," he groaned into my neck as he shifted his hips away from me.

I turned myself in his arms, snuggling up against his chest. Leaving his arms was the last thing I wanted to do, but I knew we needed to get up. The fridge was almost empty, and I had plans for him.

"Let's shower," I suggested as I traced my finger across his lips.

"Now you're talking," he grinned.

"Down boy," I teased as I felt him still hard under the sheets.

He smiled at me before he leaned forward and kissed me. It started out softly, but I soon found myself plunging my hands into his hair and opening my mouth to receive his tongue. My resolve was slipping, but I wanted to show him the surprise I'd been holding onto for a few days.

"Let's get wet..." I teased.

"Grrrr," he growled as he narrowed his eyes. "You are such a tease."

"I have a present for you, let's go."

I rolled off the side of the bed and headed for the shower with a wink over my shoulder. I hated leaving him in the bed, but I'd need crutches at the rate we'd been going.

"Alright, what's this present you promised me?"

"Well, it's pretty much a present for me, but it's for you to wear." I hoped that he'd indulge my sense of humor. I thought he'd enjoy it, but I wasn't sure how he felt about a little experimentation. He'd been open to it so far but being on the receiving end was different.

His eyes shot up to mine from his seat at the kitchen island. "Where did you get this from?"

I pulled the box from behind my back and slid it across the island to him.

"Amazon...hmmm. So probably not leather chaps," he mused, his lip twitching as he tried to keep a straight face. So far, so good.

"Those are coming tomorrow." I nodded seriously. Maybe those should be my next purchase.

His head fell back with laughter as he smiled at me. God, he was so pretty. I giggled as he blew out a noisy breath and shook his hands out.

"Just open it," I urged impatiently.

"I will," he said as he looked at the flaps of the box. "I'm just getting ready."

"Fine, I'll open it." I started to slide the box towards myself and he slapped his hand down on top of it.

"Mine," he laughed as I threw my hands up and leaned back against the counter behind me.

"Let's see." He cautiously peered inside the flap as I watched him. He pulled the first item out and held it up, reading the message. "Fuck! This is great."

He laughed as he stood up and held it to his chest. "What do you think?"

"You could probably lose the pants," I shrugged, "but I think it'll look pretty damn good."

He set it down on the counter and opened the flaps of the box wide, his eyebrows shooting up as he appraised the other item in there.

I reached inside of the box and snatched it up, holding against my chest. "This one is for me."

He swallowed heavily as I winked at him. Who knew wooden spatulas could be so much fun?

"You want me to go where?" he asked warily, a few hours later.

"Oh, come on, it'll be fun," I was borderline begging, but I didn't care.

He sighed as he pressed his forehead into my shoulder. "All we need to do is run into town quickly. We need food, not locally sourced honey."

I pouted as I leaned back from him. "Please..."

"Not the lip. Ugh," he groaned, and his warm breath fanned over my shoulder.

"Pretty please..." I was working with my best material here.

"You're lucky I..." His voice cut off abruptly as his body went still.

"You?" It could be my imagination, but it almost sounded like something else.

"Tolerate you," he sighed heavily.

I blew him a kiss as I ran to the hook by his front door to grab my purse. "Let's go Jeeves, you're driving."

He grumbled all the way to the detached garage that was a few feet away from the house. I was bouncing on my toes as he punched the code into the keypad by the door and it slowly started to rise.

"Nice ride," I cooed, lifting my eyebrows at him. He had an Audi sedan, a metallic sapphire blue color with shiny rims and low-profile tires.

"Chicks dig it," he nodded seriously.

I laughed at him and he motioned me over towards the passenger door, pulling it open for me.

"You've had lots of chicks in your car?" I teased as I tried to play along with his bravado.

"Just one. But she digs it." And its owner.

He held my hand and helped guide me into the passenger seat.

"Hmmm. It's decent," I said dismissively. "But the driver's pretty hot."

Leaning inside the door, he kissed me quickly before he stepped back and closed it. I admired the view as he slowly walked to his side of the car.

"So where exactly am I going?" he asked as he buckled himself into the driver's seat.

"It's in Mansfield. It can't be that hard to find." None of the towns around him were all that large.

The satellite radio kicked on as he sped down his gravel drive. Boy liked a little bit of speed. Evan laughed at me as I sang along to the music. The twenty-minute ride went quickly as I serenaded him with my mad skills.

When we got into Mansfield, we didn't have to look far before we ran into something.

"I thought we were going to a farmers market?" he asked quietly as he looked over at me with wide eyes.

The entire downtown area was full of vendors and hundreds of people were milling around. I'd obviously missed the memo about this not being their normal farmers market.

"We are!" I insisted.

"Looks a little bigger than that." Evan's voice was tight, and I could see his posture stiffen the further we drove into the area of town that was crowded with people. "You owe me."

"Live a little." I blew a kiss at him and opened my door after he found a parking spot on a side street.

He crossed behind the car and slipped his hand into mine before he let out a huge breath.

"You OK?"

He nodded quickly as he shot me a tight smile. "I don't people well."

"You don't have to talk to anyone," I insisted as I let go of his hand and pulled him towards me by the plackets of his denim jacket.

"I'm here," I told him quietly as I looked up into his wary eyes. "We can always leave if it's too much."

He slipped his arms around my back and rested his forehead against mine. "I'll be fine. Thanks for understanding."

He closed the distance between us and kissed me softly, humming against my lips. I knew he had some anxiety issues, so I didn't want to overwhelm him. Pushing him out of his comfort zone was going to be touchy, but I meant what I told him. I was here for him.

"You ready?"

He nodded and broke the embrace, reaching out for my hand again. As we wandered through the crowd, Evan's hand on mine relaxed. His eyes were tracking the crowd, watching all the people move about.

"So, this is actually really nice," he let out a little laugh I wasn't expecting. "It's easier when I don't know any of these people."

"Have I led you astray so far?" This could have gone one of two ways, him pulling away from me, or Evan deciding to take a chance.

He grinned at me and wiggled his eyebrows. Pulling me closer and throwing his arm over my shoulders. "You haven't led me anywhere I wasn't already desperate to go."

My smile was radiant as I gazed up at him. In a little over a week, he was like a different person. Watching him come out of his shell was gratifying to see. I loved how playful and genuinely funny he was.

Who was I kidding? I just loved him in general.

We gathered our groceries from the different food and farm stands, taking them back to the car before we explored some more.

"I told you it'd be fun," I giggled as I held onto Evan's arm. There may have been a local brewery that was providing drinks for the festival. And I may have drunk one or two... or four.

"You're hammered." He shook his head as he gave me an indulgent smile.

"Oh shush. I am not. I'm just happy."

He kissed the side of my head as we walked through the crowds and made our way closer to where there was a live band playing. The sun was beginning to set, and I was thoroughly enjoying being out with him.

We'd been so wrapped up in our own little bubble that it was good to go out in public and do something to get away from writing. Or the naughty role-playing that had ramped up his manuscript another notch.

"Just stay right here and I'll go grab some bottles of water." He'd sat me down on a bench that faced the stage. The music was upbeat, and all sorts of people were dancing. Older couples, much younger couples, kids off spinning in their own little worlds. I admired their ability to just let loose and feel the music.

"Drink this," he urged as he took off the lid and placed the bottle at my lips.

I took it from him and took several sips. His arm went around my shoulders along the back of the bench, and I scooted over until our legs were touching. Evan reaffixed the lid and placed a small bag of popcorn in my hand. We'd been snacking all afternoon from various vendors and restaurant booths, but we hadn't really had an official meal.

"Feeling better?" The smile hadn't left his face the whole afternoon.

I nodded as I grabbed his hand and placed it into my lap, interlacing our fingers. "Much. Thank you. You take good care of me."

"I'm trying." He smiled and kissed my temple. "Did you want to get some dinner here or head back to the house?"

All the restaurants in the area were filled to the brim and loud laughter rang out of their doors. I had a feeling that it might be too much for Evan.

"We can go home. I think you've gotten in your quota of peopling today," I replied as I smiled up at him.

"I like you referring to my house as home," he whispered into my neck before he laid a sensual kiss below my ear.

"I think the fireworks will start after dark. Let's stay for that and then go." We sat cuddled on the bench enjoying the festive atmosphere until vibrant bursts of color filled the night sky above us.

I looked over at Evan halfway through and he wasn't looking at the fireworks. The lights were reflecting off his eyes as he gazed down at me. I couldn't describe the feeling in my altered state, but he was making me feel something I didn't think I'd encountered before.

"You ready?" he asked quietly as his eyes flickered to my lips.

I nodded my head as I felt myself leaning towards him. He met me halfway and kissed me long and deep, cradling my face with his large hands. Something had changed between us and I wasn't sure what that would mean for the future. There were still so many things undecided.

The only noise in the car was the soft music playing through the speakers. It was filled with anticipation of what was to come when we got back to his house. His hand was tracing a maddening pattern on my knee as he drove.

"You tired?" he asked me as he held the front door open for me.

"No." My voice was quiet, but I was wide awake.

He took my hand and started to pull me towards the living room.

"But I am ready for bed."

The silent stare from him was heated as he nodded his head and followed me as I led him down the hallway to his bedroom. I stopped at the foot of his bed and turned to face him.

For the first time since we'd embarked on a physical relationship, I was nervous. My hand was shaking a little as I started to slowly unbutton his shirt. His hands found my hips and slowly rubbed circles on the bare skin above the waistband of my pants.

I could feel his heartbeat thumping against my fingertips as I worked the small buttons through the holes, one after the other. We were completely silent as we looked at each other, afraid to break the spell. When I reached the last button, he released me and slowly shrugged his shirt and denim jacket off, letting them drop to the floor.

My hands were drawn like magnets to the defined ridges on his stomach, tracing my fingers along them through the soft hair covering his abdomen. His breath caught as I released the button to his pants.

He gently stalled my hand when I reached for the zipper and pulled my shirt over my head. My bra was the next thing to go as he reached around me to unclasp it, kissing my shoulder as the straps fell away.

He lowered himself to the floor on his knees in front of me, gently kissing my stomach as he began to peel my leggings down my thighs. Helping me step out of them, he ran his hands slowly up the backs of my thighs as he reached for my panties.

"Ohh..." I panted as his lips followed their descent down my legs. After he'd tossed them to the side, he stood up and slowly pushed his own pants and underwear to the floor.

My chest was heaving as I looked at him. He truly was a beautiful man, and my mouth went dry as his erection bobbed in between us as he stared at my exposed breasts.

Evan licked his lips and swallowed as he slowly sat down on the edge of the bed and grasped my hand. He tugged me forward and brought both hands to my waist as he encouraged me to straddle his lap.

"You're so beautiful." His voice was low and sensual as he traced a single finger along my cheek, down my neck and across the peak of my nipple.

"Kiss me," I whispered as I smoothed my hands across his shoulders and into the hair on the back of his head.

His lips were parted slightly, and I nipped at the bottom one before sliding mine to nestle with his. There was no hurry as we slowly explored each other's mouths... slow caresses against each other's tongues and lips. My head was spinning, but the alcohol had long worn off. Evan was intoxicating me with each movement of his lips and the slow motions of his fingertips along my hips.

"Can I have you?" He asked in a whisper as he began to kiss along my jaw and towards my ear.

"Yes..." I moaned as I raised up onto my knees and slid onto his waiting cock. He was so unbelievably hard as I slowly settled onto his lap, his body completely encased within mine.

His hands were still gripping my hips as he began to lead me in a slow, sensual ride. I released a breathy moan as he pulled me completely down onto him and I rotated my hips before I rose slightly and repeated the action.

Ecstasy was coursing through my veins as we looked into each other's hooded eyes. Flashes danced in my vision as my climax started to gradually build, a tingling sensation moving through my body.

"Ohh..." I gasped as his fingers tightened and he began to bounce me on his stiff member.

"You feel so good," he groaned before he leaned forward and captured my lips. My pace began to quicken as he kissed me, my body chasing the high I knew that only he could give me.

"Yes...fuck me," he panted as I rose and fell continuously, pushing us both towards the brink.

My release crested first, and my hips faltered as I felt myself rhythmically clench him inside of me. He closed his eyes, tilted his head back and moaned as he thrust up from beneath me, his fingers gripping my hips tightly.

"Uhhh..." he groaned as I felt him pulse inside of me.

I slowed my hips and tucked my face into his neck, panting as he cradled the back of my neck with his hands. Our hearts pounded against each other's chests, gradually slowing as we both cooled down. I didn't want to let go as I clung to him, completely overwhelmed by my feelings for him.

He stood up with me grasping his neck and turned around, gently laying me against his sheets.

Neither one of us said anything as we settled under the covers and entangled ourselves, my head laying over his heart. My own heart had his name tattooed all over it, I was completely smitten with him. It terrified me to think about his feelings for me. I hoped his own attachment was as strong as mine.

As I drifted off to sleep, I could feel him kiss my forehead and whisper something, but it was too quiet for me to understand.

# SIXTEEN

## Evan

**Connecticut**

*Evan: I'm going to be out of contact for about a week...*
*Adrian: You better still have email access.*
*Evan: I'm taking a break.*
*Adrian: They're pushing for a book tour again.*
*Evan: I'm not contractually obligated.*
*Adrian: Someone is cranky today.*
*Evan: Just email if you need something. I'll try to respond.*

I wasn't in the mood to deal with Adrian. It was the same thing every time I finished a book. He wanted me to do a book tour because he thought it'd boost sales, even though he knew I wasn't interested in pimping myself out to sell copies. I hadn't been on a tour since my third book.

That was where I met my ex. She was a book blogger. I'd thought she was attractive. She came on strong and I'd fallen for it. She'd been uncomfortable with my going on the next one, so I'd had it written into my contract that I was not obligated to tour.

Now, I didn't want to go on a book tour for a whole other reason. I had absolutely no desire to leave Chase. I knew I could ask her to come with me, but I wasn't sure what obligations she had with her own book.

My mind was already frantic with the thought that she might not want to come back here after our trip to Boston. She'd left yesterday to attend a meeting she couldn't skip with Isobel this morning. She wanted me to leave with her, but I'd panicked and told her I'd like to have a car while I was there.

We hadn't talked about the night that we made love at the foot of my bed. It was by far the most emotionally charged sexual experience of my life. She'd ruined me for anyone else.

I was still building up the courage to tell her how I felt when she wasn't asleep.

"God, I'm an idiot."

I'd proposed staying in a hotel, but she refused and told me she'd tie me up and drag me to her condo if I didn't stay with her.

The last few days had been filled with back-and-forth email conversations between Adrian and myself, trying to get my manuscript done and ready for publishing.

I was disappointed that we hadn't had time to engage in her naked chef fantasy, but I was packing the apron in my bag along with the wooden paddle spoon.

My mind was already a nervous wreck as we got closer to our meeting with Emory. I was completely out of my depth. I was sure we could use some levity as we continued to draft the scenes we were putting into the book.

*Chase: Managed to convince Is I was just taking a week-long extended staycation.*

Neither one of us wanted our editors to get wind of this project before we were ready.

*Evan: Adrian bought it too. I didn't tell him I'd be in the city, just out of touch.*

*Chase: He doesn't run in the same circles as Emory... I'm sure we'll be fine.*

*Chase: Have you left yet?*

*Evan: Just have to put my bag in the car and I'm ready to go.*

*Chase: I miss you...*

I miss you too, sweetheart.

*Chase: I sleep better with you.*

*Evan: You mean you sleep better when you have me to use as a body pillow.*

*Chase: And what a body it is ;)*
*Evan: Tease.*
*Chase: I fully intend to follow through if you'd get in your car already.*
*Evan: Kind of hard to drive with a boner.*

She sent me a string of crying laughing emojis, but I was serious. It's kind of hard — pun intended — to drive with a rod in your pants.

*Chase: Poor baby... I'm sure you'll manage. I can kiss it better once you're here.*
*Evan: Not turning down that offer...*
*Chase: Later...we've got plans tonight.*

I sighed. I was looking forward to a quiet night with her alone.

*Chase: Emory is taking us on a scouting mission.*

Fuck...

*Chase: Do you have any leather pants?*

My palms were sweating as I hit traffic coming into the outskirts of Boston. I'd raided my closet and found something I'd hidden in the back. A gift from my sister for a Halloween costume.

Hopefully, she'd like them, because I had not thought about how uncomfortable they'd be to drive in. Especially when I was this nervous.

I'd also found some other things in my room. Her hairbrush on the nightstand. Toothbrush next to mine in the holder on the bathroom mirror. Some dirty clothes mixed with mine in the laundry basket. It helped relieve my fear of her deciding I wasn't worth it. I wanted her to come back with me after this trip so we could finish the book...together.

It took me a little while to find parking around her condo building. I knew she had a space in the attached garage, so I'd have to ask her if she could get a guest pass.

I grabbed my duffel bag and pulled my laptop bag over my shoulder. She'd told me the code to the elevator so I could let myself up to her floor.

My heart was pounding as I crossed the lobby and saw people sitting around on the couches throughout the space. It was nice, but I was feeling a little self-conscious in my get-up and wanted to get inside her condo before I lost my nerve to wear these in public.

The elevator was empty when I got on and I breathed a sigh of relief. That was the part I hated most when I lived in the city. The awkward social interactions with people in elevators, on public transportation, going pretty much anywhere with crowds. I was not a fan.

Once I got to her door, I shot off a quick text before I knocked.

*Evan: I'm here.*

I leaned back against the wall and waited for her to open the door. I could hear rustling and a thump as I stood there, and then the door slowly started to pull open.

Chase's face appeared behind the security chain and her eyes widened. She quickly closed the door and I laughed as I watched her pull it back open and scan her eyes down my form and back up.

"I didn't think you'd actually take the leather pants comment seriously!"

I smiled at her reaction and then took in her own outfit. Damn.

She looked hot. So hot.

Chase was wearing a form-fitting sparkly black minidress with long sleeves. It hugged every dip and curve and showed off her long, toned legs. Her hair was loose and full, dark eyeliner framing her luminous eyes. She was a vision, and I was not worthy.

Damn tight leather pants.

"You look," I exhaled sharply as I released the breath I'd been holding. "Amazing...really fucking amazing."

She blushed and grabbed me by the jacket, tugging me through her open doorway. "Get in here."

I grabbed my bags from the floor and followed behind her, my free hand finding her hip as I used my foot to close the door behind me.

"I missed you," I confessed quietly as I dropped my bags to the floor in the entryway.

She froze up and stopped, my chest brushing against her back. She took a deep breath and blew it out as my grip on her hip tightened.

"Screw it," she muttered as she turned quickly and pressed her hand in the center of my chest.

Then she pounced, pressing firmly until my back hit the door. Chase grabbed the back of my neck and practically forced her tongue between my lips. I could feel my cock stirring in its tight confines and wished I could get them off quickly so I could pin her to the wall again.

My arms banded around her back as I hoisted her up against me, throwing as much passion into the kiss as she was. She bit my bottom lip and groaned when I cupped her ass and squeezed her even tighter to me.

"Mmmm." We broke apart panting at her sensual moan, and I was having a hard time focusing on anything other than how sexy she looked in that short dress and her sky-high heels.

"Goddamn," I groaned, adjusting myself.

"It's your fault!" she laughed.

"How was that my fault?" She's the one that told me to wear the damn pants and then jumped me as soon as I was in the door.

"You come here looking all fuckably hot with your leather pants, and nervous eyes, and telling me you missed me," she scoffed. "So yeah, all your fault."

"So that's all it takes? Maybe I should have dug these pants out while you were back at my house," I laughed nervously, scratching the back of my neck.

"It's not funny!" She pointed her finger at me accusingly.

"It is a little funny," I told her as I chuckled at the petulant look on her face.

"We don't have time for this! The car service from Em will be here in like ten minutes and I just finished getting ready."

I raised an eyebrow at her and pulled her back towards me. Playing with the ends of her hair as she looked up at me. "Ten minutes seems like plenty of time to me."

She narrowed her eyes at me and growled.

"Although, I don't think I'd be able to take these pants off all the way because I'd never get them back on," I mused.

"You put those away."

I laughed as she continued to scowl at me. "Put what away?"

She spread her arms apart, using her palm to gesture at my face and my crotch. "Those fuck me eyes and that thing in your too-tight pants."

I started laughing harder and closed my eyes, shaking my head. "You're ridiculous."

"And you are making me want to drag you into my bedroom."

My eyebrows rose and so did something else.

"We need to go!" she practically yelled as she glanced down at my tight pants.

"Calm down," I soothed, grasping her hand and pulling her towards me. "Why are you acting all high-strung?"

"I'm nervous."

"Shouldn't that be what I'm saying?" I thought I had the market cornered on being a nervous wreck, especially between the two of us.

"Will you promise me that no matter what happens tonight you'll still talk to me tomorrow?" she pled in a quiet, nervous tone.

"Should I be scared? Where is he taking us?" Now her behavior was starting to unsettle me.

She sighed as she played with the collar of my jacket. "It's a Dom showcase."

"What does that even mean?"

"It's a private party where some of the local Doms are able to showcase the lifestyle," she explained quietly, avoiding my eyes.

"Like to the public?"

She shook her head. "No, it's invite-only. Emory belongs to a very select circle. They do these events every couple of months."

My mind was racing. Showcase implied that there would be some sort of demonstrations going on.

"Is this a sex party?" I whispered. While I'm sure it was exciting to some men, the thought of walking into a live orgy scared the shit out of me.

"Kind of, but not really...there are rules..." she trailed off as her phone began to vibrate on the entryway table. "Our ride is here. I'm sorry I can't explain more, but we need to go."

"Are we going straight there?"

My heart was beginning to pound. I wasn't sure this was such a good idea. She must have seen my reaction because she cupped my cheek and stepped close to me. "It'll be fine. Emory will explain more once we get to his studio. You won't be going in uninformed."

I gulped and nodded. I trusted her not to lead me into something I couldn't handle.

I followed along walking slightly behind Chase as she tugged me towards Emory's photography studio. It was at the edge of a trendy warehouse district that featured part of the local art scene.

My palm was slipping against hers as my anxiety started amping up. I was trying to practice my breathing techniques, but it was increasingly difficult.

"Well, we're kind of going as a group. Emory, his partner Talia, Nathan's label is a switch and his current sub."

I'd read up a little bit online about the various kinds of people involved in BDSM. Tops were Dominants, bottoms were submissive, and switch described someone who did both.

"Like I told you before, Em flirts with everyone. He doesn't mean any of it unless it's aimed at Talia. Please don't freak out on me again."

I nodded and kissed the side of her head.

"You still with me?" she asked as she looked back and flashed me a nervous smile.

"I'm trying to be," I replied honestly. This was way out of my comfort zone, but it was important to her. It was important to us.

"I know you are, baby," she smiled as she pulled the door open to the gallery that was on the street side of his studio.

I followed her past the empty desk and through a curtain at the back of the room. I'm not sure what I was expecting, but it just looked like a regular studio. Lights and backdrops set up throughout the large open space.

"We're here," Chase called out as the door closed behind us.

A very feminine squeal came from through a door at the back of the studio. "Back here, Chase!"

She tugged me with her towards the door. I was imagining all kinds of things on our way across the room. Red walls, sex swings, whips and chains. The reality was definitely not what I was expecting. Neither were the occupants of the room.

Perched on the edge of the leather bed were a pale, lanky, dark haired man and an equally pale, petite, blonde woman. She had a leather choker on and an off-the-shoulder minidress with a leather band along the top. He was dressed more casually in a pair of dark wash jeans, a black T-shirt and a black leather jacket.

In the back corner, there was a tall, olive-skinned man with messy black hair and a close-cropped beard leaning against the metal grates mounted to the wall. The woman beside him had darker skin and gorgeous, shiny, dark hair pulled up into a bun on her head. She had on a beaded crop top and a dark skin-tight skirt. He was wearing a dark red suit and his eyes lit up as Chase and I walked into the room.

"Chase! I was beginning to think you'd chickened out on us," he greeted us as he stepped forward.

"Are you kidding? I love people-watching at these things. I wouldn't miss it."

How many of these had she been to?

"I told him you were probably just running late, as usual," the woman to his side responded. I assumed this had to be Emory and Talia. He had a definite air of control to him.

"You show up late to a flogging once and you never live it down," Chase rolled her eyes as she glanced at me out of the corner of her eye.

They all laughed and then the dark-haired man crossed the room and hugged Chase, lifting her off her feet. "It's good to see you."

He kissed her cheek and then stepped in front of me. We were about the same height, but he had broader shoulders.

"Do you want me to call you Evan or Stone?"

He held out his hand to me and I cautiously shook it.

"Uh...I don't know. Whatever you want I guess..." I responded nervously.

"He's adorable Chase. Is he normally this nervous?" he asked as he smiled over at her.

"Yes," she laughed as she slid her arm inside my jacket and hugged me to her side.

"We're going to be in trouble with him tonight," Talia laughed. My eyebrows rose as she slowly ran her gaze from my shoes up to my head, giving me a look of scrutiny.

"Fresh meat." The blonde giggled as she winked at me.

"Don't let them scare you, man. It'll be fine," the other man rolled his eyes at his three companions.

"Unless Grace gets him alone," Talia cringed.

They all laughed as Chase scowled and squeezed me tighter.

"Who is Grace?" I asked her quietly.

"The devil incarnate," Chase muttered.

"Now be nice. She's our host for the evening and I'm still surprised she's letting me bring you after the last time," Emory scolded.

What happened the last time?

"I told her I wasn't a reporter like twenty times!" Chase insisted.

"You brought a hot pink composition notebook to her party," Talia laughed.

"I didn't want to forget things!" I was kind of loving how they were teasing Chase; it made me feel a little more relaxed.

"You know better now," Emory laughed as he stepped back from us. "Let's get down to business before we need to go."

Here we go...

"Grace is the host. It's at her office complex."

"Ugh," Chase huffed.

"You'll both be required to sign an NDA at the door. Standard rules apply," he continued. "No sex or nudity in the common areas. If you're not participating, you have to keep your red cuff visible at all times."

He pulled something out of his pocket and tossed it to me. "Put that on. It signifies that you are an observer. You're not allowed to participate in any demonstrations and the Doms know to leave you alone."

The non-participation part was not going to be an issue. I was already freaking out a little.

"Where's mine?" Chase pouted.

"Don't get your panties in a twist," he rolled his eyes.

"Who says I'm wearing any?" she shot back, and my eyes widened.

What the hell?!

The woman sitting in the corner laughed hysterically as she saw me visibly react.

"Don't worry so much, this is just how they are together," she told me, "you'll get used to it."

"Shit...sorry," Chase tugged on my shoulder until I leaned down, and then she whispered in my ear. "I am. That was a stupid thing to say. I'm sorry."

I blew out a shaky breath and shook my head. I wasn't used to her sassy comments being aimed at someone else.

"Anyways. Any sexual acts or demonstrations are to happen in the closed rooms," Emory told us as he continued explaining the rules. "Word to the wise. Wait until you get back home to try anything with each other. Most of the 'private' rooms have cameras and all of the demonstration sets do."

I nodded as Chase looked up at me, still looking a little wary from her earlier slip-up.

"Any questions?" he asked.

So, so many. But I couldn't find my voice. I was just going to observe tonight.

"Alright, lovelies. Let's go," he said.

"Wait! Shouldn't you introduce yourselves?" Chase stopped him.

"I'm Emory, you can call me Em," he nodded.

"I'm Talia. You can call me Tal or Alia," his companion smiled.

"Mara." The petite blonde gave me a little wave.

"I'm Nathan. Nice to meet you, man. It's about time someone tried to tame Chase," the tall, dark-haired man winked.

We all piled into a black Mercedes van parked on the curb and headed to wherever they were taking me. I wasn't paying attention to anyone in the vehicle on the way and Chase kept looking at me with concern.

"Evan, just a little word of advice. Don't make eye contact with Grace. It won't go well for anyone if you do," Emory instructed quietly.

"Psycho," Chase muttered under her breath. Apparently, she didn't like Grace very much.

I clung to her hand tightly as we entered the loading dock door of a nondescript office building. Loud music could be heard coming from behind a doorway to our left. Two large security guards dressed entirely in black leather were on either side of the door.

"Hello, Gentlemen. Emory Gage," Em told them as he confidently approached the door.

They consulted a tablet and counted off the number of people in our party before they opened the door.

"Take deep breaths," Chase whispered as I followed behind her closely.

Easy for her to say.

We all signed a standard NDA and handed them to a young woman with flame-red hair who was wearing a leather harness and black lingerie with thigh-high patent leather boots.

I followed Em as he walked into the room and we were immediately greeted by a tall brunette.

"Emory! Tal! I'm so glad you could come."

She was wearing a tight patent leather corset dress.

"Chase. Nathan," she nodded dismissively, not looking in their direction.

"Satan," Chase whispered and I smiled at her.

"Who are these two lovely creatures?" Grace said motioning to Mara and me.

Chase squeezed my hand and shook her head.

"Mara is Nathan's companion for the evening," Em told her in a bored tone.

"And this one?" She gave me a predatory grin and I stared down at Chase's shoulder to avoid eye contact. This woman was a piranha.

"Is off-limits. He's an observer, like Chase," Emory told her, his voice full of authority.

I nervously scratched my neck and swallowed heavily. I could feel her eyes narrow in on the red cuff on my wrist and was very thankful I had it on.

"Too bad," Grace sighed in a bored voice. "Anyways. I've acquired some new talent and have decided to debut him tonight."

She raised her hand in the air and snapped twice.

A man who had been kneeling beside a lounge chair dropped to all fours and crawled across to where we were standing. Sitting up to rest on his knees as he reached her side. He never once looked up. His entire chest was covered in tattoos and he was wearing a leather collar with a clip ring on it. His leather pants were stretched tight on his legs and his feet were bare.

I found myself morbidly fascinated watching him move. I'd never actually seen a 'pet' before.

"Stephen is such an obedient pet," Grace cooed as she arched an eyebrow at Nathan. Obviously, there was some history there. "We'll be in my usual room. We're performing first tonight. I promise you won't be disappointed."

Terrified was more like it.

# SEVENTEEN

## Chase

**Boston**

Evan was completely silent as he clung to my hand. To his credit, he handled the whole situation well, just watching our surroundings with wide eyes.

"Usually, it's standing room only with Grace's performances. Let's go snag some space along the wall to keep you two out of the spotlight." Emory confidently led us down a hallway to a door that was painted bright red. Talia walked directly behind him, her hand resting on his lower back and her head bowed.

Nathan signaled to Mara with his hand, and she stepped into line with him, staggered slightly behind him off to the side. "Come."

It had always interested me to watch the dynamic of the Dom/sub relationships you saw at these things. Em and Nathan were both subtle with how they expected their subs to behave. They didn't use leashes, no crawling across the floor. Just firm, direct commands, and subtle submissive mannerisms.

I was willing to bet that was why Nathan was not here with Grace tonight. She loved humiliation and very overt displays of physical submission.

Emory gestured us over to the far corner, himself and Nathan acting as a barrier between Evan, myself, and the rest of the room.

Grace worked quickly. She led Stephen in with a metal-studded leash and he'd gained a new accessory, a bright red ball gag with leather straps.

Grace made a huge production of leading him on stage, his motions cat-like. She led him over to a raised, narrow pedestal platform that had short chains with leather buckled wrist cuffs attached to either side.

He slowly rose after she snapped her fingers above his head and bent himself over the platform with his arms down to his sides. She made quick work of the cuffs and scratched his scalp after she was done. He still had the leather pants on and was shirtless.

Evan gasped as Grace walked to the side of the stage and grabbed a small hand whip with a leather tail.

"You doing OK?" I asked quietly and he nodded, eyes wide. His focus was on Grace, but he glanced down at me and squeezed my hand. Evan's grip on my hand tightened as we watched the first crack of her whip against the middle of Stephen's back.

Stephen's back arched and he groaned against the ball gag in his mouth. She continued with several quicker snaps and dark pink lines formed on the skin of his back.

Stephen remained completely motionless the rest of the time she worked him over, not even uttering a moan.

We all held our breath as she stepped back and pressed her heeled boot onto the seat of his pants. This forced him over the edge of the platform, his ass sticking up in the air as his arms stretched against his sides, bound to the platform by his leather cuffs.

Grace knelt behind him and released a set of snaps on the back of his leather pants, exposing a sliver of his ass. She stood back up and sauntered to a chest at the corner of the stage. She pulled a few things from inside of it and returned to her bound sub.

Evan gasped again from beside me as she uncapped a bottle of lube and squirted it over the edge of the large L-shaped phallic instrument.

"That's a pegging dildo," Emory told us as he glanced back.

My eyes widened as I watched her slip it under her skirt and inside of herself while we all stood there.

The large faux appendage jutted out from under her short dress, aimed directly at the exposed Stephen.

"Barbie," Evan whimpered in my ear as he pulled me against his side, pushing his face into my hair. Obviously, the thought of being the target of a large dildo was not on his list of okayed scene simulations.

As Stephen's muffled groans filled the air, I could see Evan peeking through my hair, an intense look on his face. For another five minutes, we watched Grace manipulate her new pet for her enjoyment, ending in him laying across his platform a hot sweaty mess.

"You still with us?" Emory asked as he looked at a shell-shocked Evan.

"Yes," he answered quietly with a single nod and an exaggerated bob of his Adam's apple as he swallowed. I was happy he hadn't run out of here screaming yet.

We stayed for another two hours, quietly observing demonstrations of both female and male Doms from the same back corner. Evan didn't talk, just quietly watched with wide eyes, never releasing my hand. He had let out the occasional gasp but hadn't whispered our safe word to me again since Grace.

She hadn't approached us after her performance, but I had seen her staring intently at Evan's reactions. I could tell she was intrigued by him.

"You joining us back at the studio?" Emory asked as we prepared to leave.

I glanced at Evan and he shook his head once, making significant eye contact. "No, I think we'll catch an Uber back to my place." I pulled out my phone and requested one as we all followed Em towards the exit.

The group waited with us until our ride showed up, Talia giving us each a big hug before they retreated to their own hired car service.

Evan climbed in first and held his hand out to me, scooting across the back seat as I climbed in after him. I verified my address to the driver, and we took off across town, back to my condo building.

"Are you alright?" I asked him quietly. "You've been awfully quiet."

He took a deep breath and slowly let it out. "I'm alright, it was just a lot."

"Like you don't want to do this anymore 'a lot' or just a new situation 'a lot'?" It was on my mind all night that this might turn out to have been too much for him.

"To be honest, it scared the shit out of me, but it helped that we were there in a group," he told me quietly. "It helped that you were there."

I smiled as I scooted myself against his arm, leaning my head against his shoulder. "I wasn't sure if it was too much for you to handle."

"The only part I truly didn't like was the beginning. Please say that we will stay far away from that woman..." He was just as put off by Grace as I was. She was a predator.

"I told you she was the devil," I laughed. He smiled and laid his head against mine.

"As long as we don't have to interact with that kind of Dominatrix, I am OK with this," he sighed. "I know you trust Emory and Talia. And I trust you."

"We'll go at your pace and Emory won't make you do anything you don't want to. That's not his style."

He nodded and kissed the side of my head. "I'm just ready to curl up in bed with you."

The smile that pulled at my lips was involuntary. He was his usual honest, adorable self.

"Although, I probably need a shower after wearing these pants all night," he cringed.

"Leather isn't the most forgiving material."

We both laughed and settled back into the seat, watching the lights of the city pass by. The adrenaline was starting to wear off from the evening and curling up with Evan seemed like a good idea.

Emory wanted us to start some preliminary sessions tomorrow. He was going to show Evan the tools of the trade. I had to admit, the thought of him with a whip in his hand was kind of hot.

"Thank you," he told the driver as we stopped at the curb.

Evan pulled his door open and helped me out of the car, tucking me under his arm as we walked into my building and into the elevator.

When we got to my condo, he grabbed his bags and followed me into my bedroom, slowly peeling his sweaty clothes off and neatly folding them.

He got out a pair of boxer briefs and walked around the bed, stopping where I was pulling off my jewelry and helping me unzip my dress.

"I know I told you earlier, but you really did look amazing tonight."

I reached my hand behind his neck and pulled him into me, humming as I kissed the side of it. Despite being in a room with lots of semi-sweaty bodies, Evan smelled so good.

"You looked pretty damn good yourself," I told him honestly. He had definitely carried off the leather pants look.

"I felt like a little boy playing dress-up," he chuckled.

"Little boys don't fill out their pants as well as you do," I smirked up at him.

"You're bad," he laughed, and I reached one hand down to grasp him through the thin cotton of his briefs. "Don't start something you can't finish."

"Oh, you'll finish," I told him as I dropped my dress and stepped out of it. His eyes widened as he took in my provocative underwear.

"Fuck. I did not expect you to have that on under your dress," he breathed out with wide eyes.

"Hopefully, I won't have it on too much longer," I teased as I ran a fingertip across my chest.

"You still want to shower?" His voice cracked a little as he swallowed hard.

"I may already be a little wet," I giggled as he stared at me. I was afraid that tonight was going to make things weird between us, but his eyes still held this intense heat while he looked at me.

"Come on." His voice was rough as he held his hand out to me. I took it and followed him into the bathroom. He flicked on the lights, but then turned the one on the mirrors back off, leaving just a soft glow cast by the overhead lights.

"Setting the mood?" I giggled as he arched an eyebrow at me.

"I can take one alone..." he teased as he stepped away from me.

"It's my shower!"

He sighed and rolled his eyes at me. "I guess you can come."

"I hope so," I told him as I bit my lip.

"So dirty," he whispered.

"You better clean me..." My voice was breathy as I looked over at him.

He laughed and reached into the shower to set the water. "Or maybe I should just make you dirtier."

He pushed down his underwear and stepped into the stream of water, smoothing his hair back with both hands.

"Like that's even possible," I said under my breath.

The muscles in his back moved deliciously as he tilted his head into the spray. "You just going to stare at me?"

"Are you complaining?" I asked incredulously. "And where was all this bravado earlier?"

He shrugged his shoulders and smiled at me. Evan when we were alone, was so much different than when we'd been in public earlier. "The quicker you get your ass into this shower, the quicker we can get into bed."

"Well, when you put it like that." I reached around to unclasp my bra, letting it fall to the floor. Then I shimmied my panties down my legs and kicked them behind me.

He opened his arms when I stepped into the shower and wrapped them around me, tucking my head underneath his chin. "I'm sorry if I was quiet earlier."

"Why are you apologizing?" He had no reason to be.

"I just wish I was more comfortable interacting with people. Like you are," he confessed quietly.

"Baby, you don't need to worry about that. My friends liked you. Just because I never shut up doesn't mean there's something wrong with you," I insisted. "I lo... like you just the way you are."

His head dropped into the crook of my neck and he squeezed me to him firmly. I didn't want him to feel self-conscious. He was amazing. People would like him for who he was if he gave them a chance to.

We stood there for several minutes under the warm spray of the water, just breathing each other in.

Tonight was stressful, and the next week probably would be as well. It was nice to just be with him.

After a little while, he pulled back from me and reached over to get my body wash. He lathered it up in his hands and began gently caressing my skin with his sudsy fingers. There wasn't anything overtly sexual in the way he was touching me, but it ignited something in me nonetheless.

When it was my turn, I couldn't help but pay special attention to his growing erection. He sighed and quietly moaned into my neck as I stroked him, his lips latching onto it as he eventually spilled over my hands.

Once he caught his breath, he turned me around and caged me up against his chest. His fingers gently spread me apart and started a slow rhythm, sliding against my clit. The combination of the steady pressure and his kissing and nipping at my neck eventually drove me over the edge, and I shuddered in his arms with my climax.

We washed ourselves again quickly, just quietly watching each other. I finished rinsing off and then pulled the lever down to shut off the flow of the water. Droplets of moisture were dripping from his hair and eyelashes, making his blue eyes almost glow in the dim lighting.

"Come to bed with me," I commanded quietly as I stepped out and handed him a towel. He nodded and followed me out to my bedroom, quickly rubbing himself dry and dropping his towel to the floor.

We climbed into my bed and he curled himself around me, kissing my neck and cupping my naked breasts in his hands.

I wasn't sure what tomorrow was going to bring, but I was secure in the fact that I knew he'd brave it with me.

# EIGHTEEN

### Evan

**Boston**

My internal clock seemed to be set to wake me around the same time every morning. Chase was still dead to the world as I glanced at my phone and saw it was 6:00 am. I didn't want to be completely creepy — lying here and staring at her until she woke up. My body was restless, and I needed to get up.

While I was pulling some clothes out of my bag, I had an idea. Chase's fridge was bare, stocked only with condiments. I had a feeling it was like that even when she wasn't off at my house.

I pulled up Google, found the closest market, and then looked around for keys to her door, finding them on a hook inside the hall closet. She lived in a nice building, but I wasn't leaving her sleeping alone with her front door unlocked.

The weather was nice as I walked to my destination. The air had a crisp bite to it, but it wasn't freezing. It was just enough to wake me up. I knew I wouldn't have time to get in a proper run today with my plans.

The market was bustling; there was a little coffee shop at the back with a line that was growing by the second. I'd stop there last. I wasn't sure what kind of coffee maker Chase had.

I could picture myself here, shopping for ingredients to make dinner for her sometime. It seemed that every thought I'd had lately involved her with me.

My anxiety still flared up a little at how busy it was, but if it meant that I got to bring this fantasy to life for her I was fine with pushing through it.

I was leaning down to grab a box of pancake mix when someone bumped into me from behind.

"Oh! I'm so sorry!" A slender blonde woman apologized with wide eyes.

"That's alright," I assured her as I straightened back up.

She tilted her head and looked at me strangely. "Do I know you?"

"I don't think so," I shook my head. She looked vaguely familiar, but that didn't mean I knew her.

"You look really familiar..." she mused as she squinted at me.

She'd probably read my books. I occasionally ran into people who recognized me from the book jacket picture. Most of the time I just politely said hi to them and made a quick escape, but she was giving me a look.

"Are you sure I don't know you?" she asked again, her brows pinched together.

"I just have one of those faces." I gave her a tight smile and picked up my basket, hurrying to the next aisle.

She shook her head and continued her shopping.

We ended up in front of the eggs together at the same time, she was still trying to figure out who I was. She was making me super nervous.

Thankfully, her phone rang and distracted her.

"Yes, I'm getting the eggs. I know, I'll be back soon."

I could hear a male voice coming from her phone and then she laughed loudly. "Yes, I met with her yesterday. She's in the city for a week or so. I don't know what she did to your boy."

"Oh, come on, Adrian," she scoffed, and I looked over at her with wide eyes. "It's not my job to babysit my writers or yours."

Fuck. This must be Isobel. I needed to get out of here fast.

"I'm sure he just needs to recharge," she responded to further mutterings from her phone.

"You seriously need to lighten up."

He was talking again, and I saw her cheeks start to build up a red flush.

"Oh, stop it. I'll be back soon and then we can continue where we left off last night."

My eyes widened and she glanced over at me with a confused look on her face.

I grabbed a carton of eggs and started moving quickly down the aisle, grabbing bacon and sausage links. Throwing a glance over my shoulder, I saw her turn around a corner going in the opposite direction.

My shopping basket was almost full, so I grabbed a few last items and made my way towards the checkout. I didn't need her to finally work out who I was.

Adrian would want me to work, and I was not giving up my private time with Chase or our research.

I looked over my shoulder the whole way down the block and googled a coffee shop on the other side of Chase's condo. Running into Isobel was not on my list of things to do today.

"Hi, uh. I need a few coffees," I told the barista as I stepped up to the counter. I completely forgot that I didn't know how Chase took her coffee because she'd either made it herself or had Marian giving her a to go cup every day she'd stayed at the B&B.

"Well? Are you going to tell me what they are? Or should I guess?"

Well, she was pleasant.

"Uh...an Americano, mocha latte, caramel latte, and a plain black coffee. Can you throw in some sugar and creamers too?"

"Got it," she nodded. "What's your name?"

"Uh...Evan," I stuttered.

"OK, uh Evan. Go wait over there and we'll call your name," she rolled her eyes, clearly bored with me. "Drink carrier?"

I obviously had several grocery bags in my hands. Did she think I was an octopus?

"I'm just gonna assume that's a yes," she said pointing to the opposite side of the cash-wrap. There were a few people waiting, so I stood behind them and avoided eye contact.

My phone buzzed and I pulled it out, hoping it wasn't Chase. I wanted to surprise her.

*Adrian: Where did you go? Chase is in Boston.*
*Evan: I know.*
*Adrian: Did you go back to Chicago?*
*Evan: No*
*Adrian: Feeling talkative today, huh?*
*Evan: What do you want?*

And why was he texting me if he was with Isobel anyways?

*Adrian: Just making sure you're alive. Enjoy your fortress of solitude.*

I'm not there.

"Oh Ewan?" The barista asked as I stood there staring at my phone. Adrian was fishing and I wasn't going to be the one to leak anything to them.

"Ewan? Four drinks?" she huffed impatiently. "You! On the phone. Ewan!"

My head shot up and the barista was looking at me in annoyance holding a drink tray. I'd literally just talked to her two minutes ago and she was calling me the wrong name.

Adjusting the grocery bags into one hand, I grabbed the tray and nodded at her, heading for the exit.

It was after 6:45, I wanted to get home so I could start cooking. Chase was bound to wake up soon.

The condo was quiet as I let myself in, toeing off my shoes inside the door. I gently settled all the bags on the kitchen countertop and walked to the bedroom.

All I could see was Chase's hair sticking up from the comforter, her face completely covered as she cocooned herself in it.

My bag was still open, so I crept over to it and got out the apron and set the spoon on the corner of the bed. Hopefully, she'd see it and come find me. I didn't want to make too much noise, so I returned to the kitchen.

If I stayed behind the island, then no one should be able to see me from the windows. I may have been a little paranoid of some creep with binoculars taking in the show.

"I can do this." I shook out my trembling hands and started unbuttoning my pants, pulling them off and neatly folding them onto a chair at the island.

My shirt was next, my nipples firming up a bit in the cold air. It'd be kind of weird to stand here nude — wearing an apron — with socks on, so I pulled them off too.

The boxer briefs were the last thing to go. My dick was already semi-hard at the thought of what Chase was going to do when she found me. I don't think I'd ever been spanked by a woman before, and definitely not with a wooden spoon doubling as a paddle.

At my house, I normally would have put on music to cook, but I wasn't sure if it'd wake up Chase and I wasn't ready yet.

I decided omelets and pancakes were probably the safest bet, so I strapped on my new black apron and got to exploring her cabinets.

Surprisingly, she did have nice, anodized pans and high-quality cooking utensils. I'd need to cook the bacon first and didn't want to worry about scalding my balls with hot grease, so I was happy that I'd found a package of precooked bacon in the meat aisle. The microwave would be too noisy, so I set a skillet up to crisp the bacon for a few minutes while I looked for the knives.

She had a few high-quality ceramic ones in a small knife block in one of the drawers. For someone who claimed she didn't like to cook, she sure had all the tools. I guess it'd just make it easier for me to cook for her while I was here.

Keeping the noise to a minimum, I worked my way around the kitchen island, mixing the batter, dicing vegetables, and finishing my bacon.

I hoped that the smells from the kitchen would wake her up, but maybe I'd just have to do that myself after I finished cooking. My concentration as I watched the bubbles form on my pancakes — their popping indicating it was time to flip — must have distracted me.

The moan that tore out of me with the impact of the wooden spoon against the back of my thigh was surprisingly loud. "Fuuuck!"

Chase was standing behind me with an eyebrow raised, wearing a thin satin nightgown that reached mid-thigh. "Someone is being sneaky this morning."

"Yeah, I didn't even hear you," I laughed as she tapped the wooden spoon in her palm and ran her eyes down the length of my nude body. The predatory look in her eyes made me rock hard and I had to back up a step to keep my erection from jutting into the front of the cabinets.

"You're gonna burn," she said urgently. "The pancakes, genius. You're gonna burn the pancakes."

"Oh, shit." I quickly refocused and flipped them over.

She stepped in behind me and ran her hands along my back, causing my skin to break out in goosebumps.

"I could get used to this," she cooed as her hands roamed my exposed skin.

"Me naked or the pancakes?" I asked her with a smile over my shoulder.

"You're not entirely naked..." she teased. "But pretty much just the pancakes."

"Glad I could be of service," I replied, a little sarcastically.

"Decent service would involve a drink too, just saying," she laughed as she gave me an unimpressed look.

"There's coffee on the counter," I told her, pointing back at the paper carrier on the countertop.

"Oh, I love you..." she cooed.

Did she just...?

When I turned around, she was holding the caramel latte up to her face and inhaling it with her eyes closed.

Oh...she loved the coffee. Of course.

"Do I need to give you two some privacy?" I smiled as she took a big gulp and cradled the cup to her chest.

"It's fine, we don't mind an audience," she winked.

My ego was only a little bruised as I shook my head and refocused on bringing all the bowls of fillings for the omelets to the counter by the stove. "Anything you don't want in your omelet?"

"I've told you before that I'd put just about anything in my mouth."

"Cheeky," I smiled as I looked at her over my shoulder.

"No... I think you're the cheeky one," she laughed as she leaned across the counter to poke me in the butt cheek with her long wooden paddling instrument.

"*Touché*," I nodded.

"It is a *'touché'* as well," she laughed, pronouncing it like 'tooshie.' Obviously, she was in a playful mood today. It was probably better to start out that way. It helped keep our minds off what would happen at Em's studio later.

"You're just taking a page out of Adrian's book today with all the dad jokes."

"His jokes aren't dad jokes, they're just bad jokes." She gave an exaggerated eye roll.

"Obviously, there's no love lost between you two."

"He's an asshat."

I laughed as she scowled. He was a bit of a pig; I'd just gotten used to his antics over the years.

"Oh!" I gasped.

"Yes?" she asked with an indulgent smile.

"You'll never guess who I ran into at the market."

"Someone both of us know?" She looked confused.

"You could say that." I nodded.

"Alright, I give up," she shrugged as she smiled at me.

"Isobel. At least I'm fairly sure it was her. I've only ever talked to her on the phone. And through emails."

Her eyes widened. "Did she recognize you?"

"Maybe, I kind of blew her off," I shrugged.

"Bet she loved that," she laughed.

"But... it gets better," I told her eagerly.

She motioned for me to go on.

"She got an interesting phone call I overheard."

"Do tell..." Chase encouraged as she leaned forward with her elbows propped on the island, a look of open curiosity on her face.

"She was talking to a man... and then she mentioned his name."

"Ohh! Juicy!" Her eyes lit up.

"She told Adrian she'd be back soon to continue where they left off last night."

Her mouth dropped open. "Oh my god! I'll have to call Christine to get the dirt! I always knew he had a thing for her!"

"I've got a thing for you," I winked as I slid a plate across the island to her.

"You put that thing away," she laughed as she peeked over the counter at me.

"Fine. I see how it is." I grabbed my briefs off the stool I'd left them on. I bent over to put them on and...

"Hey! I didn't say you could put those on!" She whacked me in the fleshy part of my ass, and I jumped forward.

"Getting into character already?" I laughed.

"Should I bring my new toy with us this afternoon?" she giggled.

"Well..." I mused leaning against the counter on my elbows. "You should probably break it in first."

"I will..." she mumbled with a mouth full of sausage links. "But first...I need to eat your meat."

# NINETEEN

### Chase

**Boston**

He almost choked on a piece of his pancakes as he cracked up laughing. I smiled as I finished chewing. This was a fun way to wake up.

Naked boyfriend. Dirty banter. Home-cooked meal.

Holy shit! Was he my boyfriend? I knew we'd implied we were going to see where this went, but we'd never officially labeled anything.

He kept grinning at me as I ate the rest of my breakfast. It was really good, the bacon just melted in my mouth.

"Take your time," he winked as he finished up and started rinsing off the dirty dishes. I watched the muscles in his back and sides move as he washed the things he'd used. Naked chef Evan was hot, but naked chef Evan cleaning up his own mess was smoking.

"Mmmm. That was so good. I'm so full," I told him, sitting back on my stool and patting my stomach.

"Hopefully, you haven't eaten too much meat..." he teased as he walked around the corner of the island and leaned against the countertop.

"Oh my..." I marveled, eyeing the way the front of the black material of the apron was tented. "Is someone requesting compensation for their services this morning?"

"I'm good with providing my services for favors," he winked as he bit his lip.

"It seems like you're having a hard time with something." I nodded towards his apron, which was having trouble concealing his excitement.

"Yeah..." he nodded. "I seem to have misplaced my pants."

"They don't seem to be misplaced to me," I giggled as I picked up the wooden spoon and rolled it between my hands. "I can think of something that'd keep your cheeks warm."

"Oh, really?"

I nodded and climbed off my stool, coming around to stand behind him. Damn. Compulsive running was doing him all kinds of favors. I reached my hand out and cupped his firm cheek, giving it a nice squeeze.

"You having fun back there?" he asked, an amused smile stretched across his lips.

"Not yet..." I reached around him, positioned his hands palm down near the edge of the counter, and stepped back.

"Hmm..." I mused as I looked at his posture. "Spread your legs shoulder-width apart."

He slowly moved into position, but it wasn't quite right.

"Straighten your shoulders, chest out. That's better," I coached as he did what he was told.

The look he gave me when I walked to his side to appraise his stance would've made me drop my panties. If I had been wearing any.

"You remember the safe word?"

He nodded his head slowly as his chest heaved. I could see his erection was rock solid as it protruded out in front of him. My mouth salivated with the need to touch it, but that could come later.

"You ready?" I blew out a heavy breath as I stood behind him and worked up the nerve to strike.

Before, I was swatting him as a joke, this time I was going to try to channel what Em had taught me. He'd shown me how to use whips, floggers, and canes during my previous consultations. If I was going to write about flagellation, he wanted me to learn how to do it properly.

I adjusted my grip on the handle and took a deep breath as I established firm footing within striking distance. My wrist snapped firmly and we both jumped a little bit as the wood hit the fleshy part of his ass.

"Ahhh!" he breathed out, a low hiss filling the air.

"Holy shit. You alright?" I questioned as I reached forward and massaged the area that had already started to pink up.

"Mmmhmm," he hummed through gritted teeth.

My heart was pounding as I watched the tension drain out of his shoulders.

"Again," he said quietly but firmly, flexing his arms against the counter.

I raised the spoon up again...and...

*Thwack*

"Fuuuuck," he moaned as his hips flexed forward.

I reached forward and cupped his shoulder, kissing his shoulder blade. "Too much?"

He shook his head back and forth.

I placed the paddle down on the island and took his buttocks in both hands, slowly massaging out the sting.

"Mmmm," he moaned low in his throat, the muscles in his back tensing.

"You sure you're OK?" I asked quietly.

"You hit me again and I'm gonna cum all over this cabinet."

A flash of heat ran through me at his low growl.

"Is that what you want?" I whispered as I ran my hand up his neck and into his hair.

He groaned and shook his head, letting it drop and closing his eyes.

"Evan?" Resting my forehead on his shoulder I started to kiss along his bicep and shoulder, a low humming noise building in his chest. I didn't think I'd pushed him too far, but I was afraid to use the spoon again if he was getting all silent on me.

"Fuck it," he growled as he grabbed me by the waist and hoisted me up onto the counter in front of him.

He pushed my legs apart and slid my nightgown up my thighs exposing my naked sex to him.

"Ohh!" I moaned as he leaned forward and placed one long lick along my slit and nipped at my clit.

"Mmm..." he groaned as he dove in, tonguing me like a man possessed. His firm hands pressed my legs even farther apart, forcing me to brace myself with my arms outstretched behind me.

"Yes! Oh my...yes!" I moaned as his lips closed around my swollen bud and sucked, rubbing his tongue on it frantically. My hips tried to push up and he grunted as he held me down, never letting up.

"Evan!" I moaned as I felt my muscles starting to tense.

"Mmmmm," he growled into me, sliding one of his long fingers inside and pressing firmly on a place that made me squirm again. The tips of his fingers dug into my thigh as he sent me spinning, my head thrown back as I let out a keening cry. My muscles clenched his finger tightly as I throbbed against his lips.

"Stop...stop..." I moaned as he tried to redouble his efforts, I admired his dedication, but I wanted him inside of me.

"Please..." I panted as his finger slid out and he stood up to his full height. His lips were glistening as his chest heaved. The look he gave me was predatory as he reached back to untie the apron and pull it over his head, throwing it to the floor.

He hooked his palms behind my thighs and pulled me to the edge of the counter.

"You're a goddess," he panted as he pushed a sweaty lock of hair off my forehead and then grasped his aroused member in his hand.

"Fuck me," I moaned as he positioned himself at my entrance and hesitated. He looked up and locked his eyes with mine as he slid inside.

"Oooohhh!" My eyes fluttered shut as he pushed all the way in, only to pull out and plunge back in rapidly, building up a rhythm. Sweat dripped down his chest and I watched, licking my lips as a droplet disappeared into his abs.

"Fuck," he groaned as he watched my breasts heave beneath the thin satin material covering me.

"This has to go," he growled as he pulled the straps off my shoulders, pushing it down to reveal my breasts to him. Lips descended on one breast while his hand found the other, coaxing my nipples into tight buds.

"Mmm," he groaned as he nipped at one and then kissed his way over to the other.

"Evan..." I moaned as I supported my weight on one arm and held on tightly to the back of his head with the other. He straightened himself up and my hand fell from him as he grabbed my thighs again and started to snap his hips faster.

"Touch yourself." He nodded to where we were joined, seemingly mesmerized as he disappeared inside of me.

I brought my fingers to my clit, starting out with slow circles and rapidly increasing the pace as he pushed me closer and closer to the precipice of ecstasy.

"Can you cum?" he questioned in a strained voice as his hips started to lose their rhythm, the muscles in his neck straining as he held back.

"Yes..." I moaned as I felt the spasms begin to build.

"Fuck, I can feel you," he moaned loudly as he pulled my hips off the counter and pistoned into me with vigor.

"Oh god! Chase!" he exclaimed as he pulled me tightly to him with his fingers digging into the backs of my thighs.

"Yes...yes...yes..." I chanted as I felt him pulse inside of me and I followed right behind him.

"I think I finally had my fill of meat this morning," my voice came out strained as I tried to catch my breath.

His chest shook as he held me. "You're horrible."

"That's not what you were saying a few minutes ago," I giggled. "We should probably get cleaned up. Emory is expecting us at ten."

The clock read a little after eight-thirty. Most mornings my happy ass would still be wrapped up in my bed, but Evan had changed me. In more than just my sleeping habits.

I felt like he saw me. Not the sarcasm and the jokes. He saw *me*. And he was still here.

"So...what exactly are we walking into today?" he asked as we were seated in the car headed towards Emory's studio.

"You're going to learn how to operate the heavy machinery."

"There's machinery?" He glanced at me out of the corner of his eye as his fingers tightened on the steering wheel.

"No," I giggled. "Emory is more of a hands-on guy. Old school equipment."

"Other than what we saw last night, I have no idea what the tools of the trade are."

"We decided that we wanted her to be an old-school Dominant, right? No crazy machines or torture devices?" I asked. "Just good old-fashioned control. Right?"

"Yeah, I think that'd probably be best. Anything too crazy and my readers probably wouldn't be interested," he nodded.

"I think mine will be on board with the bondage and submission, but they wouldn't want the hard kink either," I told him. "Whatever you do don't google Sybian. You can't unsee that."

"Noted," he laughed as he pulled into a parking space near the photography studio.

We were both dressed in athletic gear. Evan wore a dark gray dry-fit shirt and a pair of loose shorts and I had on a sports bra and black fitted shorts.

"You ready for this?"

"Nope." The smile on his face as he squeezed my hand let me know he was only partially joking.

Today was sure to be an eye-opener for him. I'd been exposed to this stuff before... he was totally green. I was by no means an expert by any stretch of the imagination, but I'd been on both ends of the whip.

Em had better ease him into it slowly. Evan was way more skittish than I'd been.

"Might as well get in there," he sighed.

I nodded and stepped out of the car, waiting for him by the front bumper. "Don't want to give Emory any ideas about a suitable punishment for being late."

"You're the one who took forever in the bathroom, so if anyone is getting spanked for making us late, it's you," he accused.

"Move your ass and we won't be late," I sassed as I pinched his butt.

"Hey, hands off the merchandise." He threw his hips forward to escape my pinching fingers and laughed as he jogged towards the door with me hot on his heels.

"Finally, you two are here," Talia let out a relieved sigh as we walked in the door. "He's been wearing a hole in the floor in the back."

"We've still got five minutes." My watch read 9:55. I'd made sure we didn't get too distracted this morning. Em hated when people wasted his time.

"Come on. We don't have all day," Emory urged as Evan and I walked through the curtain hand in hand.

"Do you have a meeting you didn't tell me about?" I asked before I realized my slip.

He arched an eyebrow at me and cleared his throat.

"Wow. Already in that headspace, obviously," I backtracked. "Permission to speak, Sir?"

"Granted," he nodded.

"Evan, when we're back here, as this is his space," I told him quietly. "We defer to Emory for talking and commenting. If you have a question, you need to ask respectfully after requesting permission to speak."

Evan nodded his head and looked over to Emory with his eyes cast to the ground.

"Oh, he's already halfway there, Chase," Emory smirked as he indicated for us to follow him back into the playroom.

"Unless I'm expecting someone, this door will always be locked," he told us. "I don't like to share my personal proclivities with my photography clients, so we'll always have time scheduled in advance for these sessions so I can clear my schedule."

"May I?" I asked Em as I nodded at Evan.

He gave me a short nod and watched Evan.

"This can get a little intense sometimes. I want you to know that you can always use the safe word if something is making you uncomfortable."

He nodded and grabbed my hand, running his thumb over the knuckles.

"We don't have to stick entirely to the script either. If a scene we mapped out doesn't feel right, just ask and we can work out something different."

"These are just as much your characters as they are mine," I insisted, "and I'm open to suggestions."

Evan bit his lip and nodded again. His eyes were clear, I could tell he was anxious about this, but he wasn't worried.

"OK, we're going to go through wardrobe first," Emory explained. "Every Dom, male or female, has a style. It's like with your regular wardrobe. There are things you like and not every person is going to choose the same things."

"We'll start with male submissive," he started. "Leather is typically the material of choice, that or vinyl. It depends on if you're into a fetish style or not. Some men like to wear lace or fishnets. It totally depends on their particular kink."

"How do you envision the character, Evan?" Emory asked him, his eyes filled with curiosity.

"We aren't going to show much emotion from the perspective of her male submissive. He's part of the story, but the narration really follows Frances and her journey as a Dominatrix and a trainer."

"Have you thought about what you want her personal style to be?"

"I hate to use this word, but traditional," Evan cringed. I nodded to confirm.

"So, you're thinking less harnesses and revealing — a more polished look?" Em speculated.

"I think so," Evan responded quietly.

"Here, we'll look on this tablet at a selection of Dominatrix wardrobe options." He handed the tablet to Evan and his eyes widened as he looked at it and glanced over at me. We scrolled through the options and then Evan paused the screen on one image.

"You like that one?" I asked him.

"Ye..." He cleared his throat softly. "Yes. This one."

I had to admit. It was kind of perfect for what we'd envisioned. A tightly fitted lace dress with leather accents, it revealed just enough to be enticing, but it wasn't racy by any means.

"Order your size, Chase, and have it sent here," Emory instructed.

Evan's eyes widened as he looked over at me, his cheeks a soft pink.

"Alright." I took the tablet from Evan and added it to my cart and a few other options that I thought would also fit Frances' style.

Emory moved Evan over to start showing him some of the male options and I bit my lip to keep from laughing at his bewildered expression.

"If she is going more traditional, chances are she'd want her sub to do the same," Emory explained and Evan nodded. "Leather pants are always a staple, but you already have those."

Emory smirked at Evan and his cheeks darkened.

"In most situations, those can be the go-to. But you will also need to plan for what happens in situations where spanking play or punishment comes into action."

By this point, Evan's cheeks were full-on bright pink as he glanced over at me — probably thinking about this morning. There was a little bit of heat in his eyes. I was honestly pleasantly surprised by his reaction to being paddled.

"This is a cock cage," Emory said, holding up a little leather-strapped pouch with a ring on the front. I could see Evan visibly swallow and adjust himself in his shorts. "It's designed to confine the penis and cause discomfort if it is fully erect."

"Next is what I'm suggesting you wear during a scene where she punishes her sub by paddling him," Emory gave Evan a little bit of a roguish smile. I smiled as I watched Evan squirm. "It's a leather jockstrap. I'd suggest this to keep you covered but still expose your rear. The alternative is a thong. Any opinions?"

"The jockstrap. Definitely the jockstrap," Evan tittered out nervously as he looked over to me with mild panic in his eyes.

I couldn't wait to get started.

# TWENTY

### Evan

**Boston**

Chase's amused little grin made me want to put her over my knee, but I knew I had to keep it in check around Emory.

The thought of putting on that cock cage made me incredibly uncomfortable. It just was not big enough. I really did not need first-hand experience with that part of punishment. Just looking at the thing made me feel chastised enough.

"Evan. Pay attention," he snapped next to my head and I drew my eyes back to him, trying to ignore Chase. I wanted to know what else she was ordering on that tablet.

"This is a chest harness." Emory held up some leather strapping. "There are also more full-body harnesses that go around the groin, but this is the most common type of harness. It's used for a few different reasons."

"It's hot," I heard Chase whisper from behind me.

Mental note...

"Some use it because they like how it looks. It's often worn at showcases or play parties to identify that they are into kink," Emory explained. "It can also be used as a handle of sorts used during private play. It gives the Dominatrix something to hold onto to manipulate a male sub who is larger than her. Gives her a little bit of leverage."

"That brings a whole new level to the term 'love handle'," Chase giggled from behind us.

Emory cleared his throat and gave her a pointed look.

"Sorry...don't mind me."

"Naughty girl," I whispered under my breath and it earned me a lip quirk from Emory.

"If you can't behave, Chase," Emory warned as he nodded at a large chair in the corner that had restraints on the arms and legs. "We can always tie you to the chair again."

The urge to laugh was so strong but I managed to bite my lip to stop it.

"Anyways," he rolled his eyes. "I don't think the two of you are looking to dive particularly deep into hard kink."

"No," I said in a low voice, shaking my head.

He cleared his throat again and raised an eyebrow at me.

"Sir," Chase whispered from behind me.

"No, Sir." I averted my eyes and spoke quietly.

Emory nodded at me. "So, these will probably be all I need to show you. There are all kinds of torture devices for people into pain play, but you won't need to know about those."

I nodded, absolutely agreeing with that one.

"We can always consult with Grace if you decide to add in anything with humiliation. She's an expert in that particular kink."

Oh, fuck no. That woman was intense. I knew Chase agreed with me by the little growl she let out.

"Let's move onto equipment." He led us over to the racks on the wall. "These are leather wrist and ankle cuffs. They can be attached to various things. Corner restraints on a bed, each other with a clip or tie, spreader bars, wall hooks, crosses. Cuffs are pretty much involved in most acts of bondage, usually only subbed out for rope or silk ties."

"Hold out your hand," he commanded as he grabbed a cuff off the clip and brought it to my wrist. "Buckles tend to work best. You can set them tight, but not cutting off circulation — just enough to hold. I don't recommend metal unless it's wrapped with something softer."

He left the cuff on me and I dropped my hand, feeling its subtle weight against my skin. I knew it was there, but it wasn't uncomfortable.

"These are bondage ropes." Emory grabbed a tied bundle off the hook and held it up. "This one is what I prefer. It's a nylon rope used in boating. Can be bought at a hardware store. Don't buy it from a sex shop because you'll pay through the nose for something that you can't gauge the quality on."

He nodded at Chase over my shoulder. "This is what I use for suspension."

Oh...this is probably what he used to suspend her from the ceiling grate. I shifted my feet and tried not to think about Chase suspended from the ceiling — hands bound. My shorts didn't provide much concealment and I was sure Emory would be irritated if I developed a visible problem.

"It doesn't have a lot of bite to it on the skin, and can't be used for elaborate things, but it's strong and comes in different ratings that determine how much weight and pressure it can hold."

"Chase?" he asked, looking in her direction. "Do you still have that book of knots I gave you?"

"Yes, Sir," she chirped over my shoulder.

I felt her step in behind me and place her hand at the base of my spine, sending a jolt through me at her touch. She must have been done buying the Dominatrix outfits.

"Your homework for tonight is to practice tying knots with this," he instructed, handing me the bundle of rope and moving down the line to the next thing to show us.

"Chase is familiar with these," he said, gesturing to a few things that were sitting in brackets protruding from the frame.

"This is a small flicker whip." He flipped his wrist, and it made a soft snapping sound in the air. "Your Trix will probably use a heavier duty class of whips such as a stock or bull, but you two are beginners. You need specialized training to use those effectively."

"Next session we'll let you both try this one." Chase's fingers tightened on my shirt as she let out a soft sigh. Obviously, she liked that idea. I wasn't sure which one of us being on the tail end of the whip excited her, but I was willing to try it.

"Next we've got a suede flogger," he picked up a dark leather-handled whip-like object with several long, wide pieces of sueded material hanging from the end.

"There are several different types of floggers. Some are for sensation play, others are for pain play or punishment. This particular one doesn't have as much bite to it."

"Again, we'll start you with the beginner equipment. You don't need to be accidentally drawing blood." He actually broke character and winked at me.

What?

"You'll be fine," he assured as he saw my expression. "This will all be simulation play. But...there is another king-sized bed in the back of the playroom if you two need some alone time after a session."

I could hear Chase snickering behind me.

"Next up is the cane." He picked up a long object from a hook that looked to be made of wood. "It's a little harder to use effectively. Plastic canes are good for beginners. They flex more and don't leave as deep of marks. These can be used for both pain play and punishment. I use a rattan cane for punishment."

He placed the long wooden cane back into its bracket and moved to the paddles hanging on the wall.

"Paddles come in a huge variety of materials and sizes depending on the use," he nodded. "I'll show Chase how to use the leather and silicone paddles. They're lower impact and cause less bruising."

"I already practiced with a wooden one," she whispered from behind me. I couldn't help the smile that pulled at my lips.

"Something you'd like to share with the class?" Emory asked with a facial expression almost approaching a smile.

"Uh," I stuttered as I looked back at Chase.

"He's already taken a wooden paddle. Might as well put that into the rotation too," she told him in an amused voice.

"Have you two been practicing unsupervised?" My eyes widened as I took in his defensive stance, arms crossed, legs set wide, and an unamused smirk on his face.

"Uh...not practicing, *per se*," I whispered.

"Chase?"

"Why do I have to tell you?" she asked, sounding borderline petulant.

"Because your boy here looks like he's being led to execution. Fess up."

"Theoretically, what would happen if we were playing outside of our sessions?" she asked.

"Well, normally I'd punish you both, but it's the first day and I'm assuming you don't want Evan here to flee the state."

"May I speak freely, Sir?"

Emory's eyes flashed to mine and he nodded. "You may."

"Chase and I may have had a little fun with a wooden spoon this morning," I told him honestly. I didn't want to start this out with him having a lack of trust in us.

"And you were safe?" he asked as he looked between the both of us.

"I remembered what you taught me," Chase nodded.

"She corrected my stance, massaged, and had me take a warm shower for aftercare. We acknowledged the safe word before we started," I confessed quietly.

"Then I guess you're forgiven. Please try to take this seriously — Chase — if you try to use something you aren't ready for, one of you could get hurt," he admonished.

"Yes, Sir," she nodded and I echoed it. "Of course, sir."

"Moving on." He held up a leather riding crop and I was happy I knew what that one was. "A crop can be used for all sorts of play. Most are leather, but there are also nylon ones as well."

"Last, but definitely not least, is your own hand." He held up his own weathered palm and we nodded. "It can be used for just about any kind of play. It should be established before you start to play what kind of spanking you're engaging in."

"There are types?" I asked curiously.

"Pain, humiliation, punishment, sensation, erotic...," he listed off easily. "There are also different positions."

"Yeah, there are," Chase snickered and leaned her face into my shoulder blade.

"Behave," Emory warned.

"Yes, sir," she giggled.

"Over the knee, doggy style, standing, kneeling, lying down, restrained..."

Damn...half of those were getting me a little excited. Chase and I had covered the doggy style spanking, and I guess the standing and bending over too. All at the same time...

"You ready to look at some toys?" Emory asked.

"Sir?"

"Yes, Chase," he nodded.

"Shouldn't you have Talia in here while you're showing off her prized possessions?"

"I'm sure I can manage," he said dryly.

Motioning for us to follow him, he led us to a tall chest of drawers with various sized drawers.

"Let's start small and work our way up." He pulled a little silver capsule out of a top drawer and held it up. "This is a bullet. It is featured in hundreds of different toys. It can be used in wearables, lipstick vibes, clitoral stimulators, insertables...the list goes on. It creates a strong consistent vibration."

He pulled out a relatively short thin vibrator. "This is a lipstick vibe. It's compact, can be inserted or used for clitoral stimulation, anal play."

He put it back and grabbed a large phallic object. "This is a traditional dildo. I think this one is self-explanatory. They come in glass, silicone, metal, plastic..." He pulled out a vibrator that looked like a real penis, showed it to us and laid it back down.

"This is Talia's personal favorite." He pulled out a large vibrator with a piece of silicone protruding out the side.

Was that a bunny?

"This is a rabbit. It has an adjustable speed setting for both the bunny and the shaft. The base of the rabbit has a bullet vibe inside of it. Designed to stimulate the clitoris while the shaft is used for traditional penetration."

He pressed a button and the shaft started to slowly rotate. "This one has a rotate function too."

"That looks fun!" Chase said in an excited voice.

Holy fuck. The thought of using that on her just about made me cum in my shorts.

"Don't you worry, Tal has a nice little bag of things for the two of you to take home tonight," he told her.

Who would have thought we'd get a swag bag while we were researching a Dominatrix?

"There are also electric stimulation devices, but I don't think you're looking for those."

"Next, we move onto anal play."

My eyes widened. Obviously, I'd heard about it being done, but I had never done it and I wasn't sure I wanted it done to me either.

"There are your standard plugs. They can be plastic or silicone. Made in various sizes to help stretch the user gradually. These can also have vibration features."

He pulled out a long L-shaped device that looked like what Grace had used on Stephen. "This is used for pegging. There are a few different kinds. We've got strap-on dildos, strap-on vibrators... this one is designed to be hands-free. It takes a bit of practice because the woman needs to be able to keep it inside using her Kegel muscles while penetrating the man."

"There are also finger extension pieces that can be used for penetration, with or without vibration."

I was not sure if I was into the whole pegging thing. It made my asshole clench just thinking about it.

"I think we've got one more thing that is probably relevant to your story," he said as he pulled a small ring from one of the drawers. "The cock ring."

"This can be used to delay climaxing as well as to increase erection firmness. There are adjustable ones, silicone rings, metal rings worn at the head or base, textured, cock cages like we saw before..."

"Some are just worn at the base of the shaft; others go around the balls and teardrop ones that massage the perineum. They can also be used for partner stimulation if they have a bullet vibrator attached."

"Do you two have any questions?" he asked as he packed the items back in their homes and closed the drawers.

I wasn't even sure where to start.

"What about nipple clamps?" She just had to go there. That woman sure liked to pinch my nipples.

"We can talk about sensory stimulation items. There are a few that are fairly tame." He reached into a drawer and pulled out a little metal tool with a long handle and a wheel with spikes attached to the top. "This is a Wartenberg wheel. It's used to test nerve endings in the medical field and can also be used to stimulate nerve endings under the skin during play."

"Evan, give me your hand." I held it out and he turned my hand over gently running the device over the soft skin on my wrist. It sent a tingling sensation up my arm and the back of my neck. He pressed a little harder and it hurt slightly, but the sensation was amplified.

"It feels even more amazing with a blindfold on," she whispered as her hand slipped under the back of my shirt and her thumb stroked the bare skin of my lower back.

"Sir?" I croaked.

"Hmm?"

"Is one of those in the bag?"

He smiled and winked, "I'll make sure we put one in there."

"Now we can move on to talking about nipple clamps," Emory said as he pulled a few more things out of a drawer. "When you're starting out, they are only worn for a short period of time. It cuts off circulation, so you don't want to cause nerve or skin damage."

"These are good for beginners," he said holding up a leather collar with chains attached to it, small clips with a screw attached to them on the ends. "The bullnose clips have tightening screws so you can increase or reduce the amount of pressure. "

He held up a little saw-toothed clamp next. "This kind of clamp also comes without the screws and is called an alligator clamp."

"The rest of the clamp styles I wouldn't recommend for beginners. There are clothesline clamps; they are designed like a clothespin but have a strong spring for tight application."

"Magnetic clamps may be OK to use." He reached into the drawer and pulled out a little metal circle that had two rods sticking out of either side. He used his fingers to pull the rods apart and then release one. It immediately moved to stick to the other rod.

"Subs who really enjoy nipple play can also have Thai sticks used, ones worn with weights, attached to weighted chains... The goal of all of these is to stimulate endorphin release which can make the area more sensitive and encourage stronger climaxes."

He carefully placed all the items he'd gotten out back into their drawers, closing them and then opening a cabinet at the bottom.

"This part may seem tedious, but it's a very important part of proper play and maintenance of your items," he said as he pulled out several bottles and some small towels. "We have leather cleaner and conditioner, varnish for the rattan cane, metal cleaner and sanitizer, silicone cleaner and sanitizer. Cleaning both before and after use helps keep items in good shape, helps prevent the spread of disease if you have multiple partners, and helps prevent infection."

He spent ten minutes showing us how to clean and store multiple different types of items.

"He scare you two off yet?" Talia asked as she stood in the doorway to the playroom.

"Did you close up for lunch?" he asked her. She nodded and crossed the room, kissing him on the cheek and leaning her elbow on his chest. He gazed down at her and I could see they really cared for each other.

"Are you two staying or...?" he trailed off.

Talia pulled on his arm and spoke quietly, but Chase and I could still hear her. "There were some new things that came in when I ordered the items for Chase."

His face brightened and he gave her a naughty grin. "You two can have the rest of the day off. I've suddenly got a very pressing matter to attend to."

He pulled her hips into his and whispered in her ear. She giggled and pointed towards the door to the gallery. "There's a few paper bags out behind the desk for you."

"You're welcome," she winked and then pulled Emory down to kiss her.

"I think that's our cue," I said turning around and pulling Chase's arms around me, resting my hands on the small of her back.

"I do believe we have some *'research'* of our own to do," she nodded as she reached up on her toes and gave me a soft kiss.

# TWENTY-ONE

## Chase

**Boston**

I tugged on Evan's hand and dragged him across the studio, through the curtain and into the gallery. Talia had left two large paper shopping bags with tissue paper tucked across the top of each.

"Grab one and let's go," I nodded, excited to see what goodies Talia had gotten for us. She was a bit of a sex toy connoisseur. Tal had been contracted as a reviewer for several sex toy companies as a lucrative side gig. She got all kinds of freebies, and she was always excited to share.

"Someone's eager," he laughed as he tapped my butt with his palm and reached around me to grab a bag.

"Can you blame me?" I bounced on my toes. "I want to know what she got us."

"Well, they both do seem dedicated to us doing effective research," Evan chuckled as he lifted the bag, which seemed to be packed to the top.

We heard a loud moan coming from the direction of the playroom and shared a look.

"They didn't waste any time!" Evan was trying to hold in a laugh as he looked back towards the curtain. I loved the slight pink tinge I could see on his cheeks. I was immune to Talia and Emory's amorous behavior, but then he hadn't seen it in action as I had.

"And we are wasting time," I scolded, motioning towards the door to the street. "Move it."

"Yes, Ma'am."

"I prefer Mistress," I giggled as I crossed over the threshold of the door he was holding open for me.

"Of course, you do," he told me as he gave an exaggerated eye roll.

"Don't make me spank you again..." I threatened.

"You're saying it like that would be a bad thing." He wiggled his eyebrows at me.

"Go, go, go," I laughed. We hurried out to the car and Evan helped me into my seat before opening the back door to put the bags on the rear seats.

"Hey! Why are they back there? I wanted to look," I protested.

"You'll just have to be patient." I couldn't help the wide smile on my face as he looked over at me with an amused smirk.

"We both know that's not my strong suit," I pouted.

"Think of it as delayed gratification," he countered.

"Nope, don't like that either." The deep chuckle that followed my statement abated my curiosity somewhat. Evan had handled today like a pro.

The rest of the drive back to my place, we quietly listened to music and he drove me nuts with his thumb stroking the bare skin on my thigh.

"You ready?" he asked as he parked his car in a guest spot in the garage.

"Hell yes!"

We both knew that we'd be naked within 20 minutes of getting inside my apartment. Screw research...literally. He carried the bags inside of my apartment and we settled into the couch with them on the cushion between us.

"Do you want to go first?" I asked as I sat up straight and held open the handles on one of the bags.

"We both know you're over there *vibrating* with waiting to get in there." The amused grin he was giving me showed how much he was enjoying my excitement over our new toys. I didn't even know what they were and I was ecstatic.

"I'm not vibrating...*yet*," I winked as I pulled out the tissue paper and threw it to the floor.

"Blindfold." I tossed the black silk blindfold at him and he put it in his lap.

"Oooh. His and hers cuffs." I said, pulling out two sets of leather buckle cuffs. One set was smaller and thinner and the other was larger with a wider band.

"Just what every couple needs," he laughed.

"I know, right?" Or maybe just the adventurous ones like we'd apparently become.

Next to come out was a feather tickler. I swiped it across his nose, and he grabbed the handle from me, placing it in the pile on his lap.

"Nipple clamps. Ohhh. These are the magnetic kind." Gauging by the way his pupils dilated, he was on board with trying those as well.

I pulled out the Wartenburg wheel and ran it across the back of his hand.

"Tal must really like you," I giggled as I started pulling several different kinds of cock rings out and tossing them at him.

"Whoa. Look at this one." He opened the small box and pulled it out. Pressing the small button on the end, the little toy started to vibrate across his palm.

"Yeah...so we're definitely trying that one," I told him. He nodded as he pressed the button to turn it off.

"Giant bottle of lube," I giggled as I tossed it to him. It was twelve ounces. Apparently, Talia thought we'd be busy.

"It says it's good for anal play." He winked as he read the fine print on the side of the bottle.

"Oh, you're ready to get probed now?" I teased.

"Nope...never mind," he said with a shake of his head and wide eyes.

I pulled out a few different lengths of chains that were designed to fit around the posts of your bed. Those would work well for the cuffs.

The last thing in the bag was another small bundle of rope. I'd have to go look for my knot tying book. Emory didn't mess around when he assigned you homework.

"Ready for the next one?" Evan asked as he placed the empty bag on the floor next to the couch.

"I feel like it's Christmas." I motioned for him to hand me the other bag.

"It's more like Porn-mas," he laughed.

"She didn't buy us a camera. At least I don't think she did," I laughed at his wide eyes and held up the bag.

"Alright. This one seems heavier." I pulled the tissue out and my eyes widened as I looked at the boxes lined up inside the bag.

"Flicker Whip," I read off the top of the box.

"Collapsible riding crop."

My eyes widened as I looked at one box. "She gave us a rechargeable male masturbator."

"Hopefully, it's not one of those flashlight-looking ones." Evan made a sour face. "Talk about awkward."

"Nope. Much more discreet." I shook my head as I studied the box which had pictures of a sleek, black, elongated toy featured on the side of it.

"Did she put your bunny in there?" he asked with interest. I thought he'd been intrigued by that one in the playroom.

"Rabbit, but yes. She hooked us up."

"Let me see," he said eagerly. I pulled the box out and handed it to him. It was bright pink.

"Nice. I can control this with my phone," he winked at me as he read the information on the side of the box. I think we'd turned him into a sex-starved monster in less than a month. It was a wireless, Bluetooth, USB rechargeable, and waterproof rabbit that had access to a remote-control app. It could also be hooked into remotely by the same app using a secure passcode. We didn't even have to be in the same room.

"Anything else in there?"

"Oh, look...she got you a present." I held up the box and bit my lip to keep from laughing.

His eyes widened. "Are those...?"

"Beginners set of anal plugs. Aren't you lucky?" I giggled.

"Only because I get to use them on you." He thought he was so clever.

"Who knows," I mused, tapping the box with the rabbit that was still sitting in his lap. "Maybe after you use that one on me, I'll let you do whatever you want."

"Well, then we better get started." He carefully started breaking the seal on the end of the box, opening it and pulling out the pieces.

"You realize that probably needs to be charged, right?" I told him, and a little frown appeared on his lips.

"I'm sure we can figure out something to keep ourselves occupied." He started moving the items from his lap onto the coffee table and back into the bags by our feet.

"Maybe we can try these out." He held up the small box with the nipple clamps in one hand and the vibrating cock ring in the other.

"Grab the lube. Let's go," I laughed as I took the vibrator and the charger out of his hands and stood up to head back to my bedroom.

"I'll grab the cuffs too," he called out before he followed me. I liked his style.

Evan tossed the items in his hands on the bed as I walked into the bathroom and pulled my toy wash and a small towel from under the sink.

"Get the cock ring," I told him as I turned on the water to let it warm up.

"On it." He took it out of the box and then joined me at the bathroom sink, laying down the ring on the countertop. He put his arms around my waist and rested his chin on my shoulder, watching as I cleaned the cock ring and set it onto the clean towel on the counter.

"Who knew washing a hot pink vibrator could be arousing," he whispered as he watched my soapy hand slide up and down the shaft.

"You have turned into a horn dog," I told him, thoroughly amused with his reaction to all this stuff. Some guys would have bailed being exposed to all the things he had in the last two days — even without any underlying anxiety issues.

"So, you've got your own toy wash?" he whispered into my neck between soft kisses.

"Yup," I nodded, tilting my head to the side. "I am over thirty and have been single for the last six months."

"Should I be worried I don't measure up to the toy arsenal?" he asked quietly.

"You really just want me to stroke your ego, don't you?" He tucked his nose into my neck and laughed. I could feel him pressing his hips into me from behind. Someone was getting aroused.

"Among other things," he said in a deep, husky voice.

"Someone thinks they're funny today," I smirked as I made eye contact with him in the mirror.

"You can't be the only one with the jokes," he mused. "Come on...let's get that charging and go *research*."

He reached over to grab the USB charger, plugging it into the wall outlet. Picking up the pink toy, he turned it in a few different directions with a confused expression on his face. "How the hell do you charge this thing?"

I took the toy from him and turned it for him to see. "Find this textured dot and press the jack into it."

He pressed the little cord jack in gently, a red light showing under the silicone when it was in all the way.

"It's completely covered since it's water-resistant," I explained. He nodded and took it from me, setting it down on the counter and pulling me towards him. He kissed me deeply, slowly pressing his tongue into my mouth.

"Hmmm." His head pulled back slowly. "So...who gets tied up first?"

"Who do you want to get tied up first?" I asked curiously. Let's see how brave he was feeling.

"I'm really kind of curious about those nipple clamps," he told me, searching my eyes. I had to admit I was a little curious too. I'd only done solo research with some of the adjustable clamps. I'd never had a partner before.

"OK...let's try them."

I was a little nervous as I walked back into the bedroom, taking off my socks and shoes. Evan followed suit and pulled off his own and his shirt.

"So...restraints?" He held up the bed chains and the smaller set of four cuffs.

I blew out a short breath and nodded. "Why not? Let's do it."

He picked up the chains, and we quietly attached them to all four corners of the bed, wrapping them around each post and clipping them into place. Then he picked up the set of women's cuffs.

"Fully naked or...?" he asked as one hand cupped my side and his thumb slowly ran across my ribs.

I pulled my sports bra off, enjoying the way his breath caught. My shorts came off next, leaving me standing in my underwear.

I held out a wrist and he attached the first cuff, slowly stroking my palm with his fingers and raising his hand up to kiss the center of it. He attached the second one and then knelt on the floor in front of me to attach the ankle cuffs.

"You ready?" he asked quietly.

I nodded as I carefully climbed onto the bed and laid down. My arms and legs were slightly outstretched. Evan walked around the bed, clipping each cuff onto the corner restraints.

He walked out of the room quickly into the living room. I wasn't sure what he was getting. I closed my eyes and tried to relax as I waited for him.

"Let's put this on," he said softly, holding up the silk blindfold with one hand.

I bit my lip and nodded, raising my head a little so he could slip it on. My heart was pounding as I laid there, restrained by all four limbs, completely at his mercy. It was always the quiet ones you had to watch out for, and I had a feeling Evan was tapping into his inner freak today.

"Still doing alright?" he whispered in my ear. I startled a little... he was right next to my head but not touching me. I hadn't felt the bed move at all.

"Yes," I breathed out.

His warm breath disappeared, and I tried to listen to hear what he was doing. After a few moments, I heard a crinkling noise from the other room. Naughty boy was getting something else from the bags.

"Ahhh!" I shrieked as something soft yet a little scratchy passed over my side and across my nipples. I shifted on the bed as it disappeared and then started tracing up the inside of my thigh.

My nipples were standing erect as I waited for his next move. I could hear him shifting around next to the bed, but he must've still been standing.

"Shit," I laughed and jerked one of my legs as something sharp but prickly passed over the sole of my foot. "You're mean."

I pouted and then squirmed when the same prickly sensation traveled slowly down the side of my neck. He must have gotten out the feather tickler and the Wartenberg wheel. So much for the nipple clamps. A sharp stinging sensation on the skin just outside of my areola startled me.

"Ahh," I hissed as I tried to lean away from the sensation. I felt the bed dip beside me as the stinging sensation traveled to my other breast. My nipples were painfully hard, and I could feel myself getting wet.

The room was colder than I remembered it being. They always tell you that your other senses will become heightened if you take one away and being blindfolded accomplished that.

The room got quiet as the sensations all disappeared. My breathing was the only sound I could hear. The anticipation was killing me. My legs were spread far enough apart with the restraints that I couldn't even rub my legs together to release the tension I was feeling from my arousal.

I could barely make out the soft sound of a box being opened a few feet away and I heard him lay something down on the nightstand next to my head. A little clicking noise started and then the bed dipped beside me again.

"Fuuuuu...Ooh!" I moaned as I felt a sharp pinch to my left nipple and a weight settled on it.

Clamps were intense. I could feel the blood suffusing my breasts and my hips rose off the bed seeking some sort of friction I couldn't get because I was bound.

"Shhh," Evan whispered as he slowly ran his fingertip over the part of my nipple that was sticking out of the clamp. He kissed the side of my neck and I felt him gently pull apart the rods on the clamp and lift it from my nipple. His hot mouth descended on it as the blood rushed back in.

"Oh my god..." I moaned as he laved his tongue against my sensitive skin, my other nipple standing painfully at attention. My hips jerked up off the bed again and he pressed his hand firmly above my pubic bone, holding me down.

I had no idea how subs could withstand this type of erotic torture without making a sound and keeping still. My hips and legs were thrashing against the restraints. He released my nipple and leaned back. I felt him stand from the mattress and then the weight returned.

"Oh fuck..." I exclaimed as he placed a clamp over the other nipple. He blew on the skin exposed at the tip. I was squirming again at the sharp sense of pain that was building in my skin. Something wet touched the exposed tip and then he blew his hot breath over it again.

"Shit, shit, shit," I groaned as I felt him release the pressure, the blood rushing back in. My pussy clenched as he lightly ran his finger around the engorged skin. I was close to cumming and he hadn't even touched me down there.

"Sit tight," he instructed softly as I felt his weight shift off the bed again.

"Not going anywhere," I muttered. Between the stinging in my nipples and the way I was already close to climaxing, I was in sensation overload.

I could hear shuffling beside the bed and then I heard the plastic cap of something being flicked open.

"Ahhh," he moaned, and I heard a slick sound as I assumed he stroked himself with the lube.

All the sounds stopped for a few moments and then I heard a sound coming from the bathroom. After a few moments, I felt the bed dip near my feet. Evan climbed over my leg and sat in between them.

The quiet flick sound of the bottle lid sounded again, and I heard something wet being spread. My hips jumped as I felt his fingers press gently in the center of my panties.

"Shit...you're so wet," he groaned as he pressed the wet lacy material into my center. Then his fingers gently pushed the material of my panties to the side, and I fruitlessly tried to squirm again as the cool air hit me.

A low buzzing sounded from where he was sitting, and I cried out as he held the vibrator gently to my clit. "Ahhh...!"

He slowly dragged the tip through my wetness, not pushing hard enough to give me relief, but enough that I felt myself get even wetter.

"Ohhhh...yes!" I moaned as he pushed the tip inside me, the gentle buzz starting to fill my body.

His hand slowly rotated the toy as he pushed it into me and then retreated. He built up a slow rhythm of push and pull, my hips rising slightly with each thrust.

"Holy shiiiiit...yes, yes, yes," I moaned as I heard him push a button and the speed of the toy increased. His hand sped up the motions — the rabbit part of the toy hitting my clit with each thrust. I felt myself starting to clench as I got closer to orgasming. He pressed it fully inside and twisted it back and forth, making me buck wildly off the bed and scream out my release.

"Oh my god!" I sobbed as he continued to press the vibrator into me as the rhythmic pulsing of my climax continued. It was almost too much, but it felt so good. Fire raced up my spine as I felt a sharp pinch on my nipple and the toy started to oscillate inside of me. He ratcheted the speed up another notch and I felt myself skyrocketing towards an even more intense release.

"Ohhhh! Oh, my gahh!" I screamed as I thrashed against his touch and the vibrator, a gush of wetness accompanying my release.

"Too much...too much," I moaned out, my voice was hoarse and weak from screaming through the force of both orgasms.

The vibrations stopped with a quiet click. I sighed, a little overwhelmed as he pulled the toy from me. The bed shifted and I heard a quiet thud as he laid it down on my nightstand.

He sat back down to my side and gently pulled the blindfold off me. I had tears running down my cheeks that he wiped gently with his fingertips as he gazed down at me with raw desire in his eyes. I'd never seen him look this aroused. He slowly ran a finger over my peaked nipple before he pinched it, eliciting a sharp gasp from me.

"You ready for more?" he asked as he stood from the bed and I saw his hard member throbbing, his balls encased by the vibrating cock ring.

Holy shit.

# TWENTY-TWO

## Evan

**Boston**

Chase tied to the bed, completely vulnerable but entrusting me with this side of her was the hottest fucking thing I'd ever seen. She looked completely sated after the orgasms I'd coaxed out of her with the rabbit.

I'd never played with toys before — obviously, my history was completely boring in comparison to now — but I could see why people liked them. It was hot to be able to manipulate your partner's enjoyment.

"Holy shit," she exclaimed quietly as she stared at my aroused cock with wide eyes.

It'd been a little challenging to get the cock ring maneuvered into place with a semi, but I knew as soon as I put that vibrator anywhere near her that I would be harder than steel. The little pieces of silicone were definitely doing their job...I was throbbing and hard as granite.

"Is that a no?" I asked, already knowing her answer.

"Are you kidding me?" She smiled as she rolled her eyes.

I carefully climbed back on the bed in between her legs, slowly kneading my hands up her long legs and the tops of her thighs. Her muscles were a little tense from being immobile, but she seemed alright. "Do I need to untie you?"

She leaned her head up slightly, giving me a disbelieving look.

"No, god no," she urged. "You just need to get in there."

I chuckled at the frustrated look on her face as she pushed her hips up off the bed, trying to shimmy herself closer to where I was kneeling.

"Are you sure you don't want me to undo the cuffs?" I asked again.

"Are you serious right now? If you do uncuff me, I'm using the whip in the other room on you," she threatened.

"So impatient," I scolded.

"Maybe I should make you sweat a little." I grinned as I reached forward and grabbed the feather tickler off the corner of the bed.

Chase threw her hips upwards, trying fruitlessly to line herself up as my cock brushed against her sex.

"Hmmm...where should I use this first?" I mused as I slowly lowered the feathers to the side of her neck. "Are you sensitive here?"

My hand tilted the handle slightly and ran the very tip of one feather gently over her collar bone. She let out a soft sigh, her arm jerking a little bit against the cuff.

"Or how about here?" I traced a path towards her shoulder and then down her side, barely grazing the side of her breast.

"Ahh," she hissed as her body twitched to the side. Obviously, that spot was a little ticklish.

I reversed the direction and ran it back up and she twitched again, glaring at me as I continued to trace slow patterns across her skin. The fire in her eyes shifted as I ran concentric circles slowly around the skin of her breast. By the time I reached her nipple, she was arching off the bed and moaning softly.

"Ohhh..."

"Hm...so we know you like this," I teased as I ran it around the other side, and then slowly trailed it down to her abdomen. I set it down for a moment as I looked down at her covered sex.

"I'll buy you a new pair," I promised her as I gripped the side seam of her panties and gave it a firm yank, tearing the lace. I repeated the same action on the other side and tossed the scrap of lace to the floor.

"Wonder if you like it here?" I picked back up the tickler and slowly trailed it over the sparse hair covering her mound. I used my thumb to part her hood and looked down at her little pink swollen bud.

"Right here..." I murmured as I very gently teased her clit with the feather.

"Oh my god...I hate you," she half moaned, half sighed as her hips shifted from side to side.

"I know, baby. But I think you secretly like it," I teased.

Her eyes narrowed at my wink and I knew once she was finally released from the restraints that I was in trouble. "Grrr..."

"What do you want?" I asked her as I leaned back away from her.

She huffed and rolled her eyes, her neck arching backward as I continued to tease her with the feather-light touches.

"Use your words..." I coached.

"Cocksucker," she growled at me. I smirked, trying not to laugh at her petulance.

"We both know you're the one that does that in this relationship," I laughed. "Is that what you want?"

She frowned at me.

"Do you want to suck it?" I asked as I raised up on my knees and stroked my hard cock a few times — her eyes tracking the movements of my hand.

"Ugh," she huffed as she tugged at her bound wrists lightly. She really wanted to touch me.

"If you want me in your mouth you have to ask," I coaxed.

"Fine!" Her voice was strained as she continued to stare at me and the slow motion of my wrist.

"Fine, what?"

"Fine. Stick it in my mouth," she hissed as she licked her lips and took several deep breaths.

"Well, if you're not going to ask nicely, maybe I should just continue doing this..." I said as I grasped my dick more firmly and sped up the pace of my movements.

"Ahh..." I moaned as I shifted my hips into the momentum of my hand. The blood pooled in the shaft from the cock ring was making me even harder than I was used to. Each stroke was more intense than what I'd usually experience.

"Stop!" she moaned at me as she shifted her hips back and forth again, she still couldn't quite get her legs to touch. I knew she was trying to rub her legs together.

Dirty girl. She liked watching me touch myself.

"And what should I do instead?" I asked as I shifted forward, tilted myself towards her opening, and slowly dipped the head inside her. "Should I put it in here?"

"Yes!" she pressed herself towards me and moaned as I shifted inside of her a little deeper. She was so warm and still drenched from before.

"Hmmm...I don't know," I teased as I pulled my hips back and left her warmth, her hips dropping back into the mattress.

"Maybe you'd like for it to go in here? I leaned forward and placed my thumb on her bottom lip, pressing down lightly. Her pupils dilated and before I could react, she nipped at my finger, a sharp sensation shooting through my hand.

"Bad girls may just have to watch," I chastised her as I sat back on my heels and grabbed a hold of myself again, firmly stroking.

"I think I should see how this feels," I mused as I pressed the little button on the end of the vibrating part of the cock ring. It started to vibrate on the base of my shaft, sending a gentle buzzing through me. It felt good.

"You're a dick," she growled as I leisurely stroked up and back down, sending pleasurable sensations down my spine.

"Yes...yes, he is," I laughed nodding down at my hand.

"Ughhh..." she groaned as she watched the movements of my hand, completely transfixed.

My gaze roamed her gorgeous naked body, watching intently the way her tits jiggled as her chest heaved. Her torso was a mottled pink color and her nipples rosy red. I wanted so badly to latch onto one of them, my mouth watering at the thought, but she was being a little mouthy now.

"Please," she whimpered as she watched me with rapt interest.

"Hmmm?" I moaned as I began to pulse my hips up as I stroked down. My movements weren't strong enough to get me close, but it felt really, really good.

"Please, Evan?" she begged.

"I'm sorry, what?" I teased as I tried not to make eye contact with her.

"I'll be good..." She was pouting as she tried to convince me to do something...to touch or plunge into somewhere.

"Where do you want me?" I asked as I rose onto my knees again.

Her tongue came out to wet her lips again and she bit her lip as she eyed my dick.

"In here..." She licked her lips again. "Put it in my mouth."

I arched an eyebrow.

"Please?"

How could I resist that?

I clicked the end of the bullet and the vibrations stopped.

Carefully raising my knees over her outstretched legs, I straddled her torso and shifted my knees until my cock was poised just out of reach of her mouth.

"You want it here?" I asked as I pressed on her lower lip with my thumb.

"Yes," she sighed, and I felt her breasts brush against the insides of my thighs.

"You sure?" I confirmed, knowing her answer, but enjoying the tease.

"Please stop teasing me," she whispered as she raised her head, her lips barely grazing the head.

I shifted forward just a little bit more and eased my way inside of her mouth.

"Since you asked so nicely..."

Her hot mouth enveloped the head of my cock and she hollowed out her cheeks, sucking lightly.

"Fuck," I moaned as I reached forward and grabbed the headboard with one hand. My hips slowly rocked into her mouth... she tried to lift her head to move down, but I was completely in charge of the depth and speed.

"Mmmm," she moaned as I made shallow movements, pulling myself out every few thrusts so she could breathe.

"Shit," I groaned as I felt myself getting over-excited. The ring amplified the sensations, making everything more intense.

My fingers traced down her cheek as Chase suckled the head when I started to pull out. "You're going to make me cum."

"Mmmm," she moaned as she lightly scraped her teeth against me.

"Bad girl," I scolded as I pulled out and leaned back, reaching down to pinch her nipple.

"Fuck me," she moaned as she stared up at my eyes. Her lips were swollen and pink, moisture glistening on her bottom lip. I let go of the headboard and scooted back down the bed, centering myself in the cradle of her thighs. I lifted her hips up with both hands and slipped my knees under the backs of her thighs.

She was literally dripping. I'd never seen her this wet.

"You ready?" I asked as I gripped myself and ran the head of my cock through her wetness.

"This again?" she groaned as she wiggled as much as her position allowed on my lap.

"Be nice or I'll just make you watch." I held my dick and slowly stroked it up and down.

"Ugh," she groaned. I pressed the tip down on her clit and tapped it firmly a few times, making her throw her head back and moan. "Ahhh!"

It was fucking hot to make her frustrated like this. I was going to have to hide the wooden spoon.

"Can you be nice?"

"Yes," she huffed. I smacked her clit again. "Damn you."

I pressed the button on the side of the vibrator, and it hummed to life, sending subtle vibrations down the length of me.

"Oh my god," she moaned as I pushed the head onto her clit and slid against her slightly.

She started pulsing her hips up with my movements and I couldn't hold back anymore, no matter how much I was enjoying this. I tilted my hips slightly and drew back before plunging inside of her in one smooth thrust.

"Fuuuuuck!" she exclaimed loudly as her head pressed back into the pillow, her neck arching enticingly.

I pressed my hips as far forward as I could and pulled her into me. She moaned as the vibrator pressed into her clit and her eyes rolled back before she closed her eyes.

"Oh...yes, yes, yes...fuuuuck. Yes, oh my gah," she was moaning as I pulled out and snapped my hips forward again, rotating them as I bottomed out.

"God, you're so fucking hot." I could see a deeper flush start around her chest and neck, her cries indicating that she was close.

One of my fingers traced the outside of her lips as I disappeared inside of her and I pressed it into her clit, rubbing circles as I continued to thrust into her.

"Yes, yes, yes...oh, right there. Yes!" she cried out as her hips flexed on my lap and I could feel her start to pulse on me.

"Fuck," I groaned as I sped up, her cries increasing as the vibrator continued to stimulate her through her orgasm.

"Ahhhh!" I shouted as I felt her clench me even tighter and I couldn't hold back anymore. I came inside of her in several long streams. "Fuck."

My thumb clicked off the vibrator as my heart pounded in my chest. I sighed as I looked down to where she was lying limp against the bed, arms still outstretched.

"That's... enough, sorry," I panted as I leaned forward to unhook one wrist cuff and then the other. My cock slipped out of her as I leaned back to unhook her ankles. She sagged against the bed, staring up at me with a dazed look in her eyes.

I grabbed one wrist and rubbed lightly, slowly moving my way up her forearm and towards her shoulder. She sighed quietly as I rubbed out the tightness in her joints and muscles. I switched sides and did the other wrist and up. My hands found her thighs and I dug my fingers into her muscles, trying to ease the discomfort she probably felt.

"Come here," I whispered as I gripped her hand and tugged.

"Hmm," she sighed as she opened her eyes and stared at me with a sated look.

"I'll help you." I gripped her waist and lifted her up towards me. Pressing our chests together. She placed her arms around my neck and hugged me to her as I ran my hands softly over the sweaty skin of her back.

"That was..." she sighed.

I was worried that maybe it'd been too much. I didn't even know what possessed me to do half that shit.

"That was the hottest thing I've ever done," she whispered into my skin.

"Oh, thank god," I sighed as I tucked her face into my neck.

We sat quietly for a few moments before Chase shifted and groaned on my lap.

"Want me to draw you a bath?" I asked quietly.

"That would be amazing." She kissed the side of my neck and leaned back, her fingers scratching my neck. "You going to join me?"

Smiling, I leaned forward and kissed her gently. "I may be able to be persuaded."

I gently laid her back against the sheets and kissed her forehead as I climbed off the bed, grabbing the rabbit and the Wartenberg wheel as I went.

Once I was in the bathroom, I carefully maneuvered myself out of the cock ring. My skin was a little sensitive from being restricted for so long, but it was worth every bit of discomfort.

I washed it, together with the wheel and the rabbit, with the toy wash and left them on a towel to dry before I started the flow of water to the bathtub. There was a canister of bath salts under the sink, and I figured it couldn't hurt, so I sprinkled some into the warm water. The aromatic vapors filled the bathroom as the salts dissolved into the steamy water.

When I got back to the bedroom, Chase was curled up in the sheets, her eyes closed.

"Let's go, sleepy," I coaxed a soft smile out of her as I lifted her shoulders and helped her sit up. She clung to my arm as we walked to the bathroom and I helped her into the tub. She scooted forward and I climbed in behind her, drawing her back into my arms.

"How're you feeling?" My voice was low in the quiet of the room.

"Mmmm. I was a little sore...you know...down there...but this is helping."

"I would say I was sorry, but..." I trailed off.

"We both know you're not," she laughed quietly.

"Nope. Not even a little. That was explosive."

"Are you sure you've never played with toys before?" she asked, sounding amused and a little curious.

"Pretty sure." I nodded against the side of her head.

"That was some expert level shit in there."

She bounced lightly against my chest as I laughed quietly. I'd had no fucking clue what I was doing. At all. "Glad you enjoyed it."

"We're keeping all of those," she giggled as she turned slightly and ran her hand behind my head, scratching the hair at the back.

"Mmmm. I agree. We still have much more research to conduct." I kissed along the top of her shoulder. "So...much...research..."

My hands came up to her breasts, cupping them lightly and coaxing the nipples into points with my fingers.

"Ahhh. Be gentle," she hissed, and I decreased the pressure.

"Maybe we need to take a little break, just for the rest of today," I told her. I didn't want to hurt her by pushing it too much.

"We can work on clothed research. You better practice your knots or Emory will punish your ass tomorrow," she teased. "And I'm talking in the literal sense."

"Thank you for trusting me enough to get you into all this," she whispered.

"Why are you thanking me? Of course, I trust you...I..."

Love you.

"You?" she asked softly.

"I care so deeply about you," I whispered into her hair. I was afraid to tell her how I really felt. There was no way I'd recover if she wasn't ready for me to say it yet or didn't feel the same way.

Her breath caught and she turned in my arms, a little bit of water sloshing out the side of the tub as she turned to straddle me. Chase's hands framed the sides of my face, her thumbs stroking across my cheekbones.

"I care deeply for you too," she whispered as she leaned forward and kissed me. It was firm and wet, and I couldn't remember ever kissing anyone but her...ever...and I never wanted it to be anyone but her...ever again.

# TWENTY-THREE

### Chase

**Boston**

"Wait! I thought I got to tie him up!" I exclaimed as I looked over at Emory.

He had a smug little smirk on his face as he raised his eyebrow at my tone. "Excuse me?"

"Why does he get to be the one to use the whip?"

"You're pouting like a child," Emory scolded as he stood with his arms crossing his broad chest.

Evan was standing off to the side, his head moving between the two of us as we faced off.

"I'm serious," I insisted. "I'm writing the Dominatrix. Why does he get to whip me first?"

"You know how this works," Emory responded evenly. "You have to be willing to be on the receiving end before you get to do it yourself."

"But I already know how to use it." I flicked my wrist like he had taught me, and the end of the flicker whip cracked softly in the air.

"Very impressive, Chase," Emory sighed and rolled his eyes. "He's still going first."

I narrowed my eyes at him. He was such a dick sometimes.

"Bra on or off. Your choice," Emory nodded as he looked at my chest.

"On!" Evan practically yelled. I see he was still feeling a little worried about Em seeing me unclothed. As if he didn't see models half-naked daily. Em seeing my breasts — at least in Evan's mind — was obviously going to turn him into a wild animal.

"Standing or kneeling, Chase?" Emory asked expectantly. "I'll let you pick the position."

"Kneeling," I sighed.

"Grab the rope, Evan," Emory nodded over at the tightly coiled rope he'd laid on the edge of the large leather bed that dominated the main space in Emory's playroom. "Let's see if you did your homework."

We'd spent a few hours curled up on the couch after our bath, watching TV and talking. It wasn't about anything of substance, but I felt like we weren't just dancing around the subject of being together anymore. We were together, and I was sure we were on the same page...it was serious.

Evan had laughed when I ordered Chinese food and the delivery driver expressed his concern that I hadn't been home the week before to order my usual.

After dinner, we'd sat down facing each other, going through some basic knot tying skills. Evan practiced on me until he felt like he got it right.

"Alright. What would you like me to do?" he asked quietly as he glanced over at Emory.

Emory pointed at the large leather bed in the center of the room. He motioned me over and I knelt on a small pad he'd put on the floor in front of the edge.

"We want her arms up out of the way, and a nice stretch on her back," Em instructed as he raised my arms in front of me and rested them near one of the leather straps running down the surface. "Bind her wrists and tie her into the strapping. We want her to be outstretched but with a little bit of wiggle room."

"OK, Chase." Evan sat down on the edge facing me and picked up one of my wrists, running his thumb over the underside. "Can you hold them six inches apart?"

I nodded and got into position as he took the nylon rope from Em and began looping it around my wrists. After making five even loops, he crossed the rope ends over each other, and wrapped the space in between my wrists. He crossed the rope ends again and then carefully stretched my arms over one of the straps, fastening me to the leather strap with a neat set of knots.

"Very nice. He's a quick study, Chase. Better than your first attempt to tie me up," Emory complimented while simultaneously taking a jab at me.

Evan's eyes searched mine before they flashed over to Emory.

"Don't worry," Emory assured. "It was just for practice. Talia was enjoying seeing me bound and on my knees. Doesn't happen very often."

"You hate giving up control," I nodded. Emory's submission was a rare sight.

"You should feel accomplished knowing that you're one of the very few I trusted enough to do it," Emory stated. "That's what this entire lifestyle is about...not control, not dominance... it's about trust. Trusting your partner enough to gift them with the control to make both of your desires come true."

Evan's eyes locked with mine as he said that, and I knew that I completely trusted him with all of me. My heart. My mind. My body. I knew he'd keep me safe and care for me.

"Now to select your equipment. I think she'd look particularly nice with an array of pink splashed across her pale skin from that flogger," Emory told him as he stepped closer to the wall that held all the whipping and paddling instruments.

Evan stood up and stepped out of my line of sight. I could hear them talking quietly, their voices mixed in with the gentle clanking of the metal brackets as things were moved around.

My heartbeat started to pick back up as I heard the sound of someone's feet on the floor behind me.

I closed my eyes and leaned my forehead against the leather, trying to straighten out my back and remain balanced on my knees. I knew posture affected how the hits impacted your skin.

My trust for Evan was solid, but he was new at this and I wanted to set him up as best as I could. He'd be upset if he hurt me.

"Chase, you ready?" Emory asked quietly.

I nodded. "Yes, sir."

"Evan, feet shoulder-width apart. Strike from the shoulder, not the wrist, it should be a fluid movement, not a snap."

I blew out a breath as I heard the telltale whoosh of leather cutting the tension in the air. The tail lashed across my back and I tried not to jolt as I felt the impact. It wasn't hard enough to hurt me, but I still felt the sting from my blood rushing to the surface of the skin.

"Not bad," Em appraised. "Try to follow the whole motion through this time, don't hesitate at the end, it'll distribute the impact evenly across the skin."

I took a few deep breaths as I prepared myself for the second strike. I was able to keep still as it hit this time, my adrenaline spiking as the mild pain rushed through my body. It didn't really hurt, but it made you acutely aware of all the nerve endings in your skin. I could see why this excited certain people.

"Chase, are you still OK?" Evan's voice was uncertain behind me.

"I'm good," I nodded. "Keep going."

I could hear Em whispering some corrections to Evan's stance and I braced myself.

"Ohhh..." I moaned as he landed two strikes going in opposite directions across my lower back.

"Chase?" Emory questioned with concern.

"All good," I sighed as I tried to keep myself calm. The endorphin release from the pain fading was getting me more aroused than I expected.

Before, when I'd been on the receiving end of Emory I'd felt the rush, but not this intense arousal that I experienced when I knew it was Evan working me over.

"Just a few more swings, try to evenly distribute them so you don't hit the same place twice," Emory instructed. "That's how you get bruising or skin damage. The goal is a warm even pink across the surface."

My moans were involuntary with the next set. My nipples were painfully hard, and I could see now why Em had joked about there being a bed in the back.

"Alright. I think you've got the hang of it," Emory told Evan. "Go ahead and release her."

Evan sat down in my line of sight off to my side and ran his hand gently down my hair. I gazed up at him, a little drunk on the hormones coursing through my bloodstream.

"Are you OK?" he asked quietly.

"I'm great," I whispered as I heard the door to the studio click closed.

Evan made quick work of untying the fastenings and uncoiling the rope from around my wrists. He massaged the little bit of discomfort I had out of my wrists and shoulders before lightly running his fingers down my back, admiring his work.

"I can see why you enjoyed the wooden spoon. That was a rush."

His goofy smile looked proud, and I loved how self-assured he was with this.

"It's different being the giver, isn't it?" I asked.

He leaned down and brushed his lips on my ear. "I'm so fucking hard right now."

My breath caught in my throat as I raised my head to look at him. His pupils were dilated, and he was staring at me with an intense amount of desire in his eyes. "He left to go get Talia. Told me he locked the door and we've got an hour."

"Then what are you waiting for?" I rose to my knees and pushed my hands on his hips until he scooted in front of me, and then I pulled on the waistband of his shorts.

"Shit," he moaned, lying back as he raised his hips up enough to slide them down his thighs along with his briefs.

My god was he hard, almost as hard as he'd been with the ring on. I licked my lips and glanced up at him as I hovered above his erection.

"You don't have to do...ahhh!" he moaned as I engulfed him in my mouth and sucked hard before relaxing my jaw and taking him all the way down.

"Fuck!" he yelled as he gathered my hair into his hand and held it out of my face. Evan's other hand reached beneath me and pulled up the band on my bra, freeing my breasts.

He pinched my nipple a few times, making me moan around him. His hips pulsed upwards as I took him in, building up a quick rhythm.

"I'm gonna cum," he panted as he cupped my jaw and lifted me off him.

"Up here," he told me, sitting on the edge of the bed as he patted his lap.

"Yes, sir," I winked as I took his hand and stood up. He grabbed my hips and turned me, so I was facing away from him. He pushed down my shorts and panties, helping me step out of them.

"Put your legs up here." He ran his hand across the leather and I carefully straddled him on my knees backward as his hand reached around to support my stomach.

His other handheld the base of his erection as I eased myself down onto him. I let out an embarrassingly loud moan as I settled against his lap. "Oh god, you feel so good."

He gripped my waist and began to slowly raise and lower me onto his lap, pushing up into me at the end of each downward stroke. My head fell back onto his shoulder as his hands cupped my breasts and rolled my nipples between his fingers.

"Ride me, baby," he groaned as I sped up the rhythm of my hips, grinding into his lap and rotating my hips. One of his hands traced down my stomach and he gently pinched my clit between the pads of his fingers.

"Fuck." At this point, I was frantically bouncing on him as he started to rub me vigorously.

"Yes. God yes, just keep riding me," he groaned into my shoulder. My hips faltered a little as I started to feel myself falling over the edge.

"Evan!" I moaned loudly as his hands both gripped my waist and pushed me down onto him while bucking up from the bed. My orgasm crashed over me and he groaned into my neck as I felt him pulse inside of me.

"Oh...my...fuuuuck," I panted as I tried to catch my breath.

Evan kissed along my shoulder and his hands caressed my breasts as we came down together. "That was hot."

I giggled as I kissed the side of his face and ran my hand back through his sweaty hair. "You're wearing me out, stud."

He laughed and the vibrations shook me right along with him. "We can soak in the tub again when we get home."

I loved how he didn't even hesitate to call us going back to my condo home. His place...my place...as long as he was there, it was home.

"Uhhh..." I groaned as I pulled myself up from his lap and climbed off the bed. My arms and legs were sore. I just couldn't help myself around him. "We should probably clean this place back up, I don't want to get punished and miss out on beating that fine ass of yours."

"Going straight to spanking, huh?"

"You've got a date with a leather paddle later, mister," I winked as I walked over to Em's toy chest of drawers and took out a few wet wipes. I cleaned myself up and quickly redressed, throwing Evan his underwear and then walking back over and pushing him off the edge of the leather bed. "Get your cute little butt dressed and help me clean that whip."

"So, you think my butt is cute?" he teased as he shook his underwear-clad ass at me.

"Quit it, you dork," I laughed, spraying some leather cleaner on a cloth and throwing it at his face. "Playtime can be later. We need to be respectful of Em's space."

"Yes, Ma'am." I raised my eyebrow at him and smiled. He cleared his throat and his Adam's apple bobbed as he swallowed.

"Mistress," he whispered, and his head dropped as he gently ran the cleaning cloth over the handle and the tail of the whip he'd used on me.

He could probably use a conversation with Nathan. Evan seemed to be able to switch between Dominant and submissive with a few well-placed words or commands. Maybe we could work that into the storyline somehow.

With all the playtime-induced chemicals streaming through my blood, I was already feeling the itch to write.

Frances — Fanny — had already booted Kallie out and her story was starting to work its way through my brain. I needed to remember to bring a notebook to our next session. Evan had distracted me this morning and I was off my game.

"Where'd you go?" His fingers gently cupping my chin startled me.

"Hmm. Oh. I'm just starting to get the itch to write again," I told him absently as I started to coil back up the rope we'd used.

"I love that you get it..." He pecked me on the lips, slowly caressing my lips with his own. "Writing is ingrained in us. Once the words start building it's hard to keep them in."

"You say that now, but day four of being under the influence of the imaginary people in my brain and you'll be questioning my sanity."

"Only then?" he asked, his face completely blank.

I narrowed my eyes at him and reached up to pinch his nipple. "You know what I mean. When the muse strikes, you get lost in it.

I don't want you to be disappointed if I sit with the laptop on my lap for hours at a time."

"I'll be right there with you," he assured.

I smiled as I looked up into his eyes and wrapped my arms around him. "We can be crazy together."

"I like to call it creative," he smirked.

I laughed as I squeezed him and then leaned back. We stepped apart as we heard the lock on the door click and it slowly swung open.

"Did you miss me?" Tal asked as she stepped inside and looked at how close we were standing to each other.

"Of course!" I told her enthusiastically. I always loved the energy Talia brought to any room.

"Who's ready to get spanked?" she laughed as she crossed the room to us and tapped her hand on my butt.

"It's not my turn..." I shook my head.

"Oooh. Can I watch?" she asked as she ran her eyes down the length of Evan's form. If I didn't know she was completely committed to Em, I would have been worried. She was a bit of a voyeur.

"Up to him," I shrugged as I looked over to Evan. His eyes searched mine, and I gave a subtle nod. I didn't mind if she watched. I was planning on cuffing him to the wall if Em let me choose his position.

"Uh... I... uh," Evan stuttered.

"You're so adorable," she cooed as she squeezed his shoulder.

"Thanks?" He looked at her like she was a little crazy, and then over to me with wide eyes.

This should be fun.

# TWENTY-FOUR

### Evan

**Boston**

At first, I'd been a little nervous for Talia to sit in the room while Em taught us about erotic spankings. I felt a little cold and a lot exposed as I stood with my wrists bound in front of me with the leather cuffs and hooked into the wall frame.

The room was warm, but I was exposed clad in only the leather jockstrap. My almost nudity didn't seem to be bothering anyone but me, but once Chase brought the paddle down for the first strike I didn't care. She worked my cheeks evenly until I burned and was throbbing underneath my scant cover.

Emory walked us through more aftercare options and then he and Talia left so Chase and I could get changed back into our street clothes.

"You ready to do this?" she asked, as we left through the gallery doors and walked hand in hand back to the car.

"So ready." I knew we were both dying to write. My erection subsided by the time we got into the car and I drove us quickly across town.

"You hungry?" she asked as we sat down at the kitchen counter back at her place.

"I could eat," I shrugged. We'd probably burned a fair number of calories today. I knew if we stayed longer that I'd need to figure out a running schedule. It helped clear out all the clutter in my brain so I could focus my writing.

She nodded and pulled a stack of takeout menus from a drawer in her kitchen island. "What are you in the mood for?"

"Surprise me?" I hadn't been in the city with accessible takeout in so long, I wasn't even sure where to start. She leafed through them and pulled out a menu for a Thai place.

"I'm gonna go shower," I told her as I stripped off my shirt.

She bit her lip and ran a finger across my abdomen. "I'll order this and come join you."

I wasn't sure how sore she was from the last few days, so I was planning to let her rest, but I needed to relieve some tension.

My shorts, underwear, and shoes hit the floor next to my bag and I stroked my semi-erect cock a few times on the way to the bathroom. Setting the water to warm, I stepped into the spray and ran my hands through my hair a few times.

I leaned my forearm on the tile and hung my head as I fondled myself with the other hand. This afternoon had gotten me all worked up. Emory being in the room had been the only thing that had kept me from cumming all over that flimsy jockstrap.

"Ugh..." I groaned as I worked my hand up and down, twisting at the head before rapidly traveling back down to the base.

Chase was bound to join me soon but getting caught jacking off in her shower just made me harder.

"That's so fucking hot," she whispered as she slid the door the rest of the way open and stepped in behind me.

Her hands ran down my back and cupped my hips as she molded herself to my back. She peeked around my side and eyed where I had a firm grip on myself.

"Keep going," she urged in a sultry voice.

"Ahhh..." I hissed as she ran her fingers along the ridge at my side that led to where my hand was currently preoccupied.

"Make yourself feel good," she whispered. My hand resumed a slow circuit of up and down as I felt her lips travel down my side, one of her hands reaching down to roll my sac in her fingers.

"Fuck," I groaned as my legs started to shake a little. The skin on my backside was a little sore, but I didn't even care with the naked woman wrapped around my back.

"That's it." The combination of her touch, her soft voice, and the sensual kisses on my back pushed me rapidly towards the edge.

"Ohhh..." I moaned as her hand ran over the tip of my shaft and slightly overlapped with my own. She squeezed the head as our hands worked me over, my hips starting to rut into the motion.

"Cum for me, baby," she whispered into my neck as she rubbed her tits against my back. Chase was breathing almost as hard as I was.

"Fuck...yes...ugh," I groaned as I pulsed and painted the wall of the shower with several ropes of cum.

"You feel better?" She sounded amused as she placed a few more kisses on my back. I nodded my head and tried to catch my breath. Chase straightened up, pulling away from me.

I groaned a few moments later when I felt her working shampoo into my hair, rubbing my scalp. I'd had more Chase-induced orgasms in the last two weeks than I'd had in the last two years by anyone else.

"I just needed to clear my head," I confessed. She hadn't seemed to have a problem with me pleasuring myself, but I felt a little self-conscious. I normally was not this sexually pent up.

"I get it," she told me quietly. "Food should be here in about fifteen minutes."

She kissed my shoulder and stepped back into the spray, quickly washing herself and then handing me the bottle of body wash. I lathered myself up and rinsed off. She turned off the water and leaned out the door, coming back with towels. We were quiet as we dried ourselves.

Different scenarios were running through my mind. I had a good idea of where I wanted the story to go.

"You ready?" she asked as she pushed the door open and stepped onto the floor mat.

"As ready as I'll ever be."

We dressed quickly and the delivery guy showed up shortly after we walked into the living room.

"Netflix?" she asked as we settled into the couch. Neither of us seemed to like silence to start working.

"I'll let you pick," I nodded as I pulled open a few of the containers to see what she'd ordered. It all smelled good, and my stomach growled.

"This one is hilarious." The screen was on the menu for 'Sleeping with Other People'. It had Alison Brie in it; she was pretty fucking hot.

We ate side by side, passing the containers back and forth as the movie played. When it got to the part where Jason Sudeikis' character was showing Alison's how to masturbate with a jar I was dying laughing.

"Want to do some dirty DJing later?" I whispered as I put down my empty container and took Chase's to put on the coffee table. She tucked herself under my arm and laid her head against my chest.

"I think you're gonna break me if I don't take a breather," she laughed as she looked up at me.

"Fair enough. I probably shouldn't be distracting you with that anyways. We need to start making some progress," I agreed. "Adrian and Isobel are going to get suspicious with too much more radio silence."

"Is told me I had till Friday to send her some pages." It was Wednesday.

"For the book you were working on before you came to Connecticut?"

"Yeah...it's kind of stalled. I've been a little distracted," she told me with a guilty smile.

"I would say sorry, but..."

"You're so not," she laughed.

"Not even a little. This has been the craziest past few weeks," I told her. "But I wouldn't trade any of it, even if my ass is a little sore."

"You'll live," she rolled her eyes at me.

"As long as I don't piss you off."

"Damn straight. I'll beat that ass," she cackled.

"I know you will." I wasn't joking; if I fucked up, I knew she'd lay me out.

"But seriously...I know we need to start working tomorrow, but this has been nice." Her shy little smile made my heartbeat pick up.

"It has," I wholeheartedly agreed, "but it's back to the grind."

She smirked as she looked up at me.

"Not that kind of grind. For someone who needs a breather, you're being awfully suggestive," I teased her. It was just second nature now.

"You know I'm a giant perv. That's why you love me." The way she said it, I knew she didn't register what she'd said, but I did. She glanced up at me and took in the serious look on my face. "Oh...I didn't mean like that. You know I don't have a filter."

I grabbed her shoulders and pulled her upright next to me. "I do."

"You do...?" Her cheeks turned a little pink as she stared at me.

"I know you don't have a filter," I told her, and her shoulders slumped a little. "But I do. I love you."

My heart was hammering in my chest as I waited for her to register my words and formulate a response.

"I uh..." Her eyes scanned my face.

"I do too," she whispered quietly. I wished she'd use the words, but it'd have to do. I opened my mouth to speak again, and she pressed her finger against my lips.

"You think I'd be better with words," she laughed a little as she smiled at me. "I love you, Evan. I really do."

I cupped the sides of her face and rubbed my thumbs along her cheekbones. Even with her hair half wet in a messy bun on top of her head and zero makeup, she was beautiful.

"Will you come back home with me?"

She nodded and smiled, pressing her cheek into my hand. "I'd go anywhere with you."

I pulled her towards me as I closed the distance between us. My lips found hers and I tugged on her bottom lip as I suckled it with my tongue. She climbed into my lap and we continued kissing, just enjoying being close to each other.

She'd agreed to come back with me without any hesitation. I'd been worried this whole time, but she was in this with me.

"Hey," I smiled over at Chase as she stirred on her pillow. I'd been up with the sun around 5:00 am. First, I'd made coffee, run a quick mile, and then pulled out my laptop.

"Mmmm. How long have you been up?" Her sleepy smile was adorable.

Since I met you.

"A few hours." It was almost 9:00 am, I'd thought about waking her up earlier, but I knew our sleep would be thrown off as we started to write — she might as well get used to it now.

"What are you working on?" she asked curiously.

I had about ten pages sitting in front of me filled with a detailed outline of the story we'd plotted out. I'd also started a glossary of characters with mini-bios and where they appeared in the plot. Even though it was nowhere even close to being related to the content I normally wrote...it was good.

Frances was a Dominatrix who trained other Doms and subs. She had a regular sub named Dominic that she had been with for about a decade. People within their circle start going missing and turn up dead. She doesn't know who to trust when Dominic suddenly disappears. She never anticipated being targeted by a serial killer and it may not be who she thinks.

"What did you do?" she asked warily as I gave her a proud little grin.

"Sit up." She pushed herself up and settled against the headboard. I placed the laptop onto her legs, and she began to read.

"Oh, my gah," she yawned. "You take type A to a whole new level."

I shrugged as I smiled at her. I liked having a plan. "What do you think?"

"I think this is fucking amazing. Can I hire you to write with me full time? I need an Evan to make sense of the mess in my head."

I leaned over and kissed the side of her head as I slipped my arm around her lower back. "You don't need to hire me. I'd be happy to help you."

"You're just too adorable this morning." She reached up and ruffled my hair. "Do you have any of the dialogue started or did you just work on the outline?

I used the tip of my finger to tap the screen to switch to another tab.

"Someone has been inspired this morning."

"I have," I told her as I looked into her eyes and ran my finger down the side of her face.

"Love looks good on you," she sighed happily. Her soft lips caressed mine as she ran her fingers up into my hair.

"Is that what this is?" I teased. "I thought I just looked this good all the time."

"And you've got jokes too," she giggled.

I kissed her softly and took the laptop back, saving the various open documents and closing the lid. "Do you want me to make you breakfast?"

"Have you eaten?"

I shook my head. "Not really, just some coffee and a piece of toast."

"Do you want to go out to breakfast somewhere?"

My pulse raced a little at her question. It was innocent enough, and it would be nice, but being back in the city still made me nervous.

"We don't have to," she backtracked, and I immediately felt guilty.

"No, it's OK," I assured her, determined to step out of my comfort zone. I couldn't hide away from the world anymore with Chase by my side. "Let's do it. Want to take a shower with me?"

"Do you really have to ask that question? I'm always up for ogling you naked," she laughed.

"Ah, so that's why you keep me around. We both know it's not my sparkling personality," I rolled my eyes dramatically.

"Hey...I happen to love your personality."

"I'm glad someone does," I teased. "Let's get ready."

Chase and I showered quickly, surprisingly keeping our hands mostly to ourselves. We took an Uber across town because neither of us felt like dealing with traffic. She gave the address to the driver and cuddled silently against my side in the back seat until he pulled up at the curb.

"OK, so this place looks like a college hipster spot, but they have amazing breakfast sandwiches," she explained as we opened the door to the nondescript restaurant.

"Do we need to stop at a thrift store for some ironic fake glasses or a fedora?"

"It's not that bad," she sighed.

"I'm out of touch with the youth of today."

"Alright, grandpa. You make it sound like you're eighty."

"I wasn't known for my ability to be trendy in college," I confessed. I was just as awkward back then; I just hadn't taken up hiding from it yet.

"I'm sure you broke all kinds of hearts, Mr. Soccer Star," she cooed as she batted her eyelashes at me.

"Hardly," I scoffed. "You know Raj from Big Bang Theory?"

"Yes...?"

"That was my nickname," I told her. It'd been accurate in comparison as well.

"Big Bang? Damn, should I be worried?" She giggled as she took a seat at a table near the back and picked up her menu, hiding behind it.

I pushed it down with my finger and rolled my eyes at her. "No... my nickname was Raj because I never talked to girls." Except alcohol didn't magically make me talkative like it did with Raj. "I even stopped going to parties because the girls called me the 'creepy hot guy'."

"At least they thought you were hot..." Chase shrugged her shoulders, and I rolled my eyes, flicking her menu as I released it.

"Do you two know what you want?" the waitress interrupted, looking expectantly at Chase. I could see what she meant by hipster. The waitress had gray-dyed hair pulled up into some kind of twist and a bandana tied over it. Her denim overalls and plaid shirt reminded me of what you'd see in nineties music videos.

"I'll take the fried rice."

The waitress looked over at me after she jotted down Chase's order and winked. "And you, sugar?"

My eyes widened and I stuttered out my answer as Chase snickered at me. "Uh...breakfast burger?"

"See...women just can't help themselves around you," Chase teased as she grabbed my hand across the table.

"Well...you don't need to be worried. You're the only woman I seem to be able to articulate a coherent sentence around."

A college-aged guy dropped off our food a few minutes later and we dug in.

"Oh, my guh...thi is sooo goo," I mumbled through bites of the amazingly flavorful sandwich.

"I'm assuming that was English?" she smiled indulgently.

I swallowed and stuck my tongue out at her. "You're right. This place is good."

"Of course, it is — I'm always right..." She trailed off as her eyes widened.

"Oh shit! Incoming." Chase put her hand up next to her face and looked towards the wall. I turned towards the door and saw a thin brunette determinedly making her way towards our table.

"Who is that?" I asked as I leaned across the table towards her.

"Shit, shit, shit," she muttered as the woman stopped next to our table. "Christine! How are you?"

"Chase..." the woman sighed her name in a way that made me feel chastised. "So, you are alive. I was beginning to wonder."

"Yup...still here," Chase nodded. "What are you doing here?"

"Picking up an order for dickhead. He claimed he had a craving, and his intern was 'busy'," she said in a mocking voice doing air quotes.

"Is actually let him send you on an errand?"

"Those two are being weird. She's super distracted lately and, to be completely frank, she's pissed off at you."

"Crap." Chase cringed as she looked at me.

"So, are you the reason that Chase isn't meeting her deadlines?" the intimidating woman asked, aiming an arched eyebrow at me.

"Christine, be nice," Chase warned.

"It was just a question, Chase. He's a big boy. He can answer questions."

"Uh..." Shit. She was staring at me. I was kind of afraid of this girl. She couldn't have been older than her early twenties, but she was obviously skilled at intimidating men.

"OK, so maybe he can't." She squinted at me and gave me a look. "I know you."

I shook my head and tried to make my mouth move. "I...uh. I've never met you."

"No...your face is familiar. Where do I know you from?"

"Christine, seriously. Leave the guy alone."

She turned her intense gaze back on Chase. "Fine. Maybe I'm mistaken, but I doubt it."

"Anyways," she sighed. "You better come up with something or she's gonna take it out on me."

We heard a phone buzzing and Christine reached into her pocket.

"Damn. I'm being summoned. Good to see you, Chase. I'm sure I'll see you around." She tapped onto her screen quickly and then turned to walk to the counter. The cashier handed her a large paper bag, and she took off out the door with a salute in our direction.

"Who was that?" I breathed, my heart still racing a little.

"Christine," Chase sighed as she poked at her bowl, most of the rice was gone by now.

"I got that much."

"She's one of Isobel's interns. She does copy editing," she explained.

So that's why she was so insistent she knew me.

"She seems a little..."

"Intense. Yeah," she agreed. "She's a force to be reckoned with but she's good at her job. And 'dickhead' is Adrian. She never calls him by his real name."

"Well, he is kind of a dick. Makes perfect sense."

She laughed as she poked at my half-eaten burger with her fork. "Finish up. We've got work to do."

"Yes, Mistress."

# TWENTY-FIVE

### Chase

**Boston**

*Isobel: It's Friday...and my inbox is suspiciously empty...*

*Isobel: Quit ghosting me or I'm sending Christine to your building for proof of life.*

*Isobel: Seriously Chase, I need pages, or you must apply to corporate for an extension.*

Shit. I guess I couldn't ignore Is anymore. I had three chapters done, but I was completely absorbed with writing with Evan.

*Chase: I'm sending you what I've got so far...but get me the extension paperwork.*

Fuck...now she was calling me.

"Yes," I answered cautiously. I had a feeling she was about to give me an earful.

"What the hell, Chase?" She did not sound happy with me. "So, you have nothing to say for yourself?"

"I'm stuck," I whispered. Lying to her wasn't something I was proud of, but I couldn't draw focus from our project when we were making such good progress.

"You seemed to be fine until I had to farm you out. What the hell is going on?"

I wasn't sure if I wanted to come out to her yet. She was bound to tell Adrian, and I couldn't volunteer info if I hadn't cleared it with Evan.

"I need another two months and then I promise you, I will get back to this..." I begged. Evan and I should have a rough draft proofed by then and I could devote whatever I needed to then.

"Two *more* months!" she shrieked, and I shied away from the phone, holding it away from my ear. "You were supposed to have this manuscript done and submitted in two months!"

"I know..."

"You know!" she continued yelling. "Are you freaking kidding me? Legal could cite breach of contract on this, Chase."

"They won't. I promise."

"Look, I know you've always delivered before, but I'm worried about you," she told me in a much quieter voice.

I looked over to my kitchen table where Evan was sitting — earbuds in, crazy bedhead, shirtless — wearing only pajama pants. The laptop was open in front of him, and he was completely focused on typing.

"I've honestly never been better, Is..." My confession was completely, one hundred percent honest. This just felt right to be working with him. I'd never done a full collaboration before, but with us it was seamless.

"Are you still in the city? Did something happen?"

I looked over to make sure his earbuds were still in. Evan was in the zone.

"Only until tomorrow, and I met someone," I whispered quickly. Partial truths might get her to back off a little.

"Like you met someone and you're having a hot passionate fling, or you met someone and..." she trailed off.

"I met someone and I'm fairly sure he's the real deal," I admitted. Imagining my future with anyone but Evan just wasn't a reality for me anymore.

The phone line was quiet for a few minutes. "Is he there? I'm coming over."

"No!" I shouted and Evan startled across the room, pulling a bud out of his ear.

"You OK?" he asked quietly, a small frown on his face. I nodded as I pointed to my phone.

"I'm fine." I mouthed and growled silently at Isobel.

"No," I told her. Evan was finally relaxed enough around me that he was making solid progress with everything. Isobel showing up could spook him and I wasn't willing to risk it.

"I promise I'll come to see you later next month. Right now, I just need you to give me some space."

"You can't break up with your editor, Chase," she scolded. "I know you have a personal life, but please just keep me in the loop. It's not like you to go off the rails."

"I'm not going off the rails, Is. Please stop being dramatic. I'm working on a project and I need to see it through."

"Project? Like a writing project?" Her voice sounded a little frantic and a lot excited.

"Kinda." Shit. I hadn't meant to tell her. She was way too good at weaseling information out of me.

"Send me what you've got! We can pitch it to the higher-ups and..."

"Is, calm down. You're going to have to wait on this. It's not only mine to share. I'll send you a draft once it's done."

"Not only yours to share? What does that even mean?" she asked skeptically.

I sat there and tapped my pen nervously on my thigh. Evan had resumed his frantic typing at the table.

"Chase?" she questioned again, sounding a little irritated.

"I'm writing something with someone."

"Like a book?" Her voice still had an edge to it that I didn't like.

"Yes..." I answered warily.

"Who? Is it someone who even knows what they are doing?"

I laughed. Evan knew how to do all kinds of things now. "He definitely knows what he's doing."

"He?" Now she just sounded angry. "Is this guy you're seeing just trying to use you to get his book published? I thought you were smarter than this..."

"Oh, thanks for all the faith in me," I scoffed. "Trust me, Is. He needs no help from me to get published."

"Holy shit, Chase! Really?"

"What?" My heart started beating faster as I waited for her to respond.

"Is it Evan? Are you sleeping with Evan?"

*Fuck.* I guess she really did have me all figured out. "Um..."

"Adrian has been making my life hell since his golden boy dropped off the grid."

I'm sure he's been giving you a really hard time. Emphasis on the hard...

"It's the only thing that makes sense," she insisted. "You're being all secretive, while Evan's gone radio silent."

"I'll call you later, Is. Something has come up! Bye!" Panicking, I hung up on her and turned off my phone, throwing it on the coffee table. My heart was pounding in my chest. I leaned forward on the couch cushion with my head in my hands. I took several deep breaths to calm myself down. This project was messing with me. I wasn't ashamed of it or afraid of Is finding out the truth, but I'd become consumed.

"Hey...you alright?" He sat down on the couch next to me and pulled me into his arms. "Who was on the phone?"

"Is."

"About your deadline?" he asked as he ran his hand down my back, combing through the loose hair.

"Yes," I whispered into his neck. "And no."

"If you need me to take point on this and write the first draft, I can," he offered as he hugged me to his chest a little tighter.

"No...no," I immediately disagreed. "I want to be doing this with you, I'm just overwhelmed."

He nodded and squeezed me tight, his lips on my temple.

"She knows we're sleeping together," I whispered, waiting for him to inevitably freak out.

"Oh..." He tensed up a little. Was this the moment that he finally ran?

"I didn't tell her," I insisted. "She guessed."

"It's OK," he assured in a quiet voice.

"Then I hung up on her and turned off my phone," I told him, nodding to the offending piece of technology I'd abandoned on the coffee table.

He laughed and kissed the side of my head. "She was going to find out we're together eventually."

"I know. I wasn't hiding it, but I don't like letting her down."

"Baby..." he sighed, pulling me up to look in my eyes. "I'm sure you're not letting her down. She deals with writers all the time. She knows the words don't always come according to some contract."

"I know, but..." Panic was starting to build inside of me. This was the first time I would be missing a contract deadline. I felt like a failure.

"Just relax," he encouraged, and I gave him a shaky nod. "What can I do?"

"Take me home?" My voice was quiet and vulnerable, but for once, I didn't feel safe staying in the city. I needed him to take me back home.

He kissed me gently and leaned back into me, rubbing his hand down the back of my head and tucking my face into his neck. "Right now?"

I nodded as I took a deep breath and inhaled.

"Did you just sniff me?" he laughed.

"Maybe..." I admitted as I picked at a frayed thread along the piping on the couch cushion under my legs.

"Let's go pack. If we leave soon, we can make it there in enough time to get groceries for dinner."

"Oh, take out...I will miss you so," I sighed dramatically.

"You're so weird," he laughed as he hugged me tighter.

"Pretty sure you're stuck with me," I giggled as I leaned into his embrace.

"I'm OK with that." His voice was amused, but I could tell he was quite happy with that fact. I was as well.

"Does this mean I get more naked chef time?"

He sighed and shook his head. "You've got a one-track mind."

"You didn't answer my question."

"You have to start running with me at least three times a week," he bargained.

"Three?" I looked up at him with my face scrunched up in distaste. "Two?"

He shrugged as he shook his head. "Then I get to keep my briefs on."

"Dammit." I pretended to think about it.

"Fine. No running — then shorts stay on too."

"Ugh. You suck," I groaned as I pretended to be put out.

"Pretty sure that's you." He bit his lip to keep back his laughter.

"Not if you make me go running all the time. I'll be too tired," I insisted.

He rolled his eyes at me, "You'll live."

"Are we doing this?" he asked as we both straightened up.

"Yeah," I nodded as I looked over at the front door. "I'm half terrified that Isobel will show up here any second."

"Adrian keeps texting me but I send him an 'out of office' text," he confessed.

"You don't even have an office," I giggled. Clever, clever man.

"I know...but it pisses him off. I have it saved in the notes on my phone, so I copy and paste it every time he texts or emails me."

"You're an evil genius, Evan Stineman."

"I try." The slight blush on his cheeks made me love him even more. His personality was not all that different than mine when we were alone, it was just in social interactions that we differed. I wished that he'd show this part of him to the world, but I was perfectly happy keeping him all to myself.

"Make sure you don't forget the apron," I winked as I stood up from the couch and held my hand out to him. He pushed himself up and followed me into the bedroom, lightly bumping into me from behind.

"Maybe I should order you an apron too," Evan whispered as he let go of my hand and slipped his hands around my waist.

"Maybe I don't need an apron." His arms tightened around me and I could feel his warm breath wash over the side of my neck.

"Ugh," he groaned as he kissed the back of it. "You'd never get to eat if you prance around my kitchen naked all the time."

"What about yo...oh!" I laughed as I got his double meaning. I'd never get to eat, but apparently, he'd be eating something. "You're bad."

"You seemed to enjoy it the other day."

"OK...hands off mister," I said as I pulled his arms from around me and darted to my closet. "We need to get packed."

"So are we driving separately...or...?"

"Do you want me to drive myself?" I asked as I pulled down my bag and peeked out of the closet door. He looked super nervous.

"No..." His voice was soft as he looked at me.

"OK," I nodded and placed my bag down on the corner of the bed.

"I'll bring you back whenever you want, but..."

"But...?" I asked curiously.

"You're welcome to stay as long as you want." He mumbled something I couldn't hear under his breath, but I let it go.

I'd been serious when I told Isobel I needed two months. I was OK leaving my condo behind for a few weeks or even months to write this book with him. If I was completely honest with myself... I'd probably be content with not coming back and just staying with Evan indefinitely.

"You'll get tired of me eventually..."

He crossed the room and pulled me into his arms, kissing me softly as he held me to him. When he pulled back, his eyes were no longer guarded as he shook his head. "I don't see that happening any time soon."

We woke up early to get ready for the long drive back to Connecticut, heading out just after breakfast. I missed staying in bed and snuggling with him, but we could catch up with that later.

"Are you alright with stopping for groceries somewhere along the highway?" he asked as he turned down the music coming through the car speakers.

Evan had been quiet so far on the trip back to his house, and I was kind of zoned out with my laptop open on my knees.

"Looking for something you can't find in Ashford?"

"Not really. I don't want to have to go into town when we get back. I like the anonymity of Walmart rather than the Ashford market. No one stares at me there."

"They're gonna stare at you everywhere, but I see what you're saying." I reached over and squeezed his hand.

"It's these shorts, isn't it?" he laughed, pulling awkwardly at the hem of his *very* short white athletic shorts. His other pairs had been dirty, and he obviously hadn't had time to wait for laundry.

"Well...they're not helping," I giggled. "But why the hat?"

"I didn't feel like styling my hair," he shrugged.

"And the hat was a better alternative?" I giggled as I reached over to flick the underside of the brim. He'd put on a trucker hat that was taller than a standard one. It looked awkward as it stood up from his head.

"Oh, so now that we're official you've got a free pass to tease me?" He smiled. I knew he wasn't entirely serious.

"You're the one who made the decision to wear that today...that right there gave me permission."

His hand reached for mine over the center console and I met him halfway, interlocking our fingers and smiling.

"Just wait until you wear something ridiculous; I'll be waiting for my opening."

"I wouldn't expect anything less," I assured him. If he wanted to dish it out, I'd take it. "And I'm glad you agree that hat is ridiculous."

"Love you too, baby," he cooed as he rolled his eyes at me.

After another twenty minutes on the highway, he pulled off towards a Walmart that was right off the exit.

"Ready to go get stared at?"

"Pfft. I make this look good," he laughed as he took off the hat and threw it in the back seat before he got out of the car.

"So that's why you took it off?" I giggled as I took in the bedhead he was hiding under the hat.

"Happy now?" he sighed loudly.

"Still better than the hat," I laughed as he made a face at me over the roof of the car.

"Oh, poor baby, I'm making you go out in public without your hair done," I teased. My own messy bun was probably chaotic.

"You're mean," he pouted.

I rushed around to his side of the car and pinched his butt. "That's why you like me."

I took off half jogging across the parking lot and he chased after me, landing a hard smack to my right butt cheek as he caught up with me. "Alright, feisty... behave. We're in public."

"Since when has that stopped me?"

"Let's just get what we need so we can get home." I think we were both a little tired, but at least we had each other to stay entertained on the car ride.

"Yeah, yeah." I followed him along as he pushed the cart through the produce section, filling it up with various fruits and vegetables.

"What kind of meat do you want?"

I grinned as I eyed his shorts and wiggled my eyebrows.

"OK nympho, focus. Pork?"

"Oh my god," I giggled as I leaned my head against his shoulder.

"Can you pull your head out of the gutter and tell me what you want?" he sighed loudly.

"I could..." I shrugged, "but I won't."

"Sausage?" My giggles returned and he rolled his eyes at me.

"Obviously, I'll be doing the grocery shopping alone from now on."

"Fine...fine...I'll be good," I told him as I tried to quit laughing.

"I doubt that...but I'll still feed you anyways."

I tried to keep the suggestive comments to myself for the rest of the trip through the store — aside for my commentary about the slightly curved zucchini he put in the cart. Most of the things in the cart were healthy and I realized that my usual writing snacks were missing.

"I'll be right back." I wandered off towards the aisle that had the chips on one side and the candy on the other. I grabbed my usuals and headed back to the cart and dumped the packages inside.

"You can't be serious." He looked down at my additions with wide eyes and gave me a disbelieving look.

"Hey, I can't be held responsible if Fanny goes a little crazy because I don't have my Twizzlers."

"I'm sure you'll be fine without them," he insisted as he picked up the package and took a step away from the cart.

"Put down the snacks," I warned him. You did not come between a girl and her candy stash. That was just not OK.

"But these are garbage."

"Don't care. They're mine," I shook my head as I reached for the packages.

"You're impossible," he sighed as he shook his head.

"You mean impossibly awesome. Now step away from the snacks. I don't judge your phallic snacks. You leave mine alone."

"Phallic snacks?" he laughed. "They're carrot sticks."

"If you want to put tiny orange dicks in your mouth, then you can't judge my Twizzlers."

"Fine. Keep your junk food," he conceded. "Now you're definitely going running with me."

"As long as you're the one in the lead," I teased as I pinched his ass.

"You're impossible."

"But I'm yours." Flashing him a bright smile, I gave him a cheeky wink.

"Yes, yes you are." He put his hands on my waist and pulled me towards his chest, kissing me softly on the lips.

# TWENTY-SIX

## Evan

### Connecticut

"Come on, baby," I coaxed as I tried to pry the blanket out of Chase's hands. "You promised."

"But wouldn't you rather stay in bed with me?" Her pout was almost my undoing.

We'd been back in Connecticut for almost a month, and this was the first time she'd refused to get out of bed for a run with me. "I thought we were making progress."

"We can always go later. I think you should get back into bed."

I was having a hard time denying her. She was playing dirty this morning.

"Please?"

I blew out a breath and sat down on the bed next to her.

"I promise you'll still break a sweat," she teased as she rolled to her side. Her partially covered body caused a stirring in my shorts. Her fingers started to caress her bare breasts, rolling her nipples and eliciting soft moans out of herself.

"You play dirty."

I watched with rapt attention as one hand started to travel down her chest, dipping beneath the sheets. I grabbed the covers and pulled them back as I watched her hand cover her mound.

"Help me?" she sighed as she reached for my hand and brought it down with hers, slowly parting her folds.

"Fuck, you're so wet," I groaned as I dipped two fingers inside her opening. "You're making this really hard."

"I hope so..." She cooed as her hand reached inside the bottom of the leg of my shorts, gripping my stiffening length through my boxer briefs.

"Fuuuck..." I moaned as her fingers parted the flap and her hand encircled me. She worked me up and down, her thumb spreading my pre-cum around the tip. She knew exactly how to get me going.

I thought after we started writing and came back to Connecticut that our sex life would wane, but we still couldn't keep our hands off each other. We'd tried out a few more things from Talia's bag of toys, role-playing certain scenes as we wrote.

We'd even experimented with a few new things I didn't think I'd be into. Chase made me try the leather cock cage while I watched her play with herself. It was by far the most erotic thing I'd ever seen. I'd exploded the second she released me from it and took me in her mouth afterward to kiss it better.

"Take off your clothes," she panted as I continued to slowly fuck her with my fingers, my thumb rubbing firmly on her clit.

"Shit," I hissed as I pulled her hand out of my shorts and stood up next to the bed.

Chase leaned up and kissed along the muscle on my pelvis as I slowly lowered my shorts. My cock sprung free, and she grabbed it with one hand as she kissed the head, flicking it with her tongue.

"Mmmm," she moaned as she took it further into her mouth.

I pulled my T-shirt off over my head and tried to toe-off my shoes as she started a slow rhythm with her mouth.

"Get up on the pillows," I rasped out.

She let go of me and scooted herself backward on the bed, her naked body splayed against the sheets. I finished pulling off my socks and shoved my shorts the rest of the way off as I climbed onto the bed. Her fingers were playing with her clit as I made my way on top of her.

"Keep touching yourself," I whispered as I cupped her breasts in my hands and teased her nipples with my tongue. My finger pinched one lightly as I bit down on the tip of the other and she arched off the bed moaning my name.

"Oh fuck, Evan."

"Just keep fucking yourself, baby," I urged as I moved one hand to her hips and tilted her pelvis up. Scooting myself over, I lined my cock up with her entrance, slowly slipping the head inside her lips as she continued working her clit.

"More..." she moaned as she tilted her hips up further, her legs wrapping around my sides and pulling me into her. I sat back on my knees and pulled her towards me, grasping her thighs and supporting them against my chest.

"Ahhh...you're in so deep," she moaned as I thrust against her. I grasped the backs of her knees and pushed them in towards her chest as I sped up the movements of my hips.

"Ohhh. Oh god. Yes, yes, yes..." she moaned as she continued to rub herself. "Harder."

"Yes...uhhh." I felt her clenching on me, watching as she pushed herself over the edge. I was transfixed as I watched myself slide in and out of her, pushing her knees out and spreading her legs as I continued to fuck her.

"Ohh...oh, my gah." She was moaning as she gripped the sheets on either side of her, pressing her hips up into the movements of my hips.

"Fuck, Chase. I'm gonna cum," I warned as I pressed into her repeatedly. She was tightening on my shaft again and I wanted to push her into a second release before I finally let go.

I let go of my hold on one knee and wrapped her leg around my hip, licking my fingers and pressing on her clit. She whimpered as I rubbed harder, and her moans increased in volume. The headboard was rhythmically smacking against the wall and I was so close to exploding inside of her.

"Come on, baby. Give it to me," I urged as my hips faltered.

"I'm so close..." she moaned as she pressed her hips up into my motions.

"Yes!" I roared as I felt her clamp down on me again, and I couldn't hold back. I snapped my hips two more times and gripped onto her leg tightly as I came inside of her.

My heart was beating frantically in my chest as I tried to come down. Chase's arms were thrown haphazardly to her sides, one leg still wrapped around my hip and the other I had grasped firmly to my chest. She hissed as I slipped out of her and my cock dragged against her ass.

"Oh..." she jerked a little as the tip slid against her other hole.

"Have you ever...?" My voice was cautious, but I was curious about her experience.

Her head shook against the pillows as she bit her lip. "No."

I hadn't either, but the thought of it was making me stir again.

"Do you want to?" she asked quietly as she looked up at me. I had to admit I was intrigued. The bitch who shall not be named was only into traditional missionary, so I didn't have any experience whatsoever in things like that.

"Uh..." My brain had stopped working. I was trying to work out the logistics in my head.

Chase propped herself up on her elbows, bringing her hand down and experimentally rubbing her hand up and down my shaft.

"Do you?" I asked in a loud moan as she started to jerk me. I wasn't fully hard again yet, but if she kept going, I'd get there.

"I trust you."

Holy shit. I hadn't expected this when I woke up this morning.

"And you want to right now?"

"You have somewhere else to be?" she smirked as her hand tightened on me.

"No...but..."

"Do you want to try?" She was smirking at me and reached one hand up to poke me in the chin, so my jaw wasn't hanging open.

What did I do to deserve this girl?

"But I don't know what I'm doing." My heart started to beat harder at the thought of going through with this. I didn't want to hurt her, but I also really wanted to try it.

"Then I guess it's a good thing I don't know either. We can learn together," she giggled.

My hand rubbed up and down her thigh as she continued to try to get me hard. "Shouldn't we research this before we..."

"No, Evan...geez," she laughed at me. "Do you have lube?"

I nodded as I reached over to the nightstand and pulled out a small bottle of lubricant.

"Go ahead." She nodded at the bottle. I flipped open the cap and squirted some on myself, her hand sliding more easily on my flesh with the added moisture. I coated the tips of my pointer and middle fingers too.

She brought her leg down off my chest and loosely wrapped both her legs on my hips. I scooted back a little bit and used my other hand to tilt her hips up a little. My breathing picked up as she stopped pulling on me. I was at full mast as she licked her lips and nodded at me.

"Ohh..." she moaned lowly as I lightly touched her and ran my fingers along her skin. "It's OK."

I pushed the tip of one finger in her ass and she flinched a little, closing her eyes. My finger retreated and I waited until her eyes opened again.

"I'm fine. Keep going." She grabbed my wrist and pulled my hand back towards her. I slipped my finger in again and got a little bit further, slowly twisting it a little inside of her as I pulled it out.

"Are you OK?"

She kept holding her breath every time I pushed inside. I couldn't tell from the look of concentration on her face if she was enjoying it or not.

"I'm...I'm good," she panted as she shifted her hips from side to side.

Her muscles relaxed a little as I continued to open her up. It was definitely a different sensation. It was more concentrated pressure where my finger was constricted by her.

"Are you ready?" she whispered as I pulled my fingers out. I nodded and I watched as she opened the lube up again, squirting some on my fully engorged head. "Just go slow."

"OK." Giving her a jerky nod, I grasped myself in one hand and guided my tip against her. She moaned a little as I pressed it into her tight hole and her hips shifted into my movement.

"Oh..." Her hips jumped as the head started to ease inside.

"Fuck," I panted as I sat still and let both of us adjust to the sensation. It was tighter.

"Keep going..."

I blew out a few breaths as I pushed inside a little more, feeling the resistance of her tense muscles.

"Touch yourself," I moaned as I tried not to lose it; she was so tight.

She nodded and licked her fingers, bringing them down to her clit and starting to slowly circle. After a few moments, I could feel her start to relax and I slipped a little further inside of her. I pulled back out slightly, and she hissed.

"Go." She wiggled her hips and I slid back inside her ass.

"Oh..." she squealed and pushed one hand against my chest. I tried to retreat, and her eyes locked with mine. "Just go slow."

I nodded and gripped her hips, slowly thrusting my own hips in a shallow motion.

"Shit," I groaned as I watched her hand speed up a little as I slid in and out of her.

"Ohhh..." she moaned as I continued to keep my motions shallow, speeding up a little as I felt her relax.

"I'm gonna cum." She pressed her fingers hard on her clit and rubbed her hand faster. Her entire chest was flushed red, and I was in awe as I watched myself slide in and out of her. I could feel her clench on me a little and my heart was beating out of my chest.

"Fuck, baby. That's so hot," I groaned as her hips stiffened and I watched her pussy start to rhythmically pulse. Once she started to cum, I couldn't hold on anymore and I slipped out, cumming all over the sheets as she laid there moaning.

Resting my forehead on my arm up against the headboard, I panted as I looked down on her. "You OK?"

"Fuck," she groaned as her head rolled to the side. She was panting just as much as I was.

"I'm gonna feel that later," she giggled as she ran a hand along my abs.

"I'm sor..."

"No, it was good. I obviously enjoyed myself."

I let out a breathy laugh and carefully collapsed to her side on the bed.

She had a satisfied smile on her face as she looked over at me. "Well, that was new."

I reached over and pulled her up against my chest, kissing the side of her head as she snuggled into me. "I love you."

"Mmm...I'm sure you do now."

I laughed and pinched her side.

"I love you too." Her voice was tired as her eyelids started to droop a little. "Nap time?"

I was quite sure I'd probably had more of a workout than running would have given me this morning.

"Go to sleep, baby."

She sighed and burrowed into her pillow as I reached down to pull the covers back over us. My thoughts went to the almost complete manuscript we had sitting in Google docs. Another week or so and it'd be ready to send into Is and Adrian.

I closed my eyes and pulled Chase tighter to me and tried to shut off my brain and just live in the moment.

I was asleep before I knew it.

"Are we really doing this?" We had been working on the book all day and were just about ready to submit the manuscript.

"Yeah, I think we are," she nodded as she smiled over at me.

"They're going to freak out."

"Probably," she shrugged, "but how else are we supposed to do it?"

"You set it to locked, right? Only they have access and no edits?" I was always overly cautious with the settings on documents before I sent them. You never knew when an email would fall into the wrong hands.

"Yes. I'm not an amateur," she rolled her eyes at me. We were sitting on the couch with the laptop propped on our legs. The manuscript was done, and we were getting ready to submit it to Isobel and Adrian.

"Should we turn our phones off?" Adrian would be on the phone as soon as he realized what we were sending him. I was almost afraid of his reaction; he was unpredictable sometimes.

"No, as much as I'd like to, Isobel would make Adrian drive her out here."

"She probably would," I agreed. "We definitely don't want that."

"You ready?"

"No," I groaned as I looked over at her.

"Do you want to delay sending it to them?" Her voice was filled with concern. I knew she would wait if I asked her to, but that wasn't fair to all the work we'd put in.

I growled as my finger hovered over the send button. "No. We need to submit it, but I don't know if they're gonna go crazy. What if the house won't publish it? We're both locked into contracts. What if we just wrote a book no one will ever read?"

"They'll publish it, trust me," she assured. "They fast-tracked my last book. It's trendy and people are curious about it. I think we put a new spin on the subject."

Her hand came up to caress the side of my face. "It's good, Evan."

"I know, but what if my readers all flame it?" Her audience obviously liked sexual content, but mine would not be expecting it in my current book, much less another one with much more racy content.

"The buzz from your new book has been positive, right?"

I nodded as I looked over at her. My book had been released the previous week. Some of the more conservative critics didn't endorse it, but I hadn't expected them to. Adrian kept sending me all the comments from my fan site. I didn't even have login info, so I'd stayed away from it. For the most part, my readers had loved the spiced-up version of my book and I'd gained a little bit of a female following on Facebook.

"Yeah, it's more than I expected."

"Then this will be fine. If they're not running away from prostitutes, then a fairly tame Dominatrix should be okay too." Her warm hand cupped the side of my jaw as she tried to talk some sense into me.

"Tame Dominatrix," I laughed. "Little bit of an oxymoron."

"Would you rather have modeled Fanny after someone like Grace?"

I shook my head. "Nope. Not even a little."

Emory had texted Chase to let her know Grace had been asking about us. Apparently, she'd wanted to volunteer her consulting services. Our answer had been a resounding 'hell no!'.

"Ready?"

I nodded nervously and pressed my finger to the touchpad. The little dialogue box popped up as 'document shared' and I looked over at Chase with wide eyes.

"Hold me?" I whimpered as she laughed at me and picked up the laptop, placing it on the coffee table. She leaned back and opened her arms. I laid my head on her chest, and she started to run her fingers through my hair.

My eyes closed and I relaxed into her touch as we waited. Almost on cue, both of our cell phones started vibrating across the coffee table.

"That didn't take long," she giggled as she reached for hers and tossed mine into my lap. Adrian's name flashed across the screen and I knew it was time to slay the dragon.

"Let's do this."

I sat up in the corner of the sofa opposite Chase and we both pressed call accept at the same time.

"Yes?"

"You dirty dog. I didn't know you had it in you." His voice sounded half amused and half proud as he praised me over the line.

Chase rolled her eyes as she talked quietly to Isobel.

"That's all you have to say?" I asked him, I was expecting feedback, not some macho congratulations.

"This is gold, Evan. Obviously, I still need to read through the whole thing and send it through to Sam, but I'd expect a contract to come through on this by the beginning of next week."

I could hear a female talking in the background and Adrian answering her in a low voice.

"I gotta go. I'll call you," he said quickly as he hung up.

"So?" I asked as Chase finished her call only moments later.

"She hung up on me."

Isobel must have been the female voice I heard in the background. "They're so doing it."

"Yup," she giggled as she climbed across the couch and into my lap.

That had gone better than we expected.

# TWENTY-SEVEN

## Chase

**Boston**

"Are you kidding me, Is? I can't make him do that."

"Well, if you two don't want another ten percent of sales taken off the top, you'll convince him." She was perched against the edge of her desk in front of me.

Christine was sitting in a chair in the corner of Isobel's office, typing away. Her lip kept twitching, so despite the earbuds in her ears, I knew she was eavesdropping. That girl knew everything that happened in and out of this office.

"He's gonna tell me no."

"You'd be surprised what a whipped man will do." Isobel raised an eyebrow at me and winked. She would probably know all about whipped men. Adrian may wear pants, but Isobel was wearing *the* pants in that relationship for sure.

"Is, seriously. You need to have Adrian ask if you guys are forcing this."

"Evan already told him no," she sighed.

"Then what are you expecting from me?" Evan was free to make up his own mind. I was not going to force or coerce him into anything. Knowing his name was attached to this was already taking a big leap for him; if he didn't want to do this, I was not going to force it.

"I don't know, Chase. Cut him off or something, I've been told by the legal department that if there isn't at least a six-city book tour with this one that your royalties will be cut."

"It's not like I'm struggling, Is."

"That's not the point. This could affect your next contract," she sighed. "They want to cash in on this one, and you with Evan as the face of this book is their way to do it."

"So, you're pimping us out." The nerve of both her and Adrian. I'm sure they would also be getting a nice little bonus if they convinced us to do this as well.

She shrugged her shoulders and Christine snickered from the corner. Isobel snapped in her direction and Christine pulled out an earbud.

"Can I help you?"

"Quit spying," Isobel chided. "You better not be sharing this information with Sam."

"Why would I be telling him about this? That cock monkey isn't exactly discreet."

I bit my lip to keep from laughing.

"This conversation is a fencepost." Isobel gave Christine what was supposed to be an intimidating look, but the younger woman just rolled her eyes.

"What the hell is that?"

"It's between you, Chase, me, and the fencepost."

"Is' office is like Vegas," I nodded.

"That phrase never made sense to me. It stays in Vegas as long as you don't pick up an STI," Christine scoffed as her mouth pinched up in disgust.

"Well let's pretend you're wearing a condom," Isobel rolled her eyes. "This doesn't leave these walls."

"Yes Ma'am." She saluted Is and I started laughing.

"Something funny, Mistress?" Christine winked at me and I lost it.

"Hey!" Isobel yelled as she pinned Christine and I with an admonishing look. "Chase. Seriously? I'm trying to cover your ass here."

Christine snickered as she slouched down in her chair, the laptop on her knees hiding her face. "I think she has Evan for that."

"Alright, children," Is rolled her eyes.

"The best I can do is ask him. If he says no, I'm not riding his ass about this."

Christine started laughing again and even Isobel cracked a smile.

"Perverts," I sighed in exasperation.

"Is this something you want?" Evan had come to Boston with me to meet with our publisher.

I wasn't sure what to tell him. To be completely honest, despite the long hours and travel, I liked book tours. "I'm not going to force you."

"That's not what I asked. Do you want to go on the tour?" he asked again. I tried to read his facial cues, but he wasn't giving anything away.

"I don't mind them. I like interacting with readers and meeting interesting people."

He sighed as he settled into my couch cushions. We were staying in Boston while we were in contract negations. My lawyer had already reviewed the contract and submitted a few revisions. Evan was the only thing we were waiting for. I wasn't going to pressure him into going on tour with me. I'd offered to go on a regional tour by myself, but legal said both of us or neither.

"Do I have to speak?" He wasn't saying no, but he didn't sound enthusiastic about it either.

"Well...you as a mute sub could be kinda hot. Slap a collar on you and some leather pants." Expecting at least a smile from my joke, I cringed when his face remained solemn.

"Chase," he sighed as he leaned forward and put his head into his hands.

"I'll be there," I pointed out. "Not sure if it's helpful, but Adrian will be there. Usually, they send someone from PR. But you know all this — you used to do book tours, back in the day, before..." Knowing he wouldn't respond well to the mention of Serena, my voice trailed off.

I rubbed my hand up and down his back, slipping it under the hem of his shirt and scratching his bare skin. "I can take care of any requested readings and I'll be at the table next to you for signings. You won't be alone."

"What cities do they want?"

"Bare minimum — Boston, New York, Chicago, Denver, Seattle, LA," I replied. Isobel had been awfully specific about those cities. We could add on if that's what we wanted, but those were locked.

"Shit..."

"What?" I asked quietly, continuing to rub his back.

"My family is going to want to come if we go to Chicago."

Mine would probably drive in from Minneapolis if we were there too. "And is that a bad thing? They just want to support you."

"Or my sister just wants more ammo to embarrass me publicly," he groaned.

"I'm sure it's not that bad." My brothers could be shits when they wanted to, but they never tried to diminish my writing.

"You'll see. It's her goal in life to humiliate me as many times as possible."

"My brothers like to embarrass me too."

"They're probably amateurs compared to Kelly," he huffed.

"I didn't date most of high school because they had the entire baseball team convinced that I was really their little brother," I told him with a pointed look.

"They told them you were a guy?"

"Bad haircuts in middle school provided their photographic evidence," I nodded. Those two assholes better not still have access to those photos.

"Oh my god," he chuckled a little. "That's just mean."

"Add in that everyone called me Chase and I was assigned a locker in the girls' locker room away from everyone else." High school was one big awkward suck for me. "Pretty sure half of them thought I had a dick. The boys in my class used to aim for my crotch during dodgeball in PE."

"I would have pegged you as having been popular in high school," he confessed as he looked over at me.

I laughed a little too loud at that comment. "Nope, not even a little. I was the dorky girl on the newspaper with giant glasses who no one talked to. Add in my brother's mission to keep boys away from me, and I was just a mess."

"I probably still would have thought you were cute."

"And I love that you think that, but let's be honest. You would have been out of my league."

"I was shy too," he insisted.

"For me, shy was code for a loser. For you, shy was code for mysterious and quiet," I rolled my eyes. "So, what exactly did Kelly do to you?"

He grimaced as he looked over at me. "The question is what didn't she do? She plastered nude baby pictures of me to my locker on the first day of high school, she used to make me get out of the car two blocks from school so people wouldn't realize we were related, and she told my first girlfriend I had eyesight problems because I beat off too much. She convinced her that it really does make you go blind."

"She sounds like a real keeper if she believed that," I snickered.

"She was the only girl who would talk to me. She wasn't the smartest."

"Then why did you date her?"

His cheeks turned pink, and he gave me a guilty smile. "She had big boobs."

"Oh my god. Even teenage Evan was a little pervert."

"Teenage Evan had an overactive imagination and his sister bought him a bottle of lube for his fifteenth birthday," he laughed. "And she gave it to me in front of my parents."

"Hahahaha," I couldn't hold back that laughter. "What did they say?"

"My dad gave me a package of condoms and my mom told me if I was going to 'engage in fornication' that she wasn't raising any more children and I should 'wrap it up'."

My entire body was shaking as I tried to hold back laughter. His family sounded amazing. He was trying not to laugh, but it wasn't working.

"They'll love you." He took my hand and kissed the back of it.

"So, you'll go?" I hedged, hoping that he'd opened to the possibility.

"I really, really don't want to," he shook his head, "but I'm not jeopardizing either of our careers because I'm afraid."

He gave me a wary laugh. "Do I really have to wear leather pants?"

I laughed and climbed into his lap, grabbing his cheeks and laying one on him. "Hell yes, you do! Just don't forget that ass is mine."

"Never." He put his hand on the back of my neck and brought our lips together, slipping his tongue into my mouth. I loved this man something fierce and I was so proud of him.

"Any other questions?" Isobel asked as she finished explaining our contractual obligations.

"Just one...?" Evan asked quietly.

Christine laughed softly from behind us. "This should be good."

"Can we set the order of cities?"

"Dates haven't been booked yet," she told us, "so I'm sure we can work with the PR office on this."

"I still think you should do Vegas, that'd be awesome," Adrian chimed in and I just managed to keep in a snarky remark.

"Ad, we talked about this," Isobel sighed as she turned an annoyed smirk towards him. He was eating it up. He'd been staring at her cleavage half the meeting. "We're starting with the release and doing a limited twenty-day tour with six cities. Anything other than that is up to Chase and Evan."

"You people suck," he pouted, much like the child he was. "Vegas is awesome."

"Can't you put a leash on him?" Christine sighed loudly. She and Sam were seated behind us, kicking each other in the feet and trading smartass remarks low enough their bosses couldn't hear them.

"I have no control of that overgrown frat boy," Sam scoffed.

"You speak his language. Seriously...it's painful to watch him try to be professional."

"How do you think I feel on a daily basis?" I bit my lip to keep from laughing. Adrian's own copy intern couldn't stand him from the sound of it.

"Isobel needs a shock collar for him." Biting down harder to hold in the laughter, I hoped I wouldn't draw blood. That'd be pretty hilarious. Maybe we needed to introduce Adrian to Grace.

"Do you really think they're...you know..." I could see Sam do a lewd hand gesture out of the corner of my eye.

"He must be huge. That's the only explanation that makes any sense."

"Pfft. Nope," he shook his head.

"Chase?" Isobel asked loudly, drawing my attention away from the pair behind me.

"Hm?"

"Chase!" I snapped my head up towards Isobel. She looked irritated. She could tell I hadn't been paying any attention to what she'd been discussing with Evan.

"Yes?"

"Nice of you to join us." I cringed a little at the look of annoyance on her face.

"Busted," Sam said under his breath to Christine.

"Any issues with booking travel for Chicago the day after the release party in Boston?"

"No...why aren't we doing Boston first?" It would make more sense to do the book signings here if we had the release party in Boston.

"We'll do New York and Boston last," she explained.

"I'm OK with whatever Evan wants."

"I thought maybe it would be good to be near family for the first leg," he explained as he looked over at me.

"If that's what you want."

He nodded and picked up my hand, interlacing our fingers.

"Let me double-check with travel and PR. We can get a sample schedule worked up and send it through for your approval," Isobel offered.

"Sounds good," Evan nodded and I did as well. I was following his lead on this one.

We all started to pack up our things. Christine and Sam left first, and I thought I swore I saw him smack her on the butt with a notepad just outside of the door.

"Chase...a word?" Isobel asked as she sat perched at the edge of her desk with her arms crossed.

"Come hang out in my office, man," Adrian told Evan as he patted his arm.

Evan leaned in and whispered in my ear. "Come rescue me when you're done. Love you."

He left a lingering kiss on the corner of my mouth and followed Adrian out of the room.

"So...I've got news." Isobel's face didn't give away anything.

"Good news?" I asked hopefully.

"Maybe..."

"Ugh," I whined. "What now?"

"Good news is, they granted you a contract extension." I nodded and motioned for her to go on. "Bad news is, they want a finished manuscript going to final proof in three months max."

"Shit, seriously?" That was an awfully narrow timeline if we were going to be starting a book tour soon.

"I know. I tried to go to bat for you, but they said you can cancel your contract with no penalties or fulfill the obligation."

"Three months? They do realize I'll be on tour or doing promotional work for half of that, right?"

"They are aware, but I couldn't get them to budge." The sympathetic smile she was giving me was supposed to make me feel better, but it wasn't working. This was going to be hard to meet.

"What happens if I opt to cancel?"

She shook her head and leaned towards me. "You don't want to do that, Chase."

"Three months?" I asked, my neck sweating just from the thought of how much work I still needed to complete. "I don't know if I can do it."

"At least take the weekend. Go talk to Evan. I know it seems impossible, but you've pulled through on tighter deadlines."

I nodded and blew out a breath. My mind was still focused on the project we'd just finished. There was no way I could switch gears to romantic comedy and put out a quality product.

"I'll check in on Monday, and don't even think of ghosting me like you two did before." She pointed at me and squinted. "I will hunt you down."

"Don't pretend like you weren't sneaking around. Taking a staycation, my ass," she scoffed. "Next time don't hide in plain sight. You're lucky I couldn't figure out where I'd seen your boy."

"Obviously, I was being productive." I rolled my eyes. She'd gotten a damn book out of it.

"Not the point," she shook her head and pinned me down with an unamused smirk.

"Fine. I'll let you know Monday."

She nodded and took a seat at her desk, pulling open the cover of her laptop.

Apparently, I was dismissed.

I was a little flustered as I walked down the hallway and through the open office area in the middle of the floor and to the hallway where Adrian's office was. Hopefully, Evan had fared a little better in his conversation.

I could hear Evan and Adrian having a discussion that sounded heated as I got to the corner around from his office. I wasn't sure if this was something I should interrupt, so I leaned against the wall and listened in to what they were saying.

"I'm telling you, man, I never expected something like this out of you." Adrian's cocky voice almost seemed a little proudly smug.

"Because I'm boring?" Evan's on the other hand seemed annoyed.

"No, because you've always been so concerned with brand integrity."

"I still am concerned with that," Evan insisted.

"So, you're not worried that getting into this kinky shit will damage your credibility as a writer?"

"No, Adrian, I'm not. Chase and I worked hard on this book and have put a lot of time and research into it," he told him, raising his voice a little as he spoke. "It's not sensationalized and it's not an attention grab. This was a well-planned out plot that I feel is different from everything else out there."

I was silently cheering from my hidden location at how passionately Evan was defending us and our work.

"I know it's been a while for you, and Serena mindfucked you into seclusion, but you need to protect yourself."

"Excuse me?" The growly quality of Evan's voice would have been a bit of a turn on if I didn't want to rush in there to save him from his jackass editor.

"Chase, deep down, is a good person, but she's still manipulative. I don't want to see her turn you into something you're not and then bail."

"Alright, Adrian. I know this is your misguided attempt to protect me, but I'm a big boy," Evan's voice rose again, and I looked around to make sure no one saw that I was eavesdropping. "I can handle myself. If you've got some childish grudge against my girlfriend, that's your problem."

Evan's voice got more pinched as he talked. My eyes widened and my pulse raced as he delivered his final blow. "But I'm fully intending to marry that woman, so if you don't back off, I can always find another editor."

"Fair enough," Adrian conceded quickly. "I just wanted to make sure you were prepared to follow through with this whole thing."

"God, you're a dick," Evan sighed and I took a deep breath.

*He wanted to marry me?*

"What are you doing?"

"Shit." I jumped as I turned around and faced Christine.

"Are you spying on your man?"

"No...maybe...I was coming to get him and didn't want to interrupt," I mumbled.

She rolled her eyes at me and shifted her weight, leaning against the wall across from me. "Sounds like he handled himself pretty well."

"So, you were spying too."

She shrugged her shoulders and grinned at me. "I've got to be fully informed if I want to keep these clowns on their toes."

"You're sneaky," I smiled. She really did enjoy knowing all the dirty details around here.

"A girl has got to have talents," she proudly proclaimed as she nodded toward the door. "Is Sam in there?"

"I'm not sure, I haven't heard him speak," I told her. "What's going on there?"

She got a slight pink tint to her cheeks and rolled her eyes. "I tolerate him. We were forced to 'play nice' for your little collaborations."

"Mmm-hmm. Looks exactly like 'tolerance' to me," I laughed as she tried to look annoyed.

I had a feeling the rumored romance between Is and Adrian might not be the only relationship brewing.

# TWENTY-EIGHT

## Evan

**Connecticut**

"You need to eat, baby." I pulled the headphones from Chase's head and talked quietly in her ear.

"I will, just give me a minute."

"Chase, I'm beginning to feel like your parent."

She sighed, closed the lid of the laptop and placed it on the table in front of her. "I'm sorry."

I hugged her shoulders from behind and pulled her back towards me. "You don't need to be sorry; you just need to eat something today. And you probably need to shower."

She didn't really smell...but she needed to recharge. She'd been pushing herself to meet this ridiculous deadline before we needed to leave for the book tour. I'd flat out told her we were leaving Boston if she was going to write. Fewer distractions, easier to clear her head.

Isobel had kept Adrian away from me and given us space. It would have been ideal for us to get some alone time, but she'd been absorbed in her work. I knew I was the same way when I was actively writing, but I'd never been on the other side of it. "How's the manuscript coming along?"

"I think I need a few more days...I might have the first draft done by the time we need to head back to the city."

"Are you ready for anyone to read it?" I asked curiously. I was secretly dying to get my hands on another one of her books.

"I just want to get the first draft off to Is. She's good at helping me focus and restructure my writing as needed."

I nodded my head. Despite being a gigantic ass sometimes, Adrian was good at giving me constructive feedback. "Is there anything I can do to help you try to relax?"

"Hmmm...just pulling me out of my head is nice," she sighed as she leaned back into my embrace.

"Can I run you a bath?"

"Only if you join me." She smiled as she pushed her hand up into the back of my hair, scratching my scalp lightly.

"You naked...wet...covered in bubbles..." I kissed along the side of her neck and nibbled on her ear.

"Mmm," she moaned quietly as her hand tightened in my hair.

"Finish what you were working on and come to the bedroom."

"Yes, Sir."

I laughed and released her. While I knew it riled her up a little for me to tease her by calling her Mistress, 'Sir' didn't have the same effect on me. It was all just role playing.

She opened the laptop and started saving documents. I knew that it'd probably be a while, so I went straight to my closet and dug out one of the housewarming gifts that my parents had sent.

My mother had insisted that my house needed battery-operated LED flickering candles. I hadn't been convinced but took them out when she visited and put them in visible places.

I was a single man living by myself in the woods, what mood did I need to set?

Carrying the box into the bathroom, I turned on the tap of the bathtub.

"Shit..." I hissed as I turned down the hot water faucet, so I didn't accidentally give Chase second degree burns.

My sister had given me masculine-smelling bath products for Christmas the previous year, and there was a small bottle of bubble bath in the set. It'd make Chase smell like me, but the caveman part of me was fine with that. I may even have to dig out an old soccer jersey and strategically leave it in one of the drawers I'd cleaned out for her to use.

I pulled the candles out of the boxes and put the batteries back in them, placing them around the room.

After taking off my shirt and shorts, I reached down to pull out my nicer towels on the bottom shelf of the linen closet.

"Now that's a view."

I smiled as I straightened back up. "That was quicker than I expected."

She smirked and bit her lip.

Something naughty was going on in that brain of hers and I wasn't sure I wanted to find out. "What?"

"I was going to say, 'That's what she said', but let's hope not," she giggled as her hand touched the middle of my back, slowly tracing up my spine. Her body pressed into me from behind and all I felt was her bare skin on mine. "You gave me an incentive to hurry."

"Let's go relax," I sighed as her hand traced its way along my side to cover my heart. I placed mine on top of hers and squeezed as it soared. "I love you."

"I love you too." She punctuated her declaration with a kiss to my shoulder blade and laid her head against my back.

Even though she'd been in my house for the last few weeks, I still missed her. She seemed to be making real progress on the manuscript and I was proud that she buckled down and made it happen. It was hard sometimes to write when you knew there were expectations attached to it.

"I'm sorry if I've been distant."

"Hey..." I shook my head as I pulled her arm and brought her around my side, placing her between myself and the bathroom counter. "You don't need to apologize. I am amazed at what you have been able to create in the last few weeks."

She reached up on her tip toes and placed a soft kiss on my mouth. "Thank you for being supportive. I do miss working together. That's been the hardest part. I find myself wanting to ask you for input, but I know that we're not writing this one together."

"Baby, I'm in this. I want you to know I will always support you," I told her seriously. "If you want me to read something, let me know. I would be happy to lend a second set of eyes to your book."

She nodded and smiled shyly at me.

"You ready?" She tugged at the waistband of my boxer briefs as she gave me a playful smile.

"Absolutely." I ran my hands over her bare shoulders and down her arms as she slowly lowered my briefs, my cock springing loose. She looked up at me from under her lashes and I knew this was not going to be an innocent bath time interaction.

"Mmm...I'm glad you're happy to see me," she cooed as she pushed them the rest of the way to the floor. Chase licked her lips and ran one hand over the muscles of my abdomen as she knelt down and brought her tongue out to flick the head of my cock.

"Ahhh..." I breathed out as she licked around the head and eased me into her mouth.

Chase bobbed her head a few times before she pulled back. She placed a kiss on the tip of my cock and stood up, sliding her arms over my shoulders. "I've missed this."

"Mmm...me too." Her skin was soft and warm as I ran my hands up her back and played with the ends of her hair as I kissed her again. The pleasure I got from holding her against me and sliding my tongue into her mouth was never going to get old to me.

I felt more and more passion towards Chase the more time we spent together. I knew it was too soon, but I meant what I'd said to Adrian. I fully intended to marry Chase if she'd have me.

"Should we get into the tub?" I whispered my question against her cheek. We were both a little out of breath.

"Yes..."

I leaned down and checked the water, it was nice and warm, a thin layer of bubbles skimming the surface. She held my hand as I helped her climb into the tub. I slipped in behind her and pulled her against me, placing sensual open-mouthed kisses along the skin below her ear and along her jaw. I could feel her heart hammering in her chest as I cupped her full breasts.

"Mmm...that feels good," she hummed as I continued kissing.

"Just relax." My hand traveled down the smooth skin of her abdomen and dipped into her, sliding against her clit.

"Oh god, yes," she sighed as I began a slow slippery tour of her hot sex with the tips of my fingers.

"You're so sexy..." I murmured in her ear as she arched against me, pushing her head back into my shoulder and rubbing herself against my erection. My cock was throbbing as she writhed against me, moaning softly.

"It feels so good..." Chase was gripping my thighs under the water as her hips undulated with the movements of my hand. "Fuuuck..."

I could see the skin on her shoulder break out in goosebumps as I slipped two fingers inside of her. "You like that, baby?"

"Mmmm..." Her hips surged into the motion of my fingers.

"That's it, ride my fingers." I was so hard and wanted to be inside her.

"Oh god..." she whimpered as she began to shake in my lap.

"I wanna fuck you so bad..." My cock was pressed tightly against her back, hard as a rock.

"Yes, yes, yes..." she chanted as she clenched down on my fingers.

After the pulses subsided, she raised herself up onto her knees. Chase grabbed my cock, lining herself up and sinking down onto me. I felt fire in my veins as she started to rock in my lap. My hips were bucking up into the fluid movements of hers.

"Ride that dick, baby."

"Oh...that feels so good. You're so hard." Her fingers tightly gripped the sides of the tub, the water sloshing slightly with the rhythm of our movements.

The bubbles on the surface concealed half her body from me, but I was mesmerized by the sway of her hair in front of me. She was so unbelievably beautiful. I was still in shock sometimes that she was mine.

A few months ago, I never would have imagined she was what was in store for my future. Had we not met the way we did, I wouldn't have had the courage to talk to her.

"I'm so close..." she panted as her head fell backwards and the damp ends of her hair stuck to my chest.

"Just let go, baby. Cum on me," I groaned as I leaned forward and pulled her tightly to my chest. One hand sliding down into the water to where we were joined and the other grasping one breast firmly in my hand.

"Fuck..."

She was rapidly flexing her hips front to back, the friction on my dick pushing me closer and closer to release. I tried to push my hips up to meet her in the confined space.

Her movements faltered and her head fell back to my shoulder as she moaned out with her release. "Oh...ohhhh...I'm cumming...I'm...ohhh..."

"Yes...ahhhh!" I groaned into her hair as our hips slowed their movements.

"I needed that," she sighed as she adjusted her legs and settled back into my chest.

"Feel better now?" I asked quietly in her ear.

"Much. I know I've been a little on edge and ignoring you." She had been, but coming from the perspective of someone who did the same thing when he was in the zone, it didn't bother me.

"Maybe if you would've let me relax you a few days ago, you wouldn't have gotten so tense." I knew she'd feel guilty as I teased her, but I'd been trying to get her to take a break for days now.

"At least you're here now...I kind of like having my own stress relief on call."

"Is that all I am to you?" I smiled against the skin of her shoulder. "Stress relief?"

Chase shook her head and pulled my arms around her. "No...that's just one of the perks. You...you're," she sighed as she turned her head to the side to look up at me. "You're everything."

My heart swelled at her words. She was my everything too.

"Love you." Kissing the side of her head, I tightened my hold on her.

"Love you, too. So much."

We sat quietly in the bath until the water started to cool. Chase got dressed and returned to her laptop as I got started on dinner. Our cohabitation was something I was getting used to. I wanted to wake up with her every morning and go to sleep with her every night.

We'd already informed Is and Adrian that we'd only be needing one room for the both of us on the book tour. We weren't hiding our relationship from anyone, and I think the publishing house liked that we seemed to be a united front on this one.

"Any preference on meat?" I called out to her from the fridge.

"Your meat never fails to please," she snickered as she looked at me over the back of the couch.

"That's for after dinner..."

She gave a dramatic sigh. "Oh, alright. I guess I'll have to settle for putting another kind of meat in my mouth."

"Dirty girl..." I teased. She just couldn't resist the naughty flirtatious banter.

"That's how you like it." She was right...

"Do you have everything you need to go back?" I was sitting on the edge of the bed, waiting for Chase to finish packing her bag.

We were headed back into Boston. The official launch party for our book was in two days and we needed to head into the office to go over final schedule details with the promotional marketing team.

We'd be spending tonight at Chase's condo, but the publishing house had agreed to put us up in a suite at the hotel where the party was being held for the next two nights.

"Can I leave some of these clothes here?" she asked as she looked over her shoulder at me. Her open suitcase was sitting next to me on the bed, and it was empty.

"You can keep whatever you want here. I'm hoping after the tour is over, I can convince you to come back here with me."

"You won't be sick of me by then?" The smile she gave me was warm. She knew my answer to that.

"If I was going to get sick of you, I'm pretty sure it would have happened already over the last four months."

"Has it been that long?" she smirked as she winked at me.

"Not that I've been counting or anything," I shrugged. I totally had.

"Suuure..."

"Fine. Stay behind in your lonely condo. I don't mind going back to actually being allowed to use my covers."

"I'm not the one who steals covers!" she yelled as she spun back in my direction.

"Tell that to my frost-bitten parts..."

"Pretty sure I keep your parts plenty warm." She picked up a stack of clothes that was sitting on the dresser and grabbed one shirt before putting all the rest of them back into the drawer and shutting it. I wanted to ask her to move in with me permanently, but after the last time I lived with a woman, I was a little gun shy of asking. Chase was nothing like Serena, but she'd been different too before we lived together.

"Can I leave my toothbrush here?"

I stood up and followed her into the bathroom and pulled her back into my chest, resting my chin on her shoulder.

"You can leave whatever you'd like here. As long as you come back with me, I want this to feel like home to you."

We shared a meaningful look in the mirror, and I knew my strong feelings for her were reciprocated.

"Wherever I go with you feels like home."

I smiled and squeezed her tighter, placing a lingering kiss in the crook of her neck. "You should write that one down."

"Life imitates art..." she smiled. "Maybe I already did."

"Are you quoting your new book at me?"

"No," she shook her head, "but I can see where it'd work into the storyline nicely."

"I'm glad I can provide quality source material for you."

"You're the best research assistant ever," she snickered, probably remembering all the research we'd been doing for months.

"Happy to be of service."

"It sure makes Is happy."

"She liked the manuscript?" I asked curiously. Chase would let me read it eventually, but I was having a hard time letting her go through the process her own way.

"She said that it was very romantic."

My heart swelled as I thought back to the time we'd spent together. "So, was it inspired by us?"

"Nope..." Chase shook her head and dramatically rolled her eyes.

"Brat..."

"I left out all the spanking. But the love interest is pretty much a giant dork...so you know..." she trailed off as she looked back at me, the amusement clear on her features.

"Well, I am packing some pretty impressive equipment."

"I said dork, not dick," she laughed.

"Did you know that in the nineteen fifties that dork was another word for penis?"

"Wow...have you been reading the dictionary again?" I laughed as she looked over her shoulder in disbelief at me. She knew dirty things, but etymology was my forte.

"You're just jealous you don't have the grasp on the English language that I do."

"The words I use are all the important ones," she shrugged.

"Is that so?"

"You can use as many big SAT words as you want, but if you don't know how to really use them to portray a picture... you're lost." Damn. Remind me never to piss her off or goad her into an argument.

"Are you saying I'm a hack?" I asked in mock disbelief.

"No...I'm just saying it's important to know how to use what you're working with..." She winked at me and wiggled her eyebrows.

Letting out an exaggerated sigh, I squeezed her sides. "Is everything dirty to you?"

"Was that a question?"

I shook my head and smiled at her in the mirror. "What am I going to do with you?"

"Whatever you want, big boy."

# TWENTY-NINE

## Chase

**Boston**

"Come on...it's not going to be that bad...I've met Di before. She's the sweetest."

"Why do we need public relations coaching?" Evan grumbled. The closer we got to the book tour starting, the more anxious he became.

"They want us to have a game plan ahead of time for promotion. I've had to do this every time I have any kind of press coverage."

"I'm kind of wishing that I could go crawl back into my hole now," he sighed dramatically. His custom house on the lake was hardly a hole.

I laughed as I stepped up to him and straightened the lapels of his suit jacket. We were already dressed for the party tonight because our day was going to be too crazy to have time later.

We'd met with Is and Adrian this morning. They'd be with us tonight, but they weren't going to be on location again until we came back to the East Coast. They both had too many projects in play to be able to spare three weeks entirely out of the office. Their dedicated interns had been voluntold that they were coming with us.

"You do not...I know it's making you uncomfortable, but I think it's going to be good for you to interact more with your readers. You've gotten too used to being 'Mr. Famous Recluse' — time to get back on the book-tour horse."

"If you weren't here with me, I would have fled back to Connecticut by now." The sad thing was that I knew he wasn't joking. I felt terribly guilty to be putting him through this, but he was committed.

"Then I guess it's a good thing I'm here." I leaned up slightly and kissed him softly on the lips. He gripped my hips and pulled me closer as he deepened it and took possession of my bottom lip.

I was having a hard time concentrating today. The excitement of the book launch, Evan in his fuckhot glasses... I was in cerebral overload.

"You two ready to stop making out in public places and get this over with?" Christine sighed with exaggerated annoyance as she looked over at us.

Sam frowned down at her and then smiled back over at us. "Chris, leave them alone."

"Oh...I'm sorry. If you'd like me to pop some popcorn so you can watch, I'll be right back," she snarked as she elbowed him in the arm.

I smiled against Evan's lips and leaned back a little. He looked a little mortified but also turned on. Apparently getting caught was something that excited him. Never would have pegged him for a secret exhibitionist, he continued to surprise me.

"Let's just go in with Di and they can join us when they're ready." Sam nodded towards the conference room where our meeting was being held.

"We're good...he's just nervous and I was talking him through it," I assured as I gave them both a bright smile.

"Sure. Talking...right. You were trying to swallow each other's farking tongues in a hallway and it's talking..."

"Leave them alone." Sam rolled his eyes as he put his hand on Christine's back and pushed her towards the open door. "Come on."

"Quit tugging on me, Spammy. They're adults, they can take a little bit of teasing."

"I told you to stop calling me that," Sam said in a low voice, clearly full of irritation.

"Well...I would...but I know it irritates you, so I'm not going to," Christine smiled smugly.

"Do we really have to spend the next three weeks with them?" Evan whispered in my ear.

I looked over his shoulder at Christine and Sam standing together on the other side of the hallway. They were facing each other, and she had her hips tilted towards him slightly. There was some unresolved sexual tension going on with those two.

"Want to bet how many signings we can get through before we catch them making out in a hallway?" I whispered back, so the two potential love birds couldn't hear me.

"I'm thinking LA," Evan nodded.

"I'm betting on the first day in Denver. They're about to jump each other right now."

"You're on," Evan told me with a decisive nod.

"What do I get if I win?"

"A kiss," he shrugged.

"Pfft. I don't have to win a bet to get those." He shook his head at the naughty smile I gave him as I eyed his full lips.

"Maybe you need to be cut off." He smirked as he ran his thumb along the side of my hip over the thin material of my dress.

"You wouldn't even last to the party." He huffed at my eye roll, but I knew I was right. Evan had turned out to be a very affectionate partner.

"Hmm...winner gets to pick the subject of our next book." I let out a heavy breath and he looked down at me with concern. "You OK?"

"We're going to write another one?" I had a hard time keeping the excitement out of my voice.

"I mean, it's fine if you don't want to, but I really liked wor—" The words cut off as I gripped the sides of his face and planted one on him.

"And they're making out again. I think we're gonna need a hose." I could practically hear Christine's eyes rolling back in her head.

"I think it's great," Sam whispered.

"Of course, you do. You're probably hoping for a live-action porn."

"Oh, stop it. I've never seen him like this." Sam's voice held a little bit of awe. Apparently, everyone else could see the changes in Evan as well.

"Are you going soft on me? Watching too many Lifetime movies?"

"Since when has anything on me ever been soft?" There was a bit of a seductive edge to Sam's voice, but Christine just shot right back in her usual unaffected sarcasm.

"You think quite highly of yourself, don't you?"

"You didn't seem to mind me taking my shirt off at the gym the other day. I saw you watching," Sam taunted.

Evan broke the kiss and silently laughed against my lips. The next few weeks were certainly going to be entertaining.

"Should we interrupt them?" I asked as I looked up into his much more relaxed eyes.

"I think Christine's head is going to explode if we don't go in there." He nodded at the door.

"I guess we should go act like professionals."

"Do we have to?" he whined.

"Put on your big boy panties and let's do this."

I stepped around him and started to cross towards the open conference room door. He gripped my hips and pulled me back into his chest, pressing himself into the back of my dress.

"Who said I'm wearing any...these pants are awfully snug." Wow. I'd clearly created a monster...or maybe that was just what was in his pants. Evan's game had upped significantly in the past few weeks.

"I'll have to inspect that situation later...let's do this." I reached behind me and grasped his hand, tugging him after me into the conference room where the public relations representative who was going with us on the tour was waiting.

"Hello all," Diana, our new public relations specialist, chirped from the front of the room. I loved working with her. She was unflappable. Always polite and always classy.

When things went wrong or off schedule, she just handled business in a firm way and got you back on the tracks. It was kind of impressive to watch her maneuver in a room full of the press without being pushy or rude.

"Let's all make sure we're keeping to the itineraries included in your briefing packets for each day." She'd compiled folders with details of everything we'd be doing over the next several weeks. From hotel reservations to scheduled breaks, it was all in there.

"See...I told you she's keeping us on a tight leash," Christine told Sam quietly as the leaned toward each other in the seats to our right.

"She's keeping them on the leashes," Sam whispered nodding in our direction.

"Pretty sure they keep each other on leashes," she muttered.

I bit my lip to keep from laughing at Christine.

"We could probably go MIA for an afternoon, and they wouldn't notice," he coaxed.

"And why would I want to run off somewhere with you?"

"I'm sure I could convince you to let your hair down a little," he shrugged.

"My hair already is down, ya doofus."

He sighed loudly and crossed his arms on his chest. "God, you're impossible."

"Yet you still keep following me around."

She'd obviously upset him with all the brushoffs, his voice was cold as he responded. "We work in the same office."

"So that's why you're always conveniently within earshot." Christine shot back with a sardonic laugh.

"Yeah...they won't even last to Denver at this rate," Evan whispered, his warm breath tickling my neck.

"I thought we liked to banter as foreplay," I giggled as I watched Sam and Christine square off. It's like they couldn't help themselves.

"They take the whole love/hate relationship very seriously." He nodded as he looked across me towards the two of them.

"If she hated him, she'd ignore him. I think she likes him riling her up," I told him quietly.

"I know you like it when I rile you up," he teased as his hand covered my knee underneath the table.

"What can I say...I'm a sucker for a guy who's mouthy." I could see his chest shaking from the corner of my eye.

Diana was still talking to us, but I don't think any of the four of us were paying any attention. "OK, I think that covers just about everything. Does anyone have any questions?"

All four of us slowly shook our heads as she smiled at us from the front of the room.

"Don't worry, I know you weren't paying attention to me. All the information I went over is in the front of the folders for Chicago," Diana laughed as she held up a folder. "I'm old school and would rather have everything in writing, printed out, than rely on you to pay attention to emails."

"But you're still sending us a digital copy, right?" Christine asked anxiously. She was permanently attached to her phone, so I couldn't see her getting on board with something as archaic as a paper filled folder.

"Yes, Christine. I understand I'm a dinosaur, you'll get PDFs the night before of the next day's information," Diana sighed. "I'm sure I'll see all of you tonight. Congratulations Chase and Evan."

"Thank you," I smiled and then apologized. "Sorry, we're a bit distracted."

"Not a problem. I'm used to much worse," she smiled widely.

"Thank you, Diana. It was nice to meet you." Evan was talking to someone voluntarily; that spoke volumes about how approachable she was.

"Likewise," she nodded and was out the door, meaning we had an hour left to kill before we had to be back at the hotel for our stylists.

"Nice job, Christine. Diana is already annoyed with us." I pinned her down with a scathing look. Diana could make the next few weeks easy or hard, and I wasn't going to risk Evan's first book tour in years for a moody intern.

"Hey, why is this my fault?" Christine protested. "You two weren't exactly concentrating on what she was saying either." She pointed at Sam with her thumb. "And he has a mouth too."

"That I do." Sam rolled his eyes.

"Smartass." She rolled her eyes back and stood up, gathering her laptop and her bag. "I'm going to go do my job before I'm forced to babysit you lot for the next three weeks. See you tonight."

She stopped on her way out the door and pointed straight at Evan and me. "You better not get distracted and show up late tonight. I'd like to actually enjoy myself at one of these things and not get stuck being Is' errand girl."

"Got it," I confirmed with a nod. "Don't worry. The alarm is set on my phone."

"Uh, good to see you guys. Guess I should check in with Adrian. I'm not sure he can survive three weeks on his own," Sam smiled as he gathered his things together and stood up from the table.

"Probably not," I laughed, and Evan's hand tightened on my knee as he chuckled too.

"Back to the hotel?" He arched an eyebrow at me, and I felt heat pool between my legs. I knew exactly what his intentions were.

"Don't get any ideas, mister."

"I didn't say anything." He held up his free hand and turned on the faux innocence.

"Mmmhmm. Keep it in your pants. We have enough time to grab some food and get back to the room to get all dolled up and that's all."

"You mean to get you all dolled up," he clarified.

"Nope. They'll attack you too." He was about to be styled to within an inch of his life. I was willing to bet he'd never had his face lightly contoured or his nails manicured.

"Ugh. Really?"

"Yup. They'll send a whole team. The talent has to look flawless to work the room at the party," I winked. "Romance is a whole different ballgame, Mister. We're selling an image."

"I look fine," he pouted.

"You look amazing, baby; but you're gonna have to sit back and let them do their thing." He was looking mighty fine, but if photographers were going to be there tonight, he needed to look polished *and* fine. "With the press being invited to the party, they want us to look good for pictures."

"Fine, take me to my torture."

We took his car back to the hotel, parking in the garage before we grabbed some food in the restaurant to take back to the suite, rather than risk the delay waiting on room service.

"Are you sure we can't...?" he asked as he tilted his head towards the bedroom.

"Save it for after. We've only got fifteen minutes," I smiled. Knowing that he was constantly thinking about sex now was kind of hilarious compared to the shy man I met a few months ago who could barely look me in the eye the first day.

"I can work with that." I knew he could, but then I'd need to shower again, and I'd be getting cursed out by the stylist for having wet hair.

"Oh, baby," I rolled my eyes. "Just eat your food already."

"Fine," he snarked. "Suit yourself."

Evan was very charming with the team of stylists; he had all of them eating up every word he said. The stuttering awkward man I met several months ago had come out of his shell.

"Am I pretty enough for you?" he asked as he pulled me back into his chest while we rode the elevator down to the ballroom.

"You're always pretty, baby." I looked back at him over my shoulder and winked.

"I can't wait to peel this dress off you later," he whispered directly into my ear, his voice low.

I closed my eyes and relaxed into his embrace. I couldn't wait for the end of the night either. "Promises...promises..."

"If there weren't cameras in here..." He punctuated his suggestive remark by pressing his pelvis into me. He wasn't hard, but with a little coaxing, I was sure he could get there quickly. It was tempting, but our editors would murder us.

"You've gotten brave," I giggled as his hand rubbed the material of my dress just below my breasts.

"You make me brave," he whispered into my hair. "Are you sure I can do this?" I could hear the nerves appearing in his voice as we watched the numbers count down as the elevator neared the ground floor.

"Of course, you've come so far in the last few months. And you had those ladies, and one very smitten gay man eating out of your hands earlier."

"He was gay?" Evan asked with a surprised smile.

"He kept coming up with excuses to restyle your hair and called you handsome about forty times. Pretty sure," I nodded.

"Please stay with me." His other hand gripped mine and interlaced our fingers.

"I'll try," I nodded, "but Is wants us both to work the room and talk to the press. The buzz is already starting to grow about the book. And remember, this isn't your first book launch. You were rusty at other things as well and look at you now. You've got this."

"Ugh. I don't want to talk to the press by myself. What if I say something embarrassing?" Evan was falling into his old habits of expecting himself to fail. I found myself wanting to find the person who made him doubt himself so much and punch them.

"You'll be great. Just stick to the information Adrian and Diana gave you. Do that whole quiet mysterious thing and they'll eat it up."

"Are you sure we can't go hide in the room?" I could hear him swallow hard and his body was tense behind me.

"Baby, it'll be OK. Everything after this will be busy but low key. If we can make it through tonight, then I'll be by your side for everything else."

I could feel his chest press against my back as he took several deep breaths. His heart was still racing, but I knew he could do this.

The elevator pinged as we reached our destination and I stepped forward with my hand outstretched behind me. Evan let out a loud sigh and took my hand as I led him out the doors and down the hallway.

I could hear soft music as we approached the doors, and I hoped the room hadn't filled up yet. Evan could use a few minutes to ease himself into it before the hordes descended.

"I'm fine, let's go." He walked around me and held the door open, motioning for me to go in ahead of him.

"I'm really proud of you," I whispered as I leaned up to kiss his cheek as I passed him.

"Let's hope that's true after tonight." His hand found the bare skin on my back and he guided me to the other side of the room where Is and Adrian were stationed by a small stage with a raised podium.

"Right on time!" Isobel smiled as she pulled me into a hug and then briefly squeezed Evan's arm.

"At least you two don't look like you've been screwing in the supply closet," Adrian laughed.

"Oh my god, Adrian. Just don't talk anymore," Isobel scowled in his direction.

"It was a joke. It was supposed to be funny."

"No...just no," I shook my head as I pinned him down with a scathing look.

"You put your foot in it again, dickhead?" Christine laughed as she joined us and saw us all scowling at a contrite Adrian.

"Sounds like he put his whole body in it." Sam was right behind her, looking at his boss with amusement.

"Hey, I thought you were supposed to be on my side. Traitor!" Adrian scowled at his intern.

"What sides?" Christine asked. "Seems like there's only one person making an ass out of themselves right now."

"I was trying to be funny. How come *that* one can make remarks and I get jumped on?" Adrian asked while he pointed at Christine.

I cringed as I saw her face completely change to a blank stare.

"When you get your dog to quit peeing on the floor, let me know where you want me for the night," Christine said to Isobel, completely ignoring Adrian's presence. She walked off towards the table where there was a poster stand with the book cover on it.

The table was stacked with promotional materials and copies of the book. Most of the press invited had been mailed advanced copies, but it wasn't uncommon to provide advanced copies to anyone who might put positive reviews out online.

"I'm just gonna..." He pointed over his shoulder before he followed Christine. It was probably a good thing Adrian wouldn't be with us for the next few weeks. His brain to mouth filter had degraded considerably.

"So, anyways. I will be giving a brief introduction in about fifteen minutes to the room and then we'll start the party," Isobel told us. "All the invited press was notified that this is a social function and that they are welcome to attend any of the events when you return to Boston to ask questions."

"Did you get a response from the people I asked you to invite?" Evan looked over at me with confusion as I put the question to Isobel.

"I thought we weren't inviting family to this since we're flying out tomorrow?" he asked quietly.

"We're not." I turned to face him and saw a few people enter the ballroom and got my answer. "I wanted to make sure *they* were invited."

He turned and his face broke out into a smile as we watched Emory and Talia cross towards us holding hands. Nathan was a few steps behind them.

"I thought they wanted to remain anonymous?"

I nodded, "They do, in respect of what they do behind closed doors. They're here as friends tonight."

"Thanks for inviting us," Emory greeted as he slipped an arm behind my back and kissed my cheek. Talia elbowed him out of the way and gave me a hug while Nathan gave Evan's hand a brief shake.

"You know I'll never turn down a party," Talia smiled before she turned to Evan and hugged him as well.

"It's kind of refreshing to go to one where everyone keeps their clothes on," Nathan said quietly as he scanned the room.

Adrian's eyes went wide as the pieces connected in his head. Luckily, Isobel whispered something in his ear before he said something inappropriate.

"I'm so glad you all could make it. It'll be nice having some friendly faces in the crowd tonight," I told our friends. They'd helped us get here and they deserved to enjoy their part in it as well.

The room had started to fill in and I recognized quite a few people who were prominent in the local press and blogging communities.

"I'll need to steal these two for a little while," Isobel told our three friends as she nodded at Evan and me.

"No problem. I'm sure we can entertain ourselves while they're on duty," Emory assured her.

"I can always entertain myself with an open bar," Talia said, eyeing the well-stocked bar at the back of the room.

"I think I'll manage," Nathan nodded, staring towards a group of female bloggers who'd congregated near the bar.

"You two ready?" Isobel asked as the other three headed off towards the bar.

"I don't have to speak, right?" Evan confirmed.

"No," she laughed as she nodded towards the stage. "I'll take care of it, but Di might ask you to once you're in a smaller venue."

"You're fine. Just take a breath and pretend I'm in my underwear," I whispered in his ear as we turned to follow Is to the stage.

He laughed and tugged me towards him, leaning down to whisper back to me. "I don't think you want me to give the room a show."

I giggled as he took my hand and helped me up the stairs. As he reached the top, he ran his hand down my back and casually grazed my ass.

"Hey...behave." I shook my head at him, and he shot me a nervous smile.

I tried to pay attention to Is as she was speaking, but I had to admit I was a little nervous too. I hated the first days after a release where you're waiting for the critics and reviewers to respond.

"And thank you all for coming tonight to celebrate two of my favorite authors who have created something really special." Isobel finished speaking and Adrian stepped in front of the mic.

"Let's give them a round of applause." He'd surprisingly kept his bad jokes to himself — it probably didn't hurt that Is was hovering next to the microphone like an overprotective parent.

Evan plastered on an almost believable smile and reached over to interlock his fingers with mine. I had a hard time taking my eyes off him to face the crowd.

"They'll be here all night," Isobel smiled over at the two of us. "Enjoy the spread and we hope you enjoy the book if you haven't read it yet. Hopefully, you won't be too hungover to read it tomorrow."

Is ushered us off the stage and made straight for some of the execs from the publishing house. They did the usual patting themselves on the back for associating themselves with 'such quality talent'. Evan was quiet but respectful. He commented when needed, smiled, and nodded, but I could tell he was distracted.

"You OK?" I asked as we stepped to the side and took a moment to ourselves.

"I'm just a little out of it. I forgot how overstimulated you could get at these." His eyes nervously scanned the crowd as I held his clammy hand.

"I'm sorry if we pressured you into this."

He took a deep breath and gave me a small smile. "It's alright. I just need a minute. I think I'm gonna step out for some air."

"Nathan looks like he's trying to get your attention. Go spend some time with your friends. I'll be right back." He kissed me on the cheek and snuck out the side door, his hand running roughly through his hair as it closed.

I felt bad that he was having trouble, but I knew that he was insistent on doing this. He just needed some space to try to work out the anxiety.

"Hey," Nathan greeted as he came up behind me and placed his hand on the back of my arm. "There's someone who wants to meet you and I said I may be able to arrange an introduction. Can you spare a few minutes?"

"Sure...yeah. No problem" I said distractedly as I looked towards the door Evan had left through.

"So, she's a blogger but she's been out of the literary rotation for a while," he explained as I turned away from where Evan had escaped.

"Is she someone that Is invited?"

"Not sure," Nathan shrugged. "I think she may have just heard about it through the grapevine. She wasn't wearing an ID badge."

As we crossed the room, I saw a tall, slender, dark-haired woman send Nathan a calculated look. To a casual observer, she would look harmless, but something about the way she glanced at me sent alarms off in my head. "What did you say her name was?"

"I didn't. We didn't get that far. She just asked if I knew you personally."

I nodded and sent her a tight smile as I stepped in front of her and put out my hand. "Chastity Rose."

She nodded and sent me a predatory smile. "Oh...you don't need to hide behind silly pen names with me, Chase."

"Do I know you?"

"Not exactly," she flashed that smug smile again, "but I know all about you."

"I'm sorry, I'm at a loss here. Did Isobel invite you?" I'd never seen this woman before in my life. Was she some gossip rag columnist?

"She invited someone from my office, but I told her I'd be happy to take her place tonight," she smiled as she waved her hand, looking around the room. "I was hoping to catch up with an old friend."

"Oh, is there someone here you know?" I'd almost forgotten that Nathan was still standing there. He placed his hand on my back and stepped closer to me as we both faced this woman. I think he could tell there was something off about her behavior as well.

"You could say that...but I'm sure Chase thinks she knows him better. He's certainly different than he was when I last saw him." Her voice was light but full of sarcasm and condescension. "Apparently, drawing him down to your level lightened him up a little."

"What is that supposed to mean?" Nathan asked as he stepped forward, his body acting as a defensive barrier beside me.

"Oh nothing, just that introducing him to all your kinky friends has finally made him interesting." She rolled her eyes and waved her hand.

"Excuse me?" Who did this bitch think she was?

"I'm well aware of your little 'research quest' for this book. People in this industry talk, and I'm unfortunately aware of your last book as well," she said lowly as she flashed me a dirty look and turned her nose up at Nathan.

"OK, I don't think you realize who you're talking to, but take the condescending attitude somewhere else." Nathan's voice had a dangerous edge to it; I could see the Dom side of him starting to creep out. "People who follow the lifestyle I lead don't take highly to ignorant comments like the ones you're making."

"Nathan, it's fine. I can handle this." I placed my hand on his shoulder and tried to ease him back.

"Oh, I'm sure you can...is Nathan here one of your 'boyfriends' too?" The woman rolled her eyes as she looked at my hand on his arm in disgust.

"Not that it's any of your business..." I laughed dryly as I took a step towards her with my own fake smile. "But Nathan is a friend, and my boyfriend is obviously someone who you think you know."

"Oh, honey. I know him so much better than you ever will. Your precious Evan can't even carry on a conversation in public, much less an interesting one."

My eyes widened as she said his name in a way that sounded entirely too familiar. "Who are you?"

She smirked as she leaned down towards me.

"If you're not here to support the book, then why are you even wasting my time?" I asked with a little growl.

"You're going to realize how much time you've wasted soon enough," she laughed, but it sounded forced.

"Quit with the cryptic bullshit," I snapped as I straightened my back and looked directly into her dead eyes.

"My name is Serena Woods." She put one hand on her hip and looked down at me like she was something to be respected. I knew exactly who this bitch was, and she was evil trash.

"I think it's time you left," I told her as I glanced towards the hotel security in the corner.

"Oh, I got what I came here for," she said as she pulled a small recorder from the pocket of her dress.

Nathan was quick to grab her wrist and flip the small device down into his other hand. She looked over at him with mild panic, but he just shrugged as he pocketed the device and gave her a challenging look.

"I don't know what you think you've accomplished tonight, but you need to go before Evan realizes you're here," I told her quickly.

"Protecting your precious pet?"

"I don't need to protect him, he's a grown man, but I'm not subjecting him to your little mind games," I scoffed as I narrowed my eyes at her. He still hadn't told me everything about their past, but it was clear she manipulated him and destroyed his self-esteem.

"You're a little late...I think we've been spotted." She laughed as she looked towards one of the doors entering the ballroom.

"Nathan, can you make sure security escorts her out?" I asked as I watched the door close with a shell-shocked Evan standing on the other side of it.

"I'd be happy to," he responded flatly as he nodded towards a security guard who had stepped closer to where we were standing. He'd obviously sensed we'd encountered someone here to cause trouble.

"Oh, don't worry, I'll leave. I just wanted to see the tramp who managed to get Evan to grow a pair."

I didn't even think until I was left shaking my hand after my fist landed squarely in the center of her perfectly made-up face.

"Ahh! I think you broke it," Serena shrieked as she held onto her nose, a trickle of blood spilling down her lips.

A small crowd of people had turned to look towards us, Serena now held securely by one of the security guards while another looked at my hand.

Held firmly by her upper arm, Serena was escorted out a side door while Isobel was talking to the DJ. Not everyone in the room had seen my fisticuffs routine and apparently loud music was her method of distraction.

"Holy shit, Chase! I knew taking you to kickboxing was a good idea," Christine cheered as she stepped close to my side. The security guard returned my hand but advised I put some ice on it to prevent swelling.

"I've never hit anyone before." I blinked over at her, still a little in shock.

"Well, you got the job done with that one," she told me with comically wide eyes. I scanned the room, hoping to see Evan return — I knew I needed to find him. Christine was talking, but I didn't really hear what she was saying.

Looking back towards the exit several minutes later, I saw a disappointed Sam walking towards us.

"Where's Evan?" I asked as he stepped up next to Christine and me.

"Um..." Sam scratched at the back of his neck nervously.

"Shit, Spamela, I gave you one job," Christine sighed.

"I tried, but he's fast," he looked over at her and then turned his wary eyes to me.

"Who's fast?" My heart started to beat erratically in my chest as I looked between the two of them.

"Evan. He took off in a cab."

"What do you mean he took off in a cab?" My voice was a little bit frantic at this point. Evan saw me talking to his bitchy ex and now he was gone. I couldn't even imagine what was running through his head.

"Call him!"

My phone was back in the hotel suite; I hadn't thought I'd need it tonight and I didn't have any pockets.

"About that..." Sam held up a familiar iPhone and cringed. "Adrian asked me to hold this for Evan until the end of the night."

"Fark me!" We both looked over at Christine's outburst and she shot us a death glare that warned us not to say anything.

"So, he's just gone?" Panic started to swell in my system. Evan was gone and we had no way to find him. He had a history of major anxiety issues and sometimes even panic attacks. I hadn't seen one, but he was all by himself. What if something happened to him?

"I'm sure he'll come back once he's calmed down," Christine assured, but she had no idea. Evan retreated into himself if he felt any sort of stress.

As I looked towards the doors he'd fled through, wondering what was going through his head...I wasn't so sure it'd be that simple.

# THIRTY

### Evan

**Boston**

I paced the hallway outside of the ballroom, taking deep breaths and trying to calm myself. I hated that I still got like this in situations where I was forced to interact with people I didn't know. Chase, our friends, even Adrian and Sam didn't freak me out. I knew them, they knew my limits, and they respected me.

The press and the execs had no idea I had issues with anxiety. I preferred to keep them in the dark and let them assume that my seclusion was just part of my artistic mystique, rather than I was prone to having panic attacks in large groups and generally had trouble looking people in the eye. I'd always hated crowds.

Kelly had teased me relentlessly when I didn't want to go to Disney World when I was sixteen. My dad had understood though and he had taken me to a therapist to get some anxiety meds. We also researched the weeks when the parks were least crowded and went then.

It'd still made me nervous, but I'd been able to push through because my family was supportive. Even Kelly stopped teasing me once my parents had explained the situation to her.

Chase understood my need to walk away sometimes and wasn't upset with it. Being with her the last few months had been simultaneously the most stressful and easiest thing in the world. She pushed me to want to step outside my boundaries, but she understood when I told her no. Not that it'd happened often.

I'd never had anyone in my life who just got me like she did.

"Shit. Get a hold of yourself," I muttered as I shook out my arms and took a few deep breaths, letting them out slowly. Counting my breaths always seemed to help calm me, so I started slowly and gradually had gotten myself under control enough to go back inside.

"Hey man, you doing OK?" Sam asked as he approached me from the doors to the ballroom.

Sam was a good guy. He connected with Adrian on all the fitness stuff, making me think initially he was just a younger model. I'd come to learn he was an intelligent and thoughtful guy. He'd been working with me on minor editing before Chase, and now Sam and Christine were in regular contact with the both of us.

"I think I'm alright. I've definitely felt better, but I'll manage." My chest didn't feel quite as tight now that I was out of that room.

"My sister has some anxiety issues. Take your time. I can run interference with Adrian."

"Thanks," I told him sincerely, I appreciated people who just supported you and didn't try to jump in to fix things.

He headed towards the doors and gave me a quick nod before he went back inside.

Take a deep breath in, deep breath out. In...out...

"You can do this."

I walked slowly towards the door and opened it, scanning the room as I stood there. To the left, next to the bar stood Adrian, talking to his boss. He made eye contact and subtly signaled to me with his hand. I nodded and swung my gaze to the other side of the room.

Chase was standing with Nathan beside her. I took a moment to admire the expanse of exposed skin across her back. Her dress dipped down to her lower back and I ached to be able to touch her skin when we were finally allowed to leave.

She shifted her weight and her posture changed, turning into a more defensive stance, and from what I could see of his face, Nathan looked upset. I tried to see who they were talking to and then Chase moved over a step and she came into view.

"Fuck."

Serena stood opposite Chase, looking every bit the polished, entitled, condescending bitch she'd been when I last saw her two years ago.

My heartbeat picked up and I felt my palms break out in a cold sweat as she looked up with a sly smile on her face and made eye contact with me. She said something and Chase laughed. It didn't look like a particularly humorous one, but it threw me, nonetheless.

I started to back out of the doorway, my breathing already ragged and my clothes feeling too tight. Seeing Serena was about to send me into a full-blown panic attack.

Right as I let go of the door, Chase turned fully towards me with a look of shock on her face, probably pretty similar to mine.

"Fuck, fuck, fuck."

I stumbled a little as I hurried down a hallway, through the lobby, and out the front entrance.

My pulse was racing, I felt my neck tightening up and was seeing floaters in my line of sight. I could hear the rasp in my breathing start, a tingling sensation creeping along my jaw. Pacing back and forth outside the door, struggling to pull in full breaths, my worst nightmare came walking towards me.

"I wondered where you ran off to." Her voice was sugary sweet, totally at odds with the blood crusted in one nostril and the start of some severe bruises underneath her eyes. She looked like she'd been in a fight, her dress a little wrinkled and some droplets of blood visible on one of her straps.

"Go away."

"Oh, come on, baby, don't be like that," she cooed as she took a step closer.

"Don't...d...don't call me that," I stuttered as she stepped closer to me once more.

"Still have that nervous stutter around me, I see." She pressed herself along my side and I started gasping for air. She really couldn't take a hint.

"Cause looking in the face of e...evil... freaks me out."

"You used to not be able to keep your hands off me," she said suggestively as she ran her hand down my front and stopped at my belt. "We could go upstairs, and you can teach me your new tricks."

I pushed her away and looked back towards the hotel. Sam was coming around the corner headed straight for us. My mind raced through my options as I tried to distance myself from Serena.

I knew I needed to talk to Chase, but I also needed to calm myself down. There was no way I could do that with Serena harassing me.

"L...le...leave me th...the f...uck...a...alone," I growled and gesticulated wildly as she tried to come near me again.

My whole face was tingling and now I was finding it increasingly difficult to breathe as I tried to wave her off. Sam came through the door at the same time a cab pulled up on the curb and I made a split-second decision.

Stumbling across the sidewalk, I made a break for the cab and wrenched the door open, jumping inside and slamming the door.

"G...go...please..." I panted as the driver hesitated and looked at me like I was crazy through the rearview mirror. My voice was pinched, and I was wheezing as I put my head down and tried to pull in deep breaths.

He pulled away from the curb and I could see the little meter start on the computer screen in the back.

"You gonna tell me where we're goin or do I getta guess?" he sniped. He had a very pronounced south Boston accent and he looked like he didn't put up with anybody's shit.

"Uh..." I was still having trouble drawing a full breath and I couldn't get my eyes to focus.

"Come on, man," he groaned. "If you're on something, I don't need ta get mixed up in that shit. No junkie is gonna OD in my car, nice suit or not."

I tried to calm down my breathing enough to talk, but my throat was dry, and I was feeling a little lightheaded. "I...I...I'm..."

"What the hell you on? You can't even fuckin talk."

"No...noth...nothing..." I wheezed.

"Yeah right, and I'm a priest. Come on...I don't need this bullshit. I'm dropping you off atta urgent care center."

I shook my head back and forth, but he'd already turned into a parking lot, the red lights of the 'EMERGENCY' sign blurring in my vision. He parked at the curb and got out, crossing over to my door and opening it, pulling me out by the arm and guiding me to a bench right beside the entrance to the clinic.

"I'm not even gonna charge ya. Get some fuckin help before you kill ya self."

My throat was tight as I leaned forward and put my head in my hands, desperately trying to slow my breathing. Several people passed through the doors to my side as I sat there trying to calm down.

I saw a figure approach me through my peripheral vision and looked up at a concerned looking woman wearing scrubs.

"Are you alright, Sir?"

I sat up a little and tried to respond, but it was caught in my throat.

"Are you asthmatic? Are you injured?"

She sat down next to me on the bench and put her hand on my shoulder. She pursed her lips as I shook my head and she watched me trying to force air into my lungs.

"Do you have panic attacks frequently?" she asked, guessing what was wrong with me.

I shrugged my shoulder as I felt like my chest was easing up a little bit. It was still hard to breathe deeply, but the numbness was starting to fade from my jaw.

My lips quivered as I responded. "Some...times...I...used to..."

She nodded and placed a stethoscope on my back. "I think you're OK, but can you walk? Would you like to come inside with me?"

I nodded and stood up slowly, black spots appearing in the corners of my vision.

"Just take it easy. We'll get you checked in." She led me through a set of automatic doors and to a reception desk.

"I'm going to go ahead and take him back since we're slow." She told the woman at the front desk. "Can you send someone back to get him registered?"

"Of course. I'll start a chart for him."

The woman, whose name badge indicated she was a physician's assistant, led me through a door and down a hallway, sitting me down on a chair in an exam room. She took my vitals and by then my breathing had eased enough I wasn't wheezing.

"You seem to be alright, but I'd still like to let you calm down a little back here." She nodded after she listened to my chest.

"Th...thank you."

"Do you have someone to talk to about these episodes?" she asked as she put down her stethoscope.

"Not recently," I shook my head. "I used to have a psychiatrist, but I haven't had a full-blown panic attack in t...two years."

"And something triggered one tonight?" She guessed.

I nodded as I drew in a shuddering breath.

"I won't make you go into it. But I would like to give you something tonight to help relax you."

The receptionist came back then and got me registered. I had my wallet with my identification, but it didn't occur to me that I'd given Sam my phone until I tried to give her emergency contact information.

"I'm gonna get a doctor's permission to put you on a low dose of Klonopin," the PA told me as she took my information sheet and scanned over it. "Do you have any allergies, or have you had any adverse reactions to anxiety medications?"

"No..."

She left the room and came back a few minutes later, verifying my birthdate and last name before handing me a few little white tablets to swallow with some water. "These should help relax you enough to get through this episode, but I'd recommend following up with your psychiatrist if you'll be exposed to your source of stress regularly."

"Hopefully, that won't be a problem," I nodded, but I would try to check in with Dr. Singh if I had time.

"If you start to feel any tightness in your chest, abnormal swelling, or difficulty breathing then you need to come back in." She finished her discharge instructions and then she walked me back out to the lobby.

I wasn't entirely sure where I was, and I wasn't sure how I was going to get back to the hotel without my phone.

There was a microbrewery across the street from the urgent care, and I found myself walking across the street before I thought about it.

"Hey man, what can I get you?" the bartender asked as I sat down across from him, avoiding the other patrons sitting at one end of the long bar top.

"Can I get a water, please?"

"Sure thing. You look a little weary. Want to talk about it?" He picked up a glass out of a nearby rack and started drying it. I think he could tell that I was not doing so well.

"Just been a long night. Do you have a phone I could use?"

He walked down to the other end of the bar and picked up a cordless phone, sliding it towards me. "No long distance, but you're welcome to make a local call."

I dialed the first three numbers and then realized I wasn't 100% sure of the last four digits of Chase's phone number. Smartphones made it so easy to be reliant on not remembering phone numbers.

I was also starting to feel a little lightheaded.

Laying the phone down, I drank some more water and wished that I'd bought the Apple Watch that had cell service. The Wi-Fi one wasn't going to do me any good without my phone.

The bartender kept refilling my glass and I realized I'd absentmindedly kept drinking it.

"You doing alright?" he asked, and I noticed for the first time that several of the groups had cleared out of the bar.

"I...I think so?" I knew time had passed, but I couldn't tell how much. The windows that looked out at the street showed that it was darker than I remembered it being.

"Don't worry, you've got about an hour before I need to start cleaning up. Feel free to hang out as long as you need to."

"Thanks." My voice slurred a little as I swayed on my stool. I wasn't sure how much more time had passed, but I was a little startled as my wrist started buzzing. A 'Find my iPhone' alert was flashing across the screen.

"What's wrong with you?" I asked, tapping the little square watch face. "My phone isn't lost. It's in Sam's pocket."

Alerts for missed calls and texts started flashing across my wrist. I squinted as I tried to keep up with them, but I couldn't focus on the letters.

"You're drunk Apple Watch." I tapped at the screen to dismiss all the alerts, the screen finally clearing.

"You need a refill?" asked the bartender, as he looked down at me with an amused smile.

"Whoa...where did you come from?" I chuckled as I tried to focus on his face. Bright colors surrounded his hair, and I wondered what kind of lightbulbs they used in here.

"Been here the whole time," he frowned. "Need me to call ya a cab?"

"No...no more cabs. They don't like me." I shook my head, but it threw me off balance and I had to grab the edge of the bar to stop sliding off my stool.

"You sure you're OK?" he asked skeptically. Mr. Bartender did not look amused.

"Peachy," I smiled...at least I think it was a smile. My face felt funny.

He squinted his eyes at me and looked at my glass. "Why don't I get you some fresh water."

He sighed as the door to the bar opened and I saw two blurry figures walk in, my wrist buzzing again.

"Leave me alone, stupid watch."

I laid my head down on the bar in front of me as the room started to sway.

"Is he drunk?" I heard a familiar voice and tried to lift my head again, the room continuing to move.

Or maybe it was me moving.

Either way, it was making me dizzy.

I just wanted to go to sleep.

"Nah, I've just been serving him water since he came in here a few hours ago."

I'd been here for hours?

"You're sure you didn't give him any alcohol?" That was Emory, he didn't sound happy.

"Yup, just good old-fashioned tap."

"What the hell is wrong with him?" Nathan asked. I think it was Nathan, but I couldn't lift my head.

"You don't even want to know." My voice sounded funny again.

"What's on his wrist?" Emory asked as I felt my hand move.

"Is that a hospital bracelet?"

Emory appeared right in front of my face and my eyes widened. "Evan, can we try to sit you up?"

"No..." I groaned as I closed my eyes again.

I felt someone move my arm, but I couldn't find the energy to pull it back.

"It's from the urgent care across the street."

"What happened to you?" Nathan asked. It looked like his head was floating in the air behind Emory when I squinted my eyes open.

"Tha birch attacked me." Why did my voice sound like that?

"A tree attacked you?" Nathan laughed.

"No...no...no. Rena. Tha birch."

"Serena?" Emory guessed. It sounded like he was trying not to laugh. Asshole.

"Yup."

"That bitch attacked you? Is that what you're trying to say?" Nathan asked again.

I nodded my head slowly. "Couldn't breathe."

"Is that why you were at the urgent care?" Emory was talking again. "You couldn't breathe?"

"Uh-huh." Why were they asking me so many questions? I just wanted to sleep.

"You guys are fine for now, but I need to start closing up. Can I get ya anything before I close down tha taps?" the bartender asked quietly. I could still hear him.

"I think we'll just gather up our friend and get out of your way. Thanks for taking care of him." Emory was a nice guy. Well...unless he was teaching your girlfriend how to whip you...with an actual whip.

"No problem. Quietest non-drunk drunk I've had in a while." The bartender laughed. I think they were talking about me.

"OK...up you go." I think his name was Nathan...told me as he put an arm behind my back and slowly sat me upright.

"Evan? You still with us?" Emory asked as I closed my eyes again.

"Do you think we should take him back to the urgent care center?" Nathan sounded worried, but I was fine.

"I don't think so."

"Evan? Can you breathe OK now?" Emory's fingers snapped in front of my face and I felt myself falling backward.

"Nope, I got you," Nathan laughed as he propped me back up. "Evan? You need to see the doctor again?"

"Nooo... no doctor. Just nurse." I shook my head. "She gave me little white pills."

"The nurse gave you something?" Emory asked too many questions.

I tipped forward on my stool as I tried to nod. "For my anxiety..."

Why was I giggling? Was I giggling?

"For your anxiety?" Nathan asked. That was what I said, why wasn't he listening.

"Hold up there big boy." I felt Emory's hands grab my shoulder and pull me back upright.

"The little whiiiite pills make me feel weeeiiiird." I blinked heavily as their faces swayed, getting bigger and then smaaaaller...

"Evan... we're gonna take you to my studio to sleep this off," Emory told me as he snapped his fingers in front of my face again. "Okay?"

"Mmmhmmm..." I blinked heavily and closed my eyes.

"You've still got his phone?" Emory asked. I don't think he was talking to me.

"Yeah, in my pocket," Nathan answered him.

"You support one side; I got the other."

I felt myself moving and cracked open one eye, watching the bar pass by as they got me closer to the door. The colors that moved on the walls were freaking me out. I needed to get out of here and snuggle up with...

Chase!

Fuck. She was gonna be mad at me.

The door swung outward into the sidewalk and I stumbled a little as we crossed the threshold.

"Wait...way...wait...I gotta call Chaser..." I slurred.

"I texted her that we found you," Nathan said loudly. Why was he right next to my ear? Personal space, dude!

"No, no, no. Need to talk to her now," I slurred as I shook my head, it just made the colors move faster.

"Evan, you're a little out of it right now; let's get you lying down to rest and we'll call Chase." Emory was way too close to my other side. Geez.

"No...now." I shook my head again, but I couldn't hold it up anymore.

"Man, I'm glad I never want kids." Nathan laughed.

"Did he just stomp his foot?" Emory tried to hold in his own laughter.

"Now dammit!" I yelled, but then cringed at how loud my voice was.

"OK, calm down. I'll dial it for you..." Nathan told me as he pulled my phone out of his pocket and typed in my passcode.

How did he know my passcode?

"Don't steal...my...shit." I narrowed my eyes at him, but he just laughed.

"Fine. Take it. Just press call."

"I know how to use a...oh shit..." As I tried to press the button to call Chase, I felt my knees give out and the phone started to slide out of my hand...

I watched as it fell in slow motion onto the sidewalk and bounced off the curb. There was a hollow clank noise as it hit, and I heard Emory curse as he let go of me.

"Shit." Nathan pulled me into his side as I watched Emory step over to the curb and look down.

He scratched the back of his neck as he turned back to me. "Well...you're going to need a new phone."

"Damn. Did it crack?" Nathan asked.

"Not exactly," Emory shook his head. "There's a grate here...it's about six feet under us right now."

"No! I needed that..." I whined as I clung to Nathan.

"It's gone. We'll just have to worry about it tomorrow," he told me sympathetically, but I could tell he was trying not to laugh.

Emory came back and grabbed my other side, helping lift me back in between them again. They loaded me into the back of a black SUV and I laid myself down with my cheek touching the cool leather seats. I could hear them talking as they climbed into the front seats, but I couldn't focus on what they were saying. I heard a clunk and the vehicle started moving.

My mind drifted back to Chase. I hoped she wasn't too mad at me. This wasn't how I planned on this night going. Then the thought scattered...

"Let's go lover boy!" Em pulled me upright in my seat, helping me to climb down from the SUV. He and Nathan guided me through the gallery and into the studio. Emory stopped to unlock his playroom.

"The king-sized bed in the back room?" Nathan asked as we entered the playroom. They led me past the play space, into a dimly lit alcove at the back, a large bed, covered with dark bedding, dominating the space.

"Yeah. It's already made. We should be able to just lay him down. Hopefully, he'll sleep off whatever reaction he's having."

"I'm fine...it's fine...fine fine..." I couldn't stop saying fine. It made my mouth feel funny.

"You doing alright?" Nathan asked with concern in his voice. "Em, his color doesn't look good."

"Hold on." Emory walked away and came back with a small plastic trash can. "Just in case you need to be sick."

"I don't need to..." He thrust the can into my face, and it appeared just in time. The huge amount of water making a sour splash against the can.

Ugh...

"You feel better?" Nathan asked as I peeked over the side of the trashcan. I shook my head and Emory took the trash can to a sink in the corner and rinsed it out.

"Do you want me to stay with him?" Nathan offered. Were we going to spoon?

"You don't have to do that," Emory shook his head.

"I know," Nathan sighed. "But I feel like I owe it to Chase."

"You can sleep on the leather bed out there," Emory told him as he gestured back to the playroom. "I can grab you some blankets."

"Thanks."

I slowly felt the world start to sway back and forth again and wanted to lie down.

"Evan. You doing OK?" Nathan asked as he helped me sit on the edge of the bed.

"I don't feel so good," I mumbled as he pushed the trash can into my lap again.

"Why don't we try to get you to lie down? You might feel better if you get some sleep."

My head nodded and I could feel my whole body get heavy. Nathan got me to the pillow, and I sighed as I felt the covers settle over my body. "Just a little sleep."

My eyes were firmly closed but I still felt like I was moving.

"I'll put the can right here in case you need it," Nathan whispered.

"M'kay."

Sleep came easily, but I don't know how long I slept when I felt my stomach revolt again. I was able to grab the can and throw up into it before I collapsed back into the bed and drifted off to sleep once again.

# THIRTY-ONE

## Chase

**Boston**

The next morning, I woke up with a headache and a dead phone battery. Pounding on the door of the suite woke me up and I saw the time. I had fifteen minutes until I needed to be packed to meet the car service.

"Shit." I had no idea if they'd found Evan, but he obviously wasn't here. The pounding started back up again, and I dragged myself out of the bed.

"I'm coming. Calm down," I groaned as I pulled the door open.

Christine was standing there looking relaxed for travel. She was holding a drink carrier with insulated cups in one hand and the handle of her suitcase in her other. "Oh, come on. Get your ass dressed and I'll pack up your suitcase. Isobel is on the warpath because we're running late."

"Did they find Evan?"

She bit her lip and shook her head slightly. "I have no idea. Emory's phone keeps going to voicemail and I don't know how to contact Nathan. All I know is that he's not here."

I swallowed hard and tried to keep the tears building in my eyes from falling. Worried didn't even begin to describe what I was feeling for Evan. I hoped he was alright. It wasn't like him to just fall off the grid, but with a dead phone battery I had no idea who may have tried to contact me.

"Which one is mine?" I asked as I surveyed the cups. If I was even going to attempt to adult today, especially leaving my boyfriend behind missing in the city, I needed caffeine.

"The one in the front. Caramel macchiato with two extra shots of espresso."

"At least something is going my way this morning." I sipped the coffee as I stepped back into the room and headed for my suitcase. Comfort was my motivation for my travel wardrobe. The press event wasn't until 4:00 pm and we'd be getting into Chicago around 10:00 am local time. I didn't even want to go, but I knew Is would murder me and it'd probably screw over both Evan's and my career if I missed it.

What I really wanted to do was punch that bitch Serena in the face again. Talia had told me about Serena confronting Evan in front of the hotel and then him fleeing. He had to be so traumatized by the whole thing. He never told me everything, but she seemed to be a very toxic part of his past.

Evan had moved to a different state and taken up secluding himself because the thought of running into her gave him anxiety. Then she had to go and show up unannounced somewhere that he was already on edge.

"Plotting ways to kill the she-bitch?" Christine asked, startling me out of my racing thoughts.

"How did you know?" I laughed as I put my toiletries back into the suitcase and zipped it up.

"Cause I've been plotting revenge since I woke up this morning. She crossed way too many lines. Cuntmuffin isn't getting off easy with this one."

Christine eyed the second suitcase sitting next to the bed. "What are we doing with that?"

"I don't know," I shook my head as my eyes started to burn again. "I need to check out. Do you think they'd keep it at the desk? I don't want to take it with us. He may have something in there he needs."

I sat down heavily on the end of the bed and wiped at the few tears that slipped out.

"I think Mr. Blithe will do just about anything we ask him to do."

"Who is Mr. Blithe?" I asked curiously. I didn't remember meeting anyone yesterday with that name, not that I was paying attention.

"The general manager. We're tight. I may have threatened to sic the press on him if he didn't cooperate with us last night."

"They've still got Evan's phone?" I didn't see it anywhere around the room this morning.

"Nathan took it," Christine reminded me.

"Can you try calling it?"

She tapped on her screen a few times and then held it to her ear. A frown appeared as she pulled it away and shook her head.

Christine looked thoughtful for a moment and sent off a text. "I texted Sam. He's pretty tech savvy. He may be able to send him a push alert that'll come up once he turns it back on."

"Can't you call him?" she asked as she nodded at my phone on the bed.

"Dead battery." I held up the blank screen and she nodded.

"Let's get you packed up and stop at the desk. Maybe there's a portable charger we can buy at the gift shop. If not here, I'm sure the airport would have something."

"I forgot all mine at home." Normally they were my lifeline, but I'd been so distracted with keeping Evan calm that I hadn't thought to pack them.

As I pulled both suitcases off the bed, a card slid down from the end of the sheets to the floor.

Christine knelt to pick it up and her eyes widened. "Damn, he's really got game," she laughed as she thrust it into my waiting hand.

*'There's no one I'd rather go through the adventures of life with than you. In the past four months you've managed to make a permanent mark on my heart. Thank you for supporting me unconditionally. Love, Evan'*

Fuck.

Three sentences and he'd managed to completely shatter me. Nathan had better have found him. I pinched my nose as I closed my eyes, but the tears still leaked through.

"Hey...I'm sure he's fine." Christine awkwardly patted my shoulder and my back before she stepped away. I knew we needed to get out of here before I lost it.

"Got everything?" she asked as I blew out a shaky breath and pulled out the handles on the suitcases.

"No..." I sighed as I followed her out the door and to the elevator, dragging two suitcases behind me with each of our carry-ons over an arm.

Evan needed to be here. He deserved to be here celebrating his successes too. Not lost in the city with no way for me to contact him.

Damn Serena. Damn social anxiety. Damn contracts and bureaucratic bullshit.

"So...uh. Diana sent over the itinerary this morning," Christine awkwardly tried to change the subject once we were in the elevator.

"OK?"

"You going to be OK handling the press solo?" she asked as she gave me a tight smile.

Shit. I didn't want to do any of this right now. "Don't really have a choice."

"She said that there'd be some people there from the Tribune," Christine explained. Great — largest distribution in the city and I was going to be completely distracted. "If you want to push it to later, you're in Chicago for four days."

"Wait, I thought Chicago was for three days?" The original itinerary was for three days.

"Oh, uh. Day four only has one signing in the morning. Evan asked for the schedule to be clear for the rest of the day."

"Why?" He hadn't said a word to me. It wasn't like him to start hiding things.

"No clue but Is was all smiley after talking to him on the phone. I'm assuming it's a surprise," she shrugged.

"Shit." I knew the bookstore we were going to last was near where he grew up; maybe he was planning to meet up with his family.

When the elevator got to the ground floor, there was a little crowd waiting for us off to the side of the lobby.

"Hey," Sam greeted cautiously and gave Christine a disarming little grin.

"Hi." It must be hot in here because I definitely saw some pink appear on her cheeks. Christine was not the type to blush.

"Sup?" Adrian gave me the male head jerk.

"Really? Get out of my way." Isobel elbowed Adrian to the side and pulled me into a hug. "How're you holding up?"

I shook my head and felt my eyes tear up again.

"He'll be OK. The second anyone hears anything you'll be the first to know. I'm sure they've found him," she assured. I hoped to God they did, but the radio silence was scaring me.

"Do we really have to do this?" Leaving town was the last thing I wanted to do right now. That troll had shown up at the worst time possible.

"As your friend. I say fuck it," Isobel shrugged. "But... as your boss, you have to get on that plane. If you don't, I can't salvage this."

"It'll be fine. He's disappeared before and he's always been fine," Adrian tried to console, but it fell a little flat.

"You're not helping," Is growled as she looked down at the two suitcases by my side.

"Do you want us to take that one?" She nodded towards the one with the blue luggage tag that belonged to Evan.

"No. I'm not sure what to do. I don't want to take it with me if he needs something." I shook my head as I felt myself getting choked up again. "God this fucking sucks."

"I can take it," Adrian offered.

"No, I'm going to see if the desk can hold it." He would have to come back here eventually, right?

"Let's go visit my friend Mr. Blithe." Christine smiled as she grabbed the handle of the suitcase and led me towards the reception desk.

"Did you find a charger?" Christine asked as she stood next to me in the convenience store near our gate. We'd made it through security alright, but we only had a few minutes before we needed to be at the gate for boarding.

"I'm not sure which to get," I told her as I looked at the wall of phone and laptop accessories.

"We don't have time for this. Just pick a farking charger and let's go," she sighed impatiently. She did not like being thrown off her schedule.

"Geez, control freak. Just go to the gate and we'll meet you there," Sam elbowed her out of the way and stepped in next to me.

Christine did not like people making her late. We still had a few minutes, but I knew time was tight.

I grabbed a water, a bag of Twizzlers and the portable charger before I paid, hurrying to the gate as they made the announcement to start boarding.

Evan and I were booked in the extra legroom business class. Sam and Christine were in the row behind us. Diana had used her travel points to upgrade to first class.

"Have you ever been to Chicago before?" Sam asked as we settled into our seats outside the gate.

"Several times," I nodded. "Minneapolis is only six hours away. My parents brought us for summer road trips."

"How about you, Chris?" I raised my eyebrow at the nickname. Usually no one could call her anything but her full name. Another intern had called her Chrissy once and no one ever saw him again.

"Nope. My parents thought the Hamptons were the only appropriate place to spend summers," she rolled her eyes. "Not that they were ever there to know."

"OK then." Sam looked over at me nervously as he took a seat next to Christine.

"Have you, Sam?" I asked as I glanced over at him.

"Yeah, once or twice. It's a cool city. Lots of museums and things to do," he nodded.

"Oh, look. They called our group number, so we can stop the painfully awkward small talk." Christine perked up as she stood and grabbed her bag. I was just ready to get on this damn plane. She led us towards the gate agent, and she scanned our digital boarding passes before we walked down the bridge to the plane.

Diana smiled as we passed her and we quickly sat down in our rows on the other side of the little curtain.

I opened the packaging for the battery-charging pack and plugged in my phone. Needing a distraction to get through this flight, I also pulled a paperback book out of my bag and the bottle of water.

Sam and Christine were sitting quietly behind me, but I could tell he was whispering things to her. I saw her mouth twitch through the crack between the seats. She was trying to act unaffected by him.

The seat beside me stayed empty as the plane filled. I was half relieved I didn't have to sit next to a stranger and half depressed the owner of the seat was still missing. This was going to be a long-ass day.

While the flight attendant went through the little safety spiel, my heart started racing as the little Apple icon lit up on my phone.

One missed call.

I opened the menu and saw an alert that I'd received a call from Evan's phone number hours ago.

My phone only had one bar, something interfering with the reception, but I tried to call Evan's number back anyways. I knew I needed to hurry. They were already closing the door and getting ready for takeoff.

"Come on." It rang once and then let out several beeps and showed the call was dropped. I tried again and it started ringing this time. It rang through and then his voicemail picked up. "Oh, come on...answer your phone!"

"Ma'am," the female flight attendant stood next to the empty aisle seat, giving me an impatient look. "I'm going to have to ask you to hang up the phone. You need to put your digital device in airplane mode as the cabin door has been closed for departure."

"Just give me a second," I begged, hating myself for being 'that person' who didn't obey the rules.

"I'm sorry. You'll need to make your call after we land." The defensive posture she took as I looked down at my phone was a little intimidating, but this was time-sensitive.

I pressed the call icon again and it rang through to voicemail... again.

"Please hang up and put it in airplane mode." Her voice took on a no-nonsense quality and I knew I'd pushed my luck far enough.

"OK, OK..." Swiping down, I pressed the little airplane icon and then locked my phone screen.

"Thank you," she nodded as she resumed her path down the aisle.

Unlocking the screen as soon as she was out of sight, I pressed the little airplane again and scrolled through the text messages. There were several from Isobel. A few from Talia, checking in. Some from my brothers. My sister-in-law Elle. But the one that stood out was from Nathan.

"You're such a rule breaker," Christine teased as she stuck her face to the space between the seats.

"Nathan texted six hours ago and then again twenty minutes ago."

"What do they say?" she asked eagerly in a quiet voice, trying not to attract the attention of the flight attendant again.

"I haven't opened them." My heart would be crushed if there still wasn't any news.

"Better hurry before the phone police comes back," she urged as she glanced over her shoulder.

I opened the menu and the first one made me sigh in relief.

*Nathan: Found him.*

But the second one made me worry.

Nathan: He finally stopped puking around 4 am. I'll get him headed in your direction after he wakes up.

Shit. What the hell happened to him?

"Is that in airplane mode, Ma'am?" She was back.

Turning my phone screen away from her, I swiped to pull down the control panel and selected the plane icon.

"It is now." She gave me a curt nod as I flashed the screen at her with a guilty smile.

I hoped that Evan was awake by the time I got to Chicago. I fully planned on calling Nathan for some answers.

I reached for my phone as soon as we arrived at O'Hare International Airport.

"Come on." Groaning as I took my phone out of airplane mode, I saw that I only had 3G coverage.

I pulled up Nathan's number and hit the call button. It rang twice and then the call failed. Evan's number now went straight to voicemail.

"No luck?" Christine asked as she peeked over the top of the seat.

"Maybe you'll have better reception once we get into the airport," Sam suggested with an apologetic smile.

We waited for the plane to arrive at the gate and the attendants to announce that we could deplane. I was exhausted, still had a headache and my phone was being difficult. Diana was waiting for us in the gate area and waved us over as we came out of the door.

"We need to get down to baggage claim and then there is a car service waiting," she told us quickly as she started walking towards the center of the terminal. "I confirmed our hotel early check in, and the venue is expecting us around 2 pm."

I tried to text Adrian, Emory and Nathan the entire walk to the baggage claim escalators. No one was responding and I hadn't gotten any more messages.

"Stupid fucking phone," I growled, feeling frustrated that I still didn't have any answers.

"Let me try Talia again," Christine held her phone up to her ear and rolled her eyes as she waited for it to ring.

"Hey!" She held a thumbs up as the four of us stood there and waited for our bags to arrive at the baggage carousel.

"Yeah, we just landed."

"Uh huh. Oh shit! Really?"

What was going on?

"What?" I mouthed and she waved me off.

"OK. I'll tell her. Guess we owe Nathan."

"Tell me what?" I asked impatiently as she hung up the phone and tucked it into her pocket.

"Evan's on the move. Nathan dropped him off at the hotel," she smiled.

"That's it? He's at the hotel? Why isn't he answering his damn phone?" My voice was a little high-pitched, but I didn't care. I wanted answers.

"About that..." she cringed.

"What now?" I asked with an exhausted sigh. My poor heart and brain couldn't take any more.

"He tripped and fell on the curb outside where they found him, and his phone ended up in a sewer grate."

"Oh, shit." Sam's eyes widened comically.

As if yesterday couldn't have already sucked enough, that was the cherry on top. "So, I have no way of contacting him?"

She shook her head and then we were interrupted by the alarm going off and the sound of luggage being thrown onto the belt.

"Let's just get to the hotel, you can re-group and we'll figure it out from there," Diana suggested as we stood waiting for our bags to appear.

I spent half the ride to the hotel, hopelessly staring at my phone. Even though I knew Evan was at the hotel and he was theoretically alright, I still found myself worrying about him. Was he even coming to Chicago?

"You gonna be OK?" Christine asked as we headed towards the elevators after Diana checked us all in. She had a small room that adjoined with Sam's on a lower floor, just down the hall from Diana. Evan and I were in a one-bedroom suite again, except I wasn't all that excited for this one. I had no clue if he'd even be showing up to share it with me.

"Meet us in the lobby at 1:45 and the car service will pick us up again," Diana told us as the elevator stopped on their floor. "Please try to relax."

"I will. Not sure how successful I'll be, but I'll try," I nodded.

Christine and Sam both sent me sympathetic looks as they exited the elevator and left me alone for the rest of the ride.

I felt the exhaustion hit me as soon as I reached the end of the hallway where the room was located. I had two hours to figure out what to do with myself.

"Ugh," I groaned as I saw the bottle of champagne with two flutes on the desk and the basket of gourmet snacks next to it. The card was from Isobel and Adrian and congratulated both of us on the release of the book and our successful collaboration.

Hot tears streamed down my cheeks and I felt terribly guilty for talking Evan into doing this tour. If we'd just gone back to Connecticut, none of this would have happened. We could have continued to hide in our bubble and escape this bullshit.

My suitcase felt like it weighed a thousand pounds as I hoisted it up onto the luggage rack in the closet. Normally, I'd have at least tried to unpack, but at this point I didn't really care.

Pushing the sheets down on the neatly made bed, I kicked off my shoes and unzipped my jeans, leaving them in a pile next to the bed. I climbed in and curled myself around a pillow, letting the remnants of my tears soak into the soft fabric.

"Oh, Evan. When are you going to get here?"

The alarm on my phone woke me from a restless sleep and I quickly poked at the screen trying to silence it. Still no messages. The screen only had a calendar alert for the appearances I was going to have to fake my way through for the rest of the day.

While I would have liked to slip on a pair of sweats and eat my way through the basket of goodies on the desk while watching sad movies, I knew I needed to get ready.

"Fake it till you make it," I grumbled as I went into the bathroom with my cosmetics bag and attempted to tame my hair and put on my face.

Twenty minutes later, I looked refreshed, but I didn't feel it. The ride down the elevator in silence helped me get into the right headspace. I'd done press appearances before. I'd done book signings and readings before. If I could make it through this, in a few hours I could climb back into that empty bed and just go back to sleep.

"Well, you look human, did you hear anything?" Christine greeted as I joined the others in the hotel lobby.

I shook my head as the four of us headed out to the car service. I knew if I started talking about Evan, the sadness would creep back in again.

"Alright crew. Let's focus. I know this won't be exactly to the original plan, but we can still pull this off." Diana was in full PR mode, always trying to put the positive spin on things.

"What am I supposed to tell the press if they ask about Evan?" Surely, they'd notice his absence when it was billed as a joint book tour.

"Obviously not that he's MIA," Christine said in a sarcastic voice.

"Yeah, I figured that much," I replied with an equal amount of sarcasm. I was sad and worried, not an idiot.

"We can just stick to a simple, semi-truthful statement," Diana explained. "Evan was feeling under the weather and unable to join us for the first day in Chicago. We're hopeful he'll be recovered soon and able to join us further along during the tour. What's working in our favor is that today is just print media. You don't have to perform for a live camera or do any in-depth interviews."

"It's just a simple Q and A," she reminded me with an encouraging smile "You've been briefed on what our public message about the book is, so just stick to the script and we'll be fine," she finished with a nod.

I hoped we...I...didn't get any nosy press members inquiring about my personal relationship with Evan. As long as it was about the book, I was sure I could handle it.

"Let's do this." Christine rubbed her hands together as she scooted over towards the door to the car.

Sam slipped out first and helped each of the ladies out, his hand hovering near Christine's back as I followed the three of them into the venue for the meet and greet.

"We'll be just over there with Diana," Sam nodded towards a side table where promotional items related to the book were already set up. Another table was set up beside it, piled high with a stack of books.

At least we didn't need to go anywhere after this; the first book signing was directly after in the same location.

"You did great," Diana praised after I was done with the first part of our obligations. "If I wasn't aware of the last twenty-four hours, it would never have occurred to me that something was off with you."

"Real subtle, Di," Christine snickered from her place with Sam near the promotional table.

Ignoring Christine, Diana continued talking to me as we moved away from the crowd. "Just get a drink, there are some snacks over there off to the side. We've got another ten minutes until we can expect people to start showing up for the reading."

I absentmindedly snacked on a cookie and drank some coffee as I tried to run the passage I was reading through my head again. Public speaking made me a little nervous, but I'd never had a problem once I got started.

Reading my own work to a crowd who was a captive audience used to be one of my favorite things about promotional tours. Something about sharing your characters with your readers for the first time made all the sleepless hours and weird schedules worth it.

It didn't feel quite the same this time. These weren't just my characters. Evan was just as much responsible for the development of Frances' character as I was.

"You ready?" Sam broke me out of my contemplative state, and I realized that the room had started to fill up.

A broad variety of people had filled the room and I wondered which ones were here because of me and which ones were Evan's readers.

"Diana is going to introduce you and then you'll start the reading," he told me quietly as he steered me towards the small podium.

I nodded and got into place off to the side, and waited for my cue.

"Now one of the authors of this amazing book will be reading an excerpt to you. We'll open it up to questions at the end." Diana finished and held her hand out in my direction. It was showtime.

I wiped my hands off on my pants and took the marked copy of the book from Christine as I walked to the podium.

"You got this," she whispered as I passed.

"Thank you for joining me here today, and for your support of this collaboration with another amazing author who was not able to join us today," I started, my voice shaking a little bit. "I know that Stone and I appreciate each and every reader who has supported our separate works and now this joint endeavor."

As I looked out at the crowd, I felt a sense of calm wash over me and I knew that while I desperately missed Evan, I could do this.

"Let me take you on a journey with our female lead. For those of you who have read the book, this scene is a pivotal one. It shows our main character Frances learning to step up and become completely self-reliant."

"Her partner had become such an integral part of her life, that when he wasn't there, she really had to find her inner strength to push through a difficult situation."

"*'Frances realized that while Dominic's role in her life was that of a submissive, she wasn't the one in control. His influence had seeped into every part of her being and having him abruptly taken away was leaving her questioning her sense of self...'*"

My brain read through the whole passage we'd picked out to share on autopilot. I was jolted back to reality when the group started to applaud after I finished reading the last sentence out loud.

"Let's open up the floor to some questions," Diana announced from her place off to my side.

"I've got a question..." Christine raised her hand from the side of the room and I braced myself for it, hoping it'd just be an easy starter to settle me down.

"Go ahead," I nodded.

"So, when developing a book like this, a certain amount of research goes into making sure things seem believable." She paused as she turned to face the other side of the room and then her eyes shot to mine.

"Go on..." My mind was curious as to where she was going with her question.

"My question is...how into character did you and your writing partner get while doing your research?" Of course, Christine would delve into a semi-difficult question first.

"As with my previous book, I used a consultant who practices the lifestyle. He helped the both of us develop scenes within the book and simulate them," I explained as I looked out to the crowd.

Christine's eyes kept drifting to the other side of the room, which was blocked from my view by a set of bookcases.

I was curious what she was looking at, but also kind of irritated that she asked a question and wasn't paying attention to the answer.

"As with people who practice BDSM, we both got a chance to learn how to use the tools of the trade in a controlled environment from both sides. It helped put us into our character's heads and feel the sensations they may have been feeling in certain scenes."

"Thanks," Christine smiled and made one last pointed glance at the other side of the room. She turned to Sam and smiled, and then Diana took the microphone back.

I saw a hand shoot up from the other side of the room, the face of the owner partially obscured by the person in front of them.

"I've got a question for you..." My eyes widened as I recognized the familiar voice.

# THIRTY-TWO

### Evan

**Boston**

The top of my mouth felt fuzzy as I started to wake up. My eyelids felt like they weighed a thousand pounds. I could smell food and hear low voices, but I was too disoriented to be able to distinguish anything.

"Is he doing alright?" a feminine voice asked quietly, it sounded like Talia.

"He's fine. Probably had an adverse reaction to the anti-anxiety meds they gave him, maybe the dosage was off or maybe he just took too much," Nathan told her in a barely audible whisper.

"Should we wake him up?" Emory's voice was louder, and I cringed as my head started to ache.

"Did you text Chase to let her know that he's alive but sick?" Talia asked.

"Yeah, a while ago, but she never responded," Nathan confirmed.

"Their plane already left. Adrian is trying to get Evan a seat on a later flight," Emory told her.

"Let's hope he can get there. It was strange seeing Chase so depressed. I don't think she laughed for the rest of the night."

"I'm such a fucking idiot," Nathan sighed. I didn't understand why he thought this was his fault. Serena didn't come with him. They didn't know my history.

"Hey, I talked to that crazy witch too. She just flipped a switch on a dime. There was no way for you to know who she was," Emory assured.

"First Grace, now Serena, am I just a psycho magnet?" Nathan growled in a low voice.

I could hear all three of them laughing.

"You knew Grace was a psycho before you ever stuck your dick in her," Talia taunted. Ew.

"So scary..." I mumbled as I rolled towards them and tried to open my eyes.

"He lives!" Talia cheered and I cringed.

"Even Evan knows to stay away from Grace," Emory teased as he pushed against Nathan's shoulder.

"Yeah, yeah." He smiled wryly.

"How are you feeling?" Emory asked quietly. I think he could tell the loud noises were jarring.

"Like I got run over by a car, and then they backed up," I told them in a hoarse voice.

"Here." Nathan held out his hand with two tablets on it, an uncapped bottle of water in his other hand.

"What are these?"

"Just Tylenol. Nothing like the little white pills that nurse gave you," he laughed.

"Oh my god. Never going near Klonopin again. Last night was scary," I cringed.

"I'm just glad it was us who found you." Emory's mouth twisted. Yeah, that could have been bad.

"Me too," I nodded.

"Let's get you up and showered so you can catch up with your girl." Talia gave me a sympathetic smile as I pushed myself to sit up on the edge of the bed.

"Fuck. I really screwed up."

"Oh honey, no you didn't. She's worried, but you can't feel bad about a crazy ex making you have a panic attack." Talia's voice was trying to be soothing, but I still felt like shit, both physically and emotionally.

"I'm sorry..." Nathan apologized again. "I didn't know who she was."

"None of you did. Chase barely even knows about her. I wish I could have just buried her in the past," I sighed. With an actual shovel.

"We've all got skeletons," Emory grinned. "Some are just kinkier than others."

"Yeah, Serena is the opposite of kinky." I laughed, glad that they weren't judging me by my horrible previous taste in women.

"You seem to have caught on fine. Mr. Pink Vibrator," Talia giggled.

I furrowed my brow as I looked at her. She gave us the vibrator, why was she...oh!

"Where *is* my suitcase?"

"Still at the hotel," she smiled. "They left it at the reception desk. But I should warn you that Christine was the one who found it in there last night while we put Chase to bed."

"Oh geez."

Cause that's not awkward.

"If you throw these on, I'll drive you over there and then take you to the airport if you want," Nathan offered as he gestured at a pile of clothes that'd been set off to the side.

"Thanks. Although I'm sure at this rate, I'll miss everything we were scheduled for today." Even if we left soon, it'd still take a while to get to the airport and then even if my flight was on time, it'd be cutting it close.

"I'm sure Chase can handle it," Talia assured.

It wasn't that I didn't think she could. "I just feel horrible that she has to."

"Get dressed, stud," she nodded at the clothes. "There's a shower in the bathroom over there. If you don't get out of here, you'll miss your next flight too."

Nathan moved the stack of clothes to the end of the king-sized bed on top of the black comforter, and the three of them left, crossing through the playroom and shutting the door to the main studio behind them.

My head still hurt, but at least I wasn't seeing double anymore. The shower helped to clear my head, but when I went to put on the clothes, I knew the three of them were just trying to mess with me. Under a clean pair of black socks and boxers were a pair of leather pants and a mesh shirt.

Rather than going out there shirtless, I just nutted up and put on the clothes. I slipped on my black dress shoes and folded up my wrinkled dress clothes from the night before. I was sure they smelled horrible.

"Told you he'd put it on. Nice pecs, Evan," Talia whistled as I walked into the photography studio.

"You guys are dicks." I could feel my lip twitch as I tried not to laugh.

"Oh, it was just for a little fun. Here." Nathan tossed me a black T-shirt and I pulled the mesh one off to catcalls from Talia.

"There's an Apple store on the way to the hotel. Let's go," Nathan told me and he stuffed my soiled clothes into a bag.

Forty-five minutes later, I had purchased a new phone and retrieved my luggage from the hotel.

"Thanks for doing this. I'd much rather it be you than Adrian." Nathan really was a nice guy. I wasn't sure what I was expecting, but you'd never be able to guess his proclivities just by hanging out with him.

"I feel bad that I took Chase to your ex and she said those nasty things to her." The fact that he still felt guilty showed me that he was a good person, and Emory was right, we all had skeletons.

"I can't believe she showed up. How did she even know about it?" I hadn't talked to her since I got my new phone number upon moving to Connecticut.

"Stole her employer's pass," Nathan said dryly. I didn't even know who she worked for anymore.

"I haven't talked to her in two years," I sighed. I wished that were still true.

"She must have heard you'd moved on. She came at Chase pretty hard. Your girl sure does have a nice right hook," he praised.

"Chase hit her? Holy shit!" No wonder I thought that Serena looked like she'd been in a fight when she accosted me outside the hotel. When I'd seen them together in the ballroom, Chase was laughing at something Serena had said. I'd obviously missed a lot after that.

He nodded with a proud smile. "She's probably sporting double black eyes right about now."

"Can't say that I care," I shrugged. "Have you heard from Chase?"

"A few missed calls and texts, but I haven't talked to her," he shook his head. "She wasn't answering her phone when I woke up, so I sent her a text. They were on the plane before you woke up."

"I hope she's not mad at me," I sighed heavily. If she was, I probably deserved it. It would be an understatement to say that last night had been less than ideal. It was a fucking shit-show!

"She's not. Just worried," he assured me as he pulled up to the terminal at the airport and popped his trunk.

"Thanks again."

"Go get your girl," he laughed, and I closed the door, pulling my suitcase out of the trunk and going to check-in for my flight. I'd be getting into O'Hare around 2:00 pm and hoped that I'd be able to make it to the book reading and signing before it was over.

By the time I reached Boston Logan International Airport and finally got through security and to my gate, I had twenty minutes until boarding.

"Let's see if I can get you to work." I unwrapped my new phone and took it out of the package. I plugged the power cord into a charging tower next to my seat and powered it up. The guy at the phone store had activated the SIM card and my phone number, but I still had to set it up and sync it with the data in the cloud.

Following the prompts, I finally got it to start syncing information and waited impatiently. I didn't have many phone numbers memorized, but I did know my sister's. I was going to have to beg for Kelly's help to get to the bookstore on time.

She answered on the first ring. "Do you need bail money?"

"I don't even get a hello?" I laughed.

"You never call me during the day, so I'm guessing you need something," she deduced. My sister may have been a pain in the ass, but she was a smart one.

"I need a ride from the airport," I sighed. Arranging a car would take more time than I had and who knew how long I'd have to wait for a cab.

"Wait...I thought you were already in the city. Didn't your flight get in at 10:00?"

I let out a long sigh.

"What did you do?" she asked. She always knew when I'd fucked things up.

"It's a long story..." A long, weird, messy story.

"I've got time. Do I need to make myself some popcorn?" she laughed. Of course, she'd want the dirt before she agreed to help me.

"Ugh...you're the worst."

"So, you don't need my help anymore? Gonna catch an Uber?" she teased.

"An Uber driver probably wouldn't give me as much shit as you, but I haven't had the best of luck with hired transport lately," I laughed. That cab driver was not amused. I still can't believe he thought I was on drugs.

"What exactly did you do? Expose yourself in a cab or something?" she laughed loudly in my ear.

"No, but I did basically get dumped in a parking lot by one." And roughly manhandled by a beefy cab driver onto a bench.

"What the hell happened?"

"I had a panic attack and he thought I was on drugs." Might as well rip off the damn Band-Aid and let her make fun of me now.

"Were you?"

I laughed at her blunt question. "Not until later."

"Anything good?" she laughed.

"Apparently Klonopin makes me act like a drunk person..." I confessed. And throw up profusely.

"Oh my god! I would have paid good money to see that." I cringed at the loud laughter coming through the phone, but I was sure I'd find it just as funny someday.

"It also makes me drop my phone in a sewer grate and get violently ill. Fun times..." I said dryly. Yesterday truly was a clusterfuck.

"Bahahahaha. Oh man, wait till mom hears this one."

"No! Please don't. You know she'll tell the book club." I shuddered. Those ladies were brutal. I couldn't even imagine the social media messages that they'd subsequently send to make fun of me. Not that I'd know how to check them.

"Speaking of, they got T-shirts made," she laughed. Great.

"Kill me now."

"Oh, come on. They're harmless...mostly. Mrs. Elkins apparently signed up for Tinder."

I cringed as I thought about my mother's over sixty-year-old friends on Tinder. "That's just wrong."

"She's gone on dates too," Kelly giggled. "Horny old cougar."

"Please make it stop..."

"Fine..." she sighed. "What time does your flight get in?"

I gave her my details and then we hung up because they'd started boarding. In a few hours, I'd hopefully be able to redeem myself. I missed the banter and teasing from Chase. She'd become such a fixture in my life that I missed her terribly after less than 24 hours apart.

I arrived in Chicago a few hours later. Kelly was waiting for me near the baggage claim. Holding a sign that said 'Stoner'.

"Haha. You're so funny," I rolled my eyes.

"Hey, I could have put 'Rock Hard' on it," she shrugged. I wouldn't put it past her to do it. Nothing embarrassed her.

"Why did I call you again?"

"Because you looove me." She reached up to pinch my cheek and then threw her arms around me. "How did you get so tall?"

"I've been taller than you since I was twelve," I laughed as I hugged her back. It was good to be home.

"You're still my wittle baby brudder," she cooed in that ridiculous baby voice.

"No more cheek pinching," I leaned back as she came at me again.

"Alright. Let's get out of here. Does this mean I get to meet Chase?" she asked eagerly. My family was excited that I'd finally found someone.

"I obviously didn't think this part through," I cringed, and she smacked me in the shoulder.

"We all would have met her in three days anyway. Mom is gonna be so jealous," she laughed, clearly happy she could rub meeting Chase sooner in mom's face. "Loved the book by the way. I read the pre-release copy Adrian sent me. Damn you guys are hot!"

"I'm not talking to you about this." I shook my head. It was already weird for her to have read my last book; this was just mortifying. And exactly why I had a pen name.

We got in the elevator to go to the parking garage after my suitcase came through.

"*So*, how many sex toys do you own now?" she asked with an entirely straight face as she popped her trunk.

"I'm just gonna go walk into traffic," I sighed as I pulled the handle on my suitcase back out and pretended to walk away.

"Ain't no shame in the game," she laughed, pulling me back by my shirt.

Once we had my luggage loaded, I decided to turn the tables on her. "So, have you met any nice guys lately?"

"*Touché*," she laughed. "I'll stop teasing... for now."

She told me all about her new position at her company on the way into downtown. By the time we reached the parking structure down the street from the venue, I was nervous.

"You're gonna be fine. Just stop sweating. You don't want to be like Ross in Friends with those leather pants," she laughed.

"I was hoping you didn't notice them," I told her as I pulled at the leather covering my thighs.

"Oh, I already snapped a pic of you in them to send to Mrs. Elkins."

"I hate you."

"Come on," she bounced in her seat as she turned off the car. "I want to see this hot girlfriend of yours."

We walked quickly down the sidewalk and quietly snuck in behind the crowd while Chase was reading up at the podium. I sat in the back corner behind a broad man wearing a baseball cap. A few quiet murmurs started as people looked over to me and obviously recognized me.

"She's killing it," Kelly whispered into my ear. "I like her. Your girlfriend is a fox."

"Shhh," I scolded her as I wiped my sweaty palms off on my shirt.

As Diana opened the floor to questions, I caught Sam doing a double take as he saw me. Christine's question was a good one... but I was dying to ask Chase one or two of my own. My hand shot up when they moved on and Diana pointed at me, smiling from ear to ear.

"I've got a question for you."

Chase's eyes widened when she heard my voice. I saw her hand tighten on the sheet of paper she was holding on the podium.

"Go ahead," she nodded as I stood up from my seat and came into her line of sight.

"I've heard that during writing this book, you spent a lot of time with your writing partner."

She nodded and a smile pulled at her amazingly sexy lips. "I did."

"Was that something you'd like to repeat with another collaboration? Maybe on a more permanent basis?" I asked, willing my voice not to crack.

"With him or...?" she teased.

My pulse was racing as I could see most of the room looking back and forth between the two of us.

"With me. Would you like to live with me in a more permanent arrangement?" And marry me and have my babies.

"Hmmm...I'm not sure," she teased as she laughed and stepped down from the podium.

"Go get her stud," my sister laughed as she stood up and pushed me away from my seat.

I walked quickly behind the crowd and Chase appeared at the top of the aisle of chairs as I rounded the end of them. Two quick steps and I had my hand wrapped around the back of her neck. Her arms encircled my waist and we took possession of each other's mouths in a crowded room full of people.

The noise of my sister whistling and Christine telling us to get a room was lost as I finally had Chase back in my arms.

We separated and I leaned my forehead down to hers as she framed my face with her hands.

"I missed you," she whispered, and I saw tears at the corners of her eyes.

"Does that mean yes?" I smiled.

"Hmm. What's in it for me?" Her eyes narrowed and I pulled her closer to me.

"Just me," I assured her quietly. "You'll get me."

"Sold."

# THIRTY-THREE

## Chase

**Chicago**

"When did you get here?" I whispered as I cuddled into his side. I hadn't realized how much comfort his physical presence gave me.

After the spectacle of our reunion, the two of us had returned to the podium to answer more questions. I couldn't believe he'd shown up — and in leather pants no less!

We were sitting on a couch towards the back of the bookstore. Diana had given us ten minutes to take a breather before we needed to go back up for the book signing. I felt bad that we'd made the readers wait, but I wasn't sorry for the time alone with Evan.

"My flight got in at 2:00. My sister drove me straight here."

"Kelly's here?" I was nervous about meeting her, but she sounded hilarious from the stories he'd told me.

"Yeah, she's dying to meet you, but I think she's hanging out with Christine and Sam right now," he smiled.

"Oh man, they'll all gang up on us," I laughed as I thought about Kelly and Christine teaming up their powers.

"We can take 'em," Evan grinned.

"Were you serious? You want to live together?" I was afraid that now we didn't have a room full of people staring at us, that he'd take it back.

"We already have been living together," he smiled.

"But permanently? How are you going to escape from me?" I laughed.

"I don't want to escape from you, that's the point," he rolled his eyes as he squeezed me tighter, kissing the side of my head.

"What are we going to do with my condo?"

He smiled as he leaned forward so he could look at me. "You own it, right?"

"Yeah, but it's not as big as your house. It'd be cramped living there together and I thought you hated being in the city."

"Why don't we keep it for now," he smiled.

"As a safety net?"

He shook his head. "No. So, we have somewhere to stay when we're in the city. Chances are we'll need to make trips in and why spend money on a hotel."

"Are you sure you're OK moving into the middle of the woods?" he asked quietly.

"I love your house. There's plenty of stuff to do around there," I smiled. "You know I'm going to make you actually leave the house now and again though — and not just to go running."

"I know." He held my hands and kissed my fingers. "As long as you're with me, I think I'll manage."

"I know we'll probably be needing more than a few minutes, but what happened?" There was half a day that he was missing I needed to be filled in.

He took a deep breath and pulled my legs up over his lap, leaning his head against the side of mine. "I had a panic attack."

"Oh my god. Why didn't you come get help?"

"Wasn't really thinking rationally. I went outside to get some air and she was just there," he shook his head as he closed his eyes.

"Grrr," I growled, thinking about his nasty ex-girlfriend.

"I heard you punched her in the face," he told me, sounding amused.

"I should have punched her in the throat...and some other places," I growled again.

His deep laugh filled the air and I smiled as he kissed the side of my head, running his fingers through my hair. "She'll probably leave us alone now that you've stood up to her."

"She better..." I nodded with a steely edge to my voice.

"So, go on," I coaxed as I tried to get back to our original subject with the limited time we had left.

"Abridged version — hopped in a cab, cab driver kicked me out at an urgent care center, a nurse gave me some anxiety meds that made me feel woozy, Emory and Nathan found me, I got sick and passed out, woke up this morning and had already missed you guys leaving, Nathan took me to the airport, Kelly picked me up and then I was here."

"Wow...I don't even know what to say," I told him with eyes wide at the truncated version of an exceptionally long night...and morning.

"It's OK, I know it was a little crazy. I felt horrible I wasn't there this morning." Worry lines appeared on his forehead and I reached up to smooth them out.

"I wasn't worried about that. I was worried about you. When I couldn't get a hold of you, it freaked me out. Christine told me you dropped your phone down a sewer?"

"I'm here now. And I bought a new phone. So it's all good." He put his fingers on my jaw and turned my face towards him, leaning in and slowly caressing my lips with his. My face flushed as I felt the familiar surge of energy I got every time he touched me. His touch was never going to fail to turn me on.

His other hand slowly slipped around my waist, running the tips of his fingers up my spine. I moaned a little against his mouth and he pulled me closer, biting at my bottom lip and then soothing it with firm strokes of his tongue.

"Do you have a spray bottle?" Christine asked loudly. "They're eating each other again."

"Guys. It's time," Sam laughed and we broke apart. Panting and staring at each other.

"Do we have to? Think we can sneak out of here?" I whispered as I leaned close to his ear.

He chuckled and leaned in close to mine. "I came all this way to help you do this. Shouldn't we go ahead since we're here?"

"Hmmm..."

His lips caressed the edge of my earlobe. "I promise I'll make it up to you tonight. I packed something fun in my suitcase."

I pulled back and bit my lip while I stared into his eyes. "I did too."

"Come on," Christine sighed. "You two can eye-fuck each other later."

Sam leaned over and whispered something in her ear and her cheeks turned pink. "We'll see you up there in a few. I can't promise this one won't come back with reinforcements if you try to run off."

"I'm willing to bet those reinforcements will be your sister," I laughed as Evan looked over at me with wide eyes.

"They totally will be. She's relentless," he nodded.

"But she brought you back to me." I kissed his cheek and stood up, straightening out my dress and running a hand through my hair.

"You look beautiful," he told me with a soft smile, and I felt myself blush under his affectionate gaze.

"Hopefully, I don't look like I've been fooling around in the back of a bookstore," I laughed as I ran one hand down the side of his head and flattened out where I'd messed up his hair.

"The whole room saw us making out less than fifteen minutes ago. Fairly sure our cover is blown."

We held hands as we walked through the aisles of shelving, finally appearing behind the table where Diana was seated waiting for us.

"So, they did find you," she teased as she stood up and gestured for us to sit down.

A tall brunette was standing on the other side of the room talking to Christine. She looked over at us and waved as she saw us. That must be Kelly. I was a little scared of what those two would come up with together.

"I'll go make the announcement. You two get your signing arms stretched and ready to go." Diana walked up to the podium and announced that we were ready to start signing books.

The small line that was already formed started to move up, and others from around the room joined it. Evan was nervously bouncing his leg next to me and I put my hand on his thigh to try to calm him.

"You OK?"

He nodded, his eyes wide. "Yeah, I'm just out of practice."

"You'll do great," I winked. "Just fake it till you make it, baby."

"I'll try." He blew out a breath and nodded, picking up his pen.

The first person in line was one of Evan's die-hard fans. He'd read all his work.

"Stone...it's such an honor to meet you. I've read every book you've ever written," he told Evan enthusiastically.

"Oh wow...thank you for being so supportive."

"Man, between me and you..." He leaned over the table as Evan started writing a message inside of the book cover. "I've been writing online under an alias for a while now, and I finally had the guts to start writing some sexier content when you branched out."

Evan's cheeks turned a little pink and he brought his hand to rub the back of his neck. This was making him nervous.

"That's great!" I chimed in as Evan's cheeks continued to redden.

"And I can totally see where his inspiration came from. If I had a hot writing partner like you...damn!" The guy leaned in towards me and wiggled his eyebrows.

"What do you do...I'm sorry, I didn't get your name...?" I asked.

"I'm a baker, and it's David. Can you sign it too?" He pushed the book towards me.

"Of course," I nodded.

He leaned down over the table again. "I've read a couple of yours too."

I smiled up at him and I could see his eyes dilate. "What did you think?"

"That I wouldn't mind you tying me up." He grabbed his book, tucking it under his arm, and winking in my direction as he held his hand out for Evan to fist bump.

"What did he say to you?" Evan asked as he leaned in close to my ear after David walked away.

I bit my lip and tried to hold in the laugh that wanted to burst out of me. "That he wanted me to tie him up."

He laughed out loud and leaned in even closer, his lips touching my ear. "You can do that to me later."

My eyes widened as my head shot in his direction. "Seriously?"

"Why not?" he shrugged. Our stare-off was interrupted by the next person in line. For the next hour, we talked to our readers and signed their book copies.

No one else offered to let me tie them up, but we did get some comments about how cute we were together.

"How long do you think before Isobel gets wind of us being outed?"

He pulled out his phone and opened the texts.

*Adrian: I thought the plan was to keep your relationship on the DL?*

"So, they already know," I laughed as Evan shrugged. Neither of us cared, but with the sex appeal of the book, they'd wanted us to appear as unattached.

"Can't say I really care. I get to shack up with the hottest woman in the room. I'm not hiding that," he told me proudly.

"How did they find out?"

His phone buzzed again, and he held it up.

*Adrian: Only 10 pictures I can find on Instagram. You two better start taking selfies. Make them steamy.*

"Hahaha. Is he trying to get us to take pictures of ourselves making out?"

"I'm game if you are..." Evan raised his eyebrows and bit his lip. God, he was adorable.

He held his phone out and pulled me into his side, hovering over my lips before he kissed me softly.

"Some of us are trying to enjoy a party here. Quit making me want to throw up." A feminine voice laughed as she flicked Evan in the forehead. The dark-haired woman I assumed was his sister was standing next to the table.

"Let's see if that gives them something to talk about," he laughed as he cropped the photo and texted it to Adrian. I just found it humorous that Evan still didn't know how to log in to any of his social media.

"You ready to finish this up and get back to the hotel?" I asked quietly. I was still exhausted.

"Yes please...but we have to ditch Kelly first." He whispered the last part.

"I heard that you douche canoe," his sister laughed.

"Maybe you were supposed to." I just watched as Evan devolved back into a teenager giving his sibling a hard time. Their back and forth was adorable.

"I like this girl," Christine smiled as she pointed her finger at Kelly.

"Of course, you do..." Evan laughed.

"Excuse me?" Oh shit. Christine was giving him the bitch face. "I'm just kidding. I think I'm gonna kidnap her and take her back home with us."

"That's not a bad idea. She could stay in my condo." My mind started planning a visit with Kelly back in Boston. I wanted to get to know Evan's family better.

"Yes!" Christine agreed.

"Maybe we should sell the condo." Evan shot me a wry smile as he reached behind my back and pulled me into him. I laid my head on his shoulder and we watched Kelly and Christine banter back and forth while Sam looked on with a smile.

"That bet still going?" Evan whispered into my hair.

"Why don't we just see how things play out..."

I could tell that Sam was enjoying watching Christine bond with someone. Usually, she was a little more sarcastic and snarkier around new people. It seemed that Kelly and she were kindred spirits.

"Think we can sneak out the back?" Evan's lips were tracing along the side of my neck and I felt the exposed skin on my shoulders break out in goosebumps.

"Seriously? You can't keep your hands off each other for like three whole minutes," Christine accused as she rolled her eyes at us,

"Just ignore her," he whispered in my ear as he placed a heated kiss behind the lobe.

"Who knew my brother had game?" Kelly laughed as she looked at him proudly.

"I sure as hell didn't," Christine laughed.

"I'm over here taking notes," Sam laughed as he mimed writing things down on his hand.

"Oh my god, Sam. No." Christine rolled her eyes as she bumped her hip into his.

He put his arm behind her back to steady them both and I saw something spark in the look they gave each other. It was only a matter of time.

"Why don't we ditch these losers and go get a drink. I know a great place down the street from here," Kelly suggested as she waved her hand and Evan and me.

"That sounds amazing. I need a drink after the fuckery of the last twenty-four hours," Christine sighed loudly. "Speaking of, how's your hand, Rocky?"

I looked down to my right hand and flexed it, feeling a tightness in my knuckles that was a remnant of last night. There was slight bruising along a few of my fingers, but it wasn't really all that painful. It was worth it to knock that bitch down a peg.

"What did you do to your hand, Chase?" Kelly asked curiously as she glanced around at all of us.

"Knocked out some bitches," Christine laughed under her breath.

"I didn't knock her out. I just might have punched someone..." I shrugged, blushing a little, "...in the face."

"Damn, girl. Who pissed you off?" Kelly laughed.

I looked to Evan and he nodded as I saw his jaw clench.

"Serena."

"Serena who...oh! Are you kidding me? Where did you see that nasty piece of work?" Kelly asked as she narrowed her eyes at her brother. Obviously, she felt the same way as the rest of us about her brother's ex.

Christine and Sam started laughing off to the side.

"She was there last night," I told Kelly quietly, glancing at Evan to look for signs of his previous anxiety returning.

"Is that why you had the panic attack?" Kelly asked Evan, sisterly concern written all over her face. She obviously knew his history with that twatapotamus.

"Yeah," he sighed as he rubbed the back of his neck.

"Well, at least your girl was there to lay a bitch out. I can't believe she'd go near you after the last time," Kelly growled.

"N...neither could I."

I looked over at Evan and frowned. He'd withdrawn into himself as soon as she was mentioned. I could tell it made him intensely uncomfortable.

"OK..." I yawned, my eyes watering a little. "I think we're ready to get to bed. I'm exhausted."

"Yeah, whatever. Hope you put in fresh batteries before you guys left, Evan," Christine teased with a pointed look at Evan.

He coughed and looked at Christine like she'd lost her damn mind.

"Batteries for what?" Sam asked curiously.

"La la la. I don't want to know. Let's go get our drink on. Later lame brother." Kelly blew kisses at Evan and ushered Christine and Sam out the door.

"You two get some rest," Diana instructed as she approached the table we were sitting at. "I need you both rested and focused for the next two days."

"Of course," I nodded as I smiled at her.

"I mean it. No more disappearing acts and please be on time."

We both nodded, then Diana shooed us out of the bookstore side entrance and into an Uber she'd ordered to take us back to the hotel.

"Would you mind terribly if we took a nap before..." Evan asked quietly as he traced a pattern on the exposed skin of my knee.

"Or I could help relax you to sleep and then after..." I raised my eyebrows at him.

"Fuck, I missed you," he whispered as he cupped my jaw with his warm hand and drew me towards him. We exchanged soft closed-mouthed kisses until a sharp clearing of a throat pulled us apart.

"Sorry, man." He apologized to the driver who was eyeing us through the rearview mirror. He didn't say anything, but I think the kissing had made him uncomfortable.

Once we arrived, Evan slid out of the car and held his hand out to help me onto the curb outside of our hotel. I was hungry, but I really wanted to just curl up with him in the big bed in our suite.

"Do you think we can find someone who will bring us a pizza?" I asked curiously as we stood on the sidewalk.

He laughed as he pulled me into his side. "I'm sure we could ask, baby. I love how your mind works. Offering sexual favors one minute...asking about pizza the next."

"You're so hot," he breathed into my ear.

"Oh, you stop it." His stomach growled. And I laughed as I put my hand on it. "See! You're hungry too."

"Let's go. We can stop at the desk. Maybe we can bribe someone to bring up some Giordano's," he conceded.

Twenty minutes later Evan and I were both moaning uncontrollably on the couch back in our suite.

Pants had been unbuttoned...

My bra had been removed...

And I was mid foodgasm as he fed me his deep... dish pizza.

"Oh... muh... gah...." I moaned as I took another bite. I missed pizza in the Midwest. The thin stuff on the East Coast couldn't compare.

"So good... this is what I think of when I imagine home," he sighed as he eyed the pizza adoringly.

I giggled as I readjusted my legs across his lap and leaned my head on his shoulder. "Not your family? Just pizza?"

"You've met Kelly," he laughed.

"She's awesome. I always wanted a sister," I sighed. Two older brothers were a lot to grow up with.

"You can have mine," he laughed.

"Maybe we can share."

He took our plates and put them on the table in front of him and lifted me up by the waist, turning me to straddle him.

"You know I love you..." He swallowed hard before he licked his lips and sighed.

"I do," I nodded. "You alright?"

"I might have done something." I raised an eyebrow at him. He looked a little guilty.

"Which was?"

"On the last day in Chicago..."

I nodded. "The day where we have mysterious plans?"

He nodded as he rubbed his thumbs along the waistband of my panties. "I invited our families to come to see us."

I wasn't expecting that. My brothers and their partners both had full-time jobs, my dad still worked. They'd all implied on the phone that they wouldn't have time to come visit while I was close.

"Really?"

"You're not mad?" he asked nervously.

I shook my head as a wide smile spread across my face. My hands cupped his jaw and I leaned forward to place a soft kiss on his lips. "Of course not. I have no idea how you managed to do it, but I'll take it."

"I knew you missed seeing them being halfway across the country," he said quietly.

"You're amazing," I sighed as I cupped his jaw and looked into his eyes.

"We'll see if you're still saying that when you're trying to escape my parents' house full of people," he laughed.

"As long as my niece is there I won't even notice," I smiled.

"Just your niece? No one else can hold your attention?" he teased.

I hummed as I pretended to think about it. His hands pulled my hips flush with his and he flexed up into me. "No one else is coming to mind."

"Hmm," he hummed. "Maybe I need to remind you who else will be there..."

I arched my back and my head fell backward as he nuzzled into my neck, running his nose and lips slowly up the underside of my jaw.

"Mmm. Miguel isn't into girls," I sighed with a little moan at the end. While one of my favorite people in the world, my brother's husband was sickeningly into him.

Evan ghosted his lips along the soft skin at the front of my throat, earning himself another moan. "Oh god..."

"Hmmm...he won't be there either..." he whispered as he sucked on the skin where my collar bones met.

"Fuck...Evan," I panted as he traced his palms up my sides, cupping my breasts through the material of my dress.

"So, you do remember who I am," he chuckled as he bunched the fabric up at my waist and slipped his hands underneath.

"Yes...yes, yes, yes..." I chanted as he dragged his thumbs over my nipples. My hips rocked against him, the soft slide of the leather of his pants a contrast to the zipper dragging along the center of my panties. I was hyper-aware of the rough scratch of it through the thin satiny material covering my core. I could vaguely feel the hardness he was hiding beneath, but I ached to feel him fully against me.

"Pants...off..." I moaned as he leaned forward and captured one of my peaks between his teeth through the thin material.

"Just wait a minute..." he whispered before he used his teeth to tug on it. "Let me enjoy these."

I was writhing on his lap, the bite of the zipper almost unbearable as he continued to tease me. The wetness between my legs had seeped through the material and I could feel it sliding against the leather.

"Ooohhh..." I moaned as he pinched and bit and sucked, sending shockwaves through my body.

"Let's get this out of the way," he murmured as he pulled my dress up and away from my chest, carelessly tossing it behind me.

"God, yes," he groaned as he cupped my tits in both his large hands and caressed them, licking his lips before he dove back in.

I couldn't control the movements of my hips as I squirmed in his lap, desperately wanting him inside of me.

"Pants...off...now..." My command was half moaned, half growled, as he bucked up into me.

I rose up on my knees and tugged at his waistband, sliding his pants partially down his hips. He released my chest and lifted his hips, helping me work the material down, his solid erection jutting out of his boxer briefs into the space between us.

"I can't wait," I moaned as I gripped him with one hand and pulled my panties aside with the other.

"Yes..." I cried out as I slowly eased myself down onto him, the sensation of being stretched by him causing both of us to moan loudly.

"Uhhh..." he groaned as I slowly lowered my hips, rocking then in slow, steady motions until he was able to slide all the way inside, his cock completely encased by me.

My forehead dropped forward to rest on his, as I gripped the back of the couch with one hand and the side of his neck with the other.

Our panted breaths mingled between us as I rotated my hips and began to rock in his lap. He was so impossibly hard inside of me, pulsing and throbbing as I began to pick up speed.

"Fuck me faster," he breathed out into the curtain of my hair as I pushed the both of us closer to the brink.

His large hands gripped my hips, and he clutched the side of my panties in one hand as the other encouraged me to pick up the pace.

"Ohhh...ohhh...yeeeesss..." My voice echoed in the air around us as I felt myself start to pulse around him.

"Oh, Chase...god, yes, fuuuck," he growled as he flexed his hips up into my movements, causing him to hit even deeper inside of me.

All I could think about was the way we looked as I stared down with hooded eyes at where we were joined. Each movement was driving both of us closer and closer to experiencing transcendence.

"I'm...I'm...ohhh..." I moaned loudly.

"Come on, baby. Cum on me. I want to feel you," he encouraged.

My hips frantically slid back and forth, his hard cock sliding into me with a bruising force.

I was so close.

"Yes...yes...yes..." I chanted as I tilted my hips and he started sliding along the perfect place to press on my clit.

My eyes clamped shut and I concentrated on the feeling as he tightened his hold on the material partially covering me. Stars appeared behind my eyelids as I started to pulse on him, my hips jerking as my orgasm rushed through me.

"God, yes..." he moaned as he used his hands to force me down onto his rock-solid member repeatedly.

"Uhhh..." he groaned as I could feel him pulse inside of me. The movements of our hips slowed as we heaved in quick breaths, sweat building up on our brows.

"I love you..." I whispered as I lowered my forehead to his shoulder and encircled his neck with my arms.

"That was...*fuck*...I love you so much," he panted as he put his arms around my back and held me tightly to him. His shirt was warm and slightly sweaty as I cuddled up to his chest, inhaling his masculine scent.

My eyes closed and I felt my body relaxing as our heartbeats slowed back to normal. I could feel his pulse point on my lips as I cuddled into him and it was a steady cadence that matched mine.

He sighed as he reached a hand up to cup the back of my head, slowly combing his fingers through the curls on the back of my head.

"You can't fall asleep," he whispered as he turned his cheek into mine. His stubble tickled my neck and I squirmed against him, huffing out a laugh. "Stop moving or we'll have a problem."

"Who says it's a problem?" I laughed as I kissed along his neck, stopping to run my tongue along the dip in his clavicle.

"I don't think I can again," he laughed, and I felt him shift underneath me, slipping out of me.

"I'm so tired," I whined as I snuggled back into his neck.

"You know we have this thing in the other room called a bed..." he teased.

"Too much work."

"Come on sleepy," he laughed as he sat up and started to stand up, lifting me by the backs of my thighs.

"Hey! Quit it, you're going to hurt yourself," I scolded.

"I'm fine, Chase," he laughed as he helped me stand in front of him. I pulled my stretched-out panties back into place as he watched me, running a fingertip along one of my nipples.

"You might want to pull your pants up, stud." I laughed as I looked down and saw he was already at half-mast again. "Thought you were tired."

"I am...but he didn't get the message. What do you expect when I'm staring at those?" He reached forward and caressed the underside of one breast, groaning as my nipple pebbled.

"Let's go." He pulled his shirt over his head and pushed off his shoes. The leather pants and boxer briefs were next, and then he was standing in front of me totally nude and hard.

Evan turned me around and lightly pressed on my back with his hand to guide me into the bedroom.

"I thought we were going to sleep," I laughed as his hand reached down and massaged one of my ass cheeks as he followed me into the bedroom.

"We can go to sleep after," he told me in a rough, low voice.

"Oh, yes," I giggled. "Talk dirty to me."

He grasped my waist and pulled me back into his chest, his right hand cupping my neck. "I'm gonna fuck you so hard you can't stand tomorrow. That dirty enough for you?"

"Ohh..." I moaned as his other hand possessively cupped my pussy.

His fingers pressed into the wetness and roughly slid over my clit. I moaned as he worked me over, his hips pressing his hardened cock into my back. "Fuck you're so wet."

"Oh...that feels good," I sighed as my breath caught.

"Get on the bed." He released me and walked over to my open suitcase as I scooted up the bed with my back propped against the pillows.

"Ah-ha!" he laughed as he turned around with a small set of leather handcuffs and the small rabbit vibrator I'd hidden in there.

"Well, isn't he cute..." His eyes danced with mirth as he turned the little toy around in his hand. It was different than the pink one Talia gave us before, another gift, but a little more compact in size. It had a matte black finish, only a few inches long with a little rabbit shaped tip. Evan climbed up onto the end of the bed and sat back on his knees in front of me. "Should we see how well the bunny gets along with the pussy?"

For someone who was so tired...he sure was getting a lot of enjoyment out of this. "You're such a goofball. I thought it was my turn to tie you up?"

"Next time." He winked and wiggled his eyebrows at me. "Give me your wrists."

I held them out in front of me and he carefully latched the buckles after he'd enclosed the soft leather around my wrists. He rose up on his knees and scooted back a little, grasping my hips with both hands and pulling me towards him. The pillow near my head was tossed aside so I was lying flat on the duvet covering the bed.

"Put your arms above your head."

As I slowly raised my arms up and settled them above my head, he spread my legs apart, pushing them wide and anchoring my feet flat on the mattress.

He pushed the button on the bottom of the toy, turning it on to the lowest setting, and slowly brought it to barely glance against the hood of my clit.

"Oh god," I moaned as I gripped the fabric above my head and shifted my hips toward the barely-there hum of the ears on my sensitive skin.

"You like that?" he asked as he watched his hand on my heated flesh. He pressed it a little harder into me and watched as my hips jumped off the mattress. I was still so wet from earlier, so the little ears of the rabbit slid effortlessly against me, leaving a satisfying hum through my core in their wake.

"Do you want more?" he asked as he briefly glanced up into my eyes. I nodded as I laid there moaning and panting, completely at his mercy. "What do you need?"

"You...oh..." I moaned as he clicked the base again and the vibrations increased, a flood of arousal making me even wetter.

Evan shifted forward again, lifting one leg, and then the other to rest on the tops of his thighs, our hips almost flush with each other.

He set the buzzing vibrator on the mattress next to my hips as he grasped himself with one hand and slowly eased inside of me.

"Yes..." I half moaned, half sighed as he slipped all the way inside and then reached over to pick up the abandoned toy.

"Fuck, you're so wet." He tilted his hips back a little, which in turn tilted my pelvis up. He slowly brought the tips of the rabbit ears back to my clit and circled the sensitive skin as he started to make shallow thrusts into me.

My breathing was harsh to my ears as I held onto the duvet and let the sensations wash over me. I could feel myself getting closer as the tandem sensations of him sliding inside of me and the toy pressing into me became overwhelming.

"Evan..." I whimpered as I felt myself so close to the edge but unable to go over with his gentle movements. "Harder..."

"You want me to fuck you harder?" He pulled back and snapped his hips forward, my bound hands gripping the fabric harder to keep my head from driving into the padded headboard.

"God...yes..." I moaned as he reached forward with his free hand to grasp the headboard above me and rose up slightly on his knees.

My lower back lifted up off the mattress and he began to increase his pace, driving his cock into me in steady thrusts as he tilted the vibrator and pressed it into me more firmly.

"Shit..." he groaned as he stared down at me, seemingly transfixed by the movement of my breasts with each snap of his hips. My keening cries filled the air around us as he drove me closer and closer to my peak.

"So close..." I panted as I clamped my eyes shut. My back arched up off the bed as I rode out the intense pulses of my orgasm, the buzzing of the toy directly on my clit making the spasms just shy of painful.

"Oh god...oh god..." I cried out as he continued to pound into me, his chest glistening with sweat from his efforts.

"Almost there..." he groaned as he continued to hold the vibrator down where we were joined. I watched the muscles in his arm flex as he gripped the headboard tightly, using it as leverage to drive into me with powerful thrusts.

"Fuck..." His neck arched as he threw his head back, his hips pulsing frantically as he came inside of me.

"Ohhh..." I moaned as I felt my pussy continue to clench him inside of me, a second climax bringing tears to my eyes.

My entire face was numb and tingly as he pulled his hand away, clicking the base of the rabbit and tossing it to the side.

"You OK?" He asked quietly as he leaned his head against the arm bracing him above and stared down at me.

"I don't know," I giggled as I felt the tears that had pooled in the corners of my eyes slide down the side of my face.

"OK, now it's time for sleep," he laughed as he tried to catch his breath.

My eyes drifted closed as I felt him shift back, pulling out of me and then reaching up to unfasten the cuffs on my wrists. He gently massaged the skin and then helped me sit up as he pulled the covers down behind me. I watched with heavily lidded eyes as he tossed the cuffs to the nightstand.

"Lift up, baby," he urged as he pulled the comforter the rest of the way back and helped situate me under the covers. I felt his warm chest against my back as he nudged me to my side and slipped in behind me.

My mind was foggy as he kissed my shoulder and encircled me in his arms, his hand possessively cupping my chest. "I love you."

"Mmm...me too..." I mumbled, and then I was blissfully asleep, my whole world holding me tightly.

# THIRTY-FOUR

### Evan

**Chicago**

The last two days had been surprisingly enjoyable. Chase and I had slept soundly after I'd handcuffed her and fucked her hard in that amazing hotel bed. The next morning we'd met up with Diana bright and early for another bookstore appearance and signing.

There'd been a little buzz in the local literary circle with the pictures that'd surfaced from the other night. It'd all been positive, and I loved that Chase was finally getting the recognition she deserved. She'd always had positive press before but had been written off as only a romance writer. Having her name tied to mine had awoken the critics to her ability to tell a suspenseful story as well.

It'd also been humbling to have a few of my readers tell me that they'd been impressed that my writing had grown. I hadn't even realized that my last few books had lacked a depth of emotion until Chase came along and shook up my world.

This morning we were driving to a bookstore that was close to my parents' house on the north side of Chicago.

"You doing OK?"

I glanced over at her out of the corner of my eye. We were flying solo this morning. Sam and Christine had stayed downtown to sightsee. Diana had conference calls all morning, so she briefed us on the store we'd be at and sent us on our way.

"Yeah," I sighed as I tried to loosen my grip on the steering wheel. We'd rented a car for the day, so we didn't have to rely on hiring a ride-share.

Kelly had already headed up to my parents' house to cook for the crowd we'd be expecting this afternoon when Chase's family drove in.

"Just thinking about this afternoon. I hope your brothers don't try to murder me."

Her rich laugh filled the car and I smiled despite my nerves. "They're not going to kill you."

"You know they've read the book?" I pointed out, worried that they'd think I was taking advantage of their baby sister. She'd told me how protective they were.

"Oh, they definitely have," she nodded with a smirk. "I got some interesting text messages from Drew and Miguel the day after they got their copy."

"Shit. They're not mad, are they?" I asked anxiously. She started laughing hysterically and my palms started to sweat, slipping on the leather of the steering wheel.

"No! Calm down. They were sending me links to leather dominatrix outfits," she giggled.

I took a deep breath and let out a nervous laugh. "Did you order any?"

"No, you nut. But I may have packed some lacy things inside the secret compartment in my suitcase," she shrugged.

My eyes widened and I gripped the steering wheel as I felt a twitch in my pants. I'd seen her in sexy underwear, and no underwear, but not dressed in nothing but lingerie yet.

"You're going to make me hard," I groaned as I tried to think of anything but Chase in barely-there lacy lingerie.

"And what did Ethan think of the book?" He was the one I was worried about. Ethan was the oldest and from what Chase had told me, the most resistant to her dating when she was younger. I could only imagine what he thought of me.

"Oh, you don't have to worry about him. He's already one of your loyal fanboys. He probably thinks I corrupted your art," she said in an annoyed tone and rolled her eyes dramatically as I glanced over at her.

I wasn't sure how to respond to that. I'd never expected her family to be fans of my work. "So how big of a fan are we talking?"

"Well, Elle may have teased him before they found out about you, that you were on his freebie list."

"His what?" I had no idea what list she was talking about.

"You know how sometimes couples joke that if they ever met a celebrity that they'll give their partner a free pass..." she trailed off.

"Wait. I thought Drew was the gay brother?"

"He is," she smiled as she tried to hold in her laughter.

"I'm not even sure how to respond to that," I told her honestly. I'd never been told I was on anyone's sex list before, much less the straight brother of the woman I was dating.

"Just be prepared for Elle to roast him. She's the sweetest person but she loves to give my brother a hard time," Chase told me in an amused tone.

"No wonder the two of you get along so well," I smiled over at her.

"You know you love it when I taunt you," she smiled back.

Six months ago, my life was devoid of any affection other than my immediate family, and even that was at a calculated distance. I'd resigned myself to a life of solitude in the woods with my words. Those same words that could craft a story read by millions couldn't come close to describing the way Chase made me feel. "I just know that I love you, and I'm grateful for you being in my life."

She reached over and clasped my hand that was closest and interlaced our fingers. I knew that she felt the same way. She'd always been much more social than me, but sometimes despite being surrounded by people, you can still feel alone.

When I was with Chase, I never felt alone.

"Are you sure you're not the Romance writer?" she teased as she ran her thumb over my knuckles.

"Pretty sure," I laughed. "If it weren't for you, I'd still be putting tab A into slot B. B being my hand."

Her laughter filled the car, and she laid her head against my shoulder. "You can put your tab into my slot any day."

"Are you sure you're ready to meet my mother's friends? I can take you back to the hotel," I asked warily.

"Not a chance." She shook her head as she bounced in her seat excitedly. "I can't wait to meet them."

"They're...a little much," I told her hesitantly. That might be an understatement, but they loved my mother fiercely.

"They just want to support you."

"Um, I'm pretty sure that Mrs. Elkins is a cougar," I laughed.

"So, she probably wants to be your Mrs. Robinson. I don't blame her. You're hot," Chase laughed.

A shudder ran through me at that thought. When I was younger Mrs. Elkins had been very pretty, but she was probably over 70 now. For my part, that was a hard pass.

"I'd rather my older women be in their thirties."

Chase grinned over at me, shaking her head. "Sweet talker."

"You can be my Mrs. Robinson."

She pinched my armpit and I jerked away from her touch. "I was in preschool when you were born, not college, you perv."

She snuggled back into my arm and we sat quietly listening to music the rest of the drive to the bookstore. It was in a neighborhood called Germantown on the north side of the city. My parents' house was only about fifteen minutes away.

I was able to find street parking nearby. After I parked the car and killed the ignition, I took a few deep breaths before I moved to open the door.

"It'll be fine," Chase assured me, knowing my nerves were threatening to get the best of me. "No crazy old ladies are going to scare me off. If I survived your bitchtastic ex-girlfriend, I can survive them."

"You say that now," I warned. She hadn't met them yet.

"Bitches better back off my man," she giggled as she squeezed my hand.

I knew she could handle herself, but it still made me uncomfortable that my mom's friends read all my books. I'd hoped that having a pen name would give me some anonymity, but my mom couldn't help telling all of them.

Now with the last two books, I was terrified what their reactions would be. I knew that they liked to read racy books sometimes... but it was still going to be hard to look them in the eye. I'd known most of them since I was a little kid and a few of them had kids my age.

"OK, now or never. I'll chicken out if we don't go inside."

My palms were sweating as I followed Chase into the store. I'd been inside quite frequently when I'd been home before, but it was weird knowing I was here for people to see me.

"Great, you two are here," the shopkeeper, greeted us as we walked inside. "We've really been looking forward to this."

She looked vaguely familiar; I was fairly certain I'd seen her before. "Evan, it's good to see you again. You may not remember me; it's been about a decade since I saw you last."

She laughed as I squinted at her. " I'm Dorothy — Dottie for short. I helped teach part of your AP English class. Mrs. Farmer is a friend of mine."

I'd been in all Advanced Placement classes my senior year; our teacher had contracted pneumonia that left us with a sub for most of the last part of the first semester.

"Wow, that's been a long time," I told her with an impressed nod. I couldn't believe she remembered me being in that class.

"It has," she laughed. "I'm glad to see you retained some of what I taught you over the years."

"Folks around here are pretty proud of what you've made of yourself." She squeezed my shoulder and then beamed a huge smile at Chase. "Don't tell this one's mother, but I'm so happy you pulled him out of his comfort zone. He's really grown as a writer with those last two books."

"Your secret is safe with me. He's helped my writing as well," Chase told her with a proud smile in return.

"Do you have another book coming out soon?" Dottie asked with curiosity.

"I do," Chase nodded. "My editor is working on editing the complete manuscript right now. Should be out in a few months."

"She basically wrote the whole book in six weeks. It was amazing to watch," I gushed as I looked over at my phenomenal girlfriend.

"I remember being amazed by watching a very determined young man sit with his laptop for hours on end in that corner over there." Dottie nodded towards my favorite corner in the shop. I had spent quite a bit of time when I was writing one of my earlier books in Chicago. It'd been before I officially made the move to Boston. Before I'd met Serena.

I shook off the bad memories she conjured up and turned my attention back to Dottie.

"I'm sure your fan club will be here soon, but why don't you two get the table situated where you'd like. My assistant set up the promotional materials Diana sent up."

Dottie excused herself to go talk to the few customers milling around and Chase came with me over to where we'd be doing the book signing. The store wasn't overly large, but it was packed full of all sorts of books.

"So much for being anonymous," I sighed once Chase and I were alone.

"You can only hide it so much when your picture is inside the back cover. I know I can't hide when I'm back home either," she laughed.

"I'm sorry in advance for whatever they say to you." It seemed like everyone supportive in my life enjoyed embarrassing the crap out of me.

"I'm hoping they tell me a few embarrassing Evan stories." Chase rubbed her hands together and shot me a mischievous smirk. She did love having the dirt on people.

"Kill me now," I sighed.

"Oh, come on, I'm sure you were adorable. I'm counting on Kelly to pull out all the naked baby pictures later," she giggled.

"Don't think I won't enlist Elle to do the same for you," I threatened.

"Girl has got my back. She'll never tell," she grinned.

As the time got closer to when the reading was supposed to start, the shop began to fill up. I saw a few familiar faces in the crowd and realized that, in isolating myself, I'd neglected the people I knew who supported me.

Old friends from high school, neighbors who watched me grow up, family friends. I saw all of them among the people milling about. It simultaneously made me feel warm inside and terrified. There were some pretty taboo things in my last two books, and I was going to have a hard time making eye contact with some of them.

"Alright ladies and gentlemen, let's settle down and let these two get started." My pulse raced as Dottie herded everyone to the front of the shop and handed Chase the microphone.

"Thank you all for joining us today. I, for one, am excited to be in Stone's hometown. I'm sure some of you knew him before he was this ridiculously successful, handsome, professional..."

I heard some laughter filter through the crowd and someone cough, "Evan is a dork." I was sure it was one of the guys I used to play soccer with.

"But I am honored to call him both my partner in writing and now my partner in life."

The ladies towards the back all 'awww'ed' at her words. I knew I felt a rush at her publicly claiming me.

"The last several months have been a whirlwind for us both, but I do know that he has made my writing better. He's made me push myself and try to grow as a writer."

I grabbed the mic from her on an impulse and swallowed hard before I spoke. "And we all *know* she's made my writing better."

More laughter filtered through the crowd and I smiled as I returned the microphone to Chase.

"That's probably enough of us gushing over each other," Chase laughed as she grabbed my hand and winked at me. "Let's talk about this book and our female protagonist Frances."

Chase read a passage like the one that we'd used before, her voice calm and strong, the whole room captivated by her.

"That was wonderful Chastity, let's open it up to some questions." Dottie smiled as she borrowed the microphone from Chase.

"I've got one." A tall slender figure stepped forward from the back of the room, and I immediately recognized Dorrie Elkins, one of my mother's best friends. "This is for Chase, I mean, Chastity."

Chase smiled as she shook her head. "That's OK, I think our cover is a little blown around here."

The crowd chuckled.

"So, we know that you've been working with erotic fiction for several years, and quite fantastically, I might add," Mrs. Elkins complimented. "But my question is, how does a collaboration work with two authors from such different genres? Do you each write certain parts and try to combine them? Or do you write it all together?"

"Well, for this book, we developed a structured story outline first, mapping out the scenes we wanted to include, and then we decided which one of us felt comfortable writing a draft of that scene," Chase explained.

"Then we read the scene together and edited as we needed to. Luckily, our styles seemed to fit together well," I added as I leaned in close to Chase.

"Seems that's not the only thing that fit well together with you two," Mrs. Elkins laughed and I felt my cheeks heating up.

"I've got one too," said Sharon, another of my mother's old friends, excitedly, as she pulled Dorrie's arm in her direction. "What kind of research went into this book?"

I knew that one of them was going to ask this question. I felt my throat tightening up and knew I wouldn't be able to answer this one.

"I have a consultant that I've worked with before that helped teach Evan about the BDSM lifestyle," Chase explained calmly. "He worked with us to develop Frances' inner dialogue and some of the scenes we included."

"Was there any first-hand experience you two drew from in the book?" Sharon asked with an innocent smile on her face.

I coughed and rubbed the back of my neck, my eyes dropping to the floor. I could hear low laughter coming from the third woman standing in the back, my neighbor Hazel, with her hand covering her mouth.

"We did have to learn quite a bit to get into her head, but I'd rather not reveal any trade secrets on this one," Chase winked, successfully deflecting their inquiry about our sex life, but I knew it'd take a while to calm my flaming cheeks.

The rest of the questions were tame, but Chase still fielded most of them. She was so much better with the crowd than I was.

"OK, you've got five minutes to regroup and then we'll get started with signing," Dottie told us once the questions were done. "I'll go ahead and have them start coming to the register to purchase their copies."

Chase pulled me down a quiet aisle and pushed me up against a shelf in the back corner of the store. She cupped my cheeks with her hands and forced me to look in her eyes. "You did great. I know you're not used to those types of questions, but don't be embarrassed. People are simply curious by nature."

"I just don't want my mother's friends speculating on my sex life. It's all kinds of weird."

"Honey, you know your sister has said they're a little raunchy in that group, I wasn't surprised by some of the questions, to be honest," she smiled.

"It's still embarrassing," I insisted, a little shudder running through me. They did not need to know those kinds of personal details about me.

"No. What'd be embarrassing is..." Chase started.

"Your older brother reading a book you wrote, with your boyfriend he didn't know about, whose main character is a badass Dominatrix?"

Chase spun around as two men, probably a little older than she was, walked down the aisle towards us.

"Oh my god. When did you two get here?"

The one who'd spoken was just slightly taller than Chase and shared a few of the same traits. He had bronzy reddish hair and more freckles than she did, but it was obvious by his face shape and nose that they were related.

This must be her middle brother Drew based on the matching wedding band of the handsome guy he was with. His husband had dark features and chocolatey brown eyes, his hair a rich shade of brown.

"Are you two gonna gossip all day or do we get to meet your man?" Drew asked impatiently. "We did ride six hours in a minivan to come see you."

"Where's my baby?" Chase asked excitedly.

The darker-haired man, who I was assuming was Miguel, put his hands on his hips and raised an eyebrow at Chase. "You better be talking about me."

"Oh, you are too, but I was talking about the smaller ginger-haired one who has all of you wrapped around her finger," she laughed.

"She's back at the hotel with Elle and Ethan. We stole their ride to come surprise you," Chase's brother explained, and I saw her mouth form a little pout.

"Surprise!" Miguel cheered and held out his arms. "Now give me a hug."

Chase stepped away from me and opened her arms, drawing first her brother and then Miguel into a three-way hug.

Miguel kissed her on the cheek and then leaned back to say something. "You too lover boy. Get in here."

Chase held out her hand towards me and I grasped it. "Evan, this is my brother Drew and his husband Miguel."

"I...uh, I'm glad...it's nice to meet you." I fought the urge to facepalm. Apparently, I'd forgotten how to speak.

"Oh, the pleasure is all ours. Chase has finally met her match," Drew laughed.

"I don't know about that," I told him quietly. I wasn't sure I'd ever been her match, but I was in this as long as she wanted me.

"We do. She won't tell us any gossip. That means she must really like you," Miguel grinned as he shook Chase a little in his arms.

"And I'm not going to." She stuck her tongue out at them and put her arm around my waist.

"Put that away girl, I don't need to know what freaky stuff you get up to with your little writing partner," Miguel laughed as he made a disgusted face.

"Oh, he's not little," she winked, and Miguel's eyes widened.

"Really don't need to know that," Drew laughed and cringed as he looked over at me. "You're nice to look at, but I don't need to know details about who Chase plays hide the sausage with."

"Are you two ready to get started?" Dottie interrupted our little reunion as she peeked her head around the corner.

"Of course, sorry for holding you up," I smiled at her and looked over to Chase who nodded. Dottie headed back towards the front and Miguel started laughing.

"What's so funny?" Drew asked his husband.

"Better watch out for the cougars, Chase. They're eyeing your man," he laughed.

"Speaking of cougars," Chase giggled.

"Don't remind me," I groaned. My mother's friends were still roaming free in the bookstore.

"We'll wander around. Go do your thing," Miguel insisted.

"You ready?" Chase asked as she turned to face me. I felt like she was always asking me that, and my answer was always the same.

"No."

"Well, too bad. This is the only thing keeping me from squishing some cute ginger baby cheeks, so let's go," she told me as she grabbed my hand and tugged me towards the front of the shop.

"You better listen to her or she's gonna start asking for her own ginger babies," Miguel laughed. And I wanted to give them to her one day, but I needed to get her to agree to marry me first.

"Haha. Don't scare the guy," Drew laughed as he pulled Miguel into his side.

We hadn't really discussed children, but I wasn't scared off by the prospect. I just didn't want to share Chase yet. Maybe someday.

"It'll take a lot more than babies to scare me away from Chase."

"Damn, he's smooth," Miguel cooed.

"You two try not to get kicked out and we'll see you in a little while," Chase warned them.

"I make no promises," her brother laughed as he put his arms around Miguel's waist and nuzzled his neck.

"Let's get up there before your fan club starts a riot," Chase urged as we resumed our path back towards the front.

The line for the signing table was wrapped around the small cafe and down one of the aisles of shelving. The first dozen or so people who came through were nice and super-supportive of Evan. He talked and kept engaged with people, but as the book club ladies started to creep up in the line, he started to stammer more.

"And finally, it's our turn," Dorrie smiled widely as she stopped in front of us.

"We've been waiting for this day since your mom said you'd be coming to town," Hazel nodded. "We may have called your publisher to suggest this shop."

"They said they'd love to have Evan come back to his roots," Sharron added.

"Not that we wouldn't have come to find you in the city, but we've been buying your books from Dottie for years," Dorrie explained as my head just bounced between the three of them.

"So, are you planning on introducing us to your gorgeous lady friend?" Sharon asked, wiggling her eyebrows.

"From those pictures I saw on Instagram, I think they're a little more than friends," Hazel laughed.

"You don't write smut like this if you haven't been doing some research," Dorrie winked, and I wanted to disappear underneath the table.

I sat there and just watched them as they kept talking over each other. I wasn't sure how to even get a word in edgewise.

"Sign me up for that kind of research," Hazel laughed loudly.

"My husband looked at me like I was crazy when I bought him handcuffs for his birthday," Sharon told us. "We can't all have young bucks like Dorrie."

My eyes widened as they just kept going. Chase had the biggest smile on her face as she kept glancing from them to my continuously reddening cheeks.

"I told you that Tinder would be worth my time, Hazel, but no, you refused to believe me," Dorrie taunted.

"I don't think any of us expected a swipe right connection with that fine specimen," Hazel whispered as she nodded towards the door to the shop. There was a blond man with some gray creeping into his hair staring in our direction. He was tall and fit; I was impressed that Dorrie hadn't found a creepy one.

"Wow. He is very handsome. Nice catch," Chase laughed as she introduced herself and started signing their stack of books.

"He's French. I knew I had to keep him after the first date. The things that man can do with his tongue," Dorrie told her as she leaned in.

I coughed as they all looked in my direction and broke into raucous laughter.

"Wonder what he thinks of our shirts," Hazel mused as she straightened out the plain gray long-sleeved blouse she was wearing.

"I don't care what my husband thinks of the shirt. He said I can get my motor going however I'd like to as long as I come home to him to get my tune-ups," Sharon laughed.

"I'm sure he's ready to check your oil with his dipstick," Hazel giggled. "Especially with that new prescription he came home with."

"Oh my god. You ladies are amazing," Chase laughed. I was at a total loss for words.

"We can get you an extra shirt if you'd like," Dorrie offered, laughing as they all looked at each other.

"Should we show him?" Hazel smiled as she looked over at me.

"Of course," Sharon laughed loudly and then winked at me.

"You ready for it?" Dorrie asked with a hint of mischief in her voice.

"Yes!" Chase agreed and sat up a little straighter in her chair.

The three of them turned around simultaneously and I barked out a laugh. The backs of their shirts read, 'Stone's Snow Leopards' in bright pink script, surrounded by black leopard spots.

"You're not quite old enough to be a snow leopard, Chase, but we'll still make you an honorary member," Hazel told her.

"Snow leopard?" I had no idea what she was talking about.

"Snow leopard, silver fox.... we know we've still got it," Dorrie laughed as she turned and fluttered her fingers at her Tinder boyfriend on the other side of the room. He blew a kiss back and Hazel giggled. Oh my god. Kelly was right. Dirty old cougars!

"Well, we would've liked to have a longer visit with you both, but we don't want to hold up the line. Don't be a stranger Evan. We'd love to have you and Chase as guest speakers at our book club sometime," Dorrie told us as she picked up her stack of books.

"Consider it done," Chase readily agreed. "We'll have to catch up with you in a few months after my next book is out."

They all waved and blew kisses, and then the mortification was done.

Miguel and Drew came to find us after the crowd thinned out and I was already exhausted.

"We're going to swing by the hotel to pick up the others and then we'll meet you at the Stinemans'," Drew told us as they stepped in next to Chase.

"Sounds like a plan. We'll see you there," she nodded.

They left the shop hand in hand, climbed into a red minivan parked at the curb, and took off.

"Thanks so much, you two. Would you mind signing this pile of books before you go?" Dottie asked as she tapped a small stack of hardback copies of our book.

"No problem, Dottie. We'd be happy to. Let us know if there's anything else you need from us," I nodded.

She smiled and walked back over to the register to take care of customers and I sighed as I sat down and cracked open the first book.

"You know we can't stall all day...there's a house full of people that you invited who are waiting for us," Chase teased.

"But I can try," I smirked back.

She leaned over and kissed me softly. I was terrified to meet the rest of her family, but I knew that I needed to take care of some arrangements with a few important members of our families before we left town.

# THIRTY-FIVE

## Chase

**Chicago**

"Come to auntie Chase," I cooed as I held my hands out to my sister-in-law, Elle.

"She just woke up, so she might be a little surly," she laughed.

"Oh, she'll be fine. She loves auntie Chase. Yes, you do, Princess." I did not even care that I probably sounded like an idiot. My little, almost-bald niece was adorable.

Evan was still inside with both our moms getting food prepared. We'd been at his parents' house for about an hour after we left the bookstore when my brothers showed up. I was out in the backyard with my older brother Ethan, his wife Elle, Kelly, and Miguel.

"I see how it is. We don't see you for months and the baby is all you care about," Ethan teased with an exaggerated eye roll.

"I'm glad you're not jealous," I smiled over at him.

"I've gotten used to being ignored by now. Although most people assume I'm the nanny, not the mom, since she got the red hair," Elle laughed.

"I love her ginger hair. I just wish she had more of it." I ran my hand over the downy layer of red hair on the top of my little niece's head.

"So does mom. She keeps buying her these hair clips. How are we supposed to put hair clips on a kid with no hair?" Ethan laughed.

"It'll come in eventually. She's gorgeous," Kelly said as she walked up beside us and rested her hand on the back of Sadie's head.

"I can't wait till I have nieces or nephews," she told me as she looked at me out of the corner of her eye.

"Don't look at me," I laughed.

"It's only a matter of time," she teased as she looked back towards the house.

"We've barely even decided to move in together, marriage and babies aren't happening yet," I shook my head. I hoped they would in the future, but I wasn't in a hurry.

"That keyword is yet," Kelly teased.

"I'd like some nieces and nephews too," Elle smiled and I narrowed my eyes at her.

"Traitor." She laughed at me and shrugged her shoulders. "You already have a niece."

"Miguel and Drew's dog doesn't count," Elle rolled her eyes.

"Hey," Miguel said quickly, holding his hand over his heart. "My dog is an adorable niece, thank you very much."

"Got any pictures? I wanna see," Kelly sat down beside him in the grass and leaned in as he held up his phone.

"This was when we first got her. She's a Frenchie." The grin on his face was priceless. He adored that chubby little dog.

"She's so cute!" Kelly told him as she fawned over more pictures.

"Speaking of adorable. Is something going on with your interns?" Kelly suddenly asked, swiveling her head in my direction. I laughed at the abrupt subject change.

"I'm not sure," I shrugged. "One minute they're fighting, the next they're making FMEs at each other."

"FME?" Kelly asked with a frown.

I reached down and covered Sadie's ears with my palms, which made her giggle. "Fuck me eyes."

"You mean like how Evan keeps looking at you out the kitchen window?" Elle nodded towards the picture window in the kitchen nook. Evan was staring intently in our direction with a small smile on his face.

Both of our fathers were sitting across the table from him. He looked back after a few seconds and they continued their conversation.

"You don't think our dad is giving him a hard time, do you, Ethan?" I worried. My father could be a little strict at times and I wanted him to accept Evan. He was important.

"Nah. He asked to talk to them both earlier," Ethan shook his head.

"Evan did?" He hadn't told me that he had any plans to talk to our dads. That was weird.

"Yeah. It's why I joined you lovely ladies out here," Ethan nodded.

"I'm not a lady," Miguel smirked as he looked over at his brother-in-law.

"But you gossip like one," Ethan shot back.

"You're just mad I introduced your thirsty wife to the male models on Instagram," Miguel sassed and we all laughed.

"You can hook me up with some hot male models on Instagram," Kelly laughed and reached over for a high five.

"Here, give me your number and I'll text you some links," Miguel laughed as he handed Kelly his phone.

"Does Drew know you're drooling over random guys on your phone?" I teased.

"He knows," Miguel nodded proudly. "Who do you think sends me new guys to follow?"

Kelly started laughing and I couldn't help joining in. Sadie started clapping and laughing along with us. I'm sure she'd follow some Insta hotties once she was old enough too.

"I don't even think Evan knows he has an Instagram," Kelly laughed at her social media inept brother.

"He does. He just doesn't know the password. Adrian manages it for him," I told her.

"That's frightening," she shuddered. "He still hitting on random interns?"

"Actually, we think he's hooking up with my editor," I whispered as I leaned towards her.

"Wow. You and Evan are just bringing all sorts of people together." She laughed loudly. "Does Adrian have any other hot interns since it looks like Sam is spoken for?"

I laughed. I couldn't imagine that Kelly was struggling for male attention, but I did know a certain handsome single guy she might get along with. It was too bad she lived 1,000 miles away. "Not that I know of, but what are your thoughts on tall men with dark hair? And leather pants?"

"I'm thinking I need to come to visit more," she smiled widely.

"Me too!" Elle agreed.

"If Elle is coming, so am I," Miguel nodded.

I laughed as Sadie started clapping again.

"Why don't you guys let us get through this book tour and then we can talk about visitors."

"You're going to need to build a guest house on all that land you've got," Kelly told me. It wasn't a bad idea.

"I can draw up some plans if you think Evan would be interested," Ethan offered.

"Why don't you people just let me get moved in before you start planning expansions," I shook my head. Although someday I'd love to have them all come to visit.

"I can design a kitchen for the guest house," Elle smiled widely. She was a kitchen design consultant for my brother's architecture firm. They'd had a naughty little coworker affair once upon a time as well.

"Whose guest house?" Evan sat down on the ground behind me and reached around me to tickle Sadie's foot.

She giggled at him and reached out her chubby hands toward him. "Up...up..."

"Yours," Miguel told him. "We're all coming to visit."

I turned and lifted Sadie around to Evan and he settled her on his lap. "Hey, pretty girl."

"Da!" Sadie exclaimed, clapping her hands.

"What about me? Am I not your Da anymore?" Ethan pouted as he made a sad face at his daughter.

"Oh, quit being jealous, she calls the guy who delivers the Amazon packages Da too," Elle teased.

"Because he's at my house more than I am," Ethan gave her a knowing look.

"Since when are we building a guest house?" Evan laughed as Sadie leaned in and gave him slobbery kisses on his cheek. The girl had good taste.

"Since our pushy siblings insisted they needed to come and visit," I shrugged.

"We're going to need somewhere to stay once the baby comes. Your house is too small," Kelly told him with a straight face.

"Baby..." Evan coughed as he looked between his sister and me with wide eyes.

"She's kidding. There is no baby," I shook my head.

"Yet," Miguel laughed.

"You stop it or I'm gonna tell mom you want to adopt," I pointed at him and dared him to challenge me.

"Ew." He made a face and Elle smacked him in the shoulder.

"Hey!"

"You know I love little bug, but nope. Not gonna happen," he shook his head.

"Sorry Sadie, you're just going to have to wait to get some cousins," Evan told her in his own version of the baby voice. It was pretty damn adorable.

"What were you talking to our parents about in the house?" I asked curiously as I leaned in towards Evan.

Shortly after Evan had joined us outside, our parents filled the table on the back patio with a huge spread of food. Everyone had filled up their plates and spread out across the seating available in the backyard.

Evan and I were sitting on a blanket in the middle of the yard, Elle and Ethan just a few yards away from us trying to keep Sadie from crawling over to us.

My niece seemingly had a crush on Evan, climbing into his lap at every opportunity. I couldn't blame the girl; if it was socially acceptable, I'd be in his lap all the time too.

"They were asking how the book tour had started and if we had anything planned in the cities we're stopping in," he answered quickly. He refused to look me in the eye, picking at a piece of grass just past the edge of the blanket. I had the feeling that he was hiding something, but I couldn't quite put my finger on it.

"And what did you tell them?"

He shrugged as he smiled over at me. "Just that I'd worked with Diana to figure out some things we could do in our downtime. No use in wasting our travels spending it all between bookstores and the hotels."

"Do I get to know any of these plans?" Evan was all kinds of sneaky on this trip. I was kind of impressed with his planning.

"Can't you let a guy have some surprises?" He laughed as he leaned over and kissed my shoulder.

"You better not have us doing anything crazy," I warned, but we both knew I'd do it anyway.

"You think I'm going to plan something crazy? I have a hard time getting up the nerve to talk into a microphone in front of a crowd. Since when do I do adventurous?"

I raised my eyebrows at him and bit my lip. "I can think of some pretty adventurous things you've done recently." His eyes widened as I leaned in to whisper in his ear. "Don't you remember the other night?" I drew my finger down the skin exposed by his unbuttoned neckline. "Or the time with the wooden spoon?"

He shifted around on the blanket, pulling down on one of his pant legs. "You're going to make me embarrass myself in front of both our families."

"Still not going to share what our plans are?" I asked as I bit my lip, looking at him from underneath my lashes.

He laughed as he traced the bare skin on my knee with one of his fingertips. "You're just going to have to be patient. I promise it's worth the wait."

Our next stop — Denver — was a whirlwind. Diana had us booked in back-to-back appearances and we barely had any time to breathe before she dragged us to the next venue.

"You guys ready?" Sam asked, as we waited in the hotel lobby for the app alert that our car was here.

"Tell me again why I agreed to this?" Christine sighed and looked around, an irritated look on her face.

"Because we're awesome, you would have just spent the day inside your room, and we get to drink beer paid for by the publishing house," I shrugged.

"Sounds like a win to me. Come on Chris, live a little." Sam winked at Christine and she rolled her eyes at him. Obviously, they hadn't declared their undying love for each other yet.

"I'm looking forward to a little bit of a break," Evan agreed, his thumb stroking my fingers lightly as he held my hand.

"But we have to get on a plane at the ass crack of dawn tomorrow," Christine whined.

"Since when have you gone to bed before midnight?" Sam asked with a raised eyebrow.

"Have you been monitoring my sleeping habits?" She narrowed her eyes at Sam. I knew that they'd shared a room in Boston; but there had been a mix-up when we arrived in Denver and they were put into a room with two queen beds instead of two queen rooms. Sam had offered to find another hotel, but Christine had relented and said they were adults and could figure it out.

So far Evan and I hadn't seen any additional action from those two, so the bet was looking like it wasn't going to end up in either of our favor. I wasn't holding out hope the situation would improve over the next few weeks.

"I am sleeping five feet away from you; the glow of your phone makes it hard to sleep," he rolled his eyes.

"Oh waaah, go buy a sleep mask." She crossed her arms over her chest as she stared him down.

"God, I hope the hotel in Seattle doesn't fuck up the reservations," he sighed, obviously wanting his own space.

"Oh, cause it's so impossible to spend time with me," Christine rolled her eyes as she looked away from him.

"Because I'd like to be able to go to sleep without worrying that I'm going to get glared at for every move I make," he growled at her.

Evan mouthed 'wow' at me, and I giggled as I nodded my head. They were in rare form today.

"They really should just screw each other and get it over with," I breathed into my Evan's ear as I clung to his arm. Who needed telenovelas when you had Sam and Christine to keep you entertained?

"Maybe we should just sneak upstairs while they're going at it," Evan suggested. I doubt they'd notice if we left. They'd drifted closer to each other and Christine was poking him in the chest as he smiled down at her. It appeared to me that Sam was enjoying her ire.

"Alright kids, break it up. Our ride is here. Get your asses out that door," I said, gesturing to the doors in the hotel lobby that led to the street.

We all climbed into the Uber and Evan laughed quietly as Christine made it a point to sit up front with the driver instead of next to Sam.

"Going down to Lodo?" he asked as he looked down into the rearview mirror. Lodo was the lower downtown area and the location of the historic Union Station, Coors Field where the Colorado Rockies played, the Pepsi Center where the Denver Nuggets and Colorado Avalanche played, and a wide variety of businesses and breweries.

"Yeah. We're taking a walking tour and then checking out some of the breweries," Evan nodded.

"Make sure you check out The Oxford. They do tours sometimes. It's a really neat building. One of the oldest in Denver, the oldest hotel in that area," he suggested.

"Thanks. We'll have to check it out," Sam smiled at him.

The rest of the ride from our hotel, Christina sat in the front typing into her phone, and Sam made casual small talk with us.

"So, you've got four sisters?" Evan asked him.

"Yeah... I'm the baby. They're all older and married now," he nodded. He seemed a little more sensitive than I expected, so it made sense that he had four sisters.

"I bet you've got a herd of nieces and nephews," I smiled.

"Actually, just nephews. My dad eats it up. By the time I came along he was so excited to have a son to do manly things with," Sam laughed. "He'd take me camping all the time and encouraged me to play a ton of sports."

"Evan here was a star soccer player," I teased as I squeezed Evan's arm and smiled up at his blushing face.

"I don't know about being a star, but it did help me pay for college," he chuckled nervously.

"That's cool. I played lacrosse," Sam nodded.

"Of course, you did," Christine snorted from the front seat.

I could see Sam visibly tense. He was irritated that she seemed so hostile today, but I figured it was just pent-up sexual tension between the two of them.

"Oh look! We're here," I announced cheerfully, attempting to defuse the tense atmosphere.

We thanked the driver and piled out onto the sidewalk, finding our tour guide outside the first brewery. He took us on an hour-long tour of the area, walking through it until we could see Union Station and Coors Field in the distance. Afterward, he took us to another brewery and by then Christine had loosened up with a few drinks in her.

"Oh, come on, you're telling me that you'd never used sex toys until you met Chase? I find that hard to believe," she laughed as she looked at Evan curiously.

"Why is that hard to believe? You've met me. Do I strike you as the adventurous type?" he laughed, seeming a little less tense with the alcohol we'd all consumed.

"It's always the quiet ones that are really freaks behind closed doors," Sam laughed.

"You speak from experience, Spammy?" Christine teased him and I saw his cheeks turn a little pink.

"Wouldn't you like to know?" he asked as he leaned across the table towards her and licked his lips. From where I was sitting, I could see her eyes dilate as she met him halfway, their faces only inches apart.

"In your dreams, pretty boy," Christine told him, but it didn't sound all that convincing.

Evan and I exchanged a smile and he squeezed my thigh. This was getting interesting. Maybe I would be winning the bet after all. By the time we were done with our tester flight set of beers, we were all feeling a little happier.

"We gonna try to see if we can get in a tour of the Oxford?" I asked as I glanced at the time on my phone.

"I'm up for it. We've got time," Evan nodded.

"Ugh. Actually Is just filled my inbox with pages to proof. I can't. I'll head back to the hotel and just see you guys tomorrow," Christine sighed loudly as she angrily tapped at the screen of her work phone. Isobel was notorious about sending emails at the most inconvenient times. She never worked normal hours, often sending back annotated pages in the middle of the night.

"Want some help? Two sets of eyes might help you get through it faster," Sam offered as he placed his hand on Christine's back. She didn't flinch away or step out of his touch. Obviously, she'd gotten over her animosity towards him from earlier.

"Just us, baby?" Evan asked me as I wrapped myself around his arm, nuzzling into his shoulder.

"Sounds perfect," I nodded, my voice muffled by the fabric of his shirt. It was nice to spend time with him doing things that typical couples would do. He hadn't even shown any signs of his anxiety cropping up. He was almost a different person than he'd been when we ventured out to the farmer's market months ago.

"We'll see you two nauseating lovebirds later," Christine sighed as she tucked her phone away and stood from the table.

# THIRTY-SIX

## Evan

**Denver**

Sam and Christine headed back to the hotel in an Uber after we said our goodbyes at the brewery. Chase and I headed in the other direction — to the Oxford Hotel — on foot. A tour was just about to start when we got there, but I was a little in awe of the architecture and restorations they'd done to the building.

"Oh wow, look at her," Chase sighed and I followed her eyes. There was a couple getting wedding photos taken in the lobby.

"There is a wedding today, so we'll have to sneak into the ballroom quickly, but we can get started," the tour guide explained as he ushered us towards a set of double doors.

Chase had a hard time taking her eyes off the gorgeous couple getting their pictures taken, seemingly fascinated by how they interacted with each other.

"This place is so romantic..." she sighed as we stood along the edge of the ballroom, watching the staff get everything for the reception into place.

Despite our packed schedule, my own romantic plans for Chase were coming together, Adrian surprisingly working behind the scenes to get things set up for me once we headed back to the East Coast.

The ring my father had given me in Chicago was always kept tucked into the breast pocket of my blazer in a little pouch, next to my heart. I couldn't risk Chase finding it before I was ready, so I'd left the box with him for safekeeping.

A few times over the last few days, I'd had to halt and divert wandering hands as Chase hugged or touched me, but I don't think she had any idea that a proposal was coming.

I had a hard time paying attention to the tour guide as he told us the history of the building and the several renovations it'd undergone in the last twenty years. My hand kept drifting to my pocket, fingering the ring inside of it.

The dreamy look in Chase's eyes made me second guess my plans for New York. I was ready to throw it out of the window and get down on one knee now. But I had a plan... and I couldn't wait to see it through. But first, we had to get through the next stop on the tour — Seattle.

"Wait, where are we going today? I thought we were going to a bookstore," I asked nervously. We had arrived in Seattle and this unexpected, last-minute surprise was unsettling.

"Change of plans," Diana shrugged. "Adrian set this one up, and I've got to say... with the subject of the book, it makes sense."

"He even sent a package to Sam with outfits for the both of you," she smiled.

Christine stifled a laugh as she looked over at Sam. I was worried by the shit-eating grins on their faces. An hour later, the five of us were getting out of the hired car in front of our next venue. From the outside, it looked pretty tame.

I was pulling at the seams on the sides of my newest pair of leather pants. Kelly would have a field day if she knew that I now owned four pairs of leather pants.

"I feel like a naughty librarian," Chase laughed as she pulled at the hem of her mid-thigh length, flared leather skirt.

"You look..." I blew out a breath and took in a good look at her outfit, a fitted white T-shirt was tucked into the skirt, her hair curled in loose waves, sky high black ankle boots, equally bright red lipstick and a pair of red glasses perched on her nose. I was afraid these tight pants weren't going to contain my reaction.

"Like a hot fucking badass author with a sexy boy toy," Christine laughed as she smacked me on the ass.

"Alright. I can't do this. No more gloves and what the hell are these necklaces?" I groaned as I held up the remaining parts of the get-up Adrian had sent for me to wear. He apparently thought I needed some leather gloves with the fingertips cut off and several long chains. I think he forgot our book was about BDSM and not about bikers.

"Hahaha," Christine was still laughing as Sam took the gloves and necklaces from me and shoved them into his messenger bag.

"I think you need to wear leather pants every day," Chase told me in a low, sultry voice. She grabbed the sides of my unzipped leather jacket and pulled me towards her, slowly kissing me and licking at my bottom lip.

"We'll be fine. Two hours and you can take me back to the hotel, lift this skirt up, and...." she whispered into my ear and my heart started racing.

"Stop it," I begged. "I won't be able to walk in these if you keep talking."

Diana opened the door to Gallery Erato and the four of us followed her inside. I wasn't sure quite what to expect, but it just looked like a cool restored building venue with an art gallery attached to it. Upon closer examination, you could see the various images that lined the gallery walls of all different kinds of kink and erotic photography.

"Damn, it's too bad we won't be here tomorrow. They're having a class on squirting," Christine laughed, but she didn't sound like she was joking.

I looked over to Sam and his cheeks had turned pink as he stared at Christine with wild eyes and his mouth dropped open. I had to admit, the concept of getting a woman to squirt intrigued me as well. Maybe some research was in order when we got back home.

"Let's get set up. You're scheduled to start in a half-hour," Diana told us as she led us further into the space.

"Want to go take a look around?" I could hear Christine ask Sam as she nodded back to the gallery walls. His head nodded rapidly and I heard him clear his throat before he responded.

"Absolutely. Lead the way." He gestured for her to walk in front of him and I laughed as his hand took up residence low on her back as they disappeared around the closest wall.

"You think they've given in yet?" I asked curiously.

Chase laughed as she leaned around me to look at them. "Nope. Still UST city over there."

I took one last look in their direction and they looked awfully cozy. Sam was standing with Christine in front of him. They were both facing a piece of artwork I couldn't see, but he kept leaning down to whisper in her ear and his hand rested on her hip. There was no space between their bodies. Chase was right. You could cut the unresolved sexual tension with a knife.

Three hours later I was still amped up as I stood behind Chase while she was swiping the key card to our room. The reading had gone well and I was pleasantly surprised by how full the venue had been, even if it made me nervous.

Chase had been sexy as hell as she read aloud a scene in the book where Fanny and Dominic finally decide to shed their labels and fulfill his fantasy of tying her up. I had to actively try to keep myself from getting aroused while she read the part where he fucked her as she was cuffed backward to a Saint Andrew's cross.

"Stupid card," she giggled, the light blinking red as she swiped it again.

I reached around her and took it from her, pressing myself fully against her back and turning the card around. The little green light lit up and the lock clicked as I slowly inserted the card and pulled it out.

"You have to be gentle and slide it in there. You can't just jam it in and hope it releases," I whispered against the skin on her neck.

"Oh...is that how it works?" Chase whispered as one of her hands reached between us and she squeezed my already hard cock.

With how form-fitting my pants were, I knew that it'd be hard to conceal the engagement ring, so it was zipped inside the interior pocket in my leather jacket.

The lights were off when we opened the door, and you could see the city all lit up beyond the curtains leading out to the private balcony of our suite.

"Care to join me outside?" I whispered as I placed my hands on Chase's hips and urged her to walk towards the doors that led to the exterior.

"I thought you were going to bend me over something and hike up this skirt when we got back here," she teased as she swayed her hips.

I stepped closer as she paused and I kissed along the side of her neck and sucked at the edge of her jaw, eliciting a breathy moan.

"Ohhh..."

"That's still the plan," I whispered suggestively as I pressed myself against her.

The balcony of our executive suite had a half wall that was just over waist height, another balcony above it, and solid walls on either side. It was secluded enough, but still a little risky for what I had planned.

"Do you trust me?" I asked as I fingered the clasp of her necklace and ran it along the soft skin at the back of her neck.

"Yeesss..." she moaned as my other hand came up to cup one of her breasts through the thin cotton of her shirt.

"Can I take these off?"

I took her nod as an answer and unclasped her necklace, gently placing it on the coffee table and then reaching down to untuck the hem of her shirt from the leather skirt.

Pulling it over her head, I groaned as I got a look at her sexy as fuck black lace bra. "Damn..."

Chase started to reach down to unzip her heeled ankle boots, but I stilled her hand before she could.

"Keep them on," I instructed in a low, but firm voice.

Chase hesitated once we got to the balcony doors and I kissed her shoulder softly.

"What if someone sees us?" she whispered as her hand settled on the door handle.

"We're pretty high up. Chances are no one can see us," I tried to reassure her.

"Are you sure?"

"Positive," I nodded as I stepped closer and whispered directly into her ear. "Look out there. It's gorgeous tonight."

In one direction, we could see the Space Needle, in the other, Mount Rainier.

"Isn't it going to be cold this high up?"

"Did I finally find something my fearless girl won't try?" I teased and then kissed along the exposed skin of her shoulder.

"Is that a challenge?" she laughed.

"Maybe. Did it work?"

She reached her arm up and slipped a hand behind my neck, scratching at the hair at the nape.

"Just give me a few minutes," she requested quietly.

I nodded against her shoulder and started laying soft kisses along the side of her neck and shoulder. When my hand grazed a nipple through the soft lace of her bra, it was already hardened into a firm peak.

"Does the thought of someone seeing you being pleasured turn you on?" I whispered into her soft skin. It was obvious she was turned on, but I knew this was something we'd never tried that required trust.

"Ohhh...maybe..." she panted as I pinched and plucked at her chest through the lace.

"You turn me on so much. I want to bunch up the back of this skirt and slip inside you," I told her, my voice much lower than normal. "Thrust into you so hard that your grip on the railings turns your knuckles white."

She let out a little whine and pushed her ass back into my groin.

"I want to whisper things into your ear until you can't stand it anymore and you cum all over me, biting your lip to try to keep quiet."

Her breaths were coming in shallow pants as she wiggled against me. I was rock hard, my cock pressed tightly against my briefs inside the tight leather of my pants.

"Let's go," Chase said in a breathy voice as she pushed down on the handle to the balcony door and swung it open.

The sounds of the city traffic and laughter from the hotel restaurant many floors down filtered through the air.

It was slightly windy but not as cold as I thought it'd feel. Chase shivered as we walked forward to the railing of the balcony and I helped her gently place her hands on the black metal bar.

"You alright?" I asked as I ran a hand up between her thighs and palmed her underneath the leather of her skirt.

"Yes..." she moaned as I slipped a finger under the lace and found her drenched for me. Apparently, exhibitionism was exciting for her. I had to admit it had me throbbing in my pants.

"Take them off," she whispered, and I hooked the bottom of her panties with my finger, slowly drawing them down her legs.

Her hands remained locked around the black iron bar of the balcony railing as I crouched down and helped her step out of her sopping panties. I turned and tossed them through the open doors and then quickly unbuckled my belt. It took a few tugs to get my pants pulled down to my thighs.

My hard cock sprung free as I lowered my boxer briefs, the head already weeping at the thought of what lay under Chase's skirt. She jumped a little as I stepped back in behind her, slowly running one of my hands across her abdomen.

"I love you," I whispered into her hair as I pushed the loose curls to the side and nuzzled her ear with my nose. "You're so incredibly sexy."

She pressed her head back into my shoulder and sighed as my other hand smoothed over the leather on the back of her skirt. My fingers gripped the edge of it and slowly started to draw the material upward.

"Love you...mmmm," she moaned as my hand gripped her firm ass cheek once the leather was up and out of the way.

"Hold on," I groaned in her ear as I grasped my shaft firmly in one hand and pressed it between her legs.

"Mmmm," she moaned as I stopped caressing her stomach and used my hand to tilt her hips back.

"Uhhhh...fuck," I growled into the skin of her neck as the head of my cock slid through her wet folds. One firm thrust and I was seated fully inside her, the muscles of her pussy clenching me tightly.

"Oh god, it's so big," she whispered as I held onto the side of her hip and slowly began to rotate my hips against her ass.

The lights of the city blurred as I looked out and began to make firm thrusts against her. Slowly drawing my cock out and then pushing forward, driving her thighs into the metal railing.

"Harder..." Chase moaned out quietly, the muscles in her forearms straining to maintain their grip as I started to kiss and suck along the side of her throat.

"Your pussy is so tight," I groaned into her skin as I picked up the pace a little. She widened her legs and I slipped in further with each thrust, hitting deep inside her. "You're so warm. I love how you grip my cock so tightly."

She let out a series of low moans as I talked, and my hips picked up the pace. My free hand found a place next to hers on the railing and I anchored her to me with a firm press against the front of her pelvis over the skirt.

"I want to feel you clench that tight cunt around me."

"Ohhhh..." she moaned loudly as I punctuated my whisper with a particularly hard thrust against her.

"Shhh...someone might hear you," I moaned into her ear as my lips brushed against the lobe. "Or is that what you want?"

I rotated my hips, pulling out and then thrusting all the way in. "Do you want someone to hear you?"

She clenched on me again, making stars dance across my vision. "Does it make you want to cum knowing someone can hear me fucking you?"

"Ohhhh...god...yes..." She wasn't even attempting to keep her moans quiet anymore.

That was so fucking hot.

I looked around quickly before I brought my free hand underneath the bunched-up skirt and found her throbbing clit. Her moans increased in volume again as I pressed firmly against it and began to run my finger in tight circles against the wet flesh.

"Ohhh...fuck me," she cried out as I pounded into her and felt her start to clench against me.

"That's it baby...uhhhh," I coaxed with a gruff moan as I kept up the movement of my hips.

Her neck arched as I felt her muscles clamp down on me and her hands gripped the railing harder. Through the haze of pleasure, I looked down and saw the skin around her knuckles turn white as she leaned forward, forcing her hips back into my thrusts.

"Fuck yes...cum on me, baby..." I moaned as I moved both hands to her hips and began to ram inside her forcefully.

"Oh god, I'm cumming. Fuck, fuck, fuck," she whined out as I felt her muscles start to pulse against my shaft.

"Uhhhh..." My guttural groan was long and loud as I chased my high, pushing into her with a force that made her bounce against me as she came.

"Oh fuck, Evan, it feels so good."

A few firm thrusts later and I emptied my load into her, the city lights blurring and then snapping back into focus as I gripped her tightly to me. The muscles in her legs were shaking as I drew her back into me, softly cupping her throat as we both panted, coming down from our highs.

"You're incredible," I whispered into her sweaty temple, as I held her. "Let's go to bed, baby."

She nodded and I brought my hands down to unclamp hers from the railing, slowly massaging out her tense joints.

"I don't know if I can walk," she giggled as she trembled against me with shaky legs.

I pulled out of her, my cum trickling down her leg as I bent down and scooped her up into my arms.

"Be careful," she laughed as she clung to my neck, tucking her face into the side of it as I cradled her in my arms and turned towards the balcony doors.

I kissed the side of her head as I awkwardly walked towards the bed, my pants still hitched around my thighs.

"I'm fine," I laughed as I walked around the large king-sized bed and gently laid her on top of the covers.

Chase looked up at me in the dimly lit room with a drowsy smile. The city lights were the only thing illuminating her as her wild hair spread out across the pillow.

My mind drifted to the ring tightly concealed in my jacket and I didn't know if I could wait another eight days to ask her to be my wife.

"I love you so much," I whispered as I leaned down to unclasp her bra, gently peeling it down her skin. My fingers found the zipper on her skirt next, slowly lowering it and helping her pull it off as well as her lacy underwear.

She laid there gloriously naked against the white sheets and I found my finger gently tracing the curve of one breast as her eyes fluttered closed. I stepped back and unzipped her boots, dropping them to the floor with a quiet thunk.

"Mmmm," she sighed as she blinked her eyes open and smiled drowsily up at me.

I quickly pulled off the leather jacket, carefully laying it across the chair in the corner and then unlacing my boots before I pulled them off. My shirt, pants, briefs, and socks were quickly shed before I returned to Chase and tugged the comforter out from under her dozing form.

Walking around to the other side of the bed, I slipped in next to her, gently pulling her to my chest. Her leg nestled over my thigh as she curled around me and I lightly stroked her hair as her breathing evened out.

It took a little while to calm myself down enough to sleep, but as I drifted off, I marveled at how lucky I was to find her...and I was never letting her go.

Los Angeles was the penultimate stop on our book tour, and it was challenging my anxiety in several ways.

My heart was pounding as I stood behind Chase in the admission line at Disneyland.

Christine and Sam were bickering again next to us, but I couldn't really make out what they were saying over the blood rushing through my ears.

"You OK?" Chase cupped my cheek as she stood in front of me, her chest pressed up against mine.

I nodded as my eyes drifted back and forth across the large crowd waiting impatiently for the park to open.

"We can sit down if you need to," she offered quietly as she pulled my face down to look at her and scanned my eyes. "I know the crowds make you nervous; we can try to find somewhere quiet inside."

"I'm OK. It's just..." I whispered over the tightness in my chest.

"There's a lot of people." She smiled as I nodded at her. Aside from my little bit of panicked anxiety, I was pleased that she got it and that it didn't bother her.

"You're safe with me," she said quietly as she leaned up to kiss me softly.

"Hey, tone it down, there are little kids with impressionable minds here," Christine laughed as she looked over to the two of us.

"Well, then they better stay out of earshot of you," Chase teased as she looked back at Sam and Christine.

They weren't exactly holding hands, but I saw Sam brush his fingers lightly against hers and linger. There was something going on there. If they got together before we left LA, then I'd win the bet...but I wasn't sure what I'd want the content of the book to be yet.

"Hey! I take exception to that remark," Christine laughed as she looked over at Sam and smiled. It was a real smile too, not one of her smiles that also made you want to protect your junk.

"Looks like it's time." Sam nodded towards the main gate where the staff had started scanning people into the park.

"Finally." Once we were out of the big crowd, I knew it'd be easier for me to stay calm.

I was happy we'd been able to swing this part of the trip. Diana had kept us busy, back-to-back signings and readings for the last three days, and we all needed a break.

"So, is the plan to stay together the whole day or...?" Sam asked as we walked forward in the line.

"Why don't we split up and meet for lunch?" Chase suggested.

"You mean I'm stuck with this Bozo half the day?" Christine rolled her eyes and gestured toward Sam.

"Cause you're such a peach." Sam rolled his eyes and pinched Christine's side, her shrieking and trying to lean away from him.

"Want to meet in Adventureland around one?" Chase suggested.

"Sounds like a plan, Stan," Christine nodded. "Come on, pretty boy."

She turned towards Sam and tugged on his shirt as we finally got to the front of the line.

"So, you think I'm pretty?" He grinned as she turned and stuck her tongue out at him.

"Don't let your head get too big," she rolled her eyes.

He arched an eyebrow and looked down at his pants. I laughed as she put her hand upon his chest.

"Don't."

He laughed and placed his hand over hers, and she tensed before pulling away and turning around.

Chase and I met up with them on the other side of the gate and both were avoiding eye contact.

"OK. We're going to head over to Space Mountain and then make our way over to Galaxy's Edge," Christine told us.

"We are, are we?" Sam asked with an amused smile on his face.

"Think you can keep up, big boy?" she taunted him.

"Oh, you know I can keep it up." He grinned at her as her eyes widened, briefly glancing towards his pants once more.

"I kinda wish we were staying with them to watch this bizarre mating dance," Chase giggled quietly in my ear.

"Let's just see how this plays out," I nodded.

"They're either going to kill each other before we see them next or get arrested for fucking in Disneyland," she giggled.

I snorted and pulled her into my side, quietly laughing into her hair. "I love you."

"I know you do," she teased as she squeezed my arm.

"Alright, I'd like to keep down my breakfast this morning. Let's go, Spamela," Christine pretended to be disgusted by our perfectly normal display of affection.

"Yes, Ma'am." Sam saluted and she punched him in the side.

"What do you want to ride first?" I asked as they walked away, continuing to poke at each other.

"Hmmm. Since I can't ride my favorite ride right now... Let's head to Fantasyland," Chase said with a smirk on her lips.

"Your favorite... oh!" I exclaimed as she ran her hand up my leg and squeezed the front of my pants discreetly.

"You can ride that all you want when we get back to the hotel..." I growled into her ear as she bit her lip and smiled.

By the time we met up with Sam and Christine, I had finally let go of all my pent-up anxiety. Chase made it easy to relax and enjoy myself.

We spent a few hours in Adventureland, eating and going on more rides. Chase's favorite pastime had been positioning herself in front of me while we waited in line and slowly rubbing her ass against me.

I was going to either fuck the shit out of her at the hotel later or cum in my pants like a fifteen-year-old who saw boobs for the first time.

As the sun started to set, we headed back towards Sleeping Beauty's castle.

"Oh, look!" Chase clapped as she looked over towards the walkway in front of the castle. Some cast members had held the crowd back and a young guy was standing with his who I assumed was his girlfriend in the open space. He was holding both of her hands and whispering in her ear.

"What's going...oh! Well, that's public!" Christine laughed as we stood there and watched the guy drop down to one knee.

Chase backed into me and I enfolded her in my arms as we watched the girl cover her mouth with both hands and nod frantically.

"I wonder what he's saying," Sam mused, a small smile on his face as he glanced at Christine.

"Probably something super cheesy and romantic," Christine said, sounding disgusted.

I kissed the side of Chase's neck as we watched the girl shout 'yes!' and hold out her hand to the guy.

The crowd started clapping and cheering, but I couldn't look away from Chase as she looked over her shoulder at me and we locked eyes.

# THIRTY-SEVEN

## Evan

**Los Angeles**

"I'm so farking tired. Whose great idea was it to go out last night?" Christine sighed as she settled into her airplane seat. We were on the move, yet again, about to take off from LAX.

"Yours," Sam shot back as he tried to hold in laughter.

"Shut it, you dipstick."

I looked through the seats and saw Christine smack Sam in the chest before she laid her head down on his shoulder.

The four of us had gone to a club last night and gotten entirely too drunk. Chase was feeling hungover in her baggy sweats and sunglasses.

LA was intense. Everyone was gorgeous. Everyone was oversexed and the alcohol and drugs flowed freely in the VIP lounge we'd managed to get into.

The four of us hadn't indulged in the heavier stuff, but we had drunk a shit ton of alcohol. Brilliant when you had a cross country flight at 7:00 in the morning.

"You feeling OK, baby?" I asked in a whisper as I pulled back the side of Chase's hood. She'd been trying to hide inside her sweatshirt from the small amount of light filtering through the cabin.

"No. Need sleep," she grumbled as she pulled her hood back into place and snuggled into my arm.

"You've got six hours, get some rest," I assured her.

It seemed neither of us had won the bet, but Christine definitely had a soft spot for Sam. Last night they'd been joined at the hips or at times the groin. I was both a little shocked and impressed at the dance moves those two produced when they loosened up a little.

Chase had been endlessly amused by the frustrated look Sam had worn all night as Christine rubbed up against him. It was probably pretty similar to the one on my face as Chase sat on my lap half the night in a super short dress — the wiggling just about killed me.

If I wasn't so tired, I'd probably be getting aroused recalling the hot, drunken shower sex we'd had when we got back to the hotel. I'm sure it was the only reason I wasn't throwing up right now; the endorphins flushed the alcohol out my system.

As I sat there staring out at the clouds, my brain started to formulate a plot. With all the commitments we'd had over the last few weeks, writing had been the last thing on my mind, but I was ready.

"What time is it?" Chase's sleepy voice carried softly as she rubbed her face against the sleeve of my shirt.

"Our time or LA time?"

She shook her head and groaned. "I don't even know what time zone we're in."

"You've been asleep for about three hours so sometime around 1:00 pm eastern," I told her quietly.

"How much longer do we have?" she whispered and then let out an impressive yawn.

I pulled up the flight on the interactive screen on the back of the seat and it said 2 hrs. 49 minutes left in the flight time.

"We'll get there around 4:00," I responded.

"Have you been awake this whole time?" she asked, sounding a fraction more alert, but still exhausted.

"Yeah. I got an idea, and it wouldn't go away until I got it written out," I nodded. And the quiet mixed with Chase's warm presence at my side was the perfect environment to let out all the ideas in my head.

"You gonna let me see it?" she asked as she peeked around the corner of the laptop screen.

"Let me finish this bit and then you can let me know what you think," I nodded as I flexed my fingers over the keyboard of my laptop.

"Is this for our project, or something else?" she whispered, her curiosity getting the better of her. I closed the laptop to foil her attempts to sneak a peek.

As I glanced behind us, I noticed that Christine and Sam were both passed out cold, her nose pressed into his neck and his arm behind her back as she snuggled against his chest.

"We're not in New York yet. Does that mean I won?" I jerked my head behind us, and Chase peeked through the seats, then leaned back with a smile on her face.

"Close enough," she laughed quietly, a bright smile pulled across her lips.

My arm slipped around her shoulders and I kissed the top of her head. "I promise it's good."

"You know I'm impatient when I have to wait for surprises," she smiled up at me from under my arm. I knew she wanted to know, but she could wait a little bit.

"I promise you'll like what's in store for us in New York."

She settled her head back into my shoulder and I opened the laptop back up when she dozed off again. This was a totally new genre for me, but I felt confident that I could tell our story.

I was jolted out of a deep sleep when the wheels met the runway at the airport in New York. One more day and a few hours, and hopefully Chase would agree to be my wife.

I wasn't nervous about her answer anymore, I just wanted this to be special. Maybe all her romantic notions had rubbed off on me. I never thought I'd want to go to these lengths for anyone, but she deserved a little bit of a grand gesture for showing me that the world was something I could handle.

"Are we here?" Chase stirred against my shoulder and blinked up at me sleepily.

I'd finished the outline about an hour before we were supposed to land, put away my laptop, and dozed off with her for a little while.

I could hear laughing coming from behind us, so obviously Christine and Sam hadn't decided to kill each other again.

"Yeah. We just landed, baby."

"I'm still so tired. Please say we don't have to do anything tonight," she whined with a little pout on her lips.

"We can get to the hotel and relax. Adrian and Diana have us booked for a press event in the morning, and then a reading," I told her. I was glad that today was only for travel. The time away from home was starting to add up and make us all a little weary.

"Is that all we have tomorrow?"

I shook my head, trying not to give anything away. "Not exactly."

"As long as it doesn't involve a sex shop, I'm in," I laughed because Adrian had mentioned us doing a reading at a BDSM sex shop in Brooklyn, but Diana shut it down quickly.

We were so close to being done with this tour. I was fine with the erotic gallery reading, but we didn't need to delve too deeply into the scene because we already had some positive press.

"But we could always go to a sex shop anyway. Just for research purposes, of course," I suggested.

She smiled up at me and cupped the back of my neck, pulling my face towards hers. "That's what we have Talia for. She's like a sex toy guru."

"Amen." Christine agreed as she poked her face in between the seats. "Girl knows her shit. I won't buy anything she hasn't tested."

"Do tell," Sam laughed as he pulled her back and tucked her back into his side.

"Well, you already know about the one..." she whispered quietly, but we heard her anyway.

*Oh, really?* Maybe they'd done more than we thought.

"Maybe it was a draw after all," Chase laughed. "Did you finish what you were working on?"

"I did," I nodded, but didn't give her any additional information.

"Still not going to tell me?"

"I will." I shrugged.

"Just not right now..." she sighed.

"Nope, but soon," I promised.

When we got to the hotel, Chase and I both grabbed a quick bite to eat before we went up to our room. Luckily, we didn't have to go to anything tonight. We were all too tired. It'd been a long few weeks.

"Do you want to stay in tonight?" I asked her as I looked around our spacious suite. The perks of being the talent.

"You complaining?" Chase asked.

I shook my head and laughed at her unamused look at the thought of going out into the city. "No, just trying to stay on the same page."

"Well, my page is gonna include that big bed and my pajamas." She nodded towards the large king bed that was framed by windows that looked out at the urban landscape.

"It could include that big bed and no pajamas," I told her suggestively. I would fully be on board with that option. I always felt invigorated after I'd gotten some solid work done. The flight out here had been more productive than I'd anticipated.

"Hmmm that sounds promising." Chase dropped her carry-on bag next to the bed and wheeled her suitcase next to the closet. "What else might this plan without clothes include?"

"It might involve a mandatory nudity policy for all participants and a full body massage," I shrugged.

"Massage for who?" she asked as she tilted her head, giving me an appraising look.

"The first person who can get naked."

I wasn't intending to win, so I took my time unbuttoning my shirt as Chase peeled off her sweats and threw them at me. I slipped my pants down my legs as she pulled off her last remaining piece of clothing, her panties, and threw them at my face.

"Someone really wants to win," I laughed as she climbed up onto the bed and spread herself out face down on the comforter.

"Get the hell up here, loser, and rub me," she laughed as she hooked a finger in my direction, and then pointed at my crotch. "But lose the shorts first."

"Yes, Ma'am." My briefs hit the floor with the rest of our clothes, and I climbed up on the bed, kneeling next to Chase's lower back.

I gently ran a finger down the back of her neck, tracing her spine all the way down. She shifted against the sheets as I lightly ran it back and forth across her lower back.

"You said you were going to massage me, not tickle me." She continued to squirm against the comforter at my barely-there touches.

"Don't be hating on my appreciation of your lovely curves," I scolded her, and she turned her face to look over at me.

"My lovely curves are sore, start rubbing, dude," she mumbled as her loose hair spread out around her. She'd taken out her messy bun after she'd stripped down.

I laughed as I scooted down and straddled her lower legs, my hard cock brushing against her upper thigh.

She groaned as I began to knead at her lower back with my thumbs, long sweeping strokes against her soft skin. I could feel her muscles loosen up as she lay with her head turned to the side.

"That feels good," she sighed as she shifted against the sheets, and the soft skin of her ass cheeks rubbed against the skin of my shaft. Each sigh and moan she made was making me harder and harder.

By the time I got to her shoulders, leaning forward to reach, I was weeping and painfully hard.

"Did that help?" I whispered in her ear as I pushed the hair off her neck and gently rotated my thumbs against her soft skin.

"Mmmm...maybe you need to do the front," she smiled against the soft cotton underneath her.

I stroked my finger along the side of her breast, and she let out a breathy moan. "So, you need a little attention right here?"

"A little further over," she sighed as I felt goosebumps break out across her skin.

"What about here?" I asked as I scooted back slightly and gently eased my hand between her legs.

"Oh..." Her breathy moan was enough encouragement, and I slipped my hand in further, two fingers sliding inside her.

"I love how wet you get for me," I groaned as she shifted her hips and my fingers started to thrust lightly in and out of her. The wetter she got, the harder I became, my cock begging to get inside of her. "You make me so hard. Can't you feel what you're doing to me with those sexy moans?"

She moaned as I leaned down and thrust my hard cock against the soft skin of her thigh.

"Fuck me." Her quiet exclamation into the soft sheets was my breaking point.

I leaned forward, covering her body with my own as I placed my arms on either side of her. I shifted so our hips lined up and pressed my dick between her legs. She was wet and ready for me as the head slipped inside and I moaned into her shoulder. "Fuck, I love you."

"Me too...ohhh, god," she moaned as I thrust forward into her, setting a rhythm of rocking into her that had her grasping the sheets above her head.

The angle was creating just the right amount of friction, as I slid in and out of Chase, to make my blood pump and my heart race. I reached down and slipped my hand under her, finding her engorged clit and pressing on it firmly until her hips were bucking back into mine.

"Fuck, I'm close," I whispered into her ear as I rested my forehead on her shoulder.

With a few more thrusts of my hips, she was moaning loudly against the sheets, her eyes clamped shut as she clenched around me. "Ohhhh...yes...I'm cumming..."

I couldn't hold back anymore as I wildly pushed my hips into hers, triggering an intense orgasm. "Uhhhh."

My heart was pounding against her back as I kissed the side of her neck and shoulder as we came down from our highs. Gently pulling out of her, I settled next to Chase on the bed, gently pushing the hair from her face and tucking it behind her ear.

She smiled at me drowsily and I knew that I'd made the right decision waiting until tomorrow to propose to her. She may not say it, but I knew she was a romantic and wanted the hearts and flowers.

I just hoped she wasn't disappointed if I said something embarrassing while trying to be romantic.

Isobel had managed to distract Chase for a few hours after our book reading with edits on her manuscript. It gave me the perfect opportunity to head to the airport to pick up my family. Chase's brothers, their spouses, and her parents had gotten into town while we were at our morning press event.

They were staying at a hotel a few blocks from ours. Far enough away that it couldn't spoil the surprise, but close enough we could spend time with them for the next few days.

"Hey, you!" My sister exclaimed as she ran across the baggage claim area and jumped into my arms. She laid a sloppy kiss on my cheek and I cringed as she dropped back to the floor and pinched it. "I can't believe you're going to get hitched!"

"Shhh..." I scolded her, looking around. I knew there was no way that Chase knew where I was, but I still didn't need my sister announcing things into the airport.

"She hasn't said yes, yet" I laughed as I smiled at my parents who were making their way over to us.

"Be nice to your brother, Kelly. You know he doesn't like people staring at him," my mother scolded as she smiled over at me.

"Well, he better get used to an audience, because there's no way I'm missing the big moment tonight," Kelly laughed.

"I'm sure he'd probably like some privacy while he asks such an important question," my dad told her, pinning her down with a knowing look.

"Thanks, Dad," I laughed as I hugged him and then my mom, kissing her on the cheek.

"Oh, hell no, I'm watching it whether he likes it or not. I'll climb the damn roof that overlooks that garden if I have to," Kelly insisted.

"Don't worry, I'll let you watch," I rolled my eyes at my sister threatening to go all ninja.

"Just the part with the ring, though. I don't need to see you two mauling each other afterward," she rolled her eyes and gagged.

"Whatever, dork, you're just jealous."

Several hours later, I was in an Uber with Chase headed towards the river. The Met Cloisters were located north of Manhattan in Fort Tryon Park alongside the Hudson River. It was a rebuilt monastery that they used to house some of their Medieval art collection.

Adrian was able to book us the courtyard surrounding one of the cloister gardens for a little 'business' dinner.

"Where are we going?" she asked as she looked out the window and saw the buildings make way for the trees and walking trails of the surrounding parks.

I smiled at her and took her hand, intertwining our fingers.

"Let me guess, it's a secret," she rolled her eyes.

I shrugged my shoulders and blew her a kiss as we pulled into the parking lot next to the building. It'd just closed to the public a little while ago, but I'd gotten a text that all our surprise guests were waiting inside.

"Thanks, man," I told the Uber driver as we climbed out and I led Chase to the door they'd told me to enter the building by.

I led her up the staircase into the main lobby and around the corner into the hallway that led to the Cuxa cloister garden. Our friends and family were already seated at the long tables, the wine obviously flowing by the loud laughter we could hear as we turned the corner.

Chase squealed as she saw the table come into view, most of our family members cheering as we walked up to the table. "I can't believe you guys are all here! Is told me this was a business dinner."

"And according to my expense report, it is," Isobel laughed from her seat next to Adrian at the foot of the table.

"Gotta love having a corporate credit card," he smiled with a nod.

"Did you know they were inviting everyone?" Chase asked in a whisper as she tugged on my arm and turned to face me.

"I may have had an inkling."

"Alright. Let's get this party started. I'll notify the catering crew we're ready." Adrian leaned over and kissed Isobel on the cheek, his hand dragging across her back as he turned and strode towards an open doorway in the courtyard. Guess they weren't hiding anymore either.

Sam had Christine tucked underneath his arm, chatting away with Emory and Nathan at the far end of the table.

Our families all gave us hugs before we took our seats and started dinner. Kelly was totally oblivious to the looks our parents kept giving her as she laughed loudly at something Nathan was saying to her.

"I knew he'd be into her," Chase whispered as she watched my sister and her friend already getting acquainted.

"You called it. Although I'm not sure he quite knows what he's getting himself into," I laughed. My sister could be a handful and I didn't see her as the type to take commands.

"Be nice. He deserves someone normal for once," Chase elbowed me and settled against my arm. She looked happy. I was so glad I was able to pull something like this off for her.

"I'm just not even going to comment on that one," I laughed as I watched my sister run her hand down Nathan's arm. He was grinning at her with a huge smile. It was too bad they lived a thousand miles apart.

"Elle, where's my baby?" Chase asked as she pinned her sister-in-law down with a knowing look,

"She's back in Minneapolis with my parents. Probably getting the shit spoiled out of her," Elle shrugged as she gave Chase a guilty smile.

"I don't care," Ethan laughed loudly. "We get to have a few days in a hotel without a tiny cockblocker."

I laughed as Elle swatted at his arm, pretending to be offended. I had a feeling another grandchild might not be too far away.

We spent the next half hour talking to our family members, drinking wine, and enjoying the food. After the sun set, the candles on the table and the dim outdoor lighting made the perfect setting for this get-together.

"I love this place. I can't believe that Adrian would find somewhere so romantic for a business dinner," Chase sighed as she laid her head against my shoulder.

"He didn't."

She turned towards me with a little frown.

"I did." My voice was a little shaky, but the look she gave me made it all worth it. She loved this place, and I did as well.

"I always knew you were a softy," she teased.

"Well. Not all the time, I hope," I smirked, and she started laughing. I loved listening to her sound so carefree and content.

"Go for a walk with me?" I asked quietly as I looked over towards the open courtyard.

"Do you think they'll mind if we escape?" she whispered, as she looked back at the table full of both of our families and our work family.

"I think they'd insist," I told her as I nuzzled her cheek.

"Alright. Lead the way," she whispered back with a little nod, smiling at me as I kissed her temple.

I reached out and grasped her hand, glancing back at my father who gave me a little wink and nodded his head.

It was showtime.

Chase and I walked quietly along the stone path of the cloister garden outside the hallway with the arches where our dinner was held, and towards the side of the building.

She started to turn in one direction, but I quickly tugged her the other way. "Why don't we start over here, I didn't get a chance to check out the Gothic architecture of the other courtyard when we came in."

"Alright," she laughed, "I didn't realize you were such a big fan of architecture."

My arm encircled her waist and I steered her around the corner of the building and out of sight. I knew that people would follow us, but I hoped to have a little bit of a head start. "Maybe I just want to get you alone in a dimly lit courtyard."

"Oh, do tell. And what will we be doing there?" she asked as she ran her fingers down the buttons on my shirt and let them linger on the one closest to my belt.

"Maybe it's a surprise."

"You and the surprises today," she laughed as she leaned in and gently placed her lips against mine. "I'm going to think you're a closet romantic or something."

"Maybe you've rubbed off on me," I told her, closing the distance between us and kissing her softly.

When we separated, I pulled open the door that led into the Gothic chapel and Chase tugged on my arm. "Are we supposed to go in there? Isn't the building closed?"

"I know a guy." I winked and interlaced her fingers with mine, leading her down the steps.

"It's so quiet in here. I love the stained glass," she whispered as I led her towards the door that led outside to one of the lower cloister gardens.

"Come on, let's check out the other cloister." I nodded towards the door, anxious to keep moving.

"What's the hurry?" she asked with an amused smile.

"There's no hurry, it's just a nice night," I insisted, feeling my nerves kicking in a little.

"Alright, if you're in such a rush to look at some plants," she laughed as she followed me towards the stairs that led to the lower level.

I slowed down as we reached the door that led outside. My heart was racing as I turned towards her and gently cupped her face.

"I love you," I whispered before I gave her a gentle kiss, slowly caressing her lips with mine.

"Mmm," she hummed into my mouth as she slipped her hands inside of my suit jacket and wrapped her arms around me. She laid her head against my chest, over my heart, as she hugged me.

"Your heart is racing," she whispered, and my arms tightened around her.

"That's what you do to me," I whispered as I took a deep breath and leaned back from her. "Outside?"

She nodded. "Let's go."

I interlaced our fingers and opened the door for her, letting her pass through the threshold before I followed behind her.

She looked amazing in a floaty light gray dress with her hair loose. I was one lucky bastard.

The quiet gasp she let out as the gardens came into view was worth every hour of getting this plan into place. "What is this? Is there something else going on tonight?"

"Why don't you have a look around," I suggested, my voice a little tight.

She looked up at my face and searched my eyes before she nodded and let go of my hand. I followed behind as she walked slowly along the red brick path and through the nearest archway that led to the garden.

The trees and bushes had all been covered with twinkle lights. It'd taken Adrian and Sam a few hours here this afternoon with Chase's brothers to get it all done in time.

I could tell when she saw the roses and her steps faltered. The path was lined with white and red rose petals. In the center of the cloister, there was a stone pedestal, with a single red rose lying on top of a copy of our book. It was open to the passage I'd written when I realized I wanted forever with her.

She looked back at me and I nodded, urging her to go look. I'd highlighted the line that described how I felt about her.

*"I'd die for you if it meant you got to live, but I'd happily live forever with you if we get the chance..."*

She picked up the rose from the pedestal and turned away. I glanced back and saw our family crowded against the wall, out of sight, waiting for me.

"Evan...I..." I could hear her start to talk, still facing away from me. She brought her hand up to her cheek, wiping something away and I felt a tear run down my own.

It was now or never.

Trying not to make any noise, I pulled the ring out of my pocket and lowered myself down to one knee.

"Chase..." I started, and she turned around, her hand covering her mouth.

"I...uh..." My throat felt tight as she stared at me and I knew I needed to push through the nerves.

The chance at a lifetime with her was worth more than a few minutes where it felt like I was going to have a heart attack.

"I know we've barely decided to move in together, but I want you in my home, our home, as more than just my lover."

She smiled and let out a little laugh.

"When I asked you, I knew that I wanted to marry you, but was afraid that it would be too big of a step for us at the time."

"After spending the last three weeks traveling the country with you, I know it's a step I want now. I don't want to wait."

I took a deep breath and she nodded at me, encouraging me to go on.

"Chastity Rose — and yes — a little gay birdie told me that's not just a pen name."

She laughed and looked over my shoulder to where our families were now standing out in the open.

"Screw you, Miguel." She scowled and pointed in his direction.

I laughed as I looked over my shoulder and he was blowing her a kiss.

"Anyways..." I cleared my throat.

She giggled and stepped towards me with the rose still in her hand.

"I knew that you were going to be important when I saw your picture for the first time. I knew that I loved you when you teased me relentlessly about my inability to write anything resembling a sex scene. And I knew that I wanted you forever when I wrote that line in the book."

I took a deep breath and looked up at the woman that I was determined to have in all my future plans.

"Will you please put me out of my awkward misery and say you'll marry me? Will you be my wife?"

Full tears were streaming down her cheeks as she stepped forward again and dropped to her knees in front of me.

"Yes!" she cried, and she fell into my arms, tucking her face into my neck.

I closed my eyes and hugged her tightly to my chest, tears pooled in my own eyes. She'd allowed me to grow and flourish as a person and I couldn't wait to start our own journey together with her as my wife.

"Give her the ring, doofus!" Christine called out from the stone pathway and I shook my head with a laugh.

Chase chuckled into my neck and leaned back, cupping my face with her hands and wiping the moisture from my face with her thumbs.

I brought my hand up, the ring lying flat in my palm.

"Wow..." she whispered as she picked it up with her right hand and looked closely at it in the dim light — the stone sparkling from the lights in the trees.

I took it back from her and grabbed her left hand, slowly sliding it into place.

"It's gorgeous," she whispered as she looked up at me and then back to her hand.

"Just like you," I whispered back.

"Flattery will get you everywhere," she laughed as she leaned forward and kissed me, slowly at first, before she grabbed my face and slipped her tongue into my mouth.

Applause started from the crowd behind us.

"Get a room, you freaks!" Miguel yelled as we continued to kiss passionately.

Chase laughed against my lips and pulled back, flipping him off over my shoulder.

"Do we have to invite them to the wedding?" she whispered in my ear.

"I'm afraid they're all part of the package," I sighed with a laugh as I heard Kelly start whistling and catcalling us.

"As long as you're by my side..." she smiled as she looked into my eyes.

"I wouldn't dream of being anywhere else."

THE END

# ACKNOWLEDGEMENTS

First and foremost, I'd like to extend a heartfelt thank you to my close group of writer friends, including my goats, Kelly, Miguel, and Danielle. They have been there since the beginning with this book, encouraging me and cheering me on, even when self-doubt set in and I wasn't sure these characters would see the light of day.

I'd also like to thank my husband for encouraging me to have this published, it's been such a rewarding experience to finally see it come to fruition. The laundry piled up at times, but he never said a word when I was absorbed in writing and editing.

Thank you so much to Cherry Publishing for taking a chance on this book, you finally gave me the push I needed to get my work out into the world. Vanessa, thank you for being patient with my twelve hundred emails, and for the work that you, Jonathan, and your team put into pulling this all together.

We've got some more fun in store for the characters in this universe, and I can't wait to share them with you in the coming year. Make sure to follow me on Instagram at ELKoslo_writes and sign up for my upcoming newsletter at ELKoslo.com.

I hope you enjoyed following Chase and Evan's journey in *Foreplay on Words*, it was a treat to see them come to life.

Until next time,

E.L. Koslo

Did you enjoy Foreplay on Words?

♡

Leave 5 stars and a nice comment to share the love!

You didn't like it?
♠

Write to us to suggest the kind of novel you dream of reading!
https://cherry-publishing.com/en/contact/

Subscribe to our Newsletter to stay up to date with all of our upcoming releases and latest news!
You can subscribe according to the country you're from:

You are from...

**US**:
https://mailchi.mp/b78947827e5e/get-your-free-ebook

**UK**:
https://mailchi.mp/cherry-publishing/get-your-free-uk-copy

Made in the USA
Las Vegas, NV
05 March 2022